# NO OR
# HERO

BY

RACHEL LEE

AND

# OPERATION: FORBIDDEN

BY

LINDSAY McKENNA

Dear Reader,

*No Ordinary Hero* was an adventure for me, a twist on the usual suspense. I left a question dangling at the end, hoping you would choose whichever answer best pleases you.

When two people fall in love, they often encounter differences in the way they view things, and the process by which they come to agree, or at least agree to disagree, has always fascinated me.

None of us would want to fall in love with a mirror image. How boring that would make life, to live in an echo chamber, and never experience the magic of someone else's way of seeing even mundane things.

Mike and Del face a few major hurdles because they come from such different cultural backgrounds. Love, however, is not about to leave them alone in their private worlds.

Nor is the house.

Best,

*Rachel Lee*

# NO ORDINARY HERO

BY
RACHEL LEE

First published in Great Britain 2011
by Mills & Boon, an imprint of Harlequin (UK) Limited,
Eton House, 18-24 Paradise Road, Richmond, Surrey TW9 1SR



ISBN: 978 0 263 88556 9

46-1011

Harlequin (UK) policy is to use papers that are natural, renewable and recyclable products and made from wood grown in sustainable forests. The logging and manufacturing processes conform to the legal environmental regulations of the country of origin.

Printed and bound in Spain
by Blackprint CPI, Barcelona

**Rachel Lee** was hooked on writing by the age of twelve, and practiced her craft as she moved from place to place all over the United States. This *New York Times* bestselling author now resides in Florida and has the joy of writing full-time.

Her bestselling CONARD COUNTY series (see www.conardcounty.com) has won the hearts of readers worldwide, and it's no wonder, given her own approach to life and love. As she says, "Life is the biggest romantic adventure of all—and if you're open and aware, the most marvellous things are just waiting to be discovered." Readers can e-mail Rachel at RachelLee@ConardCounty.com.

For my oldest daughter, for whom every day is a battle and every night another triumph

# *Chapter 1*

Mike Windwalker, D.V.M., came home early from work, pulling into his driveway in his battered brown van, practically a veterinary clinic on wheels. It had been a busy but short day, allowing him to leave his assistants in charge of the kennels and point himself toward a relaxing late afternoon and evening.

A well-earned bit of relaxation, considering he rarely enjoyed a day off. Not that he minded his workload. In fact he loved it because it gave him scant time to think about all the things missing in his life. And the animals he spent his time with, if not all of their owners, didn't give a damn that he was a "redskin," a full-blooded Cheyenne, an escapee from the rez.

He climbed out of the van, feeling a little stiff from an unusual encounter that morning with a bovine. The animal had been half insane but worth enough money that the rancher wanted to be sure there wasn't some treatment for the steer. In the process, he'd been kicked, although not too badly, nearly bitten—thank God he'd dodged that one—and had wrestled with twelve hundred pounds of maddened muscle while trying to get a blood sample.

He'd guessed it was rabies to begin with, but the rancher had been insistent. In the end, however, he'd simply had to put the animal down, over strenuous objections, with the flat statement that he wasn't going to risk his own life or anyone else's when the diagnosis was damn near written all over the steer.

He'd left with the body of the steer and dropped it off in his cooler so that tomorrow he could remove the brain and spinal cord to send to the state lab.

Fun day, stubborn client, and now he ached all over. Yet he still felt a lot of sympathy for the rancher, who, like most in his business, was running on a margin so small that losing one steer, just one, could be a terrifying prospect.

The only thing that had made the guy stand back and let Mike put the animal down was the possibility that if he kept that steer around, he might wind up with a sick herd—the only catastrophe worse than losing a single animal.

Mike tossed his head, causing his inky hair to fall back from his face. Despite local opinions about Native Americans, he defiantly wore his hair long. Let 'em stare. His heritage was stamped on his face, and his hair was the crowning glory. Usually he tied it back with a beaded band, but today when he left work, he'd discarded the band. His scalp was grateful.

"Hi, Dr. Windwalker!"

The light, youthful voice called to him from the

house next door, and he turned to see Colleen Carmody sitting in her wheelchair on the large front porch. The Carmodys had moved in a little over a month ago, and he'd shared a few brief conversations with thirteen-year-old Colleen, who was incurably cheerful and friendly. He'd even spoken to her mother Delia, or Del, a few times, but he tried to keep the contact to a minimum. He didn't want any trouble, and he certainly didn't want to cause any to the Carmodys. He knew his place; it had been beaten into him.

"You're home early," Colleen said with a wide, welcoming smile.

He couldn't be rude to that girl, not for anybody's sake. From inside the house he heard a banging, indicating that Colleen's mother was busy at the restoration work she did to support herself and her daughter. "Yeah," he replied, without approaching. "And I need it. I had a hard morning."

"What happened?" Colleen asked.

"A very sick steer would have liked to kill me. I didn't let him, but he almost won the fight."

The girl giggled, a delightful sound, and rolled her chair across the porch so she was a little closer. Her red hair caught some of the spring sunlight that filtered through the leaves before it crept under the porch roof, and flamed. "You don't look like you did so bad."

"That's because my bruises are under my pants. I figure I'll look like a piece of modern art in a day or two."

Another giggle answered him.

"How's your day been?" he asked. Nope, no way could he be rude to that child.

He watched, feeling a twinge of concern as he saw

the girl's smile vanish. "Colleen?" Something must be wrong.

"It's nothing," the girl said. "I just don't like this house."

"Why not?"

She hesitated, then said in a rush, "I feel like there's something else in there. I hear things. It's creepy!"

He looked from her to the two-story, clapboard house, and the blank eyes of the windows. Old house. Plenty of rot, no doubt, and maybe raccoons or mice. But something else… Some feeling he tried to shove away, because at least around here he had to be one hundred percent a man of science and bury instincts honed throughout his youth by people who believed in spirits and the sentience of even the very rocks.

"Rats?" he suggested. "Raccoons?"

"Mom checked. That's what she thinks it is."

He nodded, his gaze returning to the child. "She's probably right. But you don't think so?"

Colleen shrugged. "She didn't find anything."

"Ah." He tried a small smile. "Then maybe some mice got into the walls. They can be so hard to find once they do that."

"Yeah. That's what Mom said, too." Colleen gave another small shrug, seeming a bit embarrassed now. "I know she's probably right, but it's creepy anyway. Especially late at night."

"That would creep me out, too," he said sympathetically, letting his barriers down just a shade. "Scratching and banging from something you can't see… Nah, I wouldn't like that either."

That elicited a smile from Colleen. "You're kinda okay, Dr. Windwalker."

"Just call me Mike." He was about to say goodbye and head into his own house when the screen door behind Colleen squeaked open and a woman poked her head out.

"Colleen? Did you call me?" Then, as she saw Mike, "Oh! Hi, Dr. Windwalker."

"Just Mike." He felt nearly embarrassed that he'd kept such a distance since they moved in that they didn't even feel free to call him by his first name. Of course, he was only protecting himself and them.

Del Carmody stepped out onto the porch with a smile. And once again he felt the impact of her beauty. Black Irish to the bone, she didn't have her daughter's flaming hair but instead hair much like his, the color of a raven's wing, only shinier and finer. The impact was heightened by intense blue eyes and milky Irish skin. Right now she looked a little dusty, but that didn't detract one iota from a body that even in jeans and a loose work shirt sans sleeves showed a perfect shape, the kind of shape only a woman could achieve from hard physical labor. The kind of shape that had always drawn him, more muscular than average but still curved in all the right ways. And that smile of hers.

Things he really shouldn't notice. Couldn't afford to notice. But he saw them all anyway.

"Mike," she acknowledged, still smiling. "Didn't mean to interrupt you guys, but I heard Colleen's voice and wondered if she needed something."

"I was just telling Doctor…I mean Mike, about the mice in the house."

"The noises." Del nodded, looking at her daughter with a flicker of concern. Clearly she cared that her daughter was frightened, even if the explanation had to be utterly benign. A loving mother.

"Mice in the walls can be a beast to get rid of," he volunteered.

"Tell me about it," Del said. She came farther onto the porch and leaned against the railing. "That's where they must be because I can't find any sign of them in the attic. I just hope I can get rid of them before one dies inside a wall."

"That'll make the place uninhabitable for a while," he agreed. He felt awkward, standing so far away in his driveway, knowing the neighborly thing would be to approach. But he didn't approach white folks readily anymore. Hadn't since he was eighteen. If they came to him in a friendly fashion, fine. But he never made the first overture. And this situation, with a widow and her daughter, could cause exactly the kind of mess he'd been avoiding his entire adult life.

Awkward to stand at a distance, even more awkward to just walk away. Needless rudeness did him no favors, but then neither did unwanted friendliness. He'd given up sighing over reality years ago, though. The West was the West, and people here still harbored old hatreds.

He didn't feel sorry for himself. Others, he believed, had it far worse. But he was well aware that he was always on a tightrope, at least in this part of the country. It hadn't been so bad back east where he'd gone to veterinary school, but here…memories were long. On both sides, if he were to be honest about it.

"I hope that all my sawing and banging isn't driving you nuts," Del said.

He allowed himself a faint smile. "Not at all. I'm

usually at work during the hours you're banging away. How's it going?"

"Well, the place was in worse shape than I guessed when I looked it over before I bought it. A lot of hidden problems. But it's coming along."

"A lot of rot?"

Her blue eyes met his openly, tired but smiling. "Oh, of course. Worse than I anticipated. When I started pulling out the old plaster, I found some of the studs were in pretty bad shape, and the lath behind the plaster isn't so great either."

"It's a shame you have to replace the plaster at all."

"I know." She turned toward him, facing him. An open posture. "They don't build them like that anymore. It's killing me to have to put in drywall, but plastering would be a bigger headache than I want to buy, especially since I may have to replace all of it. I guess the roof must have leaked into the walls at some point, for a long time." She looked back at the house and then smiled at him. "This job is always an adventure."

"So's Mike's," Colleen offered. "A steer tried to kill him."

Del's eyebrows, perfectly arched, lifted. "Why in the world would a steer do that?"

"I'm pretty sure he was rabid. He got in a few kicks, but I dodged well enough that the damage is minor."

Colleen giggled. "He said he's going to look like modern art."

Del's smile widened and she chuckled. "Ouch. There are days that leave me looking that way, too."

He turned his mind away from inevitable thoughts about what might lie under her clothing, bruised and unbruised.

"How would a steer become rabid?" Del asked.

"The same way you or I could. A bite from an infected animal. I'll look for the marks when I start the necropsy tomorrow, but it could have been anything from a raccoon to a wolf."

Colleen spoke. "I bet the rancher thinks it was a wolf. They hate the wolves."

"Yes, they do." And entirely too much so, though Mike could understand their reasoning. For his own part, he prized the return of wolves to the area, both culturally and scientifically. "But it could have been something else. A rabid animal will bite just about anything regardless of size. And it's my job to find out."

"I hope it was a bat or something else," Colleen said. "I like wolves."

"I do, too." Really. Because if he found a wolf bite on the animal, there might well be other infected wolves, and the hunt would begin. Considering that as near as anyone could tell there was still only a single pack on Thunder Mountain, that would be a tragedy, both for the wolves and the ecology.

Del straightened a bit. "You must be tired," she said to him. "Don't let us keep you in your driveway."

She smiled, but instead of feeling grateful for her concern, he felt dismissed. "Thanks," he said, trying to keep a pleasant tone. "Nice chatting." Then he turned and started toward his door.

And on his back he could feel the eyes of two white women, forbidden territory.

Del watched Mike Windwalker stride away to his door, thinking he was an extremely attractive man, from his face to those narrow hips cased in worn denim. And she liked the coppery color of his skin, such a contrast to her own ghastly paleness. All her life she wished she could tan rather than freckle. Ah, well, she wasn't in the market for a man, any man.

Then she looked down at her daughter. "You getting hungry?"

"Could be." Colleen grinned.

"How hungry?"

"Um…" Colleen pretended to think it over. "Just teensy hungry right now. Big hungry comes later."

"Fair enough." She reached for the grips on the back of the wheelchair and heard an immediate protest.

"Mom! I can do it myself."

Del had to smile. Colleen's independence and upbeat attitude always made her smile…except when it made her cry for what her daughter had lost. "Okay, okay. I'll just get the door."

"I want chips!"

"Whole-grain pretzels."

"Sheesh, Mom, I have a growing brain. I need the fat."

"Smarty pants."

"I learned it in biology."

"You learn too much in biology."

In the kitchen, which was still awaiting renovations, the dust layered everything. No way to avoid it at this stage of restoration, so Del grabbed a wet rag and wiped down just enough of it to feed her daughter some pretzels without all the plaster dust. In other parts of the house, near open windows, big fans tried to suck dust out of the house. They helped but not entirely. Just as the plastic she hung over the door to the kitchen didn't completely prevent the dust from getting in.

As she was wiping around the sink, she noticed the window beside it was unlocked. She paused, wondering how that had happened. She never opened the windows in here because she didn't want to create a draft that would suck the dust in around the edges of the plastic.

Damn, she couldn't remember. For all she knew it had been unlocked for weeks or more. She might have done it in the way she did so many things, while thinking of something else. Except, she wouldn't have closed it without locking it again, would she?

Hell. As forgetful as she seemed to be getting lately, it was silly even to wonder about it. Maybe one of the workmen or deliverymen had opened it briefly.

Sighing, she reached out to flip the lock closed.

"What do you want to drink?" she asked after she'd put a couple of large pretzels on a plate.

"Soda."

Del faced her daughter. "You do this to drive me crazy, right?"

Colleen giggled. "No." But the way she giggled had given lie to her denial.

Del laughed herself. "You know what's in the fridge."

"Yeah. Darn it. Wouldn't you know I'd have a health freak for a mom?"

"Such a curse." But Del couldn't help feeling a pang. Her daughter wanted the same simple things every other kid her age wanted. Having to take extra care about her weight because her activities were limited only made it harder for both of them. "Okay," she said. "Tell you what. I'll get some diet soda at the store next time. Will that do?"

"I'll love you forever." An impish smile. "Can I have cranberry juice?"

"Always." Del pulled a bottle of low-calorie juice from the fridge, rinsed a glass to remove any dust, filled it and handed it to Colleen. "Dr. Windwalker seems really nice."

Before Colleen could answer, there was a buzz that sounded almost like laughter, and the girl pulled out her cell phone. "Yeah," she answered absently as she scanned the screen then started rapidly texting a reply. The tap-tap of the keys was a counterpoint to every waking moment of the day. "Can I go over to Mary Jo's for a sleepover tomorrow?"

"Sure, once I clear it with her mom." Colleen had adapted amazingly well to her disability—so well that Del wondered if some of it weren't just show to protect her mother—and the parents of her friends were more than ready to do the extra care Colleen required. Mary Jo's mom had even installed handicap bars in her bathroom. But Del always felt she had to clear it.

"Mary Jo says her mom says to stop worrying about it."

That sounded like Beth Andrews, for certain. "Okay, but tell Mary Jo to tell her mom to call me anyway."

"Sheesh." The word was accompanied by a small frown as the tapping resumed. "Okay, she'll call." Colleen looked up. "I guess I need to go back outside?"

"Just for a bit, sweetie. I'm done making dust for the day, but I want to get rid of some more of it and let the rest settle safely."

Colleen had a little flip tray on her wheelchair and she

had set the pretzels on it. The drink created a problem, however.

Del didn't wait for the question. "Why don't I carry your food out while you resume the neighborhood watch?"

That at least earned another laugh. Unfortunately, with all the dust, and later with the chemicals she would need to use for stripping and varnishing, it was best if Colleen remained outside as much as possible. Colleen didn't seem to mind—texting seemed to be her major absorption, and sometimes friends came over to gather on the front porch with popcorn and beverages. Three days a week she went to physical therapy. School also occupied a good deal of her time except over the summers, and Del hoped to have the messiest of the work done on this house before school let out.

After she settled Colleen on the porch, she went back inside to get out her shop vacuum and start cleaning up as much as she could. Because it was still late spring, the afternoon would start getting chilly soon, and she wanted Colleen to come inside before it did.

Back inside with the inexplicable scratchings and bangings. Those concerned her. At first when Colleen had mentioned them, Del had assumed there were vermin in the attic and hadn't been too troubled. But now, having checked everywhere she could and never having heard the sounds herself, she worried about more than vermin.

She worried about why Colleen might imagine such sounds. Worried about whether she needed to mention them to Colleen's doctor or wait a little longer to see what developed.

At the back of her mind, she never quite escaped the

feeling that another shoe was about to drop. Maybe it was just because once the worst happened to you, you never felt entirely safe again. And losing her husband and having her daughter paralyzed by an auto accident had been pretty much the worst she ever wanted to imagine.

But there was also the sense that Colleen had adapted too well and too quickly to losing the use of her legs. Oh, at first there had been plenty of tears and despair, many cries of "I wish I could have died, too." But in a matter of just a month or so, those feelings seemed to have evaporated, leaving an unexpectedly cheerful and uncomplaining daughter.

Del kept thinking that at least once in a while Colleen ought to complain about *something*. But the child never did. At least not around her. Another concern. She didn't want Colleen to feel as if she had to hide negative feelings from her, that she had to be strong for her mom. That would be an unfair and heavy burden for any child that age, including Colleen.

And then, sometimes she even worried about *herself*. Because while Colleen might be hearing sounds, Del herself seemed to be becoming a bit too forgetful, and maybe even imaginative. A couple of times in the past few weeks she'd come home after leaving the house empty to find things out of place. At least she *thought* they were out of place. And each time she had the distinct impression someone had been *in* the house.

Which was utterly insane, because she locked the place up tight every single time she and Colleen went out. There were simply too many valuable tools and construction supplies lying around to take any chance.

So she had to be forgetting where she left stuff. Not a good sign, but probably not all that abnormal either.

Del sighed heavily, pulled on her dust mask and picked up the hose to vacuum the living room she'd been working on. One room at a time to try to keep the mess under control. Damn dust still managed to seep everywhere.

Flipping houses had been a good idea overall after the accident that took Don and disabled Colleen. With the life insurance money, she'd been able to buy a fixer-upper, and with the skills learned growing up on a farm, studying architectural engineering in college, and some heavy-duty studying to fill the gaps, she'd learned most of the trades necessary to turn a mess into a desirable property. Things had gone well, mostly, although at the moment she still had one property she hadn't been able to sell in this belt-tightening time, or even to rent to someone.

But her bank account was still healthy enough, and living in the houses she worked on made the expense easier to bear. This week, however, she'd need the electrician, as well as a plumber to help with the downstairs bath she intended to add. Those would be big bills, but necessary to ensure the house was up to code. At the moment it most certainly was not.

Living in the house she was working on also made it possible to keep an eye on Colleen. She couldn't have the girl in one house while she worked on another, and her aunt Sally wasn't up to taking full responsibility. Yes, Aunt Sally helped out when needed, especially at times when Del needed to be away to purchase materials, but Sally was getting up in years and at best could only keep an eye on Colleen and make sure she got decent meals.

Although even the need for Sally's help was beginning to pass. Colleen had learned tricks for getting herself in and out of bed, getting up off the floor if she fell for some reason, and she could even manage to cook a little, though that was difficult in a kitchen that wasn't designed for someone in a chair. And in a worst-case scenario, Colleen always had her phone within a couple of inches.

Still, Del worried. How could she not? She didn't want Colleen to have another bad experience of some kind, and total independence still lay in the future.

As she vacuumed the dust that coated the living room after a day spent pulling out damaged plaster, she chewed her lip behind her mask and tried to tell herself that everything would work out for Colleen in time.

She had to believe that.

Then her thoughts drifted back to Mike Windwalker. He was a reserved guy. She'd already noted that he didn't seem inclined to chat for long with neighbors. Shy? Maybe.

But, Lord, he was good-looking. Male eye candy, and she didn't usually respond to that. Or maybe it had just been so long since she'd been with a man that her libido was acting up.

The thought made her chuckle quietly. Well, if it had to act up, it had chosen a great object for attention. She could watch that man walk up his driveway any day.

And maybe, with a tiny bit of effort, she could break through that reserve and get to know him a bit. She liked to know her neighbors, especially now. It made her feel safer, and certainly safer for Colleen.

A thought suddenly occurred to her, and she switched off the vacuum for a minute. Maybe it was the confluence of her thoughts, but Colleen had recently asked for a kitten. Who better to ask about getting one than the local vet who lived next door?

And maybe a kitten would make Colleen feel safer from those scratchings she heard. Certainly it wouldn't hurt to find out if a cat could help with mice in the walls…if indeed there were mice.

Finally she switched the vacuum on again and resumed her task. A cat might be the answer to a number of things.

Or not.

She made up her mind to talk to Mike Windwalker about it soon. A cat, or maybe a small dog, depending on what he thought might handle small vermin better. But nothing too big, given Colleen's paralysis. Something small and cuddly that would chase away the mice.

Because either there were mice in these walls or something worrisome was happening to Colleen.

And the latter was an idea she refused to entertain.

# Chapter 2

Del loved Saturday mornings because she put aside her work and devoted her full attention to Colleen. Yes, they usually had errands to run, things like grocery shopping, but it was still time spent together without the intervention of work or school. Sometimes, like today, they even took in a matinee at the movies.

Today they had gone to see a silly animated film that had made them laugh heartily, and then afterward she had dropped Colleen at Mary Jo's for the night.

Sunday was always a day off, too, for her at least, but there was church in the morning, and the inevitable socializing that went with it after the service, and then Colleen usually spent the afternoon on schoolwork. Often, by then, Del felt tired enough to need a nap.

So Saturdays were a special time for them both: no school, no work, no therapists.

This Saturday, however, as she drove home from

dropping Colleen at Mary Jo's, Del realized she felt reluctant to go home. She tried to tell herself not to be ridiculous, that these brief times to herself without work should be prized, and that she deserved the break as much as Colleen deserved to have fun with her friends at a sleepover.

But a weird kind of edginess troubled her anyway in the waning afternoon light. She couldn't put her finger on the source, and she finally decided that she must have forgotten to do something and would remember it later.

As she turned into her driveway and stopped the car, she looked up at the house and felt a totally inexplicable impulse to just drive away.

Now that was crazy! Had Colleen's talk of noises gotten to her?

She made herself climb out of the car, but still she hesitated. Not very long, thank goodness, because she heard another vehicle and turned to see Mike Windwalker pulling up next door. She waved, trying to smile in a friendly fashion, and he nodded to her as he braked then switched off his truck.

The usual thing would be for her to continue into her house. She'd greeted him, so she didn't have to remain outside. But something pushed her across the ragged, patchy lawn toward him.

He climbed out of his vehicle, wearing a dark blue chambray shirt and jeans, not very different from what she wore, and she thought that an instant of surprise passed over his strong features. If so, it vanished quickly.

"Hi," he said as she approached.

She heard an odd note of caution in his tone, couldn't

figure it out, but it didn't matter anyway because she was already committed. She'd started closing the distance between them and now couldn't simply turn away.

"Hi," she said. Now what? She couldn't exactly tell him that for some reason she didn't want to go into her house. Then she remembered the kitten question. "Can I ask you something? If you'd rather I make an appointment, I'll understand." She gave an uneasy laugh. "Asking for a neighbor's professional opinion for free is something I usually avoid."

A slow smile dawned on his face. God, he was good-looking. "I don't mind. You never know when I might have a professional question for you."

She gave another laugh. "Fair enough. Colleen's been asking for a kitten. And I got to thinking yesterday, what with the possibility of mice in the walls, that might not be a bad thing. Then I wondered if a small dog would be better."

He leaned back against his van, folding his arms, and in the process thrust his hips forward. Oh, she didn't want to notice those narrow hips again. She dragged her gaze back to his face.

"That depends," he said easily. Apparently on familiar ground, he felt comfortable. She could identify with that, since she was definitely *off* comfortable ground herself right now. "What would be easiest for you? There are some good small dogs that would take care of mice and rats, but dogs need more attention than cats. Walks and so on. On the other hand, not every cat is a good mouser."

"Really?" That surprised her.

"Really. It depends a lot on how the kitten is raised. Most learn to hunt from their mothers, whereas with some dogs, you've got a strong inbred instinct and territoriality."

"I didn't know that!"

"Most people don't. If you really want a good mouser, I can check around the local ranches for a barn cat, but that's more likely to be less a pet than a hunter."

Del sighed. "I had no idea this could be so complicated."

A quiet laugh escaped him. "You're not alone. Just ask yourself what you want more from a pet. If it's something cute and cuddly that would like to spend time on Colleen's lap, I'll find you something good."

"Well, she can't walk a dog very far yet, unless it's really well behaved. On the other hand, would a kitten hang around or take off?"

"Despite what some folks think, if you get a young kitten it can be trained to tolerate a collar, and even a leash. Not as easily with a dog, but cats are smart. When they realize they can't win, they give up."

Again she laughed, this time more comfortably. "So how long would that take?"

"I can probably do it for you in about a week."

She felt surprise. "You'd do that?"

"Of course. No charge. If Colleen really wants a kitten then I'd be glad to give her one that won't run off."

Del bit her lip. "It's just that I try to keep Colleen outside as much as possible when I'm making a lot of dust or using chemicals. I don't want her to suffer any harm. And I sure wouldn't want to bring an animal into an environment where it would have to be inside all the time with that stuff either."

"We're agreed then. Kitten or puppy?"

"Maybe I'm nuts, but if you think it's okay, I'd rather give her what she wants."

"I agree. Kitten it is. And I've got plenty over at the clinic. People drop them on my doorstep all the time. If you want, bring her over on Monday afternoon to pick one. Or let me work with a few for a week and find the one most amenable to a collar and leash."

Del thought about that. "I already know she wants a calico, so maybe surprising her would be more fun than making her wait for a week or so. Do you have any calicos?"

"Just one. They're relatively rare. But she's certainly a friendly little one. Loves to be hugged and petted."

"That sounds ideal then."

"Consider it done. But since it'll be me and one kitten *mano a mano,* rather than just picking the most cooperative animal, it might take a little longer to leash train it."

Again he had made her laugh, with the mental image of him in hand-to-hand combat with a stubborn kitten. "All right, I won't tell her."

"Probably best, unless you like to be nagged."

Her smile widened and she decided she liked Mike Windwalker. "I can't thank you enough."

"No thanks necessary. I'm always happy to find a good home for an animal."

"Well, I've kept you long enough." She started to turn away then saw her empty house waiting for her. And she stopped, unable to say why. Just that for some reason that house no longer looked as welcoming to her as it had when she bought it.

"This is ridiculous." Unaware she had spoken out loud, she was surprised when she heard a response.

"What is?" Mike asked.

She blew a long breath, impatient with herself, and now embarrassed. She should have made up some excuse, but she'd never been much of liar. "It's ridiculous that for some reason I don't want to go into that house tonight."

She was still staring at the building, but when she heard him move she looked at him. He stood straight up now, and he moved to her side, glancing at the house, too.

"I can't say," he said slowly, "that I don't understand what you're talking about."

Her heart slammed. What was he saying? Was he just trying to scare her? No, he didn't seem like the type. On the other hand, how well did she know him? "What do you mean?"

He gave a slight shake of his head, then shrugged. "Damned if I know." Slowly his dark-as-ebony eyes came to meet hers. "Want me to come in with you? Just to look around?"

She wanted to laugh the whole thing off, as if they were just joking, but somehow she couldn't. And as independent as she'd become since Don's death, she was surprised that his offer didn't put her hackles up.

Maybe because her hackles were already up over something she couldn't even define. "I must have eaten something that didn't agree with me," she said, trying to find a rational explanation for that lingering feeling of reluctance.

He didn't answer, just waited for her decision.

Finally, forcing briskness into her tone, she made it. "Sure, come on in and I'll show you around. Maybe you'll enjoy laughing at me."

"Why would I do that?"

"Because I was crazy enough to take on a project this size?"

At that he chuckled but shook his head. "I don't think you're crazy. I think you're a hard worker who isn't intimidated by huge jobs."

"Maybe I should have been intimidated with this one. Come on, I'll show you what I meant about the rot in the walls."

She thought he hesitated, but he was only a half step behind her as she led the way.

With each step she wondered what the heck was wrong with her. And why he could be so contrarily reluctant and friendly.

Walking into Del's house in plain sight of any nosy neighbor who might be watching through sheers or around the edges of curtains might not be the smartest act on the planet, Mike thought. On the other hand, he could sense how troubled Del felt, and he couldn't ignore that.

Just because some held on to old prejudices, it didn't mean everyone did. Hell, didn't this county have a couple of Native American lawmen?

But his people had been involved at Little Big Horn, something he'd had rubbed in his face for years when he was younger. Now that he was big enough to defend himself, most just plain didn't say anything, so he might well be attributing those animosities to more folks than deserved it.

But he knew damn well the prejudices were still there, whether in most or just a handful, and he hoped Del wouldn't suffer for what he was about to do. From what he could tell, she had quite enough problems on her plate.

Then he told himself to stop worrying about it. He was a grown-up and so was she. All that mattered was that she was nervous about entering her own house, and he'd learned early in life not to ignore those feelings. You might not be able to identify what triggered them, but ignoring them could get you into trouble.

As soon as he stepped through the front door, he looked around and remarked, "I can see why you bought this house."

She cocked an eye his way, smiling faintly. "Why?"

He waved one arm. "Most houses from this era are shotguns, one room behind another. But this one… Look at this wide hallway. And the stairway. In most places it would be right in the living room. It seems extravagant considering the era when it was built."

"It is." Her eyes brightened as she smiled. "I couldn't resist it because it's so different, and because it's more amenable to a modern lifestyle. When you have the shotgun floor plan, where rooms were just added straight back, it's hard to change things enough so that you're not walking through bedrooms. A real challenge. But this place is just perfect."

He lifted one eyebrow. "Except for all the hard work you have to do." That much was impossible to miss. Even the railing on the staircase had been painted, as had doors and moldings. He suspected there was plenty of fine wood to be uncovered in this house. "Somebody with money built this place."

"That's my guess, but I really haven't looked into the history of the house."

"You should. There's probably a fascinating story somewhere."

Yet, despite the architectural grace of the place, there they stood just inside the door. Mike hesitated, looking inward, trying to sense the cause for that. He'd gone through the house with her because she felt uneasy. Because something had made him feel a bit uneasy, too, yesterday, and again today. But instead of taking that walkthrough, they both stood here as if an invisible wall held them back.

His uneasiness had grown, he realized. But just a shade. Not enough to worry him. Finally, feeling the tension in the woman beside him, he asked, "Would you just like me to walk through on my own?"

He was willing, and a bit of a street fighter out of necessity. He could handle just about anyone who didn't have a gun. Although why the hell he should be worried about that he didn't know.

He paused a few seconds, searching places in himself that he usually kept hidden. There was something about this house…

Del gazed at him, her blue eyes reflecting perplexity and even some embarrassment. "What's going on?"

He got the feeling she was asking herself, not him. But he hesitated only a moment before saying, "This house feels sad."

She nodded, surprising him. "I never noticed anything before but…" She sighed. "Okay, I'm feeling really weird. I'm not an overly imaginative person. Maybe Colleen's complaint about noises is getting to me."

"Could be," he agreed smoothly, although for an instant he wanted to disagree strongly. But he'd turned himself into a man of science on purpose, and if he were to consider the empirical evidence, it was nuts to say the house felt sad. He managed a crooked smile. "I guess it must have gotten to me, too. Your daughter just doesn't seem like the kind of kid to think she has bears in her closet."

"She's not. We got past that stage before she turned four. So if she says she's hearing something, it's got to be mice in the walls."

"Or a water pipe ticking. I don't have to tell you how many sounds an old house can make."

"Plenty," she agreed. "And now I not only feel ridiculous, I feel stupid. You don't have to walk through with me. I'm sure you've got plenty to do."

He almost took it as a dismissal, which he was used to getting often enough in life. But her expression gave him pause. No, she hadn't lost her uneasiness, but she was feeling silly for it. He tried to think of a way to continue to accompany her while taking her concerns seriously. She was obviously a quite independent woman, and there was a good chance she didn't like leaning on a man, especially over an inexplicable feeling. And there was still something about this damn house.

"I'd actually like to see where Colleen's hearing the noises." He shrugged. "You never know. I might hear them and be able to identify them."

"I wish you could," she admitted. "I haven't heard them myself, at least not yet."

"So let's go hunting."

At that she chuckled and led the way.

The downstairs was quite spacious and nicely laid out. Kitchen and dining room on one side of the unusually large hallway, living room and an extra room on the other side. They skipped the extra room initially, though Mike could see color through the door that was slightly ajar.

Upstairs there were another three spacious bedrooms with walk-in closets and an unusually large bathroom that boasted an iron tub with clawed feet. A real antique, and a tub that a full-grown man could actually fit into.

"I wish this house had been available when I bought mine," he remarked. "I'd have snapped it up."

She flashed a smile. "You can always buy it once I get it fixed up."

"I may take you up on that."

The bedrooms, as yet, had clearly not been worked on, but even so their condition wasn't bad. Her room held an ordinary double bed and a dresser, and not one personal item was in view. He found that a little odd. The two others were empty.

When they returned downstairs, she led him to the room at the back end of the hall, the one they had skipped the first time through.

It proved to be Colleen's room and was a riot of color, with posters and a shiny mobile, and a bed nearly filled with pillows and stuffed animals. A lovely old table was obviously being used for a desk, high enough that the child's wheelchair could slide up to it comfortably, and it sported a good laptop computer along with books, papers and doodads. Over the bed was a bar hanging from a chain, probably to help Colleen maneuver into and out of her chair. He squashed a natural sympathetic reaction, because he sensed it would not be welcome either by Colleen or her mother. That child showed every sign of becoming just as independent as her mom.

"Does Colleen only hear the sounds in here?"

"So far. I've checked the attic and upstairs, but I haven't found any spoor, or anything else for that matter. I put in some traps but they haven't been sprung."

"Can we just stay here for a little bit?"

Del shrugged. "Sure. Why not?" She sat on the edge of the bed, leaving him to sit on a wooden chair in the corner, which meant moving an oversize stuffed rabbit.

"Does she only hear the sounds at night?"

"Mostly, but sometimes in the evening when she's in here doing homework. They've always stopped by the time I get in here when she calls me."

"That's…strange." Something warned him to be very careful here. There might be some emotional land mines he didn't want to trip by blundering around. "I like your daughter. She's so friendly for someone her age. I'm used to kids kind of glancing my way and dismissing me unless I'm caring for one of their pets."

"Kids that age are so awkward about things. Some of them anyway. Colleen has had so many adults in her life, in one capacity or another, since her accident that I think she's more comfortable with older people."

"That could be part of it. And she's certainly outgoing."

They sat a few minutes in silence and Mike realized that Del seemed to be growing uneasier, rather than less so. He wanted to ask what troubled her, but he didn't feel he knew her well enough.

"You know," Del said finally, "maybe I should sleep in here tonight. Colleen is spending the night with a friend, and it might be the perfect time to do a little more detective work."

He nodded. "Might be a good idea."

Suddenly her blue eyes, as sharp as lasers, met his. "Why did you say this house makes you feel sad?"

Crap. He'd kind of hoped she would let that go, because he never should have said it, even out of natural sympathy. "I don't know," he said finally. "It was just a feeling."

She nodded slowly. "I'm Irish enough to be superstitious. Or maybe I should say my mother raised me to be superstitious. Don't open an umbrella in the house, knock on wood, don't tempt fate, all those things. I rebelled against all of that, of course. Sometimes I even open an umbrella in the house just to prove I don't buy it."

Her lips curved almost impishly, and he had to smile back. "I hear you."

Her small smile faded. "But there's a definite atmosphere in this house I didn't notice before. I thought maybe I was imagining it because I couldn't find a source for the noises Colleen complains about. But then you said the house felt sad."

He wished he could take those words back. But he couldn't, and by saying them he'd not only revealed something about himself that he ordinarily kept private, but he'd apparently also increased Del's concern.

He ought to kick his own butt. "Sorry," he said. But he couldn't deny that he felt something in this house, because that would mean lying.

"It's okay. At least I know I'm not riding the crazy train alone." She sighed, then smiled. "Let me make us some coffee or something. We could probably sit here for hours and never hear the sound."

Long experience warned him to leave, that he'd been in her house long enough to stir talk if people had noticed. But another part of him, the real person who'd been tucked away inside out of necessity, told him to stick around. If she wanted him gone, she wouldn't have made the offer, and her suggestion that he stay intimated that she didn't want to be alone here. Nor could he blame her.

But she caught his hesitation, and he saw her fair cheeks color faintly. "I'm sorry," she said. "You just got home and I've already taken too much of your time."

This time he didn't hear a dismissal. Far from it: this was genuine courtesy. And it warmed him.

"I'd love that coffee if it's not too much trouble."

She hopped up from the bed, clearly pleased. "No trouble at all. In fact, I need to make dinner for myself, so why don't I just make it for both of us."

She hurried from the room, apparently intent on doing just that. He remained a moment longer, wondering if he'd just put his foot in it for both of them.

But the sadness in the house called to him, and he couldn't help thinking that, in her own way, Del was probably as lonely a soul as he was.

And that called to him, too.

In the big scheme of things, impulsively inviting a neighbor to stay for a cobbled-together dinner probably didn't amount to much. But for Del it was a big step. She liked to know her neighbors, yes, but rarely socialized beyond the most casual conversations. Not since the accident.

Once she'd been quite engaged with friends and a social life, but since Don's death she had begun to note how she had narrowed her world and limited the people she allowed to become close. In fact, she had even let close friends go, slowly, simply by not keeping up with them.

Afraid to make new connections because she was afraid of more pain? Yeah, and she knew it. But it didn't bother her. She had more than enough to occupy herself, and she could justify narrowing the scope of her life by the need to take care of Colleen.

So in the big scheme of things, asking Mike Windwalker to join her for dinner was nothing. In *her* scheme of things it seemed like a huge step. But, she assured herself as she began to pull things from the fridge and cupboards, it really was a minor thing. He'd offered to help her get an appropriate kitten for Colleen. Asking him to stay for a run-of-the-mill dinner hardly seemed out of line.

And maybe it was time for her to pull at least one foot out of her self-imposed rut. She wasn't opposed to healing—she just didn't seem to have time for it. Maybe she needed to make time, for the sakes of both her daughter and herself.

"What can I do to help?" Mike asked as he entered the kitchen.

"Have a seat and keep me company." She looked over her shoulder at him and said frankly, "I've turned myself into a hermit. It would be good for me to start practicing my social skills again."

He smiled as he pulled out a chair at the small table and sat. "I probably could use some of the same myself."

"I doubt it. You deal with people all day long. I deal with wood, plaster, paint and noxious chemicals. They don't talk back."

A chuckle escaped him. "You picked quite a profession."

"I enjoy it. I like working with my hands and solving the problems that go along with restoring a house."

He was silent a moment, then asked carefully, "Why'd you turn into a hermit?"

She faced him then, folding her arms and leaning back against the counter. "Truth or social quip?"

"I vastly prefer the truth to social ice skating."

At that she felt a smile tip up the corners of her mouth. A smile she hadn't expected. "Truth it is, then. My husband was killed in the accident that paralyzed Colleen. You know what they say about once burned, twice shy? I seem to have applied that lesson to everything except Colleen."

"I can definitely see how that might happen. I have a similar story, but I'll leave that for another time."

She could see his barriers snap into place, and her curiosity itched. But okay, she was willing to observe his boundaries. She expected the same courtesy for herself.

"Fair enough," she agreed and turned back to the counter. But she couldn't help wondering what his story was. "I hope you like salad."

"Any way it's made."

"Good." Because that was all she had planned tonight, a green salad with some leftover grilled chicken breast and a choice of bottled dressings. Her time was so limited these days that she stuck with basics, the quicker and easier the better, her only nod being to the healthfulness of what she prepared.

As she was standing at the counter slicing tomatoes, a bang sounded through the house.

She whirled around, her heart accelerating, and found Mike looking upward. "Door slamming," he said. "Do you have windows open or a fan on?"

"Not right now. I didn't open anything when I came home."

He rose. "Stay here. I'll go look."

"Like hell," she answered. She'd been using her chef's knife to slice, and she seated it more firmly in her grip. A weapon.

He didn't argue with her as she followed him. For that she gave him points.

"Sounded like it was from upstairs," he remarked quietly.

"It did," she agreed. In the hallway it was easy to see at a glance that all the doors stood wide open, the way they'd been left. Mike glanced at her, acknowledging that he'd noticed, too.

And then he started up the stairs, stepping to the outside of the risers so as not to make noise. She followed his example.

But at the top of the stairs, they could see all the doors were open, just as they'd been left.

He spoke. "Could something in the attic have made that sound?"

"There's nothing up there. Not so much as a box."

They both stood for a minute, listening, but no other sound disturbed the utter silence of the house.

"It must have come from outside." But even as Del spoke the dismissal, she knew she was lying to herself. That noise had come from inside, not from without. And there was no mistaking the sound of one of these solid oak doors slamming.

"Well," said Mike slowly, apparently agreeing with

her thought if not her words, "if one of those doors slammed open it would have been hard enough to leave some evidence."

Del watched as he checked in every room. She didn't need to look for herself because she knew exactly what the sound was, and it wasn't a door opening. As often as she had the windows open and fans going, she absolutely knew how these doors sounded when they slammed shut, and it wasn't the same as when they got caught on a gust and were pushed open. Not the same at all.

Mike returned in only a few moments. "Let me check the attic," he said.

She looked at him, realizing he wasn't criticizing her, understanding that he was genuinely concerned someone other than the two of them might be inside the house. Heck, the back of her *own* neck was prickling with that suspicion.

But surely if someone were in the house, they would have discovered it on their walk-through. Unless, as Mike apparently feared, someone was in the attic.

God, the idea made her skin crawl. She waited with forced patience as Mike pulled down the overhead ladder to the attic and climbed up. She heard him flip the switch which turned on three bulbs that hung from the rafters from one end of the attic to another. He reappeared only a minute later.

"Nobody could hide up there unless they're six inches tall."

"I know." And somehow that only made this worse.

Noises for no reason? She'd lived in this house for over two months now, and she knew its sounds as intimately as she knew her own heartbeat. That had been the sound of an oak door slamming. Hard. And in the usual way, they wouldn't do that even with the windows open and the fans blowing, even with a relatively strong breeze in the house.

Inevitably, she thought about the sounds Colleen had been hearing and tried to put it together. But it made no sense.

Mike closed the attic trapdoor and looked at her, his gaze trailing down to the knife she held. "Loaded for bear?" he asked lightly.

A faint flush stung her cheeks. "Stupid, huh?"

He shook his head. "I was just thinking that you look like you could take on the whole damn world. That's a compliment."

"Thanks." But now she felt foolish. She'd investigated odd sounds many times in her life, but never before had she felt compelled to carry a knife on the hunt. "Major overreaction."

"Not really. Not when you consider that Colleen has been complaining of noises. That'd raise *my* action-alert level, too."

He really *was* a very nice man. Her embarrassment seeped away and she turned for the stairs. "Let's go get that salad."

He also turned out to be a comfortable companion. She felt no pressure to talk as she finished the salad and served them at the table. She often spent large chunks of her time inside her own head, busy with her hands, and most of the time she preferred it that way. There was a soothing rhythm in her work, and it left her feeling content at day's end.

Someone who could share that silence while seeming to remain comfortable was unusual indeed.

"I don't spend much time on cooking," she said

apologetically as she put the last bottle of dressing on the table. "Healthy foods are the best I can do, as quickly as possible. Oh! I have some frozen garlic bread, if you'd like some."

"This is fine." He smiled and gestured her to sit with him. "I don't cook much at all myself. A fresh salad is a treat."

She returned his smile and motioned him to serve himself first. "With Colleen I probably keep a better eye on things than I would otherwise."

"Understandable. I think the animals in my kennel have a far better diet than I do. When I get sick of bottles, cans and frozen foods, I go to Maude's."

"Maude's is one of my guilty pleasures, too. I'm surprised I haven't seen you there."

"I don't go often." Something in his tone suggested there was a reason for that, and she wondered but didn't say anything. She didn't know him well enough to ask any personal questions.

She paused just as she poked her fork into a bit of tomato, as the sound of the slamming door sounded once again, this time in her head. "I'm sorry," she said after a moment. "I don't think I can hold a normal conversation right now."

He put his own fork down and looked attentively at her. "The noise we heard?"

"That and the noises Colleen is hearing. Yesterday I was wondering if she was imagining them, and not knowing what was worse—her imagining them or the sounds being real when I couldn't find the source." She tightened her lips. "I didn't imagine that slam."

"Hardly. I heard it, too, remember?"

She hesitated, then said, "Colleen has been through

hell. So much so that I keep waiting for her to shatter in some way. I mean, to lose your dad and be paralyzed all at once, at her age…" She trailed off as her throat tightened. Finally she found her voice gain. "Except for the first month or so, she's been an amazing trouper."

"I get that impression. So you were wondering if her hearing things was the shattering you feared?"

"It crossed my mind. Awful of me even to think that."

"No, I think it was reasonable to wonder. Look, I doctor animals, but I've seen them with post-traumatic stress reactions, too. With some of them, they seem fine at first, and then one day they start acting out somehow. Your fear was entirely reasonable. But apparently that's not what's going on."

"Apparently not. And now I've got to wonder what caused that sound. Maybe we misinterpreted something else."

"That's possible." He pushed back from the table. "Tell you what. I'm going to go through the house and slam doors. You holler out when you hear the one that sounds like what we heard."

She nearly gaped at him, then felt almost embarrassed, though she wasn't sure why. "I think I invited you to join me for dinner. You should finish eating first."

A soft chuckle escaped him. "Salad will keep for five minutes, and I'm as curious as you are. Let me go slam some doors. You sing out if one of them sounds the same."

In the doorway, he paused to look back. "Stand where you were before, if you don't mind. That way we can be sure it was the same sound."

"Okay." She was actually glad to hop up and go stand

by the counter, facing the same direction. She *needed* to solve this problem, the sooner the better. Then maybe she could put Colleen's fears to rest and silence her own concerns.

Maybe.

She stood leaning against the counter, eyes closed, listening to slam after slam, first from downstairs, then from upstairs. The bangs moved through the house, but by the time Mike returned she was certain of one thing.

"None of them, huh?" he asked as he returned to the kitchen.

She pivoted to face him. "The sound was similar on the upstairs doors. But I noticed something else."

"What?"

"The vibration passed through the whole house when you slammed them."

His eyes widened a hair. "So we heard the sound, but there was no vibration. You're right. I didn't *feel* the door slam."

"Nope." And what had been a small worry blossomed into a big fear.

"This is not good," he said.

She couldn't have agreed more.

# Chapter 3

"I don't believe in hauntings," she said as they washed up after the meal. Hunger had pretty much deserted them, and there was a lot of salad left. And haunting was the only other explanation her mind kept turning up for the sound of a door slamming when none had.

"No?" His question was neutral.

She looked at him as she handed him the last plate to dry and realized he wasn't looking at her. "Do you?"

"I was raised in a different culture."

She reached for a spare towel and dried her hands. "I'd like to hear about that if you don't mind telling me."

He shrugged one shoulder and put the dried plate in the cupboard with the rest. "I'm a man of science. I'm supposed to believe in the mechanistic view of life."

"But you don't?"

"Only insofar as it's useful."

Curious, she grabbed a couple of fresh coffee cups and filled them, putting them on the table before he could refuse and thus insist it was time to leave. She was well aware that she was taking a lot of his time, but she wasn't ready to let him go. Couldn't, if she were to be honest about it. Sitting in this house alone wondering about that noise was apt to keep her up all night.

He hesitated but didn't argue. She made up her mind right then that one of these days she was going to get to the root of the way he hesitated about so many things. But not now. She had just asked enough of him for one night.

"I'm sorry I can't offer you a more comfortable place to sit."

One corner of his mouth lifted. "I'm a table-and-chair kind of person. My family held every gathering around a table."

"Mine, too." At least a point of connection.

As soon as she returned to her seat at the table, he joined her. "So what did you mean?" she prodded gently.

"I'm Cheyenne. I know, dirty word around here."

"Not in this house," she informed him firmly.

Again that half smile of his. "How'd you avoid it?"

"I was always weird."

This time a real laugh escaped him. "Weird how?"

"Well, I got into a bit of trouble when I was six. I was in religious education class and when the teacher said Judas went to hell for betraying Christ, I asked how that could be possible, since God had planned it all and *somebody* had to do it."

"Wow. How much trouble did you get into?"

"Only a little, actually. But that was my first starring

role as the girl who asks off-the-wall questions." She shook her head a bit. "My dad took me to the memorial of the Battle of Little Big Horn when I was about fourteen, and all I could think was that Custer was an idiot."

That, too, surprised a laugh out of him. "How did your dad react to that?"

"He surprised me by saying it did look that way. When I got older I learned a word for Custer's idiocy—*hubris*. The man was full of it. I mean, even ignoring that we were busy taking all the land away from you folks, and hunting you down like animals, Custer was an idiot. When I stood where the cavalry stood, and looked down that hill at where all the Cheyenne—I seem to remember it was mostly Cheyenne along with some other Sioux tribes—all I could think is what idiot with two hundred and forty-five soldiers attacks five thousand people?"

"The battle began long before that day."

"I know." She sighed. "It's a sad and ugly story. And all the folks in these parts who talk as if you guys are still the enemy would be feeling a whole lot different if they'd been invaded. So no, we don't share those feelings in this house. Memories are too damned long anyway."

"Even among my people."

"With more reason."

"That's debatable, too."

She noticed he seemed to have relaxed, really relaxed for the first time since crossing her threshold. Well, considering the ill-considered bigotry a lot of people spouted, she could understand that. "So about how you were raised?"

"Many Native American people believe that all things are sentient, even the rocks. And many of us believe the spirit world exists right alongside us. And sometimes we get glimpses of that world."

She bit her lip. "So you believe in hauntings?"

"Honestly? I'm not sure. I'm just not ready to dismiss anything out of hand. But I'm definitely willing to help you keep looking for the source of that sound. Because however I was raised, I'd still like to find a concrete explanation."

She guessed she could deal with that. When she thought about it, what he was saying was really no different from what her religion taught: there was a spirit world, and afterlife. She just didn't believe the two intersected. "So you're not trying to tell me the house is haunted."

"I'd hardly jump to that conclusion from a single sound."

She sipped her coffee and regarded him thoughtfully. "You must feel sometimes as if you walk in two worlds."

"Sometimes."

She tried to read something in his expression, but this man gave away little he didn't choose to. Still, she could imagine that straddling two different cultures probably carried difficulties she couldn't begin to understand. And then there was bigotry. She'd heard enough talk in these parts to know that was still alive and well among some when it came to Native Americans.

"You probably could have chosen any place in the country to practice," she said after a few moments. "Why did you come here?"

"Because it was near enough that I could get home

to see my mother. At the time, she wasn't in the best of health."

"I'm sorry."

"That's life, isn't it?"

"Unfortunately, yes." She sighed and lifted her coffee mug in both hands. "I grew up here, but I almost didn't come back."

"No?"

"I met Don, my husband, in college, and he got a job in Denver. I followed after I graduated." She smiled faintly. "I'd studied architectural engineering and was lucky enough to land a job with a firm in Denver. So we married, and Colleen came along, and the world was my oyster. Our oyster. After the accident, after Colleen recovered enough to need physical therapy only a few times a week, I realized I couldn't bear to stay there any longer. It felt as if there was a reminder around every corner. So I ran back home."

His nod was encouraging, his expression sympathetic. "Has it turned out well?"

"I've been able to move on, if that's what you mean. I'm busy, I feel good most days about most things. Unfortunately, I studied architectural engineering and these days I wished I'd stayed longer and taking mechanical engineering, too. You know, wiring and plumbing. I have to hire people to do that work."

"Expensive?"

"Of course." She gave a rueful shrug. "The minute I start tearing out walls and putting in bathrooms, I have to bring everything up to code. And while I approve of building codes, it would be nice if I could do that work myself."

"I suppose going back for training would be difficult now."

"Now, yes. Maybe later on." She sipped more coffee and looked at him over the mug. "What made you decide to become a veterinarian?"

"Animals." His smile was beautiful. "From the time I was little I loved animals. They didn't always get treated very well on the rez because we were poor. Lots of strays. You know, that was an odd contrast. Spiritually we think of animals as our brothers. But in reality..." He shrugged a shoulder. "When you're having trouble feeding a kid, it's hard to find food for a dog. So there were a lot of strays. Mostly dogs, some cats, but cats actually do better for themselves on their own. I started collecting them, much to my mother's chagrin. And I found a low-paying job when I was eight, watching a neighbor's sheep, and used the money to buy dog food. I put my first splint on a dog's leg when I was ten because nobody could afford to take a stray to a vet and the only other alternative was to shoot it."

"Did the splint work?"

"You bet. Mainly because I was lucky and it was a simple fracture." He chuckled quietly. "But there was no stopping me after that. I learned a lot about caring for livestock from my elders. I read books. I scoured libraries and finally got really lucky."

"How so?"

"A vet who came to the rez sometimes to look after cattle and sheep picked up on my interest and took me on as an assistant."

"That's great!" But she saw his face shadow and realized the unhappiness inherent in that story, as well as the pleasure of having an opportunity. A complex man, one who kept a lot close to the vest.

"Yes, it was. He gave me a load of books to read, he taught me, and he made sure I studied hard enough and well enough to get into college. A good man."

"He sounds like it."

"I was lucky to have a mentor, a great mentor. People like that can make more of a difference than they may ever realize. Unfortunately, he died before I graduated from veterinary school, but at least he knew I made it."

"I'm sure he was proud."

"Despite everything."

She opened her mouth to ask what he meant, but she realized his face had closed as suddenly as someone slamming a door. She bit back the words and sat there, feeling at sea, wondering if there was any direction with this man that didn't lead to a closed door, or a hesitation, or the sense there was a lot he would never say.

Of course, that just made her even more curious, but she knew how to bide her time. She'd learned patience the hard way, with a daughter whose slow recovery demanded it.

A rumble of thunder drew her attention and she glanced toward the kitchen window, surprised to see the light had begun to turn a gray-green.

"That'll upset the dogs in the kennel," Mike remarked.

"Really?"

"About thirty percent of dogs are scared of storms. In a kennel, that thirty percent set off the rest."

"Is it the noise?"

"There's some debate about that. Some dogs seem to

start responding way too early, as if they sense a change in the air pressure."

"Amazing. Do you need to go to them?"

"No, that only reinforces the behavior. We all, me included, wish there was some way to comfort them, but there isn't. They interpret the comfort as positive reinforcement, and it makes it worse. And right now we don't have any dogs who freak out enough to require sedation. So the best thing to do is let it burn itself out."

"That must be hard to do."

"It is, I admit. I have to remind myself often enough that trying to soothe them will make it harder on them in the long run." He gave a faint smile. "When it comes to animals, I'm a natural-born hugger."

She returned his smile. "That's a good thing. I like people who want to hug kids and animals. It's the ones who don't that concern me. So you can really leash-train a cat? I'm still trying to imagine that."

"Oh, Colleen won't be able to walk her, or anything like that. But she can be trained to accept leash limitations. By that I mean if she's sitting on Colleen's lap and decides she wants to run after a bird, she won't throw a clawing, hissy cat fit because she can't get any farther than six feet. She may glare her disapproval, but before long she'll climb back on Colleen's lap, and eventually she'll stop trying to run after things outside."

"I was raised with the notion that you can't teach cats anything."

He laughed quietly. "Cats do a good job of keeping it a secret. I had my last cat perfectly trained. I fed him when he wanted, played when he wanted, and...he never

ever tried to get out the door after just a few attempts when I caught him and dragged him back in. He learned his limits. The same way he learned to stay out of the fridge when the door accidentally shut on him, catching him in the side."

"Oh, my!"

"*That* only took one lesson." His dark eyes danced. "One of the main differences between cats and dogs is that dogs are eager to please. More of a pack mentality. Cats...well, less so."

Thunder rumbled again, this time louder. This time Mike glanced at the window, and Del noticed that the kitchen was definitely darker now.

He looked at her. "Are you going to be okay by yourself tonight?"

"Because of the noise, you mean? Of course I will. It's just a noise. With my luck I'll probably find out another wall stud just collapsed or something. I'll be honest. I knew there was some rot in the place, but I didn't expect it to be quite so extensive. And then down in the basement there's this ridiculous brick wall that's starting to crumble a bit."

"A brick wall?"

"I know. Weird. I guess someone thought it would be attractive, like they started refinishing the basement and never got around to completing the job. But it's just dark. The thing is, I keep wondering if, when I tear it out, I'm just going to find that there's a big gaping hole in the concrete. That's the way everything else in this house is going." She gave a little shake of her head and a rueful smile. "At least the roof is solid."

"Maybe you just need to bulldoze underneath."

She laughed, imagining propping up the roof while

destroying the house beneath it. "Don't tempt me. But actually, there's a positive side to all this."

"Tell me."

"I get to remake most of the place. The load-bearing walls so far seem to be fine, but since so much else is a mess, I can reconfigure the floor plan in lots of ways I wouldn't have attempted otherwise. A work-through rather than a work-around." She stared past him for a few seconds, envisioning it. "This may become the house I stay in. If I'm going to do all this work, I may as well enjoy the fruits."

"What would you do differently if you decide to stay, as opposed to just selling it?"

"I'd make the kitchen more accessible to Colleen. And I'd do a complete finish-out of the bath off her bedroom so it would be perfect for her."

"Then do it."

She looked at him, surprised by his encouragement. "I've been seriously thinking about it."

He hesitated just a moment then asked, "Is she always going to be in that chair?"

"Barring a medical miracle."

"Then fix the place for her."

She gave him a rueful look. "Only if I can find the source of the sounds that are scaring her."

"True. How scared is she?"

"Scared enough. At first when I said it must be vermin in the walls or the attic, she seemed okay with it. But as time passes and I don't find anything, I can tell it's starting to frighten her."

He nodded. "This calls for some thinking, then. I'll put my mind to it and see what I can come up with." He rose from the table and rinsed his coffee cup at the sink before tucking it into the new dishwasher. "Thanks for everything. If I come up with any ideas, I'll let you know."

She saw him out and closed the door behind him, catching glimpses of him through the front window as he walked back over to his house.

A nice guy, certainly concerned about Colleen. But at the same time, she felt he hadn't been quite comfortable his whole time here.

She let out a heavy sigh and wondered if she was imagining things herself. Why should he be uncomfortable? No reason that she could see. And he'd certainly tried to be helpful.

The thunder rumbled again, like an approaching beast, and she realized she was standing all alone in a darkening house where even she, now, had heard an inexplicable noise.

For an instant she had that horrible feeling, the one most people referred to as *something just walked over my grave*.

Not good. As a single mom with a child, she couldn't let her imagination run away with her.

Not even when she was alone.

She slept in Colleen's bed that night, determined to hear whatever it was that Colleen was hearing. Or at least she tried to sleep. She kept waking from dreams that involved Mike Windwalker, and every one of them seemed to be sexy.

Man, she didn't need that. She'd buried that part of herself ever since the accident, first out of grief, and then out of the necessity of caring for her daughter and building some kind of hopeful life for them.

Yes, he was a sexy man. Yes, he was eye candy. But that didn't give him the right to turn up in her dreams, talking in that calm, deep voice of his, looking at her from dark eyes that seemed to be lit with some kind of inner flame. Nor did it give her sleeping brain the right to conjure images of him touching her, undressing her, kissing her…and waking her in a state of aching arousal.

Darn it!

Finally, sick of waking in tangled sheets, sick of waking to overwhelming need for a man's loving, she kicked her way out from under the covers and sat up.

Last night's storm still rumbled, though more quietly, and the rain seemed to have stopped. If not, it was falling so quietly she couldn't hear it through the closed windows.

The room felt chilly, but that didn't surprise her. It was still spring, nights cooled down fast and she didn't have the heat on.

Not even during her teens had she experienced these kinds of dreams. What was she doing having them at the advanced age of thirty-four? Shouldn't her hormones have quieted some?

Thunder growled again in the distance and a flash of faraway lightning brightened the room just a bit. She loved thunderstorms, and if all sleeping was going to give her was a taste of unrestrained libido, then there was no point in even trying.

Feeling grumpy—hardly surprising, she supposed—she shoved her feet into the sandals she'd kicked off before lying down in a T-shirt and shorts. When she was at this point of renovation, slippers weren't allowed, only hard-soled shoes. You never knew where a nail or splinter might turn up.

Rising, she smoothed the covers on Colleen's bed then turned to go get a drink and something to read. Maybe she could fall asleep on the sofa.

That was when she heard it.

A not very loud sound, but definitely a scratching, like fingernails on something rough.

She froze, straining her ears, and was rewarded with another rumble of thunder, one that now irritated her even more. Slowly it trailed away, as if reluctant to give up its voice, and silence reigned.

Again she heard the scratching. Faint. Weak. Impossible to say where it came from. Impossible to even be sure it came from within the room, it was so soft.

But she understood now why it disturbed Colleen so. It most definitely didn't sound like a mouse scrambling through the wall.

No, it sounded like something that wanted to get out. Something that wasn't strong enough. It was, she thought crazily, an almost plaintive sound.

And that was enough to make the hair on the back of her neck stand on end.

## *Chapter 4*

Something woke Mike. He wasn't sure exactly what it was, but it brought him bolt upright in bed, not at all usual for him.

And the instant he awoke, he knew something was wrong. Not for one second did he question the instinct. A childhood spent at the knee of his uncle, a respected medicine man, had given him lessons no amount of time among science and Europeans could erase. Sometimes there was a *knowing*. Sometimes dreams whispered a truth, or the thunder spoke a message, or even the very molecules of the air carried a warning. He didn't need to know its source to listen to it.

Rising, he stepped into his jeans and pulled on a sweat-shirt. Then he jammed his feet into the moccasins he wore around the house as slippers and began to move.

He let himself be guided, though he had no idea where he was going or why.

He *was* surprised, though, to be guided onto his front porch. The thundery night shimmered with distant lightning, nothing close enough to worry about. But in one of those flashes he saw a figure standing on Del's front porch. He tensed immediately, then in another shimmer saw that it was Del herself standing out there.

Immediately galvanized, he jumped over his porch railing and trotted her way, forgetting everything life had ever taught him about getting involved with a white woman.

"Del? Del?"

She turned as she heard his call. In the uneven, flickering light her expression was hard to read. He trotted up her steps and went to her side. "What's wrong?"

Her eyes looked like two dark holes until the lightning flashed again and he could see how wide and blue they were.

"I heard it," she said.

"The door slam?"

"No. The sounds Colleen is complaining about."

"You couldn't localize it?"

"I couldn't *stand* it."

He stilled, unsure what she meant, but troubled by the way she said it. He wanted to offer her that culture-crossing gesture of support, an arm around her shoulders, to ease her distress, but he knew better. Even if she claimed not to be a bigot, life had taught him that even that could change in the crunch. After all, Livvie's foot had kicked him, too, when he was down. Livvie's voice had cried the same insults. He understood why, and he had forgiven her eventually, but he'd learned his lesson.

Finally he asked, "Why couldn't you stand it?"

"Because… Oh, God, this is going to sound insane."

"I'm the only one listening, and I don't make that judgment. Out of my field."

She wrapped her arms around herself, shook her head once, then said, "Oh, hell, why not? If I'm crazy I need to know it."

"What exactly did you hear?"

"Scratching. But not like a mouse or a rat would do. It didn't sound like that. And I didn't hear anything moving. Nothing at all. It was just this very weak *scratching*. But…" She bit off the word and shook her head again.

"But what?"

She bit her lip, fighting with herself, he guessed. Then, "Honestly, Mike, it sounded like something was trying to scratch its way out of something. But as if it was too weak to do it. I swear it sounded almost like it was begging. And that's *nuts*."

Her gaze returned to his, vanishing and reappearing in the flicker of the distant lightning. For a second or two, he just absorbed her words, trying to add up her statements. When he did, he understood her discomfort.

He turned and looked at the house. Slowly he said, "I told you the place feels sad."

"What the hell does that mean?"

"I don't know." He looked at her, drawing back emotionally, prepared for the worst. But the worst didn't happen. Her expression was pleading, not accusatory.

"I'm going in," he said. "Colleen's bedroom?"

She nodded.

"I'll sit in there and listen."

"I'll come, too."

"No." He reached out and made the mistake of touching her forearm. Skin as smooth as satin, and the shock of the contact headed straight for his groin. Not now. Not her. No way.

"Just wait here," he said as he jerked his hand back. "Two people will make too much noise."

She nodded slowly, accepting his reasoning. He didn't tell her he was going to listen with more than his ears. Those were things you seldom shared with whites. At least in these parts.

He slipped through the open front door, his moccasins silent on bare wood and rugs both. He knew his way now and needed no more illumination than the occasional flash of the storm.

*You feel so sad,* he thought to the house. *What's your story? What happened?*

But there was no answer, and he didn't really expect one. The spirits seldom bothered to speak or explain, but his grandfather had taught him to respect them, to acknowledge them always. They were, after all, as much a part of this world as he was, seen or unseen.

In Colleen's room, he sat on her desk chair, closed his eyes and waited patiently. The rumbling of thunder in the distance was a familiar voice to him, one he had been taught to always listen to, not so much with his mind, but with his heart.

And his heart kept saying that something was wrong, very wrong, in this house.

His people believed in the sentience of everything in

the universe. Even the rocks, the water, the very air were aware. That storm in the distance was a living thing.

This house was aware. Not necessarily in the way of a human, but it was aware, and something made it sad. It had a story it could not tell, but it pierced his heart.

And maybe, just maybe, it wasn't only the house, for he could almost feel another whisper through that part of him that had been taught to listen for voices other than the human.

He sighed, trying to open himself even more, the scientifically trained portion of his brain fighting to get in the way of older teachings. If anyone around here ever heard him talk this way, he'd be out of work in a flash.

But he could not bury or deny the lessons of his youth. Nor could he quite open himself with the freedom he had known as a child, before life had gotten complicated with other philosophies, other thoughts, other beliefs.

Funny how he could go to the school on the rez, go to Mass in the mornings and hear of God, and saints and angels, and most of the folks around here held to similar notions, but if he mentioned that his own beliefs went one step farther...well. Had not the Creator created everything out of himself? Because what other materials could the Creator have used?

At least the teachers at his school had respected his tribal beliefs. Previous generations of his people had not fared so well in that regard, which until a few decades ago had driven the medicine men, like his uncle, virtually underground.

But his upbringing had benefited from more open minds, and he had managed a cultural and spiritual blending that didn't feel oppositional, that fit with reasonable comfort in his heart and mind. Not that these ideas would be welcomed around here.

His thoughts continued to meander because it was virtually impossible to silence them. Even as he tried to listen with his "other ears" to the voices that regular ears couldn't detect, his mind refused to settle.

Then he heard the scratching sound. He stiffened and waited, trying to determine where the sound came from. When he heard it again, it seemed to come from elsewhere. Weak. Distant.

Dying.

He waited longer, while the sadness of the house pressed in on him like a heavy weight, and then realized he would not hear it again. Some internal sense said whatever it might be, it had finished for the night.

He rose and went out to the front porch where Del waited. She looked cold, and he immediately felt guilty for taking so long.

"I heard it," he said.

"So I'm not losing my mind?"

"Absolutely not. I'm sorry, you're freezing out here."

She shook her head. "I could have gone in. I just didn't want to. Any idea what it is?"

"None. I thought I might recognize it, but I didn't."

"Well, okay, then. At least I know it's *something*. Colleen heard it, I heard it and now you heard it. Nobody is going crazy. So now I just have to figure out what it is."

"And we need to get you warmed up." He hesitated just briefly, too briefly for her to notice, he hoped. "You want to come over to my place? I at least have my heat on."

"Yeah." She gave a small, mirthless laugh. "One of my economies, keeping the heat off at night when it's not going to get that cold."

"Well, like I said, mine's on. Up to you. I can make us some coffee or some instant hot chocolate while you decide what you want to do about this."

She nodded then looked down at herself. "I'm not exactly dressed for a social call."

Which, of course, caused him to notice how little she wore: a T-shirt and shorts, and since her nipples had hardened prominently, he knew she wore no bra. Sexy beyond belief. He had to drag his gaze back to her face. It wasn't easy, considering the sight had caused an instant, unexpected pulse of need to head straight for his groin. In the blink of an eye, he grew hot and heavy.

He didn't need this. At all. "Want me to run in and find you something?"

She looked from him to the house. "I'm no wimp. But something about that sound seriously disturbed me."

"Me, too. Well, just come over to my place then."

She arched a rueful brow at him, barely visible in the night. "I need to lock up. I have too many expensive tools and supplies in there. And my keys are in my purse. In the house." She sighed. "This is ridiculous. I'm letting a sound drive me out of my own house."

"Most things are more unnerving at night. And more so if you're alone."

"True."

"I'll come in with you. We'll get your purse and at least a jacket."

She looked his way again. "Thanks. I keep telling myself to tough it out."

"How about you tough it out in daylight?" Then he

made an offer that must have surely risen from some unconscious part of his brain, because he knew better. “I’ll help you look for a cause in the morning, if you want.”

“That’s a very kind offer. Okay, I’ll get some sweats and my purse, and then I’ll take you up on that hot chocolate.”

He followed her back into the house and waited at the foot of the stairs while she ran up to get some clothes. At least the sense of oppression had lifted, gone as if it had never been, leaving him to wonder if somehow his imagination had run amok and had created the whole impression out of nothing.

Judging by the speed with which Del returned wearing a sweat suit, however, he suspected she didn’t feel the same lifting of the atmosphere. Or was past caring.

Thunder still rumbled in the east, louder now as if the storm was growing. Lightning which had just a short while ago merely seemed to illuminate the clouds could now be seen forking down in brilliant bolts.

After Del locked the front door, they hurried across the yard and the driveway and into his house. In the moments just before they climbed his steps, he watched a brilliant fork of lightning shoot down, and it almost seemed to him to outline a woman’s profile.

The voice of the storm? Imagination? Merely his brain constructing something familiar from lines, as brains were wont to do? Sometimes straddling worlds was a bitch.

The thought brought a faint smile of amusement to his lips as he opened his door for Del. An awkward time to feel amusement, but this was just plain an awkward time anyway. Here he was, doing what he'd vowed never to do again: get involved with a white woman.

The universe had a wicked sense of humor.

Inside he turned on enough lights to make her feel comfortable, then settled her in his living room. One of those rooms he had furnished straight out of a store, as inexpensively as he could, because he simply didn't have the patience to do anything else, or the desire to waste time. It was comfortable enough for his needs, and he supposed the fact that all the pieces matched might mean something to someone. For himself, he didn't much care.

The cocoa was instant, requiring nothing more than heating the water and adding a dollop of half-and-half for richness. He carried the mugs back to the living room and found Del curled up tightly on herself on one end of the couch.

"Feeling that bad?" he asked as he passed her a mug. She accepted it with both hands.

"No. Not exactly. I'm still a little cold. And I'm angry."

"Angry why?" He took an upholstered chair facing her.

"Because this is scaring Colleen. Because it scared me and I know better."

"Better than what?"

She arched her brow at him. "It's got to be an animal in the wall. What else could it be?"

He didn't answer, mainly because he was pretty sure she wouldn't like the kind of answer his uncle would have given her, and that was the only thing that would spring to his mind right now.

"Yeah, it sounded weird," she went on. "Strange. But

who knows what kind of effect all that lath and plaster has on sounds from inside the walls? I've never had it happen before, so how would I recognize the sound? I usually renovate one room at a time, but maybe this time I just ought to go through the whole place and strip all the walls down to the lath. If there's something there, it'll show up or leave."

"True." As long as it was an animal.

She sipped her cocoa. "This is good."

"Just instant."

"More than instant. I know, I make instant all the time."

"Well, I probably just hardened your arteries by adding some cream."

At that a faint smile curved her lips. "That's okay. Once never killed anybody unless jumping off tall buildings."

He admired the way she found humor, even when she was obviously stressed. "Tell me about Colleen," he said. "She impresses me every time I see her."

"She's an impressive kid. I honestly wouldn't have expected her to handle this mess so well."

"You mean being confined to a chair?"

"That and losing her dad at the same time. But yes, I guess most especially that." She sighed, sipped more cocoa and then unfolded enough to put her cup on a coaster on the end table. "Getting over her dad's death seemed to be the hardest part for her. Sometimes she still mentions how much she misses him."

"What happened?"

"Car accident. They'd gone together for a day of skiing. I had to stay home to work on a rush project. Anyway, on the way back it turned really cold and the wet pavement started to ice over. A car zipped around them as they were descending from the Eisenhower Tunnel, skidded and spun out. Don didn't have a chance to avoid it."

"I'm sorry." Inadequate words, but all words were.

"One of those things." She sighed, looking sad for a few moments. "You know, when you said my house feels sad, maybe it's me you're picking up on."

He started to shake his head, then let it lie. This was not the time to tell her the truth. "You and Colleen actually seem to have adjusted very well."

"Yeah. And sometimes it worries me. I keep waiting for Colleen to crash. She seems to have adjusted too well, if you know what I mean."

"It may happen from time to time," he agreed. "But some of us are born to be more philosophical about things than others. Some people just take it on the chin and move on with a smile. I've known a few."

"Are you one?"

"Unfortunately, no." He felt a rueful smile form on his lips. "I'm more the once-burned-twice-shy kind."

She nodded, and a soft smile eased her own expression a bit. "Most people are, I think. I know I am. Maybe I'm being ridiculous, but with Colleen I keep waiting for the other shoe to drop, if you know what I mean. Bad things happen. And when they happen to you, you no longer feel immune. So when she started hearing these noises, I actually—I think I told you this? I can't remember—I actually started wondering about her mental state, if things might finally be catching up with her."

"Apparently you don't need to worry about that anymore."

"Apparently not. And that's a great relief, from that

perspective. But now I know why the sound unnerves her so much, and I've *got* to get to the root of it. *I* heard it and had to get out of that house."

"I'll help you every way I can." He mentally kicked his own butt as soon as the words were out, but his nature required no less than that he help. And leaving her to deal with it alone—which he was sure she would do because trying to explain it to someone who hadn't heard the sounds would be impossible—went against everything he believed about community. "I'll help," he said again. "I may not know much about renovation, but I'm sure I can rip out walls."

That garnered a sigh from her, and she seemed to relax a bit. "That's the fun part. But if I'm going to do all that, I'll need to ask my aunt to take care of Colleen."

"You sound reluctant."

"Well, she's getting up there. Physically she couldn't do much to help if Colleen needed to be lifted."

"How far away does she live? Because she and Colleen could stay here in my house until we clear out enough of the mess."

Her eyes widened, and for an instant he almost thought tears moistened her eyes. "You're a very kind man, Mike Windwalker."

Yeah, right. And it was a damn good thing he had his legs crossed so she couldn't see the more selfish feelings on parade.

He let her comment pass because he really couldn't answer it.

Any way he looked at it, dawn couldn't arrive quick enough.

Curled up on Mike Windwalker's couch, Del felt more comfortable than she had in days, maybe since Colleen had started complaining about the noises in her room. They would get started at dawn, and she wasn't going to stop until she found the sources of those noises. For now she was out of the house, unable to worry needlessly until she could act, and Mike had made her feel that she wasn't alone.

Not that anyone was truly alone in Conard County. Neighbors were always quick to help, but they had to know you needed help, and it had to be something they could actually do. So far she hadn't told anyone but Mike about the noises, mainly because she feared for Colleen's mental state.

But now Mike had heard the noises, too, so she could rest about Colleen, and she would even have help getting at the root of the problem.

Having heard the sounds that plagued Colleen, she was more disturbed than before. When she'd been busy dismissing them as vermin in the attic or walls, it had been straightforward, ordinary. Now that she'd heard the sound herself, it didn't seem ordinary at all.

Because for some reason the only mental image that had come to her mind when she heard the noise was that of a hand, a weakening hand, scratching helplessly for escape.

And that went from beyond imaginative to downright creepy.

Still, she was a practical woman, inclined to deal with problems in pragmatic ways. The ghastly horror-movie mental image had undoubtedly arisen from a mind still half-asleep and the fact that it was dark and the house was empty.

Even pragmatic people could occasionally suffer from imagination.

She sipped more cocoa and looked around, for the first time noting that she was in a living room that appeared as if it had been put together by a decorator. Few, if any, living rooms around these parts looked like that.

"Did you actually buy all your furniture to match?" she asked.

He seemed a little surprised, then laughed. "It happened that way. Not exactly a plan."

"How so?"

"Well, I'd been living here a couple of months when I realized I no longer wanted to live like a college student, sleeping on a sleeping bag and eating standing at my kitchen counter. I even had the amazing desire to be able to sit down."

"And?"

"And then I realized I had neither the time nor the patience to furnish the place piece by piece. So I headed out to one of those big furniture stores in Casper, whipped out my plastic and said I'd take this room, that room…whatever suited me that wasn't too expensive."

She laughed. "Have you caught up with the plastic?"

"Ages ago. I was impatient, not profligate. Even so, it ran so counter to my upbringing that I felt a bit disgusted with myself for a while. But…it saved time, I can relax now, and…there's even a chance the furniture will survive until the warranty runs out."

"It looks in pretty good condition to me."

"One man doesn't put much wear on most of it. I use so little of it, actually, unless I have guests. But at least I feel like I'm walking into a home. You don't have much at your place, do you?"

She shrugged. "Honestly? With the renovations, that's the last thing I'm worried about. Back in Denver there's a storage room full of furniture. Most of it stuff Don and I inherited from our families. We used it and often talked about how we liked antiques."

He had just sipped his own cocoa and now peered over his mug at her. She felt a trickle of something she didn't want to name, for fear of where it might lead her. But damn, he was attractive, and those dark eyes of his seemed to hold entire universes in them.

"Why," he asked, "do I get the feeling that saying you liked antiques wasn't exactly true?"

"Well, it's not that I don't like antiques. It's just that we had such a hodgepodge, and I was always spending time refinishing and mending, and back then the only time I had for that was when I was already tired. I think sometimes I resented it. And nothing, but nothing, was exactly right for where it was."

"What do you mean?"

"I took some design classes while I was getting my degree. You could say it permanently affected my eye. I'd look around our place and think, oh that piece is too big for that corner, or looks too small on that wall or, or, or. I couldn't quite get it all into an arrangement that satisfied me. So Don used to tease me that I was always moving furniture. And I was. And sometimes I seriously considered moving it all onto the street and replacing it completely."

He chuckled. "But now? When you finish this house? You said you might live in it. Will it fit there?"

"Some pieces will. The rest I may leave in storage for Colleen. The truth is, we're not talking priceless antiques here. Antiques, yes, priceless no. Well-worn hand-me-downs is more like it. So the question is really whether I feel some emotional attachment to a piece. Other than that…" She shrugged.

Having a conversation like this in the middle of the night seemed about as sane as running out of her house because of a noise. She stifled a yawn, feeling her eyes tear up, and realized that Mike had calmed her enough to sleep. Even the worsening storm seemed only to provide a soothing background.

Dimly she was aware of him spreading a blanket over her. The couch was so comfy, she just snuggled in a bit more.

Sleep, it seemed, had caught her between one breath and the next.

# Chapter 5

She opened her eyes to the deep rumble of thunder, a rolling sound that seemed to come from afar, pass through the house and move on. Dim, gray light filtered through the curtains, hardly bright enough to be called day.

But she could smell the aromas of cooking bacon and coffee, and after she rubbed her eyes, she sat up and prepared to face a new day.

Her dreams, remembered only vaguely, had been troubled somehow, but they left little in their wake except uneasiness. Meaningless, and probably the result of sleeping in a strange house on someone's couch rather than in her own bed. Or even the remnants of what now seemed like a silly fear because she had heard an odd sound in her house.

When had she become afraid of sounds?

Sighing, she guessed her way to the bathroom. It

wasn't as if there was any place to get lost in a house with the shotgun floor plan. Somewhere between the front door and kitchen, a bathroom would open off the hallway. Or it would open off the kitchen. It was not as if she needed a marked trail.

Someone had evidently renovated at some point because just after she passed what appeared to be Mike's bedroom, she found the bathroom, a clearly recent addition from sometime in the past fifteen or twenty years. She did what she could with fingers, a washcloth and a bar of soap, then continued down the hall to emerge in a large kitchen with so many windows she would have bet that at one time it had actually been a porch. But that was the way these houses grew.

Mike stood at the stove, holding a fork, as bacon sizzled. This morning he wore some very old jeans, ragged at the cuffs and almost worn through at the seat, and a black T-shirt. When he heard her, he turned with a smile and she saw the yellow-and-red pattern on the front of his T-shirt, a spiral with a hand imprint on it and the words beneath it: The Sacred Circle of Life.

"Oh, I like that," she said.

He looked down. "It's from my high school. I buy a lot of my tees and sweatshirts from them because it helps support the school."

"I'll have to look into it. Colleen would probably love a shirt like that. Well, maybe a hoodie. Those seem to be her favorites."

"I don't recall if they have hoodies, but they also have other designs to choose from. How'd you sleep?" He turned back to the pan and began forking the strips of bacon onto a paper towel.

"I must have keeled over like a felled tree. The last

thing I really remember was talking to you." And him spreading a blanket over her. That little act of caring seemed hugely important somehow. Which was probably a measure of how little caring she'd been feeling in her life.

"You did kind of drop out practically mid-sentence. Grab a chair. Coffee?"

"Thanks. But first I need to check my cell." She hurried back to the living room to get the phone from her purse and came back while scanning it. No calls.

"I don't think I heard it ring," Mike remarked as he started cracking eggs into the pan.

A fresh mug of coffee sat on the table and Del sat before it, lifting it with pleasure. "Mmm, this smells so good. No, I didn't have any calls. But with Colleen, I'm almost compulsive about checking."

"I would be, too. Actually, I am. You never know when there might be an emergency."

"Do you get many?"

"Too many. Well, too many in the sense that some animal is hurt or suffering. Not too many to handle."

"So you're on call all the time?"

He smiled over his shoulder. "Where's the other vet?"

"Seems like the last one moved on five years ago or so."

"Seems like. This kind of practice isn't for everyone. For me, though, it just feels like a continuation of what I've been doing since I was knee-high to a grasshopper."

Del hardly tasted breakfast, although she tried to show her appreciation for it by eating an amount that wouldn't insult him. But her stomach was tightening, and anxiety was beginning to push at her.

She needed to arrange for Aunt Sally to look after Colleen. And then she had to get to work tearing out those walls because she wanted that noise *gone*. Bad enough it had unnerved her, but she didn't want it to bother Colleen any longer. Now that she had heard it herself, she was more than ever convinced that a creature of some sort lived in her walls.

Mike picked up on her uneasiness before they even finished. "You don't have to sit here on the edge of your chair," he said kindly.

She felt her cheeks heat. "I'm sorry. I'm not trying to be rude."

"I know. You're worried. And I meant what I said last night. If you want, Colleen and your aunt can stay here today so she's close and you don't have to worry."

"That's very generous of you." But still she thought she heard a note of reluctance in his voice. "I don't want to put you out. I..." Then she hesitated. How could she draw attention to a mere feeling she got about him without insulting him? Especially when he'd been nothing but helpful and understanding.

But Mike wouldn't let her go to her corner. "But? I hear a *but* there. Would you rather your daughter not stay in a redskin's house?"

Del gasped. She felt as if he had just punched her in the solar plexus. An eon passed before she could find the breath to whisper, "That thought never crossed my mind. What in the world...?"

He looked down at his plate. She could see his jaw work as if he were clenching his teeth. She didn't know whether to be furious or concerned. Everything inside her felt as if she'd been blindsided by a truck.

"Mike?"

He glanced to the side, away from her, then finally brought his dark gaze back. "I am," he said with an edge, "leaping to an all-too-familiar conclusion."

Then she knew exactly what to feel: sickened. She balled her paper napkin and threw it on the plate. "How dare you judge me? I'm no bigot." Then she shoved back her chair and marched down the hall to the front door.

Just before she reached the front door, she heard him call her name. Part of her wanted to just keep walking. She had seldom in her life felt so offended. But another part of her insisted she hear him out. He had, after all, been kind and helpful. He was still the man who had invited her into his home and spread a blanket over her as she slept.

Slowly, reluctantly, she turned to face him. He stood on the far side of the living room, his hands knotting and unknotting as if he didn't know quite what to do with them.

"I'm sorry," he said. "Sometimes I overreact."

"Maybe you have reason," she acknowledged. "I don't know. How would I? But I can tell you this—I've felt your reluctance since I found you talking with Colleen the other day. I don't know why you keep offering to help if it's not what you want to do. But I know one thing for certain—I don't want grudging help from anyone."

With that, she turned, grabbed her purse and marched out into the storm.

She hardly noticed the raging elements, even though it was unusual to have a storm go on for so long. The air was so full of electricity that she could almost feel it, and the raindrops were huge, striking her like a pelting of pebbles.

She didn't care. Whatever Mike's problems were, she wasn't going to let him treat her that way, accusing her of a bigotry she didn't feel even in the remotest parts of her brain or heart. Tarring her because his reluctance and hesitation kept making her wonder if his offers of assistance were genuine or forced.

She had quite enough trouble in her life, though she seldom allowed her to think of things that way. But Colleen required her all, and making a life for them, one that would guarantee that at some future time Colleen would have the care she needed, would be able to go to college and live as a reasonably independent adult, took every bit of energy she had.

She certainly didn't have much left over to tiptoe through Mike Windwalker's personal booby traps.

But then she reached the door of her house. And as she stood there, sheltered by the porch roof from the storm, she felt her shoulders sag a little. Maybe she should just dump this house for whatever she could get out of it. Maybe she shouldn't try to rescue it. After all, it scared Colleen and had even managed to scare her.

And what was this stuff about the house being sad? Mike had said that twice. What the hell did he mean?

All she knew was that where a few days ago she had loved the place, had seen it full of possibilities, now she felt an urge to just get rid of it, ditch it and move on.

And that was so unlike her as to be unnerving in itself.

She gave herself a shake and pawed through her purse for her keys. Damn it, where were they? The thought that she might have left them at Mike's made her want to beat her head on the closed door in front of her.

Good God, what was going on with her? She never reacted this way to minor frustrations. Never.

"Here."

She jumped and found Mike beside her, holding out her keys. So she had left them there. She snatched them. "Thanks." She jammed the key in the lock, twisting it.

"I'm sorry," he said.

"Probably," she agreed shortly. She twisted the key again, wondering why the bolt wasn't moving. "Damn it!"

A strong, warm hand reached out, covering hers. She yanked her hand back and Mike turned the key. This time the bolt clicked.

He threw the door open and she hurried inside, hoping he'd just go home, at least until she sorted through the internal storm that had come out of nowhere. Even as she was going off like a rocket, she wondered why. This was so unlike her.

She was stable. She had to be stable. How else had she gotten through losing Don, seeing Colleen paralyzed, all the work and stress and worry…?

She put her hand to her mouth, as if it would hold this mess of feelings inside, and tried to tell herself she hadn't gotten enough sleep last night, she'd been scared by a noise, silly or not, then insulted. Of course something had snapped.

And of course, it hardly helped that she was doubting her own sanity this past week because of the way she kept losing track of things.

But then strong arms closed around her and drew her

comfortingly against a hard chest, and a hand rubbed her shoulder as a voice murmured, "I'm sorry. I'm really, truly sorry. Don't cry."

Lord, she couldn't be crying. She never cried.

But she also hadn't realized just how damn tired she'd grown of being strong, independent, cheerful and so very, very alone.

She resisted the comfort he offered, but only for a few seconds. God help her, she needed to be held, even if only for a few minutes. She needed another pair of shoulders besides her own. Just for a few minutes. Just for a teeny slice of time.

Just for now.

She let herself weaken, let herself lean on his physical strength, gave in to the amazing feeling of arms around her, holding her. But the tears dried quickly, and in their wake came shame at her own weakness. She was stronger than this. She'd been proving it for a few years now. Surely she couldn't break over nothing. Because really, it was nothing. Nothing at all compared with what she'd been through.

She sniffled and pulled away, hating the loss of his embrace almost as much as she hated her moments of weakness. "Sorry," she said, turning away as she scrubbed her eyes. "I don't usually do this."

"Somehow I suspect you never do this."

She was afraid to look at him, afraid that if she did she'd fly right back toward the illusion of comfort his arms gave her. Because it *was* only an illusion. Mike Windwalker had barely set foot in her life, and everything about him suggested he was unlikely to remain.

"No," she said. "I don't."

Silence. She drew a deep breath, grasping for her inner strength. She looked around the foyer, trying to remind herself of all she needed to do, all she wanted to do to this house, and that she really didn't hate it, and everything would be fine because it *had* to be.

But her usual mantras failed her.

"I'm just tired," she said, as much to herself as him.

"It was a disturbed night," he agreed.

And finally she felt able to face him. He stood just inside the open doorway, as if waiting for an invitation to enter.

"Why don't you come in," she said, her voice sounding a bit thick, "and then maybe you can explain what we were fighting about?"

"Not exactly a fight." But he stepped inside and closed the door.

And at once she noticed the way the storm-created darkness seemed to close in. She didn't like it.

"Let's go to the kitchen," she suggested. "At least there's plenty of light in there."

He followed her and sat facing her at the table. She put her purse down beside her and pulled out her cell phone, setting it where she could reach it if Colleen called. If she knew anything about her and Mary Jo, though, the girls had probably spent most of the night giggling and watching movies, and they probably wouldn't even stir before noon.

With the overhead fluorescent fixtures on, the room was bright, although not yet cheerful. But at least the light held the shadows at bay.

Automatically she glanced around to make sure nothing had been disturbed. It bothered her at some level that she felt the need to do that. But right now there seemed to be more important things to contend with.

"What happened," he said, "was that I was reacting to a lifetime of experience. Perhaps unfairly."

"Definitely unfairly," she told him. "I already said I wasn't a bigot, yesterday."

"Saying it and feeling it can be two different things."

She studied his face, feeling truly curious about this man. But she didn't know how to ask, wasn't sure questions would be welcome. "I guess you would know about that better than I would."

A mirthless smile lifted one corner of his mouth. "Yeah, I would. In these parts anyway."

"I've heard the comments all my life," she admitted. "I was raised to consider them wrong. We're all human beings."

He nodded. "So when you seemed reluctant to let Colleen and your aunt stay at my place today, I interpreted it through a lifelong lens."

She nodded. "Okay. But I wasn't objecting. My problem is the way you seem so reluctant and hesitant even when you're being helpful. I feel like you don't want to be."

"Part of me doesn't."

"Then why offer?"

"Sometimes my better angels take control." He sighed, giving a little shake of his head. "I don't know if I can get you to understand. But I've been reluctant because of the possibility of people talking about you and Colleen. I'm used to what they say about me. I just don't want the two of you to get any of that crap."

"I'm tempted to say that this whole discussion sounds

like something that belongs in the Dark Ages, but I guess for you it's much more recent than that."

"Very much so. Most people don't say it to my face anymore. At least not around here, although the closer you get to a reservation, the more likely you are to have the stuff right in your face. But it's here, too."

"I know. I probably just don't hear most of it because on a few occasions I've told people to stop it."

He nodded. "Thanks. But it's still there. And I'm hesitant because it could bounce back on you and Colleen if you hang around with me too much."

"Well, too bad. If people want to treat us differently because we like you and spend time with you, then I don't want to know them."

"I've heard that before."

She heard the tinge of bitterness in his tone, and she longed to ask what had happened. But she hardly knew this man. How could she tread into what was clearly a serious sore spot? Finally she asked the question in a way he could misinterpret if he chose. "Mike?"

He sighed and put a hand to his face, rubbing his eyes with thumb and forefinger. It was almost a gesture of denial. But at last he dropped his hand. "You remember the vet I told you about? The one who mentored me?"

"Yes, of course."

"Well, he had a daughter."

And suddenly she could see it coming. Her stomach seemed to flip over. "You don't have to tell me."

"Maybe I do. Young love is foolish. I should have known better when she started flirting with me. I'd heard most of the insults by then, and I'd learned I wasn't welcome in a lot of places. I'd even been in a few fights with others my age who objected to me wandering off the rez. But maybe, in a way, I'd been sheltered, too, because I lived on the rez and went to school on the rez. God knows what I was thinking. Anyway, she finally asked me to take her to a movie. I was already getting teenaged crazy about her, if you know what I mean."

She nodded. "I remember that age well."

"I warned her people would talk. She said she didn't care. And maybe she thought she wouldn't."

"Maybe."

"I don't know how to explain it all. We were both eighteen, young, subject to peer pressure, I guess. We went out a couple of times, and her dad didn't *seem* to mind, although in retrospect I wonder if he didn't just keep silent because he figured she'd come to her senses pretty quick."

"That's awful!"

"I don't know what he thought. Or why he didn't tell her to stay away from me until later. Anyway, one night we were coming out of the movies and a group of guys attacked me. They made it pretty clear what they thought of me dating a white girl. I tried to fight back. I'm a fairly good scrapper, but there were more of them than me. And when they finally got me down on the ground, she joined them in kicking me and calling me names."

"Oh, my God!" Del's stomach cramped. "Oh, Mike!"

He shook his head. "It's done. But after that I don't find it easy to trust what people say about not caring what others think. And after that I wasn't welcomed at the vet's either. He told Livvie to stay clear of me. As if I wanted any more to do with her after that. As for her kicking me, too…well, maybe she was scared. I don't know. I never asked."

"And maybe the vet was protecting both of you by insisting she stay away."

"Maybe. I'll never know. But anyway, the point is…" He stopped.

"The point is you've got plenty of reasons to hesitate and be suspicious." She looked down at her hands. They were toughened hands, not exactly feminine with all the nicks, calluses and very short nails. But they were hands she was proud of and had no desire to conceal. She'd earned them. And as she looked at them she knew something else about herself all the way to the core. She lifted her eyes to Mike.

"I meant what I said," she told him. "This whole damn county can shun me, but I'm not going to shun you. And I'm old enough to be sure that I mean what I say."

His expression lightened, although it didn't fully become a smile. He didn't answer directly though. "When are we going to start tearing out walls?"

She almost put her head in her hand. "You know…"

"Yes?"

"That was an easy thing to threaten last night. This morning it's more complicated."

"How so?"

"Judging by the fact that noises seem to be in Colleen's room, I'd need to rip out the walls in there. Which means making a safe place somewhere else for her in the meantime."

"Ah. Okay, so we start by moving her. The dining room?"

It was a lot farther from the single downstairs bathroom, but it was also the only other room on the lower floor that she hadn't started tearing the walls out of. And it had the advantage of being on the other side of the house from where the noises were.

"That'll have to be it. I don't have any other options."

"So let's get to it."

Moving Colleen's belongings into the dining room proved to be the easy part of the job, and Mike's help was more than welcome. Not only was he strong, but he had a good eye. Before she had to tell him, he had already figured out exactly where to hang the bar over Colleen's bed so that she could maneuver in and out. In an hour, they had everything moved.

Del called a halt at the posters, though. They removed them from the bedroom, but she didn't want to rehang them. "I'll let Colleen tell me where she wants them now."

Mike nodded and laid them carefully on the bed.

They took a coffee break while Del called Beth to find out how the girls were doing. "Out like lights," Beth responded cheerfully. "Relax, Del. I'll let you know when she's ready to come home."

A call to her aunt ensured that Sally was able to come over at any time to keep an eye on Colleen.

Then she gave Mike a mask and goggles, and they went into Colleen's now-empty bedroom. First she sealed off the bathroom with plastic sheeting, then they picked up hammers and began to knock plaster loose. Before long, even with windows open and fans blowing, the plaster dust built into a nearly blinding cloud. Outside the storm continued to dump rain, which seemed only to hinder the escape of the dust.

Except every now and then a contrary gust would blow by, the dust would seem to freeze midair for an instant and then would change direction, being sucked out by the wind.

With two people it didn't take all that long. Finally they were able to stop, exhausted, and look at the heaps of cracked plaster on the floor. Only a few small pieces still clung to the lath.

Mike looked at her from behind his goggles as dust slowly settled. "That lath is so pretty I'd be tempted to sand it, varnish it and leave it."

"I've thought about it a time or two," Del admitted. "Those old-timers sure had a passion for covering up wood." Reaching out with a gloved hand, she tested some of it and found it sturdy. "The only problem is, I'm now looking at a wood wall instead of a plaster one. Admittedly it has more chinks, but still, I can't see through it." And wires were now exposed.

She crouched to look at them. "Well, it's what I expected. This whole house was apparently wired at the same time."

"Not up to code?"

"Far from it. I wondered when I bought it. In most of these old houses the wiring is outside the walls, but not this one."

"Money," he said, referring to his earlier remark about the house. "You know, it would be really interesting to look into the history of this place."

"Yeah, it would." She worked her fingers into the chink between two strips of horizontal lath and pulled plaster out. The spaces were essential so that the plaster would seep through and hold in place until it dried. The seepage she now pulled at was called a key. At the very least sixty or seventy years old, it crumbled.

She straightened, blowing a long breath. "Okay. Since it's raining so hard, I guess we leave the plaster on the floor. In the meantime I need to remove some of the lath so I can see what's going on back there."

Mike, too, touched the wall. "This seems like awfully high-quality wood to use as a backing for plaster."

"Yeah. Who knows? Maybe it was all they could get in a timely fashion. Or maybe someone had money to burn. Obviously, it wasn't built to be a bare wall, or it wouldn't have so much space between the laths."

He pulled down his mask, revealing a nose and mouth that were unsullied by the pale dust, and grinned. "I didn't realize tearing apart a house could feel like a treasure hunt."

She laughed. The hard work had eased the last of the tension from her mind and body. "It can be interesting."

Then he looked down at the oak floor. "Tell me you don't have to rip this up." He tapped it with his foot.

"No, you can see the floor joists directly under it from the basement. The ceiling will have to go, though, if we don't find the problem."

He looked up. "Well, it doesn't look as nice as the walls did. Has it been papered over?"

"At least a couple of times. Something else I'll never understand." She reached up, pointing to a seam. "Whoever did the job didn't match the seams. You can see them everywhere in the house. Lengths of paper overlay others. And then somebody painted on top of that."

"I was always told not to do that."

"Good advice. Paint on paper seldom looks good. It just seems to highlight the inconsistencies in the wallpapering. But you have the same problem with drywall, which is why you'll see me texture these walls before I paint them, unless I decide to paper them. I'm just enough of a perfectionist not to want to see shadows on walls where the wallboard is a little bent, or if the mudding shows through. Want some coffee?"

Colleen called while the coffee brewed, begging permission to stay with Mary Jo until that evening. Beth insisted she would enjoy it as much as the girls.

"Thanks," Del said finally, when she was sure it wouldn't be an imposition. "I've been tearing Colleen's room apart and moving her."

Silence. Then, "Colleen said something about hearing noises."

"Yeah. And last night I heard them, too. So you can tell her I'm going to get rid of the vermin if I have to tear out every wall in this house."

Beth laughed. "I'll do that. And if you want her to stay overnight, I can just drop by to get some clothes for her. The place must be a dusty mess."

"That's an understatement."

"Okay, when John gets back from Carl's ball game, I'll run over. I can do everything except get her to school in the morning. And I don't mind at all."

There it was again, that feeling of being cared for. Del felt her throat tighten just a bit and wondered how she'd managed for so long to overlook such little acts of kindness. Maybe because recognizing them made her feel weak? And she couldn't afford that. Ever.

When she closed her phone, the coffee was ready and

she realized she was hungry. "Something to eat?" she asked Mike.

"Tell you what. I'll run over to Maude's and pick us up a heart attack. I think we're working hard enough to survive steak sandwiches and fries."

"That does sound good. But have some coffee first. If your throat is as coated with dust as mine, you need to drink something before it all turns to plaster again."

He laughed but didn't linger, downing the coffee quickly. Then, covered in dust except for his face, forearms and hands, which he'd wiped down with a damp dish towel, he set out, promising to return quickly.

And that left Del alone in the house again. Hell. At least the growl of the storm had receded into the distance, although she could still see lighter rain falling. After calling Sally to tell her she wouldn't be needed today after all, she returned to work.

Taking a flashlight and a pry bar with her, she headed back to Colleen's room. While she waited for Mike, she could take down some of that lath. If experience was any guide, age should have caused the wood to shrink enough to make pulling out nails relatively easy.

She didn't want to use the lights in here now, either. Pulling all that plaster might have damaged wiring.

She started near the bottom, the place where she'd most likely find animal leavings if there were any. Three boards came off quickly, shedding more dust and making her sneeze and cough. "Keys" fell to the floor along with the boards, sending up small clouds. She should have worn her mask, but right now she was more concerned about finding something. Anything that would explain that darn noise.

She pulled one more board, finding it somewhat more difficult, then leaned in as far as she could, the flashlight on and sideways.

The gap between inner and outer walls was bigger than the norm. Whoever had built this house had used six-inch studs rather than the two-by-fours that were common in later construction. Another mystery. Mike was right. She ought to look into who had built this house, because they had made some interesting choices. The studs were also set farther apart, not the sixteen inches most common in modern building. Well, of course, with sturdier studs, you could make that trade-off.

And she couldn't see a darn thing that looked like rodent droppings or a rodent nest. If anything had ever lived in this wall, its leavings had long since turned to dust.

"Del?"

Startled by the unexpected voice, she jerked and banged her head. A moment later, eyes watering from pain, she sat on the floor looking up at her plumbing contractor, Edgar Dorset.

"Sorry," he said. "I thought you heard me come in."

She set the flashlight down and rubbed her head. "It's okay. What's up?"

"I couldn't remember if you wanted me tomorrow. I've got a job in Laramie, but I can put it off till Tuesday."

She looked up at the man, taking in his slightly plump figure, his "Sunday" clothes, his round face and balding head.

She *had* wanted him tomorrow because she was concerned about getting Colleen's bathroom whipped into shape. But now with the wall business… "It's okay, Edgar. It can wait a few days. If a few days is all you need."

"Oh, I can be here Tuesday." He indicated the wall with a jerk of his head. "Something going on?"

"I think I've got vermin."

"That's no fun. I had a rat die in my wall three years ago."

"I'm trying to avoid that."

"I can sure understand why." He squatted beside her and peered into the dark opening. "There's plenty of room. Have you considered trying to smoke it out?"

"I don't know. I mean this lath is so old it's probably tinder."

"Good point." He settled back a bit and smiled. "I'll think about it while I'm in Laramie. There's got to be some way to deal with this short of tearing the house down."

"You'd think."

He chuckled and stood. "See you Tuesday then, Del. Eight sharp?"

"As always. Say, if you run into Jimmy—" Jimmy was her electrical contractor "—tell him I might need him soon. Ripping out these walls might have damaged some of the wiring."

"I'll maybe see him tonight. It might be Sunday, like my wife says, but we play poker anyway."

"I don't know why it would offend the Lord more on Sunday than any other day."

His eyes twinkled. "That's my feeling. Seems like he said it was a day of rest. That's how I rest. Hannah don't always agree with that."

She could believe that. And she had wondered more

than once if Hannah had been born with a prune face. But whatever her disapproval of Edgar's poker, she loved the man to death. That much was clear.

"How soon do you need Jimmy?"

"Well, nothing seems to be shorted, so I think I can get by for a day or so just by not turning on lights in here. But I need to be sure."

"Absolutely. You still thinking about tearing out that wall in the basement?"

"Eventually." She looked at the hole she had just made in the lath and sighed. "Of course, if I can't find the vermin here I may have to go at it sooner. That brick wall seems to be right beneath us."

"True." He rubbed his chin. "I'll mention that to Jimmy, too. Unlikely that wall isn't flush up against the basement wall, though, so I'd be surprised if you'd find anything behind it. But if you decide you need to pull it out, the two of us can help." He winked. "Some things can always use an extra strong back."

She returned his smile, but she wasn't exactly wet behind the ears. Both Jimmy and Edgar could always use extra work, even if it was carting bricks out of the basement. The offer of help would come with a bill attached. Not that she would blame them for that. They all had families to support and bills to pay.

Edgar took his leave, but just as Del was about to pry loose some more lath, she heard Mike call her from the kitchen.

"Del? Lunch is here and it's hot."

The news caused a Pavlovian response. At once her stomach growled and her mouth started watering. Straightening, she automatically brushed her dusty hands against her jeans, then realized the jeans were even dustier. *Duh.* Just another sign of lack of sleep.

She washed up at the kitchen sink and joined Mike at the table where he'd set a couple of foam containers and two tall soft drinks with straws. When she opened her container, the incredible smell of the steak sandwich and fries reached her nose and she drew it in with pleasure.

"Colleen would be so upset if she saw me eating this."

"Why?"

"Because we have to watch what she eats. She's… less active now, obviously."

Mike's gaze softened. "That has to be tough."

"At her age? You better believe it. But she's pretty good about it most of the time. Every now and then we break the rules. But mostly we have to eat healthy stuff."

He looked down at his sandwich. "I don't think the sandwich is all that unhealthy. But the fries…" He shook his head. "I'm always having to tell dog owners that if they want to share fries with their pooch, one fry is plenty. They're not big enough, most of them, to justify human-size servings."

Del grinned. "I don't think I've heard it put that way before."

"Neither have a lot of dog owners." He smiled at her, then lifted his sandwich. "We all want to pamper our pets. I'm a sucker for it myself. Those big sad eyes, that wagging tail…hard to say no to. But for most dogs, if you're going to break down, a taste is more than enough. Heck, you can even give your dog a piece of chocolate-chip cookie. But just a piece."

"I thought chocolate was poison to them."

"It can be, if they get enough of it, and what constitutes enough is based on their body size. What would kill a Chihuahua obviously wouldn't kill a Great Dane."

She bit into her own sandwich, savoring it. "Thanks so much for this. It's wonderful."

"You're more than welcome. I'm not exactly being generous here. I've been thinking about one of these all morning. Did I see Edgar Dorset leaving when I pulled up?"

"Yeah. He was supposed to do some plumbing for me tomorrow but he got offered a job in Laramie and wondered if I could wait until Tuesday. Considering this whole process just took a sharp, unexpected turn, I can wait on the plumbing for a day. He was nice though. He said if I needed help with the brick wall in the basement, he and Jimmy would be glad to lend their backs." She smiled. "Invoice attached, I'm sure."

"I'm sure. Who's Jimmy?"

"Jimmy Morton. He's my electrician."

Mike's brow knit. "I don't think I've met him."

"Well, I don't usually see him about much. He seems like a lonely man, actually, but then my only contact with him is when he's working. I guess he and Edgar play poker together, so maybe I'm all wet." And how normal and natural it seemed to be sitting here gossiping about other folks in the county. It had been a long time since she'd done that.

She rolled her shoulders to loosen muscles and reached for another fry. Oh, the sin! Colleen would surely kill her if she found out. She looked up to find Mike's attention was focused on his meal, which gave her a few moments to study him.

And once again she felt the pull of attraction. He was a magnificently attractive man and she wondered if he even realized it. Probably not, as skittish as he was.

But it had been a long time since she'd noticed a man that way, and she decided not to fight it. Mike would evidently fight it enough for both of them if he happened to feel the same attraction.

But she found herself enjoying the way his muscles moved under his black—well, it had been black this morning, but now it was so full of plaster dust it looked more like a dark gray—T-shirt. And he was unquestionably handsome. Hadn't she once heard someone say that the Cheyenne were beautiful people?

As soon as the thought crossed her mind, she pulled back from it. There was a judgment in that statement, regardless of who had said it and how it was meant. She looked down and bit her lip, realizing that Mike probably had ample reason to be wary, especially if thoughts like that could occur to her. Maybe there was some of that ugliness buried deep in her own mind.

"Something wrong?" he asked.

"Not a thing." Not a thing except she had realized she'd picked up some mental lint she didn't want, and nothing, of course, except that she was starting to become too entirely aware that he was a man and she was a woman. The kind of awareness she had lost in the aftermath of tragedy.

An awareness she didn't need or want, at least not now. Her priorities had to lie in a different direction.

She hastened to eat another fry so he wouldn't find cause to question her again.

*Just focus on the important stuff,* she told herself.

Like Colleen and the noises in her room. No time to be remembering she was a woman with needs and wants. Not for at least a few years.

But she could still enjoy the view. The thought made her smile secretly. That much was allowed.

# Chapter 6

The rain let up during the afternoon, so Mike helped her carry the chunks of plaster out to the huge commercial trash bin she kept in her garage. Whenever she filled it, she called the removal people to tow it away and leave her with a fresh one.

Removing the plaster proved even more time-consuming than knocking it off the walls in the first place. By the time they were done, it was late afternoon and more clouds were crowding in.

But Mike didn't look in the least tired. He knocked dust off himself and asked, "What next?"

"Frankly, if I don't find something in the walls, I don't know."

They went back into the house together, and Del started snapping on lights in the hallway, in the kitchen, even work lamps in the living room. The darkness of the day got to be a drag, and in some way made her edgy.

"Well," Mike said once light flooded all the downstairs rooms except the one they had spent the day tearing apart, "we could try a campout."

She stopped and looked at him. "A what?"

"A campout. You've got the walls torn out. All the activity might have frightened the vermin away temporarily. So we could sit in that darn room tonight and just listen."

"I could also spray something in the walls to kill whatever it is and live with the odor."

"Weeks or maybe longer depending on how big it is."

"Damn." She stared down at her toes. "Well, it must be big."

"Why do you say that?"

"Because every now and then I find things moved after I've been out a little while. And some of the stuff isn't exactly lightweight."

She raised her gaze slowly and found him totally arrested, staring off into space.

Finally he said, "Why didn't you mention that before?"

"Because…well, it sounds nuts. It has to *be* nuts. I probably just don't remember where I put stuff."

"Maybe."

She wished she hadn't said anything. She didn't like the way he stared past her, as if he didn't want to meet her gaze.

But finally his dark eyes came back to her and he said quietly, "Have you considered the possibility that someone is trying to scare you?"

She gasped in shock. "Why would anyone…? Mike, that's crazy. That's paranoid!"

"Maybe so." He shrugged one shoulder. "But given the sounds, and given stuff being moved, I wouldn't be too quick to dismiss it."

She wanted to argue with him. She wanted to believe that he was seeing this whole thing through some level of distrust because of the way he had been treated.

But she had heard the sounds. Colleen had been frightened by them more than once. And things *had* been out of place. Just enough, and just often enough, that she had started to scan every room when she entered it after being gone for a while, sort of like a personal mental health test. *Did I remember correctly where I put it?* She'd even started to pay closer attention every time she put something down.

"Damn," she said, and took two steps so that she could sag onto the bottom step of the wide staircase. "Damn."

"I'm sorry." He sounded stiff. "I don't mean to upset you. That was thoughtless."

"Oh, stop it," she sighed. "Just stop it. Why would it be any crazier that someone might be trying to scare me than that I'm suddenly losing my ability to remember where I put things? I mean, the latter sounds like a bigger problem than the former."

"I could see how you might think that."

She shook her head. "But there's absolutely *no* reason for anyone to want to scare me. Nobody else would want this house in its current condition."

"Then I'm wrong."

But she couldn't quite agree. Losing her mind or being deliberately scared by someone. She preferred the latter, frankly. The thought that she was becoming forgetful had been bothering her. But if she went the other way, there was a question that had to be answered.

"Why did that thought occur to you?"

"I don't know." He spread his hands. "Random brain misfire? Psychic intuition? Maybe because I said something earlier about how tearing the walls out felt like a treasure hunt?"

She started to nod thoughtfully. "I guess that makes a kind of sense. I suppose someone might think there's something of value hidden in here."

"Oh, it's ridiculous." He turned, saw a wooden chair against a wall, and dragged it over, straddling it and folding his arms across the back so he was close and could look at her. He sighed. "It just popped out. In the first place, somebody would have to have a *reason* to think something of value is hidden here. Which would mean a former occupant, or relative of an occupant. And what would you say if someone came up to you and said, 'I think Grandma left her life savings in a tin can under the floor?'"

Almost in spite of herself, Del grinned. "Frankly, I'd tell them that if I found Grandma's savings, I'd give it to them."

"Exactly. Most people would do precisely that. So it's ridiculous to think someone would go to such great lengths to scare you out of the house. I mean, even if Grandma *did* leave her savings in here somewhere, it's unlikely to amount to more than a few hundred dollars. If it hasn't rotted away."

"True." But she couldn't fail to note the way he seemed to be talking himself out of the idea more than her. Yet he was the one who had brought it up. But he was also the one who had said the house felt sad.

"Brain misfire," he said again. "I must be watching too many true-crime shows or something."

"Well, as far as I know, the only things of value in here are my tools and supplies. I always lock the house so nobody gets tempted, but the most you could hope to walk out of here with, as long as I don't leave the house for long, is an expensive bunch of drill bits and socket wrenches. That kind of stuff. If anybody wants any more, I'll have to be away long enough for them to bring in a moving van." She shook her head. "Frankly, I worry more about bored kids getting in here and vandalizing things."

"Makes sense."

"Which brings us back to vermin in the walls. And I have to get rid of whatever it is, because I'll be damned if I let Colleen get scared at night." She sighed. "I don't know about you, but I'm getting tired. Time to call it a day."

"How about that campout I suggested? If we keep watch together, maybe we can pinpoint the sound."

"You mean sit up all night? That would kill tomorrow."

"Or take turns. Did it wake you last night?"

"Maybe. I'm honestly not sure. I was restless to begin with." Having dreams that would make her blush if she let herself recall them. She felt a faint coloring of her cheeks, probably not enough for him to notice.

"Is it waking Colleen?"

"Sometimes."

"Then maybe we can count on that. I've got a couple of sleeping bags we can use."

"Okay. It's worth a try." Just then she heard a car pull

up out front. "That must be Beth coming to get Colleen's clothes."

He rose immediately. "I'll just go home and shower and get those sleeping bags."

Then he made her heart ache: he went out the back door rather than the front, and she didn't doubt for a second that he did so in order to avoid being seen by Beth Andrews.

Despite what she had said, he still didn't want anyone to talk about her and Colleen because of him.

If she let herself think about it, she was quite sure she might have cried.

Mike crossed the backyards and let himself into his own house. And while he had backtracked from his suggestion that someone might be trying to frighten Colleen and Del, he wasn't sure he believed his own rationalization.

No, there was no logical reason to assume such a thing. At least not one he was aware of. That didn't mean it wasn't so.

Nor had the thought been a mere mental misfire. No, it had been an intuition. The kind of intuition he'd been taught as a child not to ignore.

Which left him with a huge cultural gulf he simply didn't know how to begin to bridge with Del. Most of the things his uncle had taught him as a child, most of the things he had experienced along those lines, were utterly dismissed by the European world. They had no room in their science for the spiritual or mystical.

So how could he even hope to explain it without convincing Del he was a nut?

He climbed into his shower, letting the hot water beat

away all the fatigue along with the day's dust. His past, he thought, not only lay behind him, but it very much lay between him and the world he had adopted.

Maybe he should have listened to his uncle when Walking Crow had told him that he was called, that when the animals spoke to him they were summoning him to be a medicine man. Instead, bullheadedly, he had refused to listen.

But when in his life hadn't he been torn at least to some degree? Torn between old ways and new ways, torn between his traditional beliefs and the ones he learned at school. While the parochial school had by his time learned to treat his tribal beliefs with respect, the inescapable teaching remained that there was only one true faith…and it wasn't the faith of the Morning Star People.

He'd melded it all somehow, and sometimes even felt comfortable with it. Until something happened like today, when intuitions rose and goaded him, and he could not ignore them. When the old ways told him one thing, and the logic of the new ways entirely another.

And sometimes he wished Walking Crow were still around, so he could pick up a phone and call his uncle and talk things over.

Something was going on here, but because he'd turned his back on the old ways to a large degree, he didn't know enough. Not nearly enough.

After he dressed in fresh clothes, he picked up the sleeping bags, left over from when he'd still been in school and he and some buddies had occasionally taken off for a weekend to hike and camp. He filled a canvas tote with snack foods because he didn't want to burden Del and headed back to her house. Across the backyards. Feeling a bit like a kid who was doing something wrong.

Stupid.

He found Del in Colleen's room. She had apparently had time to finish vacuuming the room and was now running damp rags over everything, one rag in each head.

Her face looked a little pinched and tired, and he felt badly for her. He doubted he had been anywhere near as much help as he might have been today.

He dropped everything on the clean floor and said, "Let me finish that. You run up and take your shower."

She barely managed a smile. "Sorry, I'm beat. And I can't wait to get this dust off. It's starting to rub me raw in a few places."

"Then go. You're not alone now. Shout if anything worries you. In the meantime, I'll just finish wiping stuff down for you."

It was easy to see where she had wiped and where he needed to finish up. He felt glad for the simple, mindless task. His thoughts had started to follow disturbing paths, paths that made him feel both mentally and physically edgy.

Finally he paused for a moment in his wiping and closed his eyes. Upstairs he could hear water running, and outside the night was deepening, punctuated by flashes of lightning. In here, a couple of flashlights were all that held darkness at bay.

And some of that darkness seemed to be seeping into him. Something was wrong in this house. Very wrong. And damned if he knew what.

And what an irony it would be if he proved unable

to help Del because he had a long time ago refused to follow the Red Road to become a medicine man.

Of course, had he done as his uncle wished, he wouldn't be here now either.

Sighing, he opened his eyes and resumed wiping at the walls and anything else that looked dusty. The air had cleared considerably, and a fan at the window still sucked the remaining dust out of the room.

And upstairs Del was naked in the shower. Tightening his mouth, he wiped harder. He couldn't afford to think about that. Couldn't allow himself the feelings and needs she so easily evoked in him.

What was wrong with him? Once wasn't enough to tell him where this would lead if he followed his desires?

And Del sure as hell didn't need this from him now, if she ever would. Right now, it was most important to get to the bottom of what was frightening Colleen. What had managed to frighten Del enough that he'd found her standing outside her own house in the dead of night, reluctant to return.

And he'd heard that damn sound himself. Clearly. More like weary fingers, nails short or gone, making a half-hearted attempt to get attention.

It sure hadn't sounded like animal claws. He had enough experience to know those sounds as intimately as the sound of his own breathing.

So what the hell was it?

Light suddenly bounced around the room and he turned quickly. Del stood in the doorway carrying a camp lantern, one of those battery-operated things with a fluorescent tube. She wore sweats again, but they seemed to caress her figure rather than conceal it. "Can you breathe?" she asked.

Oh, yeah, he could breathe, and right now he smelled a woman fresh from the shower, still warm from the heat of the water, scented with soap and shampoo. Her hair hung wetly, as if she hadn't bothered to dry it with more than a towel, and even in the light from that single lantern and the flashlight on the floor he could tell her skin was flushed a healthy pink.

And in that instant he wanted her so much that he gripped the damp towels in his hands until his fingers ached. Not even reminding himself of Livvie's taunts could batter down the sudden surge of aching need.

"Yeah," he managed to say, aware that his voice sounded oddly thick. He cleared his throat and looked away before he could make a fool of himself. "Yeah," he said again, more firmly, even though he was lying because right now it felt as if there wasn't any air left in the room, or in the entire universe. Primitive rhythms beat in his blood, in his loins. He forced himself to take another swipe at the walls.

"It doesn't have to be perfect," she said, coming into the room. "As long as we beat the dust down enough to breathe."

"Just a bit more." Just a few more swipes until his self-control mastered his more basic urges.

And offering to stay the night here had surely been one of the *stupidest* things he had done in a long time. He knew better, far better. This woman had a huge "off-limits" sign around her, practically painted in neon. Even if he removed the likelihood that she and her daughter might suffer for getting too close to him, there was her situation. He wasn't ignorant enough or selfish enough not to realize what she was up against already in her personal life. She didn't need additional complications of any kind. Least of all him.

So he finished wiping the wall, avoiding looking at her, avoiding the very thing he had set himself up for. Yeah, he needed to go beat his head on a wall until he managed to pound some sense into it, until his head ached so much more than his manhood. He needed to forget he wanted Del Carmody more than he'd wanted anything in a long time.

Behind him he heard her moving around. When at last he felt he had a leash on himself, he turned around to find she had spread the sleeping bags out. And she hadn't spread them on opposite sides of the small room. Oh, no. Somehow they were only a foot apart on the floor.

Did she have even the least idea?

No, probably not. Why would she? She obviously trusted him, and somehow he had to live up to that. Crap. Right now he had never felt less like living up to anything.

He cleared his throat again. "Where should I toss these rags?"

She came to him immediately and took them. "I'll just spread them on the washer until I'm ready to do a load. Use the bathroom there." She nodded to Colleen's bathroom, behind a closed door, and he headed in there.

The room showed signs of age and wear, with chipped tiles and a tub that looked as if it had seen better years. But just like the bath upstairs, the room was unusually large. People didn't build them like this anymore. No, you were lucky if you could squeeze into a modern bath.

He washed his hands and forearms and returned to the bedroom. Del was already sitting on one of the sleeping bags, and she offered a smile as he emerged.

"I really appreciate you being willing to do all of this," she said.

He hesitated only a moment, feeling like the wolf in *Little Red Riding Hood,* before sinking to sit cross-legged on the other sleeping bag. "It's what neighbors do," he answered, both seriously and to try to remind himself that that was their *only* relationship. Distance. He needed to keep the distance.

"Not every neighbor," she said. "This room isn't exactly crowded with helping hands."

He tightened his mouth and gripped his knees with his hands, keeping them safely occupied. "Maybe some aren't aware you could use some help."

At that her smile faded a bit. "True. I don't generally go waving my problems in people's faces. But I don't think you do either."

"No," he admitted.

"My husband always said I was cussedly independent. I'm not sure he always meant it as a compliment." Her face shadowed, but then she managed another smile. "Mostly I like the independence of doing my own thing. When I need help I hire it. But…this is different."

"We'll get to the bottom of it somehow."

"I have to. It's either that or move, and the way I've got this place torn up… Well, I suppose I could move us into the house I finished four months ago, but I'm trying to rent it."

"Do you need the income?"

"From the rental? It would help. I'm okay for now,

but there'll come a point when paying the mortgage on two houses will drain me."

He nodded. "It must be a load."

"Not when things go right." She unfolded her legs and stretched out on the sleeping bag on her side, her head propped on her hand. "I imagine your childhood was a lot different from mine."

"Life isn't *all* that different on the rez."

"I didn't mean it like that."

He felt an immediate pang of guilt. "Jumping to conclusions again."

"Yup." But she smiled at him. "Still, I grew up in the local culture. Your experience had to be somewhat different. For me, I guess the equivalent would have been being born to an immigrant family." She suddenly held up her hand, "And don't tell me you folks weren't the immigrants. I know that."

He chuckled because he had to. "Well, we were immigrants, too."

"Ah, but there was no one else here when you arrived."

"There's some debate about that, too."

Her interest clearly perked. "Really?"

He shrugged. "Depends on if we're being politically correct. Many of my people aren't pleased when others suggest we weren't here first. But there's some evidence in South America that a wave of immigration actually came around from Australia, long before the time dates given for my people. They may have reached as far north as Central America. And there are those Olmec heads."

"I've seen photos of them and always wondered."

"Other than to clarify prehistory in the Americas, I

think it's pointless to argue about it. My people clearly migrated here, too, whether it was twelve thousand years ago or twenty-five thousand."

"And apparently all of us came out of Africa."

"So it would seem. At this point, getting proprietary about things that happened so long ago seems like it should be of interest primarily to academics."

"Well, we *do* know who was here when the Europeans arrived."

He smiled slightly. "Indeed, whether it was the first group of Europeans, or the second, or the third…"

The way he said it made her laugh. "I guess that's another debate."

"Endlessly."

She appeared to hesitate then said, "If I'm treading on toes here, let me know. But you said a couple of things, and they got me curious. Like when you said this house is sad."

He should have anticipated this. It was bound to come. The question was how frank he wanted to be. And then he decided to just go for it. If she didn't like it, or treated it as merely interesting lore, what did it really matter? It would start drawing lines, and then he could stand behind them. Safely. Away from the temptation to repeat one of the biggest mistakes of his life.

"My uncle, Walking Crow, was a medicine man. He thought I should follow in his footsteps."

"Why? Tradition?"

Mike shook his head. "It's never tradition. It's about abilities. About being called to take a journey and learn things that aren't part of your kind of thinking."

"And you were called?"

"My uncle thought so. I was drawn to animals. I don't

recall my earliest experiences, but he told me when I got older that I shouldn't ignore the call of the wolf."

Del sat up. "Meaning?"

"I awoke night after night to find a wolf standing in my bedroom. Or so it seemed."

"Was it real?"

He hesitated. There was only so much he could share, as his people kept their beliefs very private. And with good reason, given how most non-natives reacted to them, either with disdain and disbelief, or some kind of New Agey cultism.

He spoke carefully. "In the terms of my people, it was real. It was a summons. But I refused to take the Red Road, and instead followed my own path."

Del leaned forward, intent. "Why did you refuse?"

"Because…" Again he hesitated. "Because the Red Road is a difficult one and would require a commitment I wasn't sure I wanted to make. By the time I finished kindergarten, I had conflicting worldviews. Maybe because I was young I wanted to follow the new ways, not the old ones."

She nodded thoughtfully, clearly interested in what he had to say. But how much could he say? He couldn't betray what his people chose to keep private.

"So what exactly do you mean by the Red Road?"

Ah, now there was a problem. He sought ways to explain to her without revealing matters he shouldn't share with an outsider. Finally, he sought refuge in the dry terms of anthropology. "Have you heard of the shamanic path?"

She shook her head. "Not really."

"Well, let me start by saying my people don't like the

word *shaman*. Mainly because it's a Siberian word and has been flung around rather liberally by academics."

"Okay."

"I'm just using it here because…well, you'd probably connect with its meaning better than if I resort to our preferred translation, which has plenty of baggage of its own."

"And that is?"

"Medicine man or woman."

"Spiritual leader, or healer?"

"Or both. Anyway, if you look into the subject you'll find the so-called shamanic path, or journey, is strikingly similar across cultures and continents. But the main thing to remember is that it's a journey. It's not something you do once—you do it all your life."

"That *is* a commitment."

"And it's not easy. It involves suffering, sacrifice and a willingness to look into other realities that can be terrifying. Altered states of consciousness, if you prefer the clinical term. I may have been called, but I didn't answer. I learned one thing at home, and another at school, and finally I opted for what I was learning at school. I sidestepped into the so-called rational world."

Her brows lifted a bit. "Why do you say *so-called?*"

"Because mysteries and spirituality exist whether science can explain them or not. This *rational* world denies those experiences and calls them hallucinations."

She nodded slowly, absorbing what he was saying. He gave her credit for not arguing with him. "I get the feeling you regret your choice."

"Once in a while. But not often. I mostly feel that I'm doing what I was meant to do."

"That's a good feeling to have."

She was letting him out of the noose of tightening questions, and he felt grateful to her. But at the same time, just talking about it raised the questions he'd never really answered for himself—like whether he had indeed made the right choice.

Del spoke. "It must have been a hard decision to make, to go against what your uncle thought you were called to do."

"There's nothing like being young and headstrong."

Another smile graced her face. "True. I was supposed to marry the son of the rancher next door, thus combining the two ranches. Clearly, I didn't live up to expectations."

"Did your folks object when you went off to college?"

"Pretty much. They figured I'd meet someone there and never come home to the ranch permanently. They were right. After my parents passed away, I sold the ranch to the rancher's son next door."

The way she said it made him chuckle. But he felt compelled to add, "I'm sorry about your parents."

"I miss them. What about you?"

"My parents are gone, too. Mom died last year. And my sister married a Seminole and they live in Florida now. I fly down to see them once a year."

"In the winter, I hope."

"Of course. If I'm going to take a trip to the Sunshine State it has to be in February or March, right about the time I've decided I'm going to hate the cold and snow forever."

"And it does start to feel like forever about then." She sighed a little, as if thinking about it, then said, "You've had an interesting life. Very different from mine."

"I could say the same for you."

She laughed. "I guess you could." Then she looked around at the shadowy room. "I'm starting to feel edgy."

"Any particular reason?"

She shook her head. "I wish. It's just a feeling."

"This whole house gives me feelings."

It must have been an opening she had been waiting for, because she immediately asked, "What did you mean when you said the house feels sad? What *exactly?* Some kind of mystical feeling?"

"I can't explain it." He wanted to evade her question, realizing that they were probably about to get into a conflict for which there could be no easy resolution. Yet he knew evasion would be exactly the wrong answer now. For them both. "It just feels to me as if this whole house is weeping for something."

"And you don't get that feeling in your house."

He shook his head slowly.

"Well, damn." All of a sudden she jumped up from the sleeping bag and hurried from the room.

He thought about sitting right where he was, waiting for her to deal with this however she needed to. Then he considered just how much that woman had on her plate, from strange noises in her house to a paralyzed daughter.

He couldn't do it. With a sigh, he rose and went to meet his fate head-on.

# *Chapter 7*

Del stood in the kitchen, trying to make coffee even though she was shaking. She didn't know if she was mad, or if she felt he was trying in some way to con her, or what. Just because Mike Windwalker had been the vet in town for the past few years didn't mean he was someone she could trust.

All that stuff about being a medicine man. She had been willing to accept it as part of his cultural heritage, but now she wondered if he hadn't been making up stuff to try to impress her some way…or to scare her.

After all, it had been Mike Windwalker who had suggested that someone was trying to scare her out of her house. She couldn't imagine any earthly reason why anyone should want to do that, so why had that even popped into his mind? Because *he* was the one trying to scare her away?

"Del?"

"I don't want to talk right now." She almost spilled coffee as she scooped it into the filter.

"Then I'll talk. I'm sorry I upset you, but I can't pretend to be somebody I'm not."

She turned then to face him, seriously annoyed though damned if she was sure why. "And just what are you?" she demanded. "All this talk about feelings and shamanism, and then trying to scare me out of my house because you say it feels sad? I'm supposed to swallow that?"

His jaw dropped a little, and then his dark eyebrows drew together. "I'm not trying to scare you out of your house. In case you hadn't noticed, I've been busting my back trying to help you find out what's going on."

"Sure. And dropping little hints in my ear about feelings you get, about how somebody might be trying to scare me out of this place. Suggestions."

"They're not suggestions! I'm not trying to convince you of anything. I'm trying to help solve the problem."

"If they're not suggestions, what are they?" She wanted an answer, and it had better be a good one.

He looked away for a moment, then faced her again with a steady gaze. "They are what they are. Feelings. Intuitions. Something I was taught to be open to since my earliest childhood. This house speaks, for those with ears to hear, and you can like that or not. It doesn't change what I sense."

"Why would *you* sense it and no one else?"

"You already sense it. Your daughter has heard noises. You've heard them. *I've* heard them. Something is wrong with this house."

"There's plenty wrong with it. And I'm fixing what's wrong with it."

"But there's something you can't fix with all the hammers and nails in the world. If you think I'm trying to get you out of this house, if you *really* believe that, I'll leave now."

She couldn't immediately answer. For some reason what he had said had knotted her emotions in some way and she couldn't fully untangle the skein of feelings and thoughts. But as he started to turn away, clearly intending to leave, she knew one thing for certain.

"I trust you," she said. Words that came from her heart, more than her brain. Her brain kept saying she must be nuts, all this talk of intuition and feelings and the house speaking…

But her heart believed something very different.

He faced her again, slowly. Reluctantly. "Are you sure about that?"

She almost winced when she heard the edge of bitterness in his tone, and she knew where it came from. God, she felt about two inches tall. "Look, I'm not criticizing your heritage. Let's get that clear."

"Really?" He folded his arms.

"Really. But you're asking me to accept things I don't believe. You've lived in my world. I haven't lived in yours. So suppose you tell me how someone from *my* world is supposed to believe that this house is sad? That a house, an inanimate object, is capable of having feelings?"

"That'll take the Golden Gate Bridge, to span that gap." Again, an undercurrent of bitterness.

And that bitterness pierced her. The study of architectural engineering had *not* prepared her to cross culture gaps. It hadn't given her even the smallest of tools for dealing with the gulf that lay between them now. "Help me," she said finally. "I'll try."

Then she turned to finish making the coffee, letting him decide for himself whether to continue this conversation or leave. Because she just didn't know what to say next.

It was beyond any experience in her life.

When she had switched on the coffeemaker and washed her hands, she turned again from the counter and found Mike still standing there. Even in the bright fluorescent lighting, he somehow looked archetypal, mysterious. And in the course of this single evening, he had indeed become mysterious to her, no ordinary man with ordinary thoughts or an ordinary life. At least not the ordinary kind of man she was used to.

"In my culture," he said finally, "there are no inanimate objects."

She caught her breath. "What do you mean?"

"We believe that consciousness imbues everything. The stones, the earth, the air, the water, even this house. That storm outside, the wind, the fire, the lightning. All of it is aware. When we cut a tree we give thanks to it for its sacrifice. We thank the rocks when we use them to build a fire pit. We thank the rain for choosing to moisten our fields."

She nodded but remained silent, afraid of interrupting him. More than anything, she felt a need to understand him.

"This house is aware," he said flatly. "Not like you or I, but it *is* aware. And something has made it sad. It weeps. And if you want to know what my uncle would have said about it, I can tell you."

She nodded again.

"He would have said we need to find out what happened to sadden this place."

For long moments there was no sound but the distant rumble of thunder and the nearby sound of the coffeemaker. She stood there, trying to absorb what he was telling her, trying to fit his worldview into her own.

"I'm trying," she said finally.

"I know it's not easy. It's alien to you. I'm not even asking you to believe. Just telling you something about who and what I am. About how I see things."

She knew then that she had to cross that gulf somehow. Because if she didn't find a way, right now, Mike Windwalker would once again return to his private life, would once again become the hesitant, reluctant man she had first met.

But there were no words. She couldn't say she agreed with his beliefs. She couldn't, certainly not having just been exposed to them for the very first time.

So without words, all she could do was show him acceptance. She crossed the kitchen to him and put her arms tentatively around him.

"I'm sorry," she said. "I was frightened and confused."

And slowly, very slowly, he lifted his own arms and hugged her back. "You don't have to accept it," he said quietly.

"Yes, one way or another I do. Because accepting it is accepting you."

"That's a lot to ask of yourself."

"No, it's actually very little. I don't have to believe it. I don't have to see the world the same way you do. But I *do* have to respect your beliefs."

It seemed to her that his arms tightened, so she tightened her own around him. He smelled so good from his recent shower, and he felt so good against her. She wanted to believe that he could be a haven, however temporarily, because it had been so long, too long, since she had had one.

She recognized the weakness in herself, and knew that soon she would have to take up her burdens again, because they were *her* burdens. But she let herself feel, for just these few minutes, that she didn't have to shoulder them alone.

For one wild moment she wished she were just an ordinary woman herself, as free as a bird, but the instant she thought it, she felt guilty. Nothing could make her wish Colleen out of her life. Nothing.

So she stepped back and turned to pour coffee for them. "How," she asked, hoping her voice didn't sound as thick as it felt, "would we go about finding out why the house is sad?"

"Good question. My suggestion would be to find out what we can about previous owners, whether there were any tragedies."

Such a prosaic answer. What had she been expecting? That he would offer to seek a vision? Talk to the house? She could have laughed at herself if she hadn't already put her foot in it enough for one night.

"Okay," she agreed. "We can check the newspaper morgue in the morning. Or I can. I guess you need to be at work."

"Unfortunately. I have a full day scheduled. But you might save a lot of time by asking Velma, the dispatcher at the sheriff's office."

"I should have thought of that! Or Nate Tate. That

man must know about everything that's happened in this county in the past sixty years."

"Yeah, he probably would."

"I'll start there then, right after I take Colleen to school."

They carried their coffee into Colleen's former bedroom and settled onto the sleeping bags, sitting cross-legged and facing each other.

Again, Del felt as if something were trying to close in on her, something that hovered in the shadows beyond the camp lantern. And then a thought trickled across her awareness, a thought she usually ignored.

"You know, maybe the sadness you're sensing is me."

"Why do you say that?"

"Because, well, I'm sort of aware that my grief over Don was truncated because of what happened with Colleen. I had to focus all my attention on getting her through that. There was a counselor who worked with both of us for a while, and she said, basically, that the devil would get his due. That I had to find time for my own grieving."

He nodded but said nothing, clearly giving her space and time. She took both, but probably in a far larger way than he meant them. Because *this* was not the time either.

"Who's getting first watch?" she asked.

"I'll take it," he answered promptly. "I think your night last night was far more disturbed than mine."

So she pulled back the flap on the sleeping bag and lay down with her back to him, pulling the cover over herself, hunching her shoulder a little as if to hold him away.

No, she hadn't had much time for grief. But right now

she did, and for the first time in a long time, she let the tears fall silently. In a few hours, maybe in the morning, she could be strong again.

But right now she felt an overwhelming need to shed tears for her lost husband and her daughter.

If there was any sadness in this house, she thought, it only echoed her own.

During the night she awoke to feel strong arms around her, a strong body pressed to hers from behind. The feeling was at once startling and familiar. She felt Mike's warm breath near her ear, a steady sound as if he slept, too.

But weren't they supposed to remain awake to listen?

She didn't want him to roll away. No, she wanted him to stay right there. It had been so long since she'd felt this kind of comfort, and this was the second time in a single day that he'd managed to remind her just how much she missed it.

She tried to remain still, so as not to wake him, afraid the almost magical moment would end, proving that it really was an illusion. And it was. She knew that. But it was an illusion she wanted to cling to.

Her breathing must have changed.

"You were dreaming," he murmured near her ear. "It didn't sound happy. Sorry if I woke you."

She wasn't, but she couldn't say so. "I don't remember any dream."

"It didn't sound like one you'd want to remember. Go back to sleep."

"It must be my turn to keep watch."

"No. I'm not at all sleepy yet." A moment of silence, then, "I can move away."

"No. Please." So many empty, worried, frightened, lonely nights lay behind her. The last thing she wanted right now was to add yet another one.

He gave her a little squeeze and continued to hold her, almost as if he was feeling the same way: too many lonely nights haunted him.

What a pair, she thought. He was afraid of connections because life had taught him, probably more often than he had told her about, that he was unwelcome because of his heritage. And then there she was, afraid of the same thing, for probably the same reasons. Because if she were to be honest about it, the idea of putting her whole life on hold until Colleen grew up was kind of ridiculous. The only valid reason she could have for that kind of decision was fear that she might fall for someone who wasn't good for Colleen. Beyond that…

Beyond that she'd been hiding. Because she was afraid. Because her heart had been ripped out once, and she didn't want to risk it again.

*At least,* she told herself, *be honest about what you're doing.*

And much to her surprise, she heard herself say, before she was even aware of the thought, "Do you date?"

She thought she felt him stiffen a little, but she couldn't be certain. Then he said, "Not often."

"Me neither. I was just thinking that I'm afraid."

"Of dating?"

"Of caring."

"I can sure see why."

"Ditto."

"Ouch." But he said it without any real emphasis, as if he knew perfectly well that he was hiding from pain.

She gave him marks for that. "Unfortunately," she said quietly, "I think I've been making Colleen my excuse."

"How so?"

"Too busy. She needs me, and I can't divide my time that way. Oh, there's probably a whole list of reasons that are buried in my subconscious."

"Probably. That's only human."

"But for you it's different. Why don't you just go home and find some nice young woman who won't kick you and call you names?"

A long silence answered her.

"I'm sorry," she said presently. "None of my business."

"No, I was just thinking it over. The trouble is, I'm not sure why. Maybe because I worked so hard to get away, to walk into this world and be accepted, at least partly, for my skills. Maybe I ran away from the past."

"Another common human thing to do," she murmured. "We all have our ways of hiding."

"Too true." He was quiet for a while and shifted his hold on her, bringing her closer until the back of her head rested comfortably in the hollow of his shoulder. "I don't have a lot of people left at home that I would consider close. No real reason to go back. I did a pretty good job of separating myself. Maybe it was the stupidity of youth."

"I don't know that I would call it stupidity. A lot of us grow up wanting to escape whatever rut we think we're in."

"True. And we rebel against expectations, and

traditions. I don't know. I *do* know that when I go back to visit it feels like I have to look at the same old questions over and over again."

"Which questions?"

"About who I am. What I am. And how I fit."

Struggling against the confines of a sleeping bag that seemed to want to hold on to her like duct tape, she managed to turn over until they were face-to-face. She could barely make him out in the darkness, but she could see the glint of his eyes and the shape of his head. Even the suggestion of his mouth and nose.

"I can't imagine it," she said. And instinctively she reached up to brush her fingers against his cheek. "It would seem to me that you should fit anywhere you choose to. I guess that's where I have an advantage. No big deal that I didn't want to be a ranch wife. A much bigger deal for you not to stay within your culture and become what your uncle wanted."

"And that's just the beginning."

She turned that around in her mind as she waited for him to say more, but he remained silent. And then a thought occurred to her. "Do you feel *guilty* for leaving?"

"Just a bit."

"But why?"

He snorted quietly. "My ancestors didn't choose to abandon their culture or their way of life. It was forced on them. And those cultures are slowly but surely changing and evaporating. Well, maybe not so slowly. Remember, it hasn't been all that long. Three, maybe four generations for some of us. Less for others. So when I walked away, I put another nail in the coffin of my people's ways. So yeah, it makes me feel a bit guilty. The fire is dying. The light is going out. The bits that we've managed to cling to have for many become a tourist attraction, or a quaint mythology. Kids want to bust out of the limited opportunities on the rez. They want the whole oyster, just the way I did. Perfectly natural, I guess. Sadly, for native populations there are only two choices left—live the old ways and die out, or build a casino and live the antithesis of the old ways."

"I hadn't thought about it that way."

"No reason you would." He stirred a little as if resettling himself into a more comfortable position. "It's inevitable. Eventually we'll be little more than someone's record of us in an ethnography. Time marches on, things change, and the stories I was told while growing up will eventually be nothing but stories."

"But that's not a good thing, is it?"

"Of course not. Why else do I feel guilty? There are a lot of things well worth preserving in native cultures. Unfortunately, the world doesn't seem to work that way. The sands of time bury us all sooner or later."

"And you feel like one of those sands?"

"Sometimes."

"But not all the time?"

"No, not always. But I feel a pull, and one of these days I may do more than send donations. I may go back there to stay."

That frightened her a bit, though she wasn't sure why. "To do what?"

"Oh, I could teach. I could look after animals. There are lots of things that need doing. Always." He sighed quietly. "But the fact remains that while there are twelve thousand enrolled members of the Northern Cheyenne, fewer than five thousand remain on the reservation."

"So a lot of others have moved away, too?"

"Yup. A steady drain, until one day we're gone."

"That is so sad." When she thought of extinctions, she thought in terms of biological species, but he was talking about something very different. "You're watching an extinction," she whispered.

"Exactly. Slowly and steadily. And it'll take a lot more than me going back to stop it. Cheyenne blood will last a lot longer than Cheyenne culture."

She nodded against his shoulder, absorbing what he was saying and feeling a definite pang of sorrow.

"I guess," he said after a moment, "that we'll become museum curiosities, if we aren't already."

"That's awful!"

He surprised her with a quiet chuckle. "It's awful, but it's inevitable. Whatever we preserve will eventually survive only in museums. I suppose the good thing is that there's an effort under way to preserve it at all. And my people have been changing for a long time anyway."

"What do you mean?"

"We're Algonquian. We started out back east, moved to the upper Midwest, then continued our westward journey, most likely because of pressures coming from the East and all the Europeans. We were farmers, then we became Plains hunters. So we've been adapting all along. Who knows how much of our current culture was adopted along the way as we migrated."

"That's very philosophical."

"Show me a healthier way to look at it. Because I sure as hell can't stop it any more than you could return to a sod hut in the nineteenth century."

"So true. And that's where my ancestors, at least

in the local area, started. In a sod hut. It's still on the property, but now it looks more like a hill. When I was a kid, I tried to dig into it. You know, like an archeological site. I was sure stuff must have been left behind in there when the family finally moved into a house. My dad stopped me though."

"How come?"

"Because he was afraid there might still be hollows inside, and that it could collapse on me."

"So you became a renovator instead, still hunting for treasures."

She gave a short, soft laugh. "I guess so. In some ways it's not that different. I find treasures from time to time. Old postcards, an earring. Once I even found a locket."

"What did you do with them?"

"I keep them in a little box. Somehow I don't feel right about throwing them away. Maybe in some silly way I feel that someone someday might show up who would find meaning in them."

"That's an intriguing thought."

Then she heard him murmur a total non sequitur. "Tell me to stop."

Before her brain could even begin scrambling around to figure that out, his mouth met hers. At first the touch was tentative, as if he expected rejection, but rejection was the last thing in her heart or mind.

Every bit of awareness she'd tried to shove into her subconscious over the past couple of days leaped to the forefront of her mind and body. Instead of pulling away, instead of protesting as he wanted her to, she leaned into his kiss, seeking a much deeper connection.

Electricity sparked along her nerve endings. Synapses

long asleep awoke in a huge wave of hunger and desire. Yearning filled her, yearning for a man's touches, and man's possession. All the things she'd been without for so long.

And perversely, the very caution in him that had tried to warn her away now seemed like a promise of safety. Whatever happened between them here and now would not go any further. He would pull back to save himself, and in so doing would save her *from* herself.

And that perverse sense of safety unleashed the explosion of need. She leaned into him, against him, twining her arm around his neck, wanting him closer, needing him closer. Reveling in the feeling of a man's hard body pressed tightly to hers, even through layers of clothing and sleeping bag.

A quiet groan escaped him, she felt a shudder run through him, and then he gave up the battle, just as she had.

Right here, right now, all the barriers dissolved into a more primitive force than culture or race. And all those barriers had never seemed more irrelevant. They were just imaginary, man-made boundaries to the elemental need to mate, man and woman.

His kiss deepened as she welcomed him. She felt his leg lift to drape heavily over hers. The sleeping bag was between them, but at that moment it was the only acknowledged barrier. Anything else had instantly vaporized in the heat of longing.

God, she wanted him. Wanted this stolen night, these explosive moments of passion. If there would be a price later, she was past caring.

His hands worked their way inside her sleeping bag, then up under her shirt until skin touched skin. The sensation was electric, and so, so good. Her back seemed to come alive under his touch, more nerve endings awakening to the thrill of being alive.

And how long had it been since she had allowed herself to feel that?

Too long, because almost as soon as skin touched skin, she felt a deep, almost painful throb between her legs as her body took over.

Her brain became incapable of any thought except a yearning to be touched, *here,* or *there*… She nearly held her breath in anticipation, every ounce of her being focused on those fingers that stroked so lightly against her back, trespassing no farther although she wanted him to trespass everywhere.

She could feel the tension and heat building in him as well, could sense in the way his body tightened, in the pressure against her abdomen, and sensing his need inflamed her own.

She was wanted. God, it had been so long since she'd been wanted….

His hand slipped around, up under her bra, cupping her breast in heat. Desire zinged through her and she arched against his legs. Needing no more invitation, he caught her nipple between thumb and forefinger, brushing it, twisting it gently, sending more shock waves running throughout her body.

She ached. Oh, how she ached. She pressed herself harder into his hand, tried to bring her hips to meet his, felt the rocking response of his body against her. She managed to clutch his shoulder, telling him with her grip that she wanted it all, every bit of it, right now.

He groaned softly and deepened his kiss, now pushing his leg hard up between hers, pressing on her aching core, and it felt good, so good that she became instantly damp.

She burned for him, and somewhere deep inside, some part of her was holding its breath in anticipation, wishing away clothes, wishing away everything that separated them.

"Mike, please!" It was the only way she could tell him. A plea for more and yet more. He mumbled something she couldn't quite make out.

Then a loud bang sounded through the house.

At once they both froze. Mike swore, and before she could make a sound he had leaped to his feet. She struggled against the sleeping bag that seemed to have become the arms of an octopus, grabbing at her and refusing to free her.

Still struggling, she blinked as the camp lantern came on and she cried a protest as she saw he was about to leave the room.

"No, wait!"

He paused, looking back at her, his face cast into eerie shadows by the lantern he held low. "No, stay here," he said. "If someone's in the house…"

*If someone's in the house?* He'd spoken the words quietly, but they seemed to ring deafeningly in her head.

If someone was in the house, the last place she wanted to be was tangled up in a sleeping bag, alone.

By the time she got out of that damn sticky sleeping bag, Mike had vanished. She could tell where he had gone only by the dim glow from the lantern as he moved through the downstairs rooms.

By the time he reached the staircase, ready to ascend, she was there, determined to go with him. He looked at her, as if he wished she'd listened to him, but he didn't argue.

Together they climbed the stairs, with him just two risers ahead of her. She kept her feet to the outside of the risers, so as not to make them creak, and he did the same.

She was convinced, absolutely convinced, that someone had to be in the house. The windows weren't open so there was no way on earth the wind could have blown one of those doors shut.

And she was mad. Sexual arousal and adrenaline weren't far apart on the biological scale, at least to judge by what she felt. She was angry that someone might be trying to scare her, although she couldn't imagine why anyone would, and furious that those precious moments with Mike, that wonderful budding sense of being a woman again, had been truncated.

A switch had just been flipped, from her earlier concern that Colleen was uncomfortable to one of sheer fury. Whoever was responsible for this crap would pay.

Maybe she was forgetful. Maybe she laid down tools and other equipment in her preoccupation and forgot where she'd placed them. She could accept that explanation for things seeming to move around. She could even accept that vermin in the walls could make the noises that frightened Colleen. But a door slamming? Twice now?

Unless they found a window open, there could only be one explanation.

They got to the head of the stairs and Mike reached out, flipping on the lights. No more tiptoeing in the dark. Getting out of here now would involve someone rushing past them or scrambling out a window and over the front porch roof, any one of which would be a dead giveaway.

But nothing happened.

Room by room they walked through the upstairs and found nothing at all.

Del felt her lips tightening with anger. This could not continue. She would not allow this to continue.

Except she had no idea at all how to put an end to it.

Back downstairs, in silent agreement, they went to the kitchen. It was nearly 5:00 a.m. The sun would be coming up soon, and apparently the night was over, at least as far as sleeping went.

Still furious, Del went to put on a pot of coffee. Mike disappeared for a few moments and returned with a bag. He placed it on the counter and began pulling out an assortment of snack foods: chips, pretzels, even a tray of raspberry Danish from the local bakery. "What would you like?" he asked.

"Sugar. Energy."

"Danish it is." He ripped the plastic wrap off the aluminum tray and hunted up some small plates and a knife.

"That wasn't vermin," she said. She leaned against the counter, facing the coffeepot, her head resting against a cabinet.

"No," he agreed.

"And don't tell me the house is sending a message."

"Never crossed my mind."

But she sensed the stiffening in him, as if she had just insulted him. Damn it. Were they always going to have to tiptoe around sensibilities?

"Look," she said, "I didn't mean anything critical by that."

"No?" He sighed and put two plates of Danish on the table. "Maybe not."

"I didn't. But if I'm going to have to measure every word against some form of political correctness, we're going to spend a lot of time being angry."

"Or I could just leave."

"Oh, that'll solve a lot," she said, pivoting abruptly to face him. "Just walk away. That always clears the air."

"Del…"

But she interrupted him. Something had been building in her, some point of snapping rapidly approached. She didn't know why, unless the past four years were finally catching up with her, aggravated by sounds she couldn't explain, a frightened daughter and now a neighbor who, while he seemed to be trying to help her, had also added a whole additional area of concern.

"Look, I'm me, and you're you," she said. "We have different backgrounds. I don't have a particular problem with that, regardless of what you seem to think. And if I'm tired and a bit crabby and I say something not exactly right, I'd appreciate it if you would not put five hundred years of ugly history on *my* shoulders."

Silence hung so thickly in the room that she felt it nearly impossible to draw a breath. Mike didn't move a muscle. His face revealed not a single thing.

Well, she thought, that had blown it. Too little sleep, too much worry, noises she couldn't explain, and it had all come together to make her blow up like some fringe lunatic over absolutely nothing. She should apologize. If nothing else, she should at least apologize.

But then he astonished her by saying simply, "You're right."

She sucked a breath so deep it felt as if she must have stopped breathing throughout the silence as she waited for his reaction. "What?" Stupid question, but his words seemed out of sync with what was going on inside her.

"I said, you're right. I think of it as being smart and not getting involved in dangerous situations, but in point of fact I'm walking around with a bunker mentality, waiting for the next artillery round to land. And damn near everything hits me like an artillery shell. My own emotional version of shell shock."

"I'm sorry," she whispered, feeling more than anger now, something that overwhelmed anger completely. Whatever her problems, she could scarcely imagine the life experiences that had taught him this.

"You have nothing to apologize for." He passed his hand over his face before continuing. "You're right. I overreacted to something you said because you're upset and worried, and you have every right to be. And I've been muttering on about how this house feels sad—and I won't take that back because it *does*—so why wouldn't you expect me to say something like the house is slamming doors? It must all sound like mumbo jumbo to you."

"But that's the thing," she said with a surprising amount of vehemence, maybe bordering on a plea. "It *doesn't* sound like mumbo jumbo. It's just a different way of looking at things I've basically always believed! In my faith there are angels and saints, and even, if I'm willing to go that far, demons. If that's part of my belief system, then why not the things you said earlier? It even makes a kind of sense."

His eyebrows lifted, as if it surprised him that she should say such a thing. "What do you mean?"

"Well, like you said, if God created the universe, what did he create it out of? Why not awareness in rocks and trees? Different awareness, maybe, but why not? I'm having less trouble with that idea than you would think."

"Wow."

"Wow?"

"Wow." The faintest of smiles touched his lips. "Just don't go New Agey on me."

"I'm not sure New Age is all wet." She sighed. Her eyes felt as if they were full of sand, and her body just wanted to sag in the wake of her anger. "I mean, I don't buy most of it, but who am I to say it's totally wet? Why do you object to New Age?"

"Because they try to glom on to bits of my people's beliefs and twist them to their own purposes."

"Well, I'd resent that, too. I'm sorry I sniped at you, but I'm not going to accept the possibility that the door-slamming sound originated with anything except a human being."

"I agree. And that seriously concerns me. So before this day is over, we're going to move Colleen into my house with your aunt, or find some other suitable arrangement. And if you don't talk to the sheriff about this, I will."

At least it was a plan. It wouldn't solve the problem, but it would take the biggest worry off her plate: Colleen. Right now she wouldn't bring Colleen back into this house for any reason. She didn't want her daughter scared any more than she was already.

"I don't know about talking to the sheriff," she said. Behind her, the coffeepot popped and released a blast of steam, letting her know it had finished brewing. She pulled some mugs from the cupboard then carried them and the pot of coffee to the table.

Mike sat facing her as she poured coffee. "Why not go to the sheriff? Something's not right."

"Obviously. But what have I got? The sound of a slamming door? And maybe some forgetfulness about where I put things? What could the sheriff possibly do about any of that?"

"I guess you're right." But he didn't look happy about agreeing. "And Colleen?"

She looked up from the piece of Danish she was cutting with her fork. "I agree. She's not coming back into this house until I get to the bottom of this. She's been through enough. But how do I get to the bottom? What if it's just somebody playing a practical joke?"

"I doubt a practical joker would be running around at this hour of the morning."

"Me, too." And that sense of creepiness started to return.

"But that leaves us with the huge problem of why someone would be trying to scare you or your daughter."

She put her fork down, facing the horrible sense that reality was spinning out of her control and that for once she couldn't grab the reins and bring it back in line. "I don't think I've done anything to make anyone that mad. And I seriously doubt Colleen has either."

"I'd be shocked if either of you had. So it's got to be something about this house."

Back to the house again. But she was out of arguments. She couldn't put this down to forgetfulness, early onset senility, distraction or mice in the walls. It had gone well past that. Especially since Mike had heard the sound both times.

So she wasn't going crazy, Colleen wasn't going crazy, and the likelihood that someone was pulling a prank was minimal at best. Heck, it wasn't as if Colleen had even reached the age where she might have friends who wanted to wrap toilet paper on the trees out front. And making strange noises in a house in the predawn hours went well past that.

"Man," she whispered.

"Eat," Mike finally said. "The calories will help. When do you have to get Colleen?"

"I need to pick her up around six-thirty so I can bring her back here to shower and change before school."

"Okay. I have surgeries starting at seven, but I'll do what I can to finish out early today. Maybe cancel some appointments."

She lifted her eyes to him again. "Then what?" she asked. "Then what?"

"I don't know," he admitted. "But we've got to figure out something. And soon."

# *Chapter 8*

Colleen was happy to see her, even though it meant another day of struggling through school. And Colleen did struggle. She didn't complain about it, but Del had heard from teachers how the other kids bumped her around because her wheelchair got in the way. The only thing that seemed to have improved over the past couple of years was that no one picked on her anymore for it. They just got impatient, and going down a crowded hallway could be a problem. When the school had decided that Colleen should change classes just before or after the other kids, she had objected, claiming that everyone would be mad at her for getting special privileges. So she struggled through crowded hallways surrounded by kids who sometimes seemed blind to the fact that there was a girl in a wheelchair among them.

Del didn't understand it, but since Colleen's accident she had noticed how often people treated the disabled poorly, getting impatient with their slowness or the obstruction they seemed to cause. And maybe worst of all, how the disabled became invisible to those rushing around them.

Unfortunately, she had to take Colleen home before school. Much as she didn't want her daughter in that house right now, she had to. Colleen needed a shower, and there was only one place she could get one, and only one person who could help her with it. She wouldn't embarrass Colleen any further by asking anyone else to help with dressing and undressing, maneuvering into the chair in the shower, or washing her.

Colleen had already suffered enough indignities for a lifetime, and to some extent had to suffer them each and every day at the hands of her own mother.

"You moved my room!"

No way to hide that.

"Only until we get rid of whatever's making the noises. You can tell me later where you want your posters and things."

"It's farther from the bathroom."

"I'm sorry."

Colleen was frowning, clearly unhappy that she hadn't been consulted, but when Del accompanied her through her torn-up room, the frown faded to be replaced by a giggle.

"What's so funny?" Del asked.

"You sure made a mess for one mouse."

If only it were just a mouse, Del thought, but she managed a passable laugh in return. "It was going to happen sooner or later. You've been through this enough times to know."

Colleen sighed. "Yeah. Someday maybe we can live in just one house for a long time?"

Del felt her heart squeeze. "All this moving bothers you?"

"A little." Then, as if catching herself, Colleen looked up at her. "It's okay. It's what we have to do, right?"

"Right." But was it? It had initially been necessary because she couldn't afford two mortgages, but now she was paying two anyway. And then she was always afraid to leave a house unoccupied for long while she was working on it because there were so many useful things to steal.

And maybe that was too paranoid?

Or maybe not. Hell. She could hear that slamming door echo in her mind as she helped Colleen bathe and dress for school.

And she decided not to tell Colleen that there was going to be another change that very afternoon. She'd do it later, when she picked her daughter up from school.

As she did every morning, she lifted Colleen into the passenger seat of her truck and put the wheelchair in back in the bed. As she did every morning, she reversed the process at school, then stood and watched as Colleen wheeled herself along the sidewalk, up the ramp and through a door that a teacher opened for her.

Her throat tightened. She squeezed her eyes shut and sent a message winging heavenward, about how unfair life had been to this little girl.

As soon as she did, she felt guilty for it. She'd seen kids in the hospital and in therapy who had it far worse. But sometimes trying to feel grateful that it wasn't worse felt damn near impossible.

Finally, as she heard the bell ring inside the building,

she climbed back into her truck and pulled out her cell phone. In just a short time, she heard Nate Tate's gravelly voice answer.

"Hi, Sheriff, it's Del Carmody."

"Del! Hot damn. You work so hard I never get to see you around. And what's with the sheriff thing? It's Nate to you now."

She felt a smile crease her face, and so many memories came flooding back. Just the sound of Nate's voice was comforting. She had a string of memories of all the times he came into her classroom, before he had retired and she had moved away, to talk about the law, about not being stupid behind the wheel, or just to give students a glimpse of how the sheriff's office worked, and what it was like to be a deputy.

And then there were the other times, good times. Nate had six daughters, and Del had gone through school with some of them. And that had meant pajama parties, and barbecues, and birthday bashes. There was a time when it hadn't been unusual to see twenty or even thirty girls crammed into the Tate house, all giggling and laughing. There had even been one memorable time when they'd camped in the backyard, trying without much success to keep the volume down so the neighbors wouldn't complain, only to be sent inside in a rush by an unexpected thunderstorm.

"How are you holding up?" Nate asked her now. "You ought to come by some time for coffee."

"Well, I was going to ask if I could do that sometime today. I'd like to pick your brain."

"Brain's always open for picking. If you're not busy right now, come on over. The coffee is fresh."

"Thank you. I'm on my way."

The Tates still lived on the edge of town, their ranch-style house set on a large lot surrounded by similar houses from the same era. Every so often, the town grew in a spurt. Del didn't know what spurt had caused this particular subdivision, as it had been here as long as she could remember. At the other end of town, the relatively new semiconductor plant had caused another spurt of growth: houses and apartments both.

Nate hadn't changed much in the course of the past twenty years or so, at least not to Del's eye. The man had always seemed ageless. And Marge, his wife, while a little plumper around the middle, showed her years only in the gray hair that had replaced her once-fiery mane. Both of them welcomed Del warmly, and soon she was on the sofa, holding a mug of coffee, with a plate of small pastries on the table at her elbow.

"How's Colleen doing?" Marge asked immediately.

"Surprisingly well," Del admitted. "I keep waiting for her to erupt one way or another, but she doesn't."

"Some people," Nate remarked, "roll more easily with the punches than most. Maybe she's been blessed that way."

"I hope so." And indeed Del did. Not a thing could be done about her daughter's paralysis, so the best she could hope for was that Colleen could remain upbeat and happy.

"So you wanted to pick my brain," Nate said presently, when the social niceties were out of the way. "What about?"

Del looked down into her mug, uncertain how to even begin. Sitting here in the Tate house, the whole thing sounded ridiculous even as she tried out words in her mind.

Finally Nate spoke again. “There isn’t much I haven’t heard, Del. Some of it far stranger than you could even imagine.”

At that she looked at him and smiled. “I believe you. It’s just… Oh, I don’t know. I was going to ask you if anything had ever happened in that house I’m working on over on Jackson. Anything bad.”

His face didn’t reflect even a smidgen of surprise. Instead he asked, “What’s going on?”

She sighed. “Nate, it sounds insane.”

“A lot of things do. So just tell me what’s going on. The best place to start is usually the beginning.”

“Well, it started with Colleen hearing noises in her room. I thought we had mice or something, and for a week or so I tried to ignore it, thinking they’d go away as I continued pulling down walls. I looked around, of course, but couldn’t even find any sign that something had been in the attic. And Colleen was getting frightened.”

Nate nodded encouragingly and Marge left her bentwood rocker to come sit beside her and pat her hand comfortingly.

“Anyway,” Del continued, “Colleen went to spend the night with a friend on Saturday, so I decided to sleep in her room and see if I could identify the noises. I heard it. And I don’t mind telling you, it scared me, too. So much so I ran out of the house and didn’t want to go back in. Mike Windwalker saw me outside on the porch and came over to see what was wrong. He sat in Colleen’s room, too, and heard the same thing. Crazy as it may be, it absolutely did *not* sound like animal scratching. It sounds…well, it sounds almost like human fingers. Soft, not like claws.”

"Okay," Nate said. "I don't think you're crazy. What happened next?"

"Mike and I spent all Saturday ripping out the plaster in Colleen's room until I could pull enough lath loose to look in the walls. I couldn't find any sign that animals had ever been in there. And by then we'd heard some other noises, too."

"Like what?"

"Doors slamming. Heavy doors. Except none of the doors in the house had slammed. And when we made them slam, we realized it shook the house. We could feel the vibrations when we did it, but none when we just heard it."

Marge squeezed her hand, and Nate frowned faintly.

"That's strange all right. Anything else?"

"Just that I seem to keep misplacing things. I'm probably just not being as attentive as usual what with Colleen being scared."

"Could be." Nate's eyes remained both kind and thoughtful as he looked at her. "What aren't you telling me?"

Del almost jerked backward in surprise. No wonder this man had been such a good sheriff. How could he guess there was more? She hesitated, because she didn't know how Mike would feel about her spreading this.

"You can't tell anyone else," she said finally.

"I won't." Nate smiled. "I've been keeping this county's secrets most of my adult life. So has Marge."

"I'll leave if you want," Marge said gently.

"No, no, it's just that I don't think this is the type of thing Mike would want getting around."

"It won't," Nate promised.

"He says the house feels sad." She felt her own jaw thrust forward, almost belligerently, because if he said one thing critical about Mike she was going to…going to what? Nate wouldn't do that. He'd been the man to hire the county's first two Native American deputies.

He asked, "And that's why you wanted to know if something bad had happened in the house?"

"Basically. Or anything else. I mean, right now we're both pretty convinced that someone is trying to scare me, but we can't figure out why. And we thought maybe if we looked into the house's history, we might get a clue. Obviously the place was built by someone with money. Could someone think there's some kind of treasure in there?"

"I've never heard even a rumor like that." He sat back and rubbed his chin, obviously ruminating. "Something in the house that someone wants to find first? Possible. Some reason someone wants to scare you out? Equally possible. Or some just plain mean person wants to make your life more difficult? Much as I hate to admit it, I've known people like that. Somebody might have taken some wild notion about you or even your daughter. Some folks are that low. Someone might even object to the noise of your renovations and be too mealymouthed to just come out and tell you."

Del nodded slowly. "I hadn't even thought about that. I asked my neighbors to let me know if I disturb them, but so far no one's said anything."

"Hmm." Nate fell silent for a few minutes. "Well, that's one hell of a hodgepodge of things. Can't even be sure all of them are related."

"I know. I feel silly for even troubling you with it."

At that Nate smiled. "If I didn't like folks troubling

me with things, I wouldn't have stayed sheriff for so long. Marge'll tell you."

"I certainly will." Marge smiled warmly. "And lately, he's been getting a bit cranky because he misses the action. So you see? Coming here was a good thing to do."

"I'm not getting cranky," Nate protested mildly, but he winked at Marge as he said it. "I'm going to need to think this over, Del. Something's obviously going on. These occurrences happen at any particular time?"

"Mostly in the evening or during the night, but we did hear a door slam in the afternoon. And we couldn't find a thing."

Nate nodded. "As for Mike saying the house is sad…well, he may be right. I'm the last one to question that kind of intuition. But what would leave that impression?"

Marge shook her head. "I don't remember anything unusual connected to the house. I seem to remember Barb Barrow died there, but she was old and that was nearly forty years ago, wasn't it?"

"That's right. They found her in bed. Looked like a peaceful passing and she was ninety-five. Hardly enough to make a house sad."

Del was surprised that Nate didn't seem to have a problem with the idea that Mike thought the house was sad. Quite the contrary, he seemed to consider it an important clue. She had expected skepticism, although no bigoted comments, not from Nate Tate.

"I've got to give this some thought," Nate said after a moment. "As far as I know, nothing unusual has ever happened there."

Marge spoke. “Barb Barrow was fairly well-to-do. Didn’t she and her husband build the place?”

“I think so.” Nate’s gaze grew distant with thought. “But she wasn’t batty. I vaguely remember the probate proceedings. There was enough money in her bank account that I doubt she left any in the walls or under floorboards. It wasn’t like any of her heirs claimed there was missing jewelry or something. Besides, this is an awfully late date for someone to want to hunt for valuables like that.”

“Maybe,” Del said, “I should check the newspaper morgue.”

“Easier to go to the library,” Nate said. “Miss Emma will have everything at her fingertips. Meantime I’ll talk to a few people, put the old ear to the ground.”

When she left a half hour later, Del felt considerably better. Why? She didn’t know, except Nate Tate had a way of making people feel more relaxed, as if he’d somehow take care of things. And maybe he would. If one of her neighbors was mad about noise or something, Nate would surely be able to find out.

Although the idea of any of her neighbors running around in the middle of the night trying to scare her seemed ridiculous beyond belief.

In fact, the whole situation seemed ridiculous. Standing in the bright morning sunlight outside the library, in a world washed clean by the heavy rains, she would have found it easy to believe she had imagined everything. All of it. Except Mike had heard it, too. And Colleen.

And Colleen was scared.

*The house was sad.*

If she allowed even the possibility that the animism

with which Mike had been raised had even one iota of reality to it, then the house could be sad. And if the house was sad…

Squaring her shoulders, she marched into the library. Miss Emma, as she was known to everyone, sat at her small desk behind the circular wooden counter. She looked up and greeted Del with a smile. "Well, it's been a while," she commented as she rose to greet Del. "I thought you were too busy to read."

"Unfortunately, I usually am. But that's not why I'm here. Nate suggested you might be able to help me out. I need to know if anything bad ever happened in the house I'm working on now."

Emma's green eyes narrowed thoughtfully. "The old Barrow place, right?"

Forty years since elderly Mrs. Barrow had died, and yet the place would probably forever be *the old Barrow place*. That was one of the things Del loved about living here. "That's it."

"I don't recall anything offhand, but I can look. I helped the editor get most of the newspaper morgue onto microfiche and indexed on the computer."

"That must have been some job."

Emma laughed. "I'm always coming up with ideas like that. These days librarians are seldom overworked. Between TV and paperback books, most people show up here only when they need to do some serious research. The more databases I can develop, the busier I keep myself."

"Well, now that's a comment on modern life."

Emma, still smiling, shrugged. "It's easier for most people to click something online and have it delivered to their doors. But for research, there's nothing like your local librarian. Tell you what, it'll give me something to do today, and I'd probably be faster than you at working my way through the database, so why don't I research the address for you? I'll call later, whether I find anything or not."

"That would be wonderful!"

"I'd actually enjoy it. And I've been working on putting together a really detailed history of this county, so who knows? Maybe I'll find a good story to add to my book."

Which left Del standing on the street at nine-thirty in the morning and few choices. She knew she should go back to the house and work. She shouldn't allow a few noises to scare her off. At the very least she could wedge doors open so she could be absolutely certain they weren't slamming around. Maybe if she kept looking she'd find something in the walls, like a raccoon. Something big. Something she'd later laugh about and wonder how she could have missed it.

At least that was how she tried to buck herself up.

But it didn't prevent her from making a stop at the hardware store first. Once there she bought some new window latches. Maybe she ought to consider having the locksmith come out to rekey the locks on the doors. No need to replace them when the current door locks were reasonably new and could be rekeyed.

Feeling a bit better, she drove home, her first task to check every window latch in the house.

Pulling into the driveway, though, she felt a prickle of apprehension, which she hadn't felt even a few days ago. Sunny skies, beautiful weather, and she sat in her truck feeling as if severe storm clouds were gathering around that house.

No, she definitely wasn't bringing Colleen back into that house unless she got to the bottom of these noises.

Sighing, she grabbed the bag from the hardware store and let herself into a house she had once loved and now was coming to hate.

Ridiculous, she told herself. *You're being ridiculous.* The house couldn't do anything to her, even if *was* sad. She knew that.

Stepping through the door, however, felt like stepping into another universe. Even the sun spilling through so many windows, brightening the dusty wood floors, shining off walls and paint, couldn't make her feel comfortable.

Window latches. All of a sudden, she decided she wasn't going to be cheap about it. Every window would get a new latch, no matter how good the old one might seem. And if that meant another trip to the hardware store, so be it.

Before she started her task, however, she called her aunt Sally and made sure the woman wouldn't mind watching Colleen at Mike Windwalker's place. Of course Sally didn't mind. There was a time when the woman would have insisted on bringing Colleen to her place, but Sally was no longer as steady, strong or nimble has she had been just a few years ago. The idea of staying at Mike's house seemed actually to appeal to her.

That taken care of, Del went to work. She needed a screwdriver and a chisel, and she stuck a rubber hammer in her tool belt. Some of those latches had been painted around so many times over the years, she was sure they were probably stuck to the wood beneath.

Because of the latch she had found open on Friday,

she decided to start in the kitchen. There were a great many windows, a lot of them big enough for a grown man to crawl through easily. The current locks could be jimmied open from the outside with a chisel, but the new ones wouldn't allow that.

When she finished in the kitchen, she was startled to see that it was already two-thirty in the afternoon. Time to wash up a bit and go get Colleen and then Sally.

At least she hadn't heard any noises.

Sighing, she wiped perspiration from her forehead with her sleeve then went to the sink for a quick scrub down. No time for a shower.

Colleen was already waiting in her chair on the sidewalk when Del pulled up. She looked so tired that Del felt her heart squeeze as she climbed out of the truck.

As soon as she reached Colleen, she squatted in front of her daughter so they were nearly at eye level. "You okay, sweetie?"

"Yeah."

"But you don't look like it."

Colleen gave her a moment of panic by looking away and biting her lip. Slowly her green eyes tracked back.

"What is it?" Del prompted gently.

"I don't want to go home," Colleen admitted in a muffled voice.

"Why not?"

Colleen hesitated again, then finally blurted, "Those noises. I hate those noises. And I'm tired of pretending they're just a mouse."

Del's heart skipped a beat and she sat back a little, balancing more on her heels. "Want to talk about it here or in the truck?"

"But I don't want to go home!"

Del sighed. "You're not going home. Not for long anyway."

"What do you mean?"

"We're going to get Aunt Sally, and then the two of you are going to stay at Mike's house until he and I get rid of the noises."

Colleen frowned. "You're not kidding me?"

"About something this important? Do you think I would?"

Slowly Colleen shook her head, and her shoulders relaxed a bit. "No, but…"

"But what?"

"We have to live in that house. What if you don't get rid of the noises?"

"Then we'll go back to the other house."

"Promise?"

"Promise." If for no other reason than Colleen had enough on her plate, and Del could no longer believe it was just a mouse. Putting Colleen back in that house before the problem was solved would be utter cruelty. "Have you been worrying about this all day?"

Colleen gave a reluctant nod.

"Why didn't you tell me just how much the noise was disturbing you?"

"Because I don't wanna be a wuss. Because you need for us to live in the house you're fixing."

Those words nearly broke Del's heart. How much pressure had she been putting on this child without realizing it? "What I don't need is for you to be miserable and scared. Stop trying to be strong for me, sweetie."

"Why? You're always strong for me."

Oh, crap. Del looked down at her knees, not knowing

what to say. Had she been too strong? If so, it had all been veneer. Had she set a bad example? Thrust too much on this child's shoulders by always trying to be upbeat and positive about every damn thing?

Dropping her knees to the pavement, she leaned forward and wrapped her arms around Colleen, hugging her tight. "I'm sorry," she whispered. "I thought I was doing the right thing for you. But it's the wrong thing if you feel you have to hide your fears and pains from me."

Colleen answered with a hug. "Sometimes I'm so scared, Mommy. So scared."

Del's eyes burned, and tears started to run down her cheeks. "Me, too, sweetie. Me, too."

Del waited for the tears to pass and for Colleen's hold on her to loosen. By then the buses were gone and the schoolyard nearly empty. Only then did she lift her daughter and the chair into her truck and set out for Sally's house.

"Okay," Del announced as they rolled slowly down the residential street, "we start a new policy of honesty today."

"What's that?"

"I'm not going to pretend to be strong when I'm not feeling that way."

Colleen's answer was slow in coming. "Do you know how not to be strong?"

"Yeah. I've just been hiding it. From you, from me, from everyone."

"So you weren't kidding when you said you get scared?"

"I get scared all the time. I've just been keeping it to myself."

"What scares you?"

"That you might not be happy. That your daddy's gone. That there are noises in the house and I don't know why."

Colleen remained silent as they drove past rows of houses, until finally she blurted, "It seems like you always smile. Like no matter what happens you find a way to make it sound better."

"There's nothing better about some of the things that have happened to us, Colleen. Nothing better about them. And I guess I should have admitted that to you."

Colleen thought that over. "Okay. I know I'm still a kid, but I'm not little like I was when the accident happened. You don't have to pretend that everything is always okay."

Del felt a renewed ache. "I'm sorry. I thought I was making things easier for you."

"I know." Another pause. "Daddy's dead, Mom. Sometimes I have a hard time remembering him. But you remember him, don't you?"

"Yes. Yes, I do." Her voice broke and she didn't try to conceal it.

"So that has to be harder for you than for me. I'm lucky because I don't even remember the accident."

"I'm glad."

"And I'm paralyzed."

"Yes." Now Del's throat was almost too tight to speak.

"So if it's okay, I'd like to be sad about that sometimes."

"Of course it's okay!"

"I didn't want to upset you."

If she hadn't been driving, Del would have closed

her eyes with the pain. "I'm sorry. I made you feel that way, didn't I? Of course you're allowed to be sad about it. Mad about it. Whatever you need to feel."

"Mom?"

"Yes."

"Most of the time I don't think about it too much. You know?"

"I know."

"But sometimes I get really sad about it. Just so you know."

"I've been a little worried that you haven't gotten mad or sad since the first couple of months."

"Well, I kinda realized that we'd *both* lost Daddy, and I figured, well…it seemed wrong to make you hurt more."

Del hit the brakes and pulled over to the side of the street. As soon as she put the truck in Park, she reached over and hugged Colleen as tightly as she could.

"It's okay, Mom," said an extraordinarily wise thirteen-year-old. "We were just trying to take care of each other."

"Yes." She could taste her own salty tears. "I'm sorry. I was trying to do everything right, and I guess I did everything wrong."

"Nah." Colleen almost seemed to brush it off, but she gave her mother another tight hug. "Don't we have to get Aunt Sally? And I really get to stay at Mike's place tonight?"

"For as long as it takes me to figure out what's wrong with that house. And if I can't figure out what's wrong, I swear we're moving."

"Good deal," Colleen said as they separated. "I can live with that."

Del was sure her eyes were still red when they picked up Sally, who managed to squeeze onto the bench seat with Colleen in the middle. And Sally's mind was elsewhere.

"So Collie and I are spending the night at the vet's house, eh?"

Oh, man, Del thought as she heard her aunt's suggestive tone. She was already going through a wringer because of her conversation with Colleen, and now her aunt was going off the deep end? "Aunt Sally…"

"Don't bug Mom," Colleen said. "I just gave her a hard time."

"Well, he's such a handsome man. I keep wondering why he doesn't date."

"Because of nosy people like you," Del blurted in sudden annoyance. And she was happy, so happy, to hear Colleen giggle.

"What did I say?" Sally asked.

"He's just helping Mom find out what's wrong with the house. Right, Mom?"

But this time there was a certain knowingness to Colleen's tone. Del fought an urge to beat her head on the steering wheel. "I hardly know him," she said finally.

"That's the most interesting type," Sally remarked.

And Colleen giggled again.

Del took what comfort she could from the fact that the tense moments were past now. Sally dropped the subject of Mike, and Colleen seemed content now that she knew she didn't have to go back into that house until the problem was solved.

And she was utterly amazed to see Mike's van in

his driveway when she pulled into hers. He came out before she could even finish parking and crossed the lawn smiling.

A cautious smile, maybe because of Sally, but a welcoming one however restrained.

Del hopped out of the truck and hurried to greet him. "I didn't expect you home already."

"I told you I'd shorten my day somehow. All that was left was some routine checkups and vaccinations, easy enough to postpone." He went to help Sally out of the truck while Del pulled the wheelchair out of the truck bed.

"We've met," he said to Sally.

"Yeah, you took care of my cat until she died last year," Sally said. "I'm starting to think about getting another."

"I have a couple dozen you can choose from."

Sally rolled her eyes as Del unfolded and locked the wheelchair. "Darn cats breed like rabbits."

"Seems like it sometimes."

And then as easily as if he did it every day, Mike reached into the truck and scooped Colleen up in his arms.

"Okay?" he asked her.

She grinned. "More than okay. You're cooler than Mom."

"No way," he protested, a laugh in his voice.

"Moms aren't allowed to be cool," Colleen said. "It's some kind of law."

He settled her in her chair then let her arrange herself. Apparently, Del thought, he'd noticed more about how to handle Colleen than she would have guessed. Colleen insisted on doing as much as she could for herself, and had gotten quite good about adjusting her position in the chair and putting her legs where she wanted them.

She looked up at Mike with a grin. "So I'm staying at your place?"

"You bet. And I got it all ready for you and your aunt."

"Awesome! What did you do?"

Mike's smile broadened. "Come on over and I'll show you."

So Colleen wheeled down the driveway to the sidewalk and then up Mike's drive. No ramp to the porch, of course, so Mike gripped the handles on her chair and pulled her up backward while Del steadied her aunt by tucking her arm through hers.

Inside, the living room looked as if a genie had visited. A stack of brand-new videos rested on the player, and he'd even rolled up his area rugs so Colleen could move freely. There were also some new teen novels by the sofa, which had been made up like a bed, and a couple of teen magazines.

"This so looks like a pajama party," Colleen announced, smiling.

"That was the idea. Your aunt Sally can sleep in my bedroom. I even cleaned it all up for her. Fresher than a hotel room."

Del followed him as he showed Sally and Colleen through the house, but there was one problem: the bathroom. Then she saw the safety bar leaning in one corner in an unopened package.

"Oh, Mike," she said softly, as Colleen and Sally looked around in the kitchen.

He followed her stare. "Essential," he said with a

shrug. "But I wanted you to help me put it up because I don't want to make a mistake. Too dangerous."

"That is so, so kind of you. I was wondering how we'd do this part."

"I do think of some things. The shower…well, you have a seat for that, right? We can move that over here?"

"No problem at all." She already liked this man, but now her heart seemed about ready to burst. He'd thought of everything, and all without being asked.

"You'll tell me what else I need to do? I want Colleen to feel as comfortable and independent as I can possibly make her here. I would have hung a bar over the couch, but I don't know where to find one."

Her heart swelled even more. "We can bring over the one from my house. Obviously she won't be needing it there until we get this problem solved. Mike? You're really thoughtful."

She almost thought his cheeks colored. Hard to tell with the coppery tone of his skin, though.

"Nah. These are minimal things. Just let me know if you notice something else."

She went back to her house to get her toolbox to install the safety bar, and Mike accompanied her. With that simple act, he both reminded her of the threat that now seemed to lurk within her house, and the fact that she didn't have to face it alone.

By the time they got back to Mike's house, Sally and Colleen had begun to bake chocolate chip cookies in Mike's kitchen. Somehow she suspected the ingredients hadn't just been lying around.

Sheesh, this was turning into a day for throat-tightening emotions. First over her conversation with

Colleen, and then over Mike's obvious concern for her daughter.

While she and Mike worked on installing the bar, she turned over her talk with Colleen in her mind. The worst of it, she supposed, was that she'd set a bottled-up example that wasn't good for a child Colleen's age. Why hadn't Colleen had the anticipated reactions, the *normal* reaction to what she'd lost? Because her mother had bottled her own away, as if one mustn't do that.

Damn. She gave a screw an especially hard twist, then jerked in surprise when Mike's hand touched hers. "What's going on?" he asked.

"Later." She jerked her head toward the kitchen, to indicate Colleen and Sally. They at least gave her an excuse. She didn't know if she wanted to discuss any of this with anyone else yet. If ever.

Fact was, she'd gotten used to not discussing anything emotional with anyone.

She swore softly as she drilled in the last screw. Then she straightened and tested the bar with her full weight. Yup, it was good.

She packed her tools away then went to the hall and called toward the kitchen. "I have to go back to the house to get Colleen's clothes and a few other things. I also need to do some work. Is that okay?"

"Go!" Colleen called back. "You don't want to see me eat cookie dough."

"Probably not, so I'll pretend I didn't hear that."

"Good."

Mike accompanied her again. Once they were outside, he asked, "Did I do a bad thing by getting the stuff to make cookies? I know you said you have to watch what Colleen eats."

She managed a smile for him. "Once isn't a catastrophe. Right now I want her to have fun, sneak more cookies than she should, and just plain enjoy herself."

He walked silently beside her until they reached her front door. Finally he asked, "Did something happen?"

She hesitated as she unlocked the door. Should she tell him? "Oh, why not?" she asked herself, almost under her breath. Her insides felt as if they'd been tossed into a dryer and tumbled until up felt like down. "I guess I've been a bad mother."

"In what way?"

They stepped into the foyer and she closed the door, shutting out the world. Shutting in whatever was going on in this house. For some reason, she had to suppress an inexplicable shudder.

"Colleen and I had a talk," she said finally. She couldn't even look at him. "It seems I've been too strong."

"In what way?"

"I've been so busy trying to pretend everything is okay for Colleen's sake, that she felt obliged to do the same for me. Today she called me on it."

"Ouch."

She looked at him then. "Ouch?"

"Yeah." He shook his head just a bit. "Here you've been trying to do the right thing, be strong, hold it all together, and now you feel guilty for it. That's an ouch."

"Yeah. It is." She sighed. "I need to gather up her clothes. I need to bring the shower chair over. God knows how long it's going to take to get to the root of all of this. Emma's looking at the library for information on the house. I'm replacing all the window latches, and so far I've only gotten to the kitchen windows. I'd like to get that done today."

"I'll help in every way I can. But first?"

She finally looked at him. Before she could ask, he opened his arms and drew her into a snug hug. "I think a bit of this is in order," he said huskily.

Any urge to resist, to remain in her personal pond of private misery, evaporated as his arms closed around her. How could she have forgotten how good a hug could feel, or how much she could need one?

"I don't know what's wrong with me," she said against his shoulder, then drew in his wonderful scent, a scent that had become so pleasingly familiar just last night. He smelled so good…

"Want me to guess?"

"Sure, why not."

"How about that you've spent the past few years doing everything in your power to protect your daughter, and now something is going on in your home and you don't know how to protect her. You don't know what to do, and you feel like you're floundering for a solution."

She thought about that, then leaned in even closer. "You're good. That's probably at least part of it."

"Well, the other part might be that you've been fighting all these battles for a long time, pretty much by yourself. Even strong people can't always go it alone."

"Isn't that what you're doing?"

"I haven't had the kind of load you've been carrying."

"But you're all alone."

"Yeah. I'm alone. I go to work and I avoid other possible complications. Life simplified to a ridiculous point, I guess. You've got considerably more on your plate. You can't just go to work, come home and shut the world out."

She looked up at him, suddenly realizing something. "We're peas in a pod. We just have different ways of hiding."

"Apparently so. And I'm beginning to wonder if I'm ever going to outgrow that eighteen-year-old kid."

"Maybe you already have." She hugged him back, smiling wanly. "You're all mixed up in *my* life now."

"Yeah. And I'm not regretting it. It's funny, but when I decided to move back here, rather than start a practice out east, I told myself I was going to face down all those old demons. Then all I did was avoid them."

"I don't think you entirely avoided them."

"What do you mean?"

"You put yourself in a very public position here. It's not exactly the same as hiding in a cave."

"True, but I've avoided other stuff." His dark eyes were tight around the corners, but the tightness began to ease. For a moment, he looked about ready to say something else, but then he cocked his head and looked past her.

"Come on," he said suddenly, letting go of her. "Let's get Colleen's stuff together. We've got work to do."

She caught his arm, surprised by the sudden change in him. "Mike?"

He shook his head, but said with urgency, "Just a feeling. Let's just get going. *Now.*"

# *Chapter 9*

Mike's urgency propelled Del despite the fact that a couple of disturbed nights and some heavy work over the past few days had left her tired. Normally at this time of day she'd be wrapping up, getting ready to make dinner and settle in for a restful evening.

Instead, after carrying the necessary items over to Mike's for Colleen, she and Mike worked their way through the house, changing locks on windows. Darkness was falling by the time they reached the last room, her bedroom. Del took a minute to pull out her cell phone and call Colleen. Everything was fine, she was assured, and then Sally got on the line to ask when the two of them were coming over, as she'd roasted a chicken and it was about to come out of the oven.

"Thanks, Sally. I want to change one last lock, then we'll come over."

"Just make sure you don't take so long that it's all cold."

"I won't. Promise. It's just one lock."

The window in her bedroom was a tall one, overlooking the backyard. She could reach the lock easily enough to simply turn it, but she needed more leverage and a closer position to wield a screwdriver, so she knelt on the broad window ledge.

The next thing she knew she lay on the floor on her back, looking up at Mike, who kneeled beside her.

"Don't move," he said, and he started to feel her arms and legs as if checking for broken bones.

"I didn't know you did people, too."

"There are times I'd prefer a fellow vet to some of the medical doctors I've seen."

"What happened?"

"The window ledge popped off and you took quite a spill. You hit your head on the bed frame, but you were out only a few seconds. Are there two of me?"

"I wish. Two of you would be wonderful. But no, you're still a singleton, and it's Monday, and I'm okay."

He started to smile. "The old brain and mouth are working great."

His touch was purely professional, but she could not help but be aware of his hands moving along her limbs. With every touch, a small campfire seemed to ignite. Great timing.

"I don't think anything's broken," he said presently. "Now try to move your toes and fingers."

They all wiggled obediently. "Everything's fine."

"Okay. Then let me help you sit up slowly."

As he put his arm behind her shoulders and started to lift her to a sitting position, he said, "Let me know if your neck hurts. Even a small twinge."

"Nothing," she told him when she reached a sitting position. Then she raised an arm to feel the back of her head. There was an ache there, but she'd felt worse. "Goose egg tomorrow."

"You'll probably be sore in more places than that."

"I can deal with that. I just need to get that lock changed."

"I can probably manage that. I'm not totally useless, you know."

She looked at him. "Am I doing it again?"

"Doing what again?"

"Trying to accomplish everything by myself when other people want to help? Trying to be superwoman when it's not even good for my kid?"

"I dunno. Are you?" There was a twinkle in his eye. "Come on, you can supervise, but I'm taller and in my humble veterinarian opinion, you just lost your leverage when that shelf popped off."

"I can't argue with that."

He held her elbow to steady her as she rose to her feet. "It's okay," she said when she was standing. "The room isn't spinning or tilting. You can take off your vet hat now."

"Good. Now I can play at your job."

A couple of steps took them back to the window. The ledge, about eight inches wide as was common in many older homes, had indeed popped off. In fact, it had cracked right where it ran under the window.

And what Del saw when she looked down made her gasp. "There's a book in there!"

Bending, she lifted the slim volume and used her sleeve to wipe the dust from it.

"Why would someone hide a book?" Mike asked.

"I don't know. Unless..." She opened the cover carefully and looked at the fly leaf.

It was stamped with a gold *Journal,* and beneath that was a handwritten name: Madeline James.

"Oh, it's someone's diary."

"Fantastic!" Mike leaned closer and looked over her shoulder. "Imagine some teenager finding a place like that to hide her diary from her parents."

"Yeah. And imagine her forgetting it was there." Del had to smile. "Colleen would think of something like that in her more impish moments."

"I have no trouble believing it."

She looked at him. "Let's take a look at it after we finish the lock."

*"After dinner,"* he reminded her. "I gather Sally wants us over there soon."

"True." She tossed the diary on the bed. "I don't think Madeline James would mind us looking at it after all this time. Besides, I don't even know who she is."

They went to work and finished the new latch in just about ten minutes. Satisfied that now no window in the house could be jimmied, she and Mike collected her tools and the diary and headed downstairs.

Mike watched as she put the tools away. "You're compulsive about that, aren't you?"

"Putting my tools away? You bet. There's nothing

worse than knowing you have a screwdriver and not being able to find it."

"So that makes it even weirder that stuff is being moved around."

"Yup." She locked the box and stood. "Except it *is* possible that I get slack about it sometimes."

"I doubt it." He compressed his lips. "I was just thinking."

"Yes?"

"Everything has a place at my clinic. Everything. I know where every damn piece should be, whether it's in a drawer, in the sterilizer, whatever. I never have to look around wondering where I left something. That kind of practice is essential, and objects disappear only when someone else moves them. Every time I get a new assistant for example, we have to go through the 'everything has a place and everything in its place' routine. And for a week or so, things will disappear."

She nodded. "What are you driving at?"

"That once you've formed habits like that, you don't break them unless something major distracts you. I don't think you've been getting careless. So you know what?"

"What?"

"We're coming right back here after dinner. And we're going to keep watch again."

"That was my plan." She sighed and brushed her hands against her jeans. "Miss Emma hasn't called, so I guess she hasn't found anything out about the house yet, one way or another."

"What did Nate say?"

"He's putting his ear to the ground."

"I hear he has fantastic hearing. Wish I knew him better."

"Maybe we can remedy that after we solve our mystery. I should have him and Marge over for dinner." Then, looking around the mess that was the house, she gave a laugh. "Well, maybe after I get things in shape."

"Feel free to use my place."

They locked up then crossed the yard to his house. Del felt a pang when she saw all the light pouring out of his windows, an inviting sight. Then she remembered that since she'd moved in next door, she'd rarely seen more than a single light burning in one of his windows.

Loneliness and solitude stank.

They ate in the large kitchen, the four of them gathered around a nice dinette. Sally had apparently decided to pull out all the stops: roasted chicken, mixed vegetables and mashed potatoes with gravy.

Colleen seemed to be in much better spirits, probably owing to the fact that she didn't need to spend the night at home with the noises. And maybe an unusual amount of sugar from cookies had added to it.

She chattered cheerfully about her weekend with Mary Jo, talking about musical groups Del had never heard of, about movies Del had never seen, and boys.

Boys?

Del zeroed in, listening more intently. She had known that would happen eventually but…but… Not only was Colleen so young, but she was also paralyzed, and Del lived in fear of the slights and disappointments that would come her daughter's way over the next few years.

But at the moment, Colleen's interest seemed to be more general than specific, so maybe they could avoid the inevitable pain for a while longer.

Mike raved so much about the dinner that Sally began to blush and offer to cook for him anytime. Afterward Sally insisted on doing the dishes, so Del and Mike took the time to hang Colleen's trapeze bar over the couch and watch her try it out. She settled onto the couch with a big smile and a happy sigh.

"Have you decided on a movie yet?" Mike asked her.

As soon as they had a movie running and the DVD player remote in Colleen's hand, they headed back to Del's house with the diary. For some reason she'd been unwilling to leave it behind when they went for dinner, and now it seemed to be almost burning her hand.

They made a pot of coffee then sat at the kitchen table.

Del passed her palm over the cover of the diary, feeling its nubbed leather surface. "This feels like an invasion."

"Well, we can just skip here and there. It's not like we have to read the whole thing."

"True." She looked from the journal to him. "It's probably nothing but a lot of teenage angst and dreams."

He hesitated, then said, "I think it's more."

"A feeling?"

"Yeah. Like the house."

She realized she was having a similar feeling, and that it was holding her back from opening the book. "Mike?"

"Yes?"

"I'm getting a bad feeling about this."

"I know. I am, too."

"I'm not a fanciful person."

He looked straight at her. "And you think I am?"

"No, that's not what I meant. Maybe you're accustomed to getting these feelings. I'm not. That's all I meant. So when I get a feeling like this..." She hesitated. "Can I tell you something?"

"Of course."

"The day that Don and Colleen went skiing...all day long I had this feeling that something terrible was going to happen. I couldn't shake it. I tried to tell myself I was imagining it, made myself focus on work. I don't get these feelings. But that evening when the officers showed up at the house..." She shook her head, unable to continue.

"You weren't surprised," he said.

"No. It was almost as if at some level I'd been getting ready for it all day. As soon as I heard the bell ring, I knew what it was. Even though it could have been any one of my neighbors or friends."

A tear escaped, rolling down her cheek. She dashed it away impatiently. "God, I seem to be crying all the time lately."

"Maybe you have some catching up to do."

Maybe she did. She sniffled, blinking away one more stray tear, then drew a deep breath. "Let's do this."

The cover made a cracking sound as she opened to the first page. Girlish handwriting slashed impatiently over the pages, and she realized that indeed this was a teen diary. Madeline seemed to be about sixteen or so, and she gushed about friends, boys, going to the movies and all the other stuff a girl her age would find fascinating.

With Mike leaning close enough that their shoulders brushed, they skimmed pages quickly. There were time gaps, sometimes long ones of several months, then they reached a section where Madeline gushed about her upcoming wedding, pages of details about dresses and bridesmaids and flowers.

"Who is she marrying?" Mike asked finally. "She doesn't really mention him. You'd think she'd be going on about her fiancé, too."

"Yeah." Del leaned back, giving her eyes a break. With the passage of time, Madeline's handwriting had become smaller and had lost some of its neatness. "More coffee?"

"And another pair of eyes if you have them."

"Are you reading my mind?"

"Always possible."

Then as she grinned at him, he moved in and kissed her. A gentle kiss, almost questioning. After their moments last night when only the sound of a slamming door had kept them from going much further, Del was at once surprised and touched. Surprised that he should be uncertain, touched that he thought it possible she might have changed her mind since last night.

But she hadn't. So she leaned into his kiss and looped her arm around his neck. He responded by wrapping her in a tight hug and kissing her more deeply, his tongue finding hers in a mating dance as old as time. She felt desire sink heavily to her center, a feeling so strong that it almost made her squirm with need.

Then, with obvious reluctance, he broke the kiss. His face inches from hers, he said, "I don't think this is the time or place. If a door slams again, I may become impotent for life."

The way he said it made her giggle, a sound surprisingly like Colleen's. She leaned toward him and kissed him lightly. "I can't say I blame you."

"Coffee," he repeated. "I'll get it."

And right then she absolutely hated this house. Absolutely hated whatever was wrong with it, because otherwise she'd be heading upstairs to lie down beside Mike and share lovemaking with him, something she hadn't wanted since Don died. Something she wanted more now than she could ever remember wanting it before.

Instead she had strange noises and a diary which, frankly, wasn't all that interesting.

She glanced at the wall clock above the sink as Mike poured the coffee. "I need to go help Colleen get ready for bed soon."

"Sure. Just say when. If you want, I can stay here."

"Maybe fifteen minutes." She reached for the fresh coffee and sipped it gratefully. "What's your bet on how much we learn from this diary?"

"I think we need to keep reading."

"Yeah." She sighed. "That feeling. It's still nagging at me, too."

"I'd like to point out that so far I haven't read a single thing that would require that diary to be hidden from anyone."

Del arched her brow. "So you think things changed later?"

"Most definitely. Because Madeline felt she had to hide it securely, and we're not talking about between the mattresses or beneath the socks in a drawer."

"You're right." She glanced at the clock again, feeling reenergized. "Let me go take care of Colleen right now. I'll be right back, unless you want to come over with me."

"Can I confess I've been thinking of chocolate chip cookies?"

So they went together, and she noticed that it was he who this time picked up the diary, as if reluctant to leave it in the house.

But she had changed all the window locks, and as far as she knew she and her aunt Sally were the only ones who had keys. So nobody could possibly get in, right?

Back at Mike's, they found Colleen quite ready for bed, although she was still in the midst of an animated movie. Sally was sitting in an armchair, with one of the magazines she had apparently brought with her.

Mike found the cookies and put a half dozen in a small bag, and then they headed back to her house. Once again at the kitchen table, they resumed reading.

That was when the horror began to unfold. Madeline went from thrilled about her marriage and the excitement of being a newlywed to something furtive and ugly. Bubbling with excitement gave way to terser notes, a record of being increasingly abused. Threatened, yelled at, controlled and finally beaten.

And the final note: *I'm leaving. Tomorrow. I can't hide this anymore and I don't want to. He could kill the baby! I hate him, I hate him, I hate him…*

Page after page filled with "I hate him" until there was nothing at all.

"Good God," Del whispered. "Oh, God."

Mike reached for the book and closed it. The sound seemed almost final.

They sat silently as minutes ticked by. Del felt as if she'd just been touched by a toxin so awful she wanted to wash it off. The anguish in the final entries, so few and so sparse, had hit her as hard as if she'd witnessed it all. It was as if she could mentally fill in all the gaps that Madeline had left in her tale.

Mike rubbed his eyes with thumb and forefinger, sighing heavily. "I guess," he said eventually, "that's why she hid it."

"I guess."

He leaned back in his chair, drumming his fingers absently on his thighs, staring into space.

"She wanted us to find this."

Del's gaze snapped to him. "What?"

"Don't you feel it? She wanted us to find this. For someone to know..."

Del wasn't ready to leap quite that far. "You can't know that."

"She wanted someone to know what happened to her. I feel it. Laugh at me if you want, but the house isn't quite as sad now."

Since she'd never really felt the house's sadness, she wanted to argue. Then she noticed the qualifier in what he said. "Not as sad? You mean it's still sad?"

He nodded slowly. "There's a lightening, but it's not finished."

"Hell." Del nearly snapped the word, then felt immediately awful. "Sorry. It's just..."

"Just that you can't handle my way of looking at the world."

"No!" She glared at him. "It's not that. If you want to listen to rocks, that's fine by me. My problem is that you keep saying something is wrong in this house, my daughter is scared of this house, I've started to hate the place, and I don't know how the hell to fix any of that!"

"I don't *listen* to rocks. Not the way you mean."

"You don't know what I mean, obviously, or you wouldn't be getting all offended. What I meant was, I have no problem with your *beliefs*. I have a problem with the mess I'm in, and I don't know how to fix it. I don't really know where to start. Stop hearing me through your filters. I'm open-minded. If you say the house is still sad, the house is still sad, whether I feel it or not. But damn it, I need some way to *fix* this."

"Del..."

"I don't necessarily mean fixing the house's sadness. Have you forgotten that there's good cause to believe that someone is getting in here for some reason? That there are noises I can't explain? That my tools move? And excuse me if I don't think a *house* can do all that."

She jumped up from her chair, wrapping her arms tightly around herself, and began to pace the kitchen. "What do I do? Tearing out walls isn't going to fix it. Moving out is impossible, at least at this point. As long as only Colleen and I can live in this place while it's torn up, I need to keep trying to rent the other place I just finished so I can meet my bills. Colleen doesn't want to come back here. I promised she didn't have to until I solved the problem. This is one huge heaping stinking mess!"

She reached a counter and came to an abrupt halt, leaning forward on her elbows and putting her forehead in the palms of her hands. "Damn," she whispered. "Damn, damn, damn."

"Maybe I'm not good for you."

"Oh, cut it out," she said wearily. "You've been good for me. I was all alone and now I'm not. You saved Colleen from spending another night here. You opened your home to virtual strangers, you helped me tear out walls and cart a ton of trash. If you haven't been good for me, then nobody could be."

Silence answered her. Then, amazingly, strong arms closed around her from behind and lips found the nape of her neck. A shiver trickled through her, one of pleasure. Oh, Lord, here? Now? In this house?

"Del." He murmured her name and kissed the nape of her neck again. Another thrill ran through her.

"Nothing's adding up," she whispered.

"What do you mean?"

"I'm so upset and yet I…want you. Now. Here."

"I want you, too," he said huskily. "Here. Now. I'll risk it if you will."

She straightened then, turning within the circle of his arms to look at him. Reaching up, she touched his cheek, tracing his beautiful cheekbones, tracing his wonderful lips. "Am I going crazy?" She whispered the words.

"No crazier than I am."

She felt so off-kilter from the past few days, but one thing shone through as strong and certain: she wanted him. She wanted to lie naked with this man and learn his body as well as she knew her own. She wanted to know every secret that could make him sigh or moan. She wanted to feel her body hum once again to longing and rhythms she'd abandoned four years ago.

He seemed to read her answer in her eyes. "Just be sure," he asked. "Just be very sure."

"I'm sure."

"And no matter what we hear, we ignore it."

"I'll ignore everything short of a human being walking into the room."

At that he smiled faintly and dropped a kiss on her nose, then on her lips. "The house will leave us alone tonight."

And she didn't care how he knew that. When he took her hand and guided her toward the hall and the stairway, she felt as if strength was entering every muscle. A troubled thought flickered through her mind, because he brought the diary with them. He seemed so protective of it.

But whatever compelled him to do that, she soon forgot. Standing in her bedroom, in a pool of moonlight, she watched him close and lock the bedroom door.

"Maybe," she said, "you should block it somehow." And then she laughed.

He laughed, too, and the whole mood changed. From a heaviness, in an instant they moved to a lightness, a readiness to smile as if they were embarking on a wonderful journey and could hardly wait.

He pulled her dresser over, though, so it would prevent the door from opening. "Good enough?"

She laughed again. "I defy anyone mortal to get in here."

"That's all we need then. I may have animistic tendencies, but ghosts don't scare me. They can whisper, they can talk, but they can't hurt us."

And for some reason she spread her arms and said to the house, "Give us tonight. Just tonight. I promise we'll work on finding out what happened tomorrow."

Mike stepped toward her, smiling. "That wasn't so hard, was it?"

"Ah, but will the house listen?"

"For tonight."

He kissed her again, long and deep, then stepped back. Button by button he began to open his shirt. Smiling, she felt the courage to do the same, reaching for the buttons on her work shirt. At the same moment they dropped fabric to the floor.

"You're beautiful," he murmured. "So beautiful."

"So are you."

He reached out and ran his fingertips lightly across her midriff. At once her center clenched with delight and another shiver of longing passed through her. "Oh, Mike," she whispered raggedly.

In the moonlight, half dressed, he looked like a god to her. His chest was smooth and perfectly muscled, telling her that being a vet wasn't light work.

He ran his fingers along her shoulders and down her arms.

"Can I tell you a secret?" he asked softly.

"Sure."

"I've always been drawn to women who work

hard with their bodies. Women have such beautiful musculature."

"Only a doctor could say that."

A quiet laugh escaped him. "I know some men look for softness, but for me a woman with an athletic body has always been more appealing. It's one of the first things that attracted me to you."

"I hope you like callused hands."

"Love 'em."

Then like a magician, he unhooked the front clasp of her bra and her breasts spilled free.

"Perfect," he murmured, and before she could answer, he swooped in and took one of her nipples in his mouth, sucking strongly. An instant cord of electricity ran from her womb to her core, causing a resonant throbbing that drew a groan from her.

The world tilted, and she found herself on her back on the bed. He popped the snap on her jeans and tucked them down along with her panties until they caught on her work boots.

"Oh, crap," he said, sounding amused.

"What?"

"Damn boots have laces, and right now I'm feeling ham-handed." But he dealt with that by pulling the boots off, still tied.

And then she lay naked in the moonlight while he stood over the bed, drinking her in with his eyes. "I wouldn't change one thing about you," he said.

"Not even my mind?"

"Most especially not your mind."

A kind of peace flowed through her when she heard that. They might have arguments in the future because of their different worldviews, but he didn't want to change her. She could live with that. But as soon as that feeling of peace hit, it was followed by something much less peaceful.

"Are you going to leave me here by myself?"

Another laugh escaped him, short and thickened, and he kicked away his own boots then reached for the snap on his jeans. He paused then, looking down at her.

"Quit teasing," she whispered. "Mike, quit teasing."

"I just don't want to stop looking at you."

"Try feeling me instead."

The words seemed to galvanize him. He stripped his jeans then stood for a few moments in the moonlight, giving her a chance to drink him in. "Do I meet your approval?"

"More than you can know." She thought she'd never seen a man so perfect. A man so ready for her. That gave her another delicious thrill. She held out a hand, and at once he joined her on the bed, driving the rest of the world away, replacing it with the most basic and elemental reality: that of a man and a woman coming together for the first time.

Skin against skin. Was there a more glorious feeling in the world, than two bodies joining this way? It felt to Del as if every cell of her skin responded to every brush of his from head to toe, demanding that she just let go and give in to primal need.

His lips painted her with fire, moving along her neck and then lower as her hand sought to discover him, moving over the rippling, bunching muscles of his back, then lower until they found his waist and the powerful muscles of his rump. There her hands paused, trying to grasp, trying to bring him closer still. But he wasn't yet ready to yield. Instead his lips continued their magical quest, first from one nipple to the other, sucking so strongly that her entire body responded, arching toward him, demanding fulfillment.

But even as he sucked her to a near frenzy, his hand wandered over her midriff, over her belly until it found the damp nest between her legs. There his fingers played her as if she were an instrument, stroking, teasing, promising but never delivering.

Soft moans escaped her, and a kind of delightful frustration filled her. Had she ever been ready so fast? Doubtful, but she was ready now, yet he kept her waiting, hovering on a brink that was almost scary in its height, knowing that one step, just one step, would carry her off into the chasm.

She hardly realized that her hands began to nearly claw him as she voicelessly begged for more. Her legs clamped around his hand, rocking against him, trying to find the answer she so needed.

Until finally, finally, he rose over her.

He swore. "I don't have a condom."

"I do…I do…" She knew they were old, but she didn't care. All that mattered was that nothing stopped them now. Reaching out, she fumbled at the drawer in the night table. He took over, pulling out the box, tearing open a packet as he straddled her.

Then she reached out and took the latex from him, refusing to be denied the experience of feeling him as she rolled the protection smoothly onto his staff. Loving the way he groaned at her touch. The way he threw back his head as if it was almost too much to bear.

And then he lowered himself over her, finding her breast with his mouth at the same moment he thrust into her. It was like the completing of a circuit. The thrill rocketed through her, holding her taut in its grip as he plunged, filling a long empty place, as he sucked a breast that had not nursed in too long.

With one hand she clasped the back of his head; with the other she gripped his rear, urging him on, wanting him deeper inside her than he could possibly go.

He thrust again and again, and any one of those thrusts could have pushed her over the edge, but she fought to hold the moment back, to cling to this amazing, aching, overwhelming anticipation as long as possible.

But her body betrayed her. With a cry she tumbled over the edge, and just moments later he followed her with a deep groan.

And then the house felt happy.

And sated.

With her body still clenching with aftershocks, Del clung tightly to Mike. She never wanted to let go.

# *Chapter 10*

Morning arrived all too quickly. After a night of cuddling and lovemaking, Del didn't feel quite so much anger and dislike for the house.

But a change in her feelings didn't solve any problems. She showered quickly, changed into fresh work clothes, then took Colleen to school. Mike went off to work, promising to try to get back early again to help her.

Edgar and Jimmy showed up at eight-thirty. Edgar went to work on installing the new shower in the downstairs bath so that Del would no longer have to lift her daughter over the edge of the tub to sit in her shower chair.

"That'll save my back," she told Edgar.

"I can see how it would. I don't know how you've managed all this time, Del."

"I have a strong back, I guess." She glanced over her shoulder to see Jimmy checking all the exposed wiring in Colleen's former bedroom, using a meter to look for shorts. Then she went back to helping Edgar pull the tub out after he disconnected the plumbing.

At once Jimmy was there. "Let me do that, Ms. Del. That tub's heavy."

"Must be one of those old wrought-iron ones," Edgar grunted as he shoved. "Shame to throw it away."

"I just want to get it out to the garage," Del said. "If not today, at least we can get it out of the way for now. I figure I can probably sell it."

"Don't doubt it," was Jimmy's response as they worked on tugging the tub through the door. It took the three of them nearly a half hour to get the tub through the kitchen and to a place near the back door.

"Cripes," Edgar said, wiping his forehead with his sleeve. "Let's let it rest for now. We can move it the rest of the way later."

So it was back to work in the bathroom, this time extending plumbing up the wall to a good height for a showerhead.

"Okay," Edgar said finally after he'd welded the last copper pipe. "Let's go get the enclosure."

Del had had it delivered through the outside cellar doors so it was in the basement. She and Edgar headed down the stairs together and found Jimmy down there.

"Is something wrong?" Del asked immediately.

He shook his head. "Not sure. I'm getting low voltage on the electrical lines in the bedroom, but I can't figure out where the bleed is. And if you have a short, you should blow a fuse. You *are* going to replace this box with circuit breakers, right?"

"Of course," Del answered. "Code."

"Yeah, code." Jimmy shook his head, peering at the fuse box with a flashlight.

Del felt a tingle along her nerve endings. "Jimmy?"

He looked at her. "Yeah?"

"Could this cause a fire?"

"It's always possible. But you remember when you bought the place?"

Del nodded.

"There weren't no bleed then. And I'm not finding one in the rooms where you took out the walls. Damn." He stepped back from the fuse box, closed it and scratched his head. "I don't like this, Ms. Del."

She stood there uncertainly. "Jimmy, my strong suit isn't electricity, but how could something be causing a power drop in Colleen's room? I mean, just plugging something in for example…something that really sucks power…wouldn't that cause just a temporary drop? Like when a major appliance turns on? The way the lights dim when I first ramp up my table saw?"

"You'd think." He looked at her, shrugging.

"And a short would blow the fuse?"

"It's supposed to." He scratched his head again. "I don't like this," he repeated. "Something in the wiring ain't right. Something's bleeding power steadily, but not enough to be an outright short."

"Does that make it any less dangerous?"

"Can't say. Gotta find the problem."

"What do you suggest?"

His answer was short and to the point. "Don't sleep here."

She swore softly and turned to find Edgar just standing there, listening. Well, of course. Edgar was a plumber. This probably made just about as much sense to him as it did to her. She wasn't totally ignorant of electricity, but she couldn't for the life of her imagine how this could be happening.

"Okay," she said, looking at Jimmy again. "Try to find it. In the meantime, I'm going to help Edgar with the shower. If you need me, just holler."

Jimmy nodded and turned his flashlight back to the wiring that emerged from the fuse box, beginning to follow it along the basement ceiling in the general direction of Colleen's room.

"Oh, and Jimmy?"

"Ma'am?"

"We discussed using conduit for the new wiring, right?"

"Yup. Surely did. Beginning to think we may have to tear it all out."

"I've suspected that from the beginning. I doubt any of this would meet code."

"Likely not," he agreed.

Edgar helped her open the box containing all the parts of the new shower enclosure, then together they carried the foam-wrapped panels upstairs to Colleen's room.

She and Edgar leaned the panels carefully against the walls then made one last trip for the bottom and assorted odds and ends. During that time, Jimmy had moved back upstairs and was following a meter along a wall.

Unlike the old tub, the new shower came with a pan that sat below the enclosure's tile floor to catch any overflow and prevent water damage. Edgar attached it to the floor and then sealed any possible gaps around screws with thick, gooey caulking. Once they got the wall through which the plumbing lines would project firmly in place, the rest went swiftly.

By two, the shower was completely installed and the water was running. Edgar flashed her a grin. "Tomorrow the toilet."

Rubbing her lower back, Del leaned one shoulder against the wall. "I'm thinking about taking the fixture I bought back and exchanging it for something that would be easier for Colleen to use."

He lifted his brow. "You're not going to turn this house over like the rest?"

Good question, she thought. Good question. She had promised Colleen she wouldn't have to live here until she got rid of the noises, and she hadn't been able to find out a damn thing about the noises. Cool. Very cool.

"I don't know," she said finally. "I probably should. Either way, yeah, we can put in the new toilet tomorrow. And maybe the sink."

He nodded. "Okay. See you in the morning."

But he didn't pick up his tools, and she knew why. In this business, payment didn't wait.

He followed her into the kitchen, where she took her business checkbook out of a drawer and wrote him a draft for the day's labor.

As he was leaving, Jimmy came down from the upstairs.

"Did you find anything?" she asked.

"No." He didn't look happy. "I'm coming back in the morning. Something's wrong and I don't like it. Just don't you sleep here tonight, Ms. Del."

"I won't," she promised. She asked what she owed him and he shrugged it off.

"Ain't fixed nothin' yet," he said. Then he nodded, picked up his tools and left.

And she was alone in the house. A glance at her watch told her she needed to race to pick up Colleen. No time for even a quick wash.

Hurrying, she checked all the locks, then set out for the school.

Colleen seemed a lot happier knowing she didn't have to go back to the house. A quick call to Sally resulted in a short shopping list, so they hit the grocery. She even yielded to Colleen's pleas for some diet soda.

And by the time she got everything taken care of, it was after four and Mike still hadn't come home. Almost as soon as she thought of him, though, her cell phone rang.

"Hi, Del," Mike said. "I'm sorry, but I had an emergency. It might be an hour or more before I can get home."

"That's fine. I think I'm almost done with work for the day. I may go back and clean up a bit, though."

He paused. "Why don't you wait for me?"

"I'm just going to get some trash out. It won't take ten minutes. I'll see you soon."

There were words she wanted to say, words she wanted to hear from him, but she gathered he wasn't alone. Last night he had called her *darling,* and *sweetheart,* but over the phone she was *Del* again.

She felt a pang as she said goodbye, then told herself not to be ridiculous. Now, if he came home and didn't call her *darling* or *sweetheart,* she'd have something to wonder about.

"Sally?"

"Yes, dear?"

"I'm going over to the house to carry out some trash."

"That's fine, dear. I'll get started on dinner soon."

As she crossed the lawn, she decided to call Miss Emma at the library.

"Still haven't found a single thing about that house," Emma responded cheerfully. "Apparently nothing newsworthy ever happened there. At least nothing I've found yet."

"I can't thank you enough for looking."

"Actually, I think I'm having fun, and probably taking longer than necessary because I keep getting distracted by other stories."

Del had to laugh. "Would you like to search something else for me?"

"Sure, why not?"

"Who was Madeline James?"

"Hmm." Emma's tone grew thoughtful as Del climbed the steps and started to unlock the front door. "Now that *does* sound familiar. Did I go to high school with her?" But she apparently didn't expect an answer. "I'll look her up. Why do you need to know?"

"I found her diary."

"Oh! I bet she would love to have that back. Those things look so silly to us when we're young and look back on them, but when we get older they can be downright fascinating. I'll let you know what I find."

"Thanks, Miss Emma."

"My pleasure, Del. I've actually been having a ball."

Del wished she could say the same. Instead she headed for the basement to pick up the cardboard that had encased the shower enclosure. She could have asked

Edgar to help get rid of it, but she hadn't wanted to pay for the extra time. Pulling a utility knife from her pocket, she snapped it open and began to cut cardboard to manageable sizes.

*A fire hazard because there was a power bleed somewhere in the house.* That really shook her, because she'd had Jimmy check it out before she bought the place. She'd been worried about the wiring from the start, given the place was so old. And while she might expose Colleen to the dust and mess of renovation, she would *not* expose her daughter to a dangerous dwelling. She'd had the building inspector in, and Edgar and Jimmy both before she'd even made an offer. No one had thought the place dangerous *then*.

She had guessed she would probably need to replace the wiring, given the age of the place and the fact that she was bound to do damage tearing out the rotten walls, but to learn she had a voltage drop in Colleen's room, something which Jimmy couldn't locate, seriously troubled her.

As she cut cardboard and stacked it neatly, she tried to remember anything she might have done to cause the problem. The only trouble with that, of course, was that Jimmy should have found the bleed easily enough in the walls she'd already torn out.

So what else was there?

She went back to the fuse box, opened it and studied it with the help of a penlight she always carried in the breast pocket of her work shirt. Maybe there was something wrong with it. Well, there had to be, didn't there? She couldn't imagine how she could have a power bleed somewhere without blowing a fuse. The very idea struck her as counterintuitive.

When the refrigerator compressor came on, the lights dimmed just briefly until the current draw leveled out again. It happened fast, something she almost didn't notice. So how could you have a persistent bleed that wouldn't be compensated for unless you had a major short, one that should blow a fuse?

All the fuses looked okay, as they should considering she had put in fresh ones when they moved in.

She squatted, flashlight in hand, staring up at the fuse box as she tried to remember her all-too-brief studies in wiring and electricity years ago.

What could create a persistent power drop that couldn't be compensated for? Some kind of resistor?

Yeah, a resistor. But they made heat, which was how they expended the energy they pulled out of the system. Light and heat, just like a lightbulb.

Well, how could something like that have happened all of a sudden and all on its own?

She knew she should wait for Jimmy to come back in the morning. He was the expert, after all, the one with the license and years of experience.

But she hated problems she couldn't solve.

Straightening, she started to follow the wiring from the fuse box, just as Jimmy had. Not that she really expected to see anything. If it was obvious, Jimmy would have found it.

Walking slowly, she peered up at the wires. They all were insulated, and she didn't see any breaks in the insulation. A couple had been capped off with plastic, having been cut and thrown into disuse. A couple headed for the overhead bulb fixtures that were attached to the overhead joists, and which cast little enough light in the basement.

Everything looked absolutely normal, and she was just about to give up when her flashlight trailed across one wire.

It went *behind* the brick wall.

Her opinion of the person who put up that wall sank another notch lower. Not only lousy mortar that was crumbling, but unevenly laid bricks, too. And now, apparently, the builder had just sealed up an outlet box. Stupid.

She considered cutting and capping the wire right then and there and couldn't understand why the guy who had built the wall hadn't done it himself. If water got in there…

Sighing, she traced the wire back to the fuse box and tried to determine which fuse it was attached to. Well, of course, the basement fuse. She'd have to turn out all the lights down here if she wanted to cut that one wire.

Shoot.

Well, it had survived this long.

She shoved her knife back into her pocket and pulled out her cell phone to call Sally and tell her she'd be over in a few minutes, that she just wanted to take care of a bit of business first. Like tearing down enough of that wall to see where the wire went. As crumbly as the mortar was, the only thing she needed to fear was carelessness.

But just before she could flip her phone open, it rang.

"Hi," said the voice of Emma Dalton, the librarian. "I found Madeline James!"

"Really? Where is she?"

"Well, that's the thing. She left town about fifteen

years ago, and other than a couple of postcards she sent to her husband and friends, nobody's heard from her."

"Nobody? No family?"

"Her parents died right after she got married. And then after about two years, she took off. The story is she couldn't stand life around here anymore, that she wanted more adventure and more money. She was certainly pretty enough to marry it."

"But..." Del's mind balked. "That's weird."

"Well," said Emma, lowering her voice a bit, "I was thinking that, too. Jimmy reported her missing about two days after she left, and then a week later he got a postcard, so they stopped looking for her."

Del's heart seemed to stop. "Jimmy? Jimmy who?"

"Jimmy Morton."

Her neck prickled. Del turned slowly and looked at the brick wall, dark and ugly in the light from two sixty-watt bulbs. "Jimmy Morton, as in the electrician?"

"The same. He divorced her about a year later, but they couldn't even find her to deliver the notice to. Not the first time this has happened."

"I'm sure." Del hesitated, a chill creeping along her spine even as her mind refused the thoughts that were trying to surge to awareness. "Did anybody else ever hear from her?"

"According to the report I read, two of her best friends got cards, too. Hold on, it's in one of these old police reports."

Del waited patiently until she heard a rustle as Emma came back on the line. "Yes. Several of her friends received postcards, too. It seems she'd been thinking of leaving Jimmy for a while, so none of them were surprised. Anyway, the report said they verified the handwriting was hers, so no question of abduction or anything like that. The girl simply kicked up her heels and left."

"Well, her diary said she was going to leave."

"A shame we can't get it to her. She'd probably look back at it now and laugh."

*I doubt it,* Del thought as she said goodbye to Emma.

So Jimmy had lived in this house once, with his wife. Odd that he'd never mentioned it.

Or maybe not so odd. Why would he want to bring up such a humiliating, painful memory?

*Stop it,* she told herself. Cripes, why was her imagination running away from her? The woman had said in her diary she was leaving. She'd told her friends she was leaving. She'd sent postcards from wherever she'd gone, and her friends said it was her handwriting.

So no mystery, right?

"Right," she said aloud to the empty basement.

Except there was a mystery *now.* A mystery with the electrical power, a mystery with strange noises, and Jimmy himself who had said it wouldn't be safe to stay in the house until he found the electrical problem.

An electrical problem that made no sense whatever to her unless someone had created it. Or invented it.

Her phone rang again, jarring her, and she looked at it. Mike. "Hello?"

"Hi, sweetie." Apparently he was alone now, and the endearment made her smile. "I'm still hung up, but not for much longer, I promise."

"What happened?"

"Dog meets car. As usual, the dog took the worst of it."

"Will it be all right?"

"I'm pretty sure, but we had to do some extensive surgery and I'm going to help clean up. I'm also waiting for one of my assistants to come in to watch the poor guy overnight. Forty-five minutes. Maybe an hour. Tell Sally I'm sorry, if she made dinner."

"She did. I'll tell her. She'll understand, Mike."

"I hope so. Be there just as soon as I can."

She disconnected and called Sally to let her know.

"Not a problem," Sally answered. "Casseroles keep well. When are you coming back?"

"I just need to check something. Is Colleen okay?"

"She's doing just fine. She did ask for that LMNO music thing of hers."

"Her MP3 player. Tell her I'll bring it. I can't believe I forgot to get it for her yesterday."

"She'll live. She's watching some comedy reruns right now."

Del's cell began to beep. "Sally, my phone's dying. Be there as soon as I can."

She shut the phone, turned it off to save the last of the battery and shoved it into her pocket. *Okay, get the cardboard out, go clean up for dinner and wait for Mike.*

Except she no sooner reached the foot of the basement stairs when her neck started prickling again.

Was this what Mike meant when he said the house felt sad to him? Or was it something else?

She turned slowly, looking around the basement, seeing absolutely nothing except some tools, ladders, the stack of cardboard she'd just made and a couple of boxes holding bathroom fixtures she intended to install tomorrow.

An empty room that certainly didn't feel empty.

And a brick wall that made absolutely no sense.

No, she wasn't going to start *that* job tonight.

Oh, yes, she was.

Okay, just around the wire, just to see if maybe it was capped off right behind the brick. That much she could justify. If there was any place in this house that could have an electrical drain that Jimmy hadn't noticed during his first inspection, that would be it. After all, it had rained a lot over the past few days. Something back there might be damp.

Picking up a hammer and chisel, she dragged a stepladder over to that end of the wall. She could have reached the top bricks while standing on the floor, but she didn't want to risk the possibility of bricks falling on her head when the mortar crumbled.

Just before she struck the first blow, she had a thought. More light would be useful. Very useful.

Sighing, she climbed down and went back upstairs to get a couple of her work lights. Back in the basement, she hung them to the side on nails in the rafters so they were in a position not to blind her as she looked at the bricks.

The first brick came loose with one blow of the hammer against the chisel. Not caring if she damaged it, she tossed it to the floor, where it made a surprisingly high-pitched *thunk* as it hit the cement.

Bricks, she had noted over the years, had different voices according to how dense they were and the amount of firing they'd received. Differences in quality made for differences in voices.

She scraped the remaining mortar away and saw that the wire continued to run behind the bricks.

Great. She touched the basement wall behind and felt a definite dampness. This wall absolutely had to go.

But she also felt a shuddering wave of relief. The thought she had refused to entertain just a short while ago while speaking with Emma surged up along with the relief. Nothing was hidden behind that wall. Nothing. There was no room. The brick she had removed had rested flat against the cement wall behind it.

Feeling almost weak with relief, she leaned against the ladder and put her head down for a moment. How could she have even suspected such a thing? Too many TV shows, she decided. Too damn many.

She was appalled that her own mind had even dredged up such a notion, particularly about a man she had worked with over the past several years. One who seemed nice.

God! She lifted her head, telling herself to just head back to Mike's and enjoy a nice dinner.

And that was when she saw it. Looking along the length of the wall for the first time, perhaps aided by the work lights she had hung, she saw a definite bulge in the brick wall. Not huge, but as if something were pressing on it, working it slowly away from the wall behind.

It was not big enough to conceal anything, but she was curious anyway. Climbing down from the ladder, she used her hammer, tapping gently along the wall, listening to the sounds. And when she got to the bulge, those sounds changed. Deadened.

There was definitely something different back there.

She tried rationalizing. Maybe someone had put this wall in because part of the basement wall had given way.

But that didn't make sense. As a repair job for that kind of problem, this was a terrible idea. Bricks just didn't offer the same kind of strength. Even a well-mortared cinderblock wall with reinforcing rods would have been within the scope of a home handyman.

Of course, during her renovation career, she'd found a whole lot of really strange repair jobs.

Sighing, she tapped the wall again and heard that deadened sound. Why did she think this was going to turn into one helluva repair job?

She laid the palm of her hand against the bulging bricks and felt dampness. Water was definitely getting in.

And if water was seeping upward into the exterior wall, then she had truly big trouble on her hands.

Feeling suddenly frustrated, she banged her hammer hard against the bulge. A brick cracked. She banged again, determined to know what she was up against here.

Three more bangs and some of the bricks broke enough that she could pry them out with her hammer's claw, and then she dropped her hammer to work with her fingers. At once she found wet mud.

"Holy hell," she muttered. She pushed her hand in a bit farther and felt tree roots, more mud, something hard and pitted. "What the…?"

Water began to trickle out of the mud.

"You shouldn't have done that."

Startled, she fell to her hands and knees, then looked around to see Jimmy. "What are you doing here?" she asked, confused by his sudden appearance. "I thought you were coming back in the morning."

"I told you not to sleep here tonight."

The prickling on the back of her neck reached an uncomfortable level. "I'm not going to," she said. And Jimmy looked…odd. Not like himself.

"That wall could fall on you now," he said.

She glanced at it and realized he was right. Pulling out those bricks had destabilized it, and water was coming through the opening even faster now.

"I'll brace it," she said. "In the morning we can rip it out. There's a hole in the concrete behind it."

"I know."

That was the moment when the prickling turned to a chill. Trying to be furtive, she felt around for her hammer. Damn it, where had it gone?

"It'll be such a tragedy when they find you tomorrow," he said.

"Tragedy?" Her heart was racing like a horse's at the end of a derby. "Why should there be a tragedy?" Although now she knew, absolutely knew, that her imagination hadn't run away with her.

"Buried under that brick wall you should never have tried to take down by yourself."

She poised herself, ready to spring. But before she could reach her feet, Jimmy ran at her carrying her sledgehammer.

Oh, God! Somehow she managed to shove herself away from the wall just before Jimmy hit her. He hit the wall himself, and more bricks cracked.

But it gave her time, just enough time to get to her feet. "Jimmy," she said, pretending she knew nothing, "what's wrong with you?"

A weapon. She needed a weapon. Some way to protect herself from that sledgehammer. Some way to knock it out of his hands. Fast. She'd have to move fast.

All she had was a utility knife. And her hammer… She looked away from him just long enough to locate it. Out of reach, at least right now.

But he wanted her to be buried under bricks. So if she started to swing around in a way that would bring her back to the wall…

She edged carefully, circling. He followed her, something at once intent and vacant in his gaze. A quick glance at the floor told her that she might be able to get him to the wet spot that was growing as water trickled through the hole in the wall.

A wet spot that would be as slippery as ice, as she knew from experience. This floor in this basement had never been roughened. At some time or other, it had been covered with a smooth concrete coat. Perhaps with intent to paint it.

All that mattered was that she might be able to get him to slip in that water.

Taking a huge risk when she judged the time right, she jumped toward him. Instinctively he leaped back and hit the water. His feet slipped and he struggled for balance.

Del kept right on charging, head lowered until she butted him in the chest. She heard the sledgehammer fall.

And then she was on the floor, rolling around with Jimmy as he punched at her and then tried to get his hands around her throat.

But hard work had made her strong. She shoved her forearms up between Jimmy's arms and snapped them outward with enough strength that although she didn't have the leverage to break his grip, he loosened it.

She drew a deep breath then turned her head and bit him as hard as she could on his wrist.

He yelped and let go, instinctively pulling away from the pain. It was enough to allow her to shove at him and try to wiggle from beneath him.

She almost made it, then he came back at her, more enraged than ever.

Damn, she thought wildly, falling hadn't been a good idea. She couldn't get leverage anywhere on her back. But then she realized one of his legs had fallen between hers. Gasping another deep breath, she yanked her knee upward as hard as she could manage.

Jimmy howled and reared away from that awful pain. Struggling, Del managed to roll over, her hands clawing to find the hammer she'd dropped.

She heard the scrape of the sledgehammer and knew Jimmy, nearly paralyzed with pain as he must be, had found his weapon again. Panic nearly swamped her, adding to her strength. She managed with a single shove to yank her legs from beneath him.

If she could just get to her feet before he did, before he got enough leverage to use that sledgehammer…

Oh, God, she had to get out of this. Who would take care of Colleen?

Rage joined fear as fuel as she thought of her daughter. Scrambling, she got her feet beneath her, her gaze fixed on Jimmy, who was rising again, hammer in hand.

Damn! She thought wildly, trying to weigh options, realizing that one blow of that sledgehammer would put her down.

"Del?" The call seemed to come from far away. It sounded like Mike, but it was too soon for Mike. Feeling like a threatened animal, she watched Jimmy straighten and realized there was only one thing she could do.

With her legs still bent, her feet beneath her, she sprang at his knees, hitting him with her shoulder right at the kneecaps.

And hit him hard. She lost her wind at the impact when she landed on her stomach. Her shoulder hurt almost as if it had been broken.

But now Jimmy was on the floor again, on his back, unable to use that sledgehammer to any real purpose.

*Stand,* she ordered herself. *Stand.* But she couldn't catch her breath. Her body seemed almost paralyzed. And Jimmy had started to move again.

God, why couldn't she breathe?

Then, the most welcome sound in the world.

"Del? Del!"

The thudding of footsteps on the wooden stairs. With a great gulp she finally gasped for air, and her limbs began to move again.

And Jimmy reared up to his feet, staggering a little as he tried to lift the sledgehammer.

And then the most beautiful sight in the world.

Mike came flying by like a defensive end to make a rushing tackle. Like someone who had played the game and knew exactly how to do it.

Jimmy fell backward again, with an *oof* as the wind was driven from him, and this time his head cracked on the concrete.

And suddenly, unbelievably, everything went still.

# *Chapter 11*

"Del? Del? Oh, God, honey, open your eyes!"

Had she passed out? She didn't think so. Groaning, she opened her eyes and realized she was facedown on cold concrete. She started to roll over, but Mike stopped her.

"Wait," he said. "You might be injured."

"My shoulder hurts," she mumbled and kept turning over anyway, grimacing, but pretty certain she was just bruised. "Jimmy?"

"He's out like a light. But it won't last. Cops are coming. Just don't move. I need to be sure he doesn't get up again."

"You were wonderful," she said hazily. "Great tackle."

"I played a little in college. My God, what was going on here?"

"I'm not really sure. He attacked me."

"I could see that."

Mike moved away from her as another groan sounded in the basement.

Del lay staring up at the ceiling joists, coming down from the adrenaline, feeling weak and shaky. But when she heard the scrape of metal on concrete, she stiffened. "Mike?" Another wave of panic.

"It's okay," she heard him say. "If he moves I'm gonna use this hammer on his head."

"Oh." Why did she feel so woozy? Seconds ago she'd been more focused than almost any time in her life, focused on survival. Now she felt as if she couldn't collect her thoughts.

"The cops," she said.

"I already called them."

Wow, she must have blacked out for a minute or so. Moving carefully, she felt her head, but found only the lump from falling against the bed. "Did I pass out?"

"I'm not sure. You weren't responsive for a little while there."

"I got winded when I hit the floor."

"Or maybe the pain put you out for a short while."

After what she'd just been through, anything was possible, she thought. Shock. Pain. Lack of oxygen from her fall.

A shudder passed through her and she winced as her shoulder screamed. The compulsion to get up off the cold, hard concrete was overwhelming, though, and she managed to push herself into a sitting position.

"I'm not sure you should get up," Mike said.

"I need to." She scooted over to the wall so she could sit leaning against it. Away from the brick wall where a steady stream of muddy water kept pouring onto the floor.

Then, in the distance, she heard sirens. And finally the thud of footsteps upstairs. Moments later three deputies burst into the room: Sarah Ironheart, Micah Parish and Virgil Beauregard. All of them people she knew, for which she was intensely grateful.

"Well, hell," Micah said, taking in the scene. "What happened?"

"Jimmy attacked me," Del said. "And I think you'll find his ex-wife behind that brick wall." She lifted a hand to point. "Will someone please tell Colleen and my aunt that I'm okay?"

Then she closed her eyes and leaned her head back. She was done. Finished. Kaput.

"How did you figure that all out?" Mike asked as he sat beside Del's gurney in the emergency room. X-rays had shown no broken shoulder, but she was waiting for a sling for her arm because it had become so painful to move.

"Yeah," said a familiar voice. "I want to know, too."

Del turned her head to see Gage Dalton, the county's sheriff, in the doorway. "Hi, Gage."

"How are you feeling?"

"I'm going to be fine as soon as they immobilize this arm. Did you guys find anything?"

"Plenty. We found remains behind that wall. Sorry, your basement looks like a bomb exploded. I'll make sure the county cleans it up once we're done with the scene."

Del let her head fall back on the pillow and sighed.

"I guess I'm homeless for a while now. Unless I move back into the other place."

"Move into mine," Mike suggested. "Aunt Sally can go home then, and you can have my bedroom."

Del figured she liked that idea a whole lot more than she should.

"So," Mike repeated, "now we both want to know how you figured out there was a body behind that wall."

"Thank Emma," Del said, looking at Gage. Emma was his wife. "I asked her to do some research for me. Mike and I found a diary belonging to Madeline James, and Emma was kind enough to look into it. She called me just before Jimmy attacked me, to tell me that Madeline had been married to Jimmy and that she left town fifteen years ago. Except for a few postcards right after she left, nobody heard from her."

Gage nodded. "Guess I need to question my own wife a bit."

Del managed a weary smile. "Anyway, that brick wall had been bothering me for a long time. And Jimmy claimed we had to stay out of the house because there was some kind of electrical problem. Only after he left, I couldn't figure out how such a problem would have developed, especially since there hadn't been one when we moved in, so I started looking around. I saw a wire running behind that brick wall, which bothered me because it might get damp behind there, and I pulled out a brick to follow the wire. The cement wall behind was damp, which meant water was getting in somehow, and then I saw the bulge in the wall, pulled out a few bricks, found dirt and water… But I'm running on. I admit I'd already had the ugly thought that maybe Madeline hadn't just disappeared. And then Jimmy attacked me, and it was the only way I could put the pieces together."

Gage nodded. "Jimmy admitted it. He's been trying to scare you out of that house since you mentioned you were going to get rid of that wall."

"Really?" Del felt appalled by the whole thing. "That man scared my daughter with creepy noises?" She started to sit up, furious, but Mike gently pushed her back.

"Easy," he said. "Easy."

"I don't know about noises," Gage replied. "He did say he kept moving things around when you weren't there, trying to make you feel unsafe."

"All he did was make me think I was getting forgetful. It was the damn noises that brought everything to a head. How in the world did he make them?"

"I don't know," Gage said. "Maybe he didn't, but I'll be sure to ask."

Del sighed and felt an infinite wave of weary sorrow wash over her. "No wonder the house felt sad."

Gage didn't reply directly to that crazy-sounding statement, but Mike smiled faintly at her.

"So you found Madeline?" she asked.

"Yep. We certainly did. And Jimmy admitted it. Seems he found some postcards she'd written, apparently meaning to send them just as she was leaving town. So he knew she was going, and he got furious and beat her to death."

"My God!"

"Well, I don't know if he meant to kill her. But one way or another, he did."

"He was beating her for a long time. I'll give you her diary."

"That'll be helpful." Gage shook his head. "Anyway, when the deed was done, he panicked, hammered a hole in the basement wall, buried her, then put up the bricks. And he used the postcards she'd written, mailing them from Laramie, to cover."

Del shuddered, then winced as her shoulder hurt. "That's so ugly. I never would have imagined Jimmy could do such things. At least not until tonight. But I still want to know how he made those sounds."

Gage leaned against the door frame and folded his arms. "What sounds?"

"Scratching inside the walls. Doors slamming when no door slammed."

"I can't imagine," Gage said. "If he used some kind of sound system, you'll find it when you tear out walls, won't you?"

"I guess. But I still want him to admit it."

"I'll see what I can do. And I'll try to clear out your house as soon as possible, but it might be a couple of days."

Del closed her eyes for a moment. "I don't know if I want to live there anymore. My God, a woman was buried in my basement!"

"But she'll rest now," Mike said quietly.

Del looked at him and something in her heart, in her perceptions, shifted. "Yes," she said finally. "She can rest now."

And maybe that was the most important thing.

The sun was up when Mike took her home. Colleen was waiting impatiently and demanding to stay home from school. Sally, oddly enough, had packed her battered suitcase and announced she was no longer needed.

Del hesitated. And Mike took charge.

"You're going to school, Colleen. Your mother can't lift you right now, but I can, so we'll skip your shower this once and I'll drive you to school. And take Aunt Sally home."

Sally didn't twitch a muscle, but remarked, "I put fresh sheets on your bed, Mike." It was only as she headed for the door that she gave Del a knowing wink.

Del was too weary to pay any attention. After last night, running on absolutely no sleep, she couldn't deal with anything more, even something as silly as a wink from Sally.

The shower might be impossible at the moment, but Del still had one good arm, and it was enough to help Colleen get dressed.

But Colleen reached out and gripped her forearm, stopping her. "Mom?"

"Yes, honey?"

"You're really okay?"

"Just some bruises."

Colleen slipped an arm up around her neck, and they hugged. "Mom?" she whispered.

"Yes, honey?"

"Don't…don't go away like Daddy did."

Del lost it. She started sobbing, and she hugged her daughter as tightly as she could with one arm. "I'm safe," she whispered brokenly. "I'm safe and I'm not going anywhere. I'll be right here when you come home from school. I promise."

"The bad guy is in jail, right?"

"Right. And Mike will protect me just like he did last

night." It was a rash promise, one she wasn't entitled to make, but it seemed necessary.

But then she heard a sound and looked over Colleen's head to see Mike standing there. She could have sworn his eyes seemed a little damp. "I'll protect your mom," he said to Colleen. "I promise."

He took Colleen to school and then drove Sally home, and it seemed to Del to take forever. She was exhausted, she hurt and, by God, she didn't want to be alone.

Although if she were honest, she wasn't really alone. There were enough cops swarming over her house right next door that help could have arrived in an instant.

But life had taken too much from her, and after last night she wondered if she would ever feel safe again.

But then Mike walked through the door and she realized she could. And would. At least with him.

He scooped her up and sat on the couch with her on his lap. He showered kisses all over her face. She answered eagerly, needily, knowing deep within that this was a man she didn't want to lose.

Yet she had absolutely no reason to think he wanted her in the same way. Her heart squeezed as she remembered all his objections to getting involved with a white woman. And she couldn't blame him for that. Everyone learned lessons, and lessons learned the hard way stayed the longest.

Mike's cell phone rang. He swore. "Dammit, if this is work I'm going to…" He didn't complete the thought as he fished his phone out of his breast pocket.

Del's heart sank. Of course this was a workday for him. He probably had all kinds of appointments. Should probably, in fact, be at the office right now.

The thought of spending the day without him, all

alone with nothing to think about except what had happened last night and how much she missed him, nearly scared her.

"The sheriff," he said, looking at the screen on his phone. He flipped it open and spoke. "Howdy, Gage. What's up?"

He listened for a while, then said, "Okay, I'll tell her."

"Tell me what?" she demanded as he tucked his phone away.

"Jimmy denies all knowledge of sounds in the house. And since he's admitted to everything else…" He let the sentence dangle unfinished.

Del closed her eyes, trying to absorb it. "Maybe…"

"Maybe," Mike said. "Maybe. Some things just never get answers, Del. Never."

She met his gaze. "Tell me. Do *you* think it was Madeline?"

"I don't know. But in my world that's possible. Can you live with that?"

She put her fingers to her forehead, thoughts scrambling around inside her head like worried mice, escaping every effort to grasp them. And then she knew, absolutely knew, something deep inside herself.

"If…if it was Madeline, we'll never know."

"No," he agreed.

"But if I were her, I'd sure want somebody to discover what happened to me."

"I would, too."

She drew a deep breath, then let it go. "I guess I can live with that mystery."

"Mysteries can be good things. They help remind us of the magic in life. That we don't know everything."

She nodded, accepting it. "I can deal with that."

"Then there's something else I'd like you to deal with."

She raised her eyes to his, found them dark, warm and inviting. Such beautiful eyes. "What's that?"

"I realized something last night when I came charging down those steps and saw you in so much danger. Hurt and not even moving."

"What's that?"

"I think I love you, Del. Because right then, when I thought you might be gone, I realized I didn't want to face this morning without you."

She caught her breath. All weariness vanished, replaced by a dawning of joy she had thought she would never know again. "Oh, Mike!"

"I realize we've hardly had a chance to know each other. I mean, a handful of days is hardly a courtship. But I want to take it slow. I want to date you. I want to be sure Colleen wants me around all the time. And then… and then, assuming you start to feel the same way about me, and everything's okay by Colleen, I want to marry you. Because honest to God, Del, I faced life without you last night, and it's just not worth living."

For a few moments she couldn't even find her voice. Her heart pounded wildly and a tear rolled down her cheek.

"Oh, hell," he whispered. "I made you cry. It's okay. Forget I said anything."

"No." It came out as a gasp, but then again, more strongly. "No. I won't forget. Because I want the same thing, too, Mike. The very same thing. I think I love you."

The smile on his face was beautiful. She'd always

found him beautiful, but right now he gave new meaning to the word. That gorgeous smile. She couldn't imagine a day without it.

Still smiling, he scooped her up and carried her carefully to his bedroom, where he laid her gently down.

"We'll sleep now," he whispered. He lay beside her and drew her carefully into his arms. "Then we'll wake up together and go get Colleen. Which is the way I want to wake up every single day for the rest of my life."

She couldn't think of a better future. Snuggling in, she smiled and closed her eyes.

Happiness had found her once again.

* * * * *

# OPERATION: FORBIDDEN

BY

LINDSAY McKENNA

First published in Great Britain 2011
by Mills & Boon, an imprint of Harlequin (UK) Limited,
Eton House, 18-24 Paradise Road, Richmond, Surrey TW9 1SR



ISBN: 978 0 263 88556 9

46-1011

Harlequin (UK) policy is to use papers that are natural, renewable and recyclable products and made from wood grown in sustainable forests. The logging and manufacturing processes conform to the legal environmental regulations of the country of origin.

Printed and bound in Spain
by Blackprint CPI, Barcelona

Dear Reader,

The creation and idea for this story comes from my dear friend, Marchiene Reinstra, an Interfaith Minister. Although born in India to Dutch missionary parents, Marchiene lived the first eight years of her life in Pakistan on the Afghanistan border. She has fond memories of that country and its people. It was from her experience and memories about the Afghan people that I developed my hero.

I love Marchiene's perspective on the world. As an Interfaith Minister, she is steeped in many different world religions, including the Muslim faith. Her contention is that all the great religions, while having their fanatics, also have a core group who truly practice what they believe. Marchiene knows quite a bit about the Sufi branch of the Muslim faith. They are the mystics of their faith. She said that the Sufis work from their heart. Everything they do is in praise of God.

My prayers are that one day, all peoples of the world can live in harmony, peace and respect with one another. And with that in mind, please enjoy *Operation: Forbidden*. Let me hear from you at www.lindsaymckenna.com.

Warmly,

*Lindsay McKenna*

As a writer, **Lindsay McKenna** feels that telling a story is a way to share how she sees the world. Love is the greatest healer of all, and the books she creates are parables that underline this belief. Working with flower essences, another gentle healer, she devotes part of her life to the world of nature to help ease people's suffering. She knows that the right words can heal and that creation of a story can be catalytic to a person's life. And in some way she hopes that her books may educate and lift the reader in a positive manner. She can be reached at www.lindsaymckenna.com or www.medicinegarden.com.

# *Chapter 1*

Emma was in deep trouble. She'd just signed up for a second tour at Camp Bravo on the front lines of the Afghanistan war. And now this. Her commanding officer, Major Dallas Klein, had just requested her presence. Right now. That couldn't be good. She swallowed hard, and her heart began a slow pound of dread.

"Go on in, Captain Cantrell," the assistant said, gesturing to the C.O.'s office.

Emma nodded, took a deep breath and opened the door. She stepped inside and quietly closed it behind her. "Reporting as ordered, ma'am," Emma said, coming to attention.

Dallas Klein looked up from behind her desk.

"At ease. Have a seat, Captain," Dallas said, pointing to the chair near her desk.

"Yes, ma'am," Emma murmured. Sitting at attention,

she clasped her hands and waited. Her boss frowned as she lifted about ten files and put them into her lap. The woman sifted through them, and Emma instinctively knew they had something to do with her. She almost blurted out, *What kind of trouble am I in now?* but didn't. Compressing her lips, Emma held on to her last shred of patience.

"Here it is," Dallas said, opening one file and pushing the others aside. "Captain, you're the only woman in our squadron that speaks Pashto. You took a one-year saturation course before you came over here. Correct?"

"Yes, ma'am." Emma nodded.

"Good. And you continue to use the language?"

"Of course. I get a lot of practice with the Afghans who are allowed to work here on our base."

Dipping her head, Dallas looked down at the thick sheaves of paper in the file. "Very well, Captain. I've just had a highly unusual request dropped on me. And ordinarily, I would tell high command to go stuff it, but this time, I couldn't." Dallas scowled over at Emma. "You really gave your career a black eye last August by rescuing that Special Forces sergeant off a hill under attack. I know Nike Alexander had the idea, but you were the XO at the time, and you implemented her request."

Emma wanted to roll her eyes. God, didn't Klein forget anything? She remained silent; the major wanted her to respond, but what could she say? Yes, she'd screwed up, but she'd also saved a life. Emma knew when to keep her mouth shut, and she held the major's flat stare. Emma had never confessed to what the major just said. If she had, she would probably have been court-martialed. The better choice was to remain alert but mute.

"Well," Dallas growled, jerking open another paper from the file, "I have a way for you to save your career, Captain Cantrell."

Brows raised, Emma was interested. "Oh?"

"Actually," Dallas said, "the Pentagon chose you because you speak Pashto, the common language here in Afghanistan. And frankly, I'd like to see you distinguish yourself in some way so you can eventually go up for major and make the promotion." Dallas thumped the file with her index fingers. "I believe this is a very good way for you to salvage your army career, Captain Cantrell. I hope you think so, too."

Perking up, Emma leaned forward. "I'm interested."

"I thought you might be." Dallas opened up the file to another section. "This is a very special mission. What I don't like is that you'll be out of my squadron for six months. You'll be part of a team working on a unique Afghan project known as Operation Book Worm."

Emma almost laughed and struggled to keep a straight face. "Operation Book Worm? Ma'am?" Dallas appeared completely serious, not a hint of a smile or joking demeanor. And God knew, members of the Black Jaguar Squadron played tricks on each other all the time. Black humor was alive and well in this combat squadron. It kept them all sane. Laughter instead of tears.

"This is not a joke, Captain Cantrell, so wipe that smirk off your face."

"Yes, ma'am." What the hell was Operation Book Worm?

"Okay, here's the guts of the mission. You're being assigned to Captain Khalid Shaheen. He's the only

Afghan currently allowed to fly the Apache combat helicopter. He's been flying with another Apache squadron in the Helmand province of southern Afghanistan until this operation went active."

Emma's brow bunched. "An Afghan flying one of our Apaches?" She'd never heard of such a thing. And she was being assigned to this dude?

Dallas held up her hand. "Just sit and listen. I don't want you interrupting me, Captain."

"Yes, ma'am."

"Captain Shaheen is a thirty-year-old Afghan. He's responsible for creating Operation Book Worm."

Emma nodded and said nothing. How was this mission going to help *her* career?

"Captain Shaheen comes from one of the richest families in Afghanistan. He is a Princeton graduate and has a master's degree in electrical engineering. He graduated with honors. The army persuaded him to spend six years with them and he proved ideal flying Apache helicopters. The Pentagon is relying on Captain Shaheen to persuade other Afghan military men to come to the United States to be trained at Fort Rucker, Alabama. Once they've earned their wings in Apaches, they will come back to Afghanistan to start fighting and defending their own country."

"Afghanistan does not have an air force."

"No, but Shaheen is the bedrock for starting one."

Emma considered the pilot with new respect. "That's a tall order."

"New ideas start with one person," Dallas said.

"And what is my activity with him?"

"There's more. His sister, Kinah Shaheen, was also educated at Princeton. She's twenty-eight years old and holds a Ph.D. in education. She has made it her mission in this country to provide education to young girls. As you know, under Taliban rule, girls weren't allowed any type of education. Kinah is armed not only with a hell of an education, but her family's money and a fierce determination to get girls back into school."

"Wow," Emma said, "that's an even taller order. I've been here long enough to see how women are suppressed when it comes to education. In the past, the Taliban killed teachers and tribal elders or chieftains of villages who allowed girls to be schooled."

"I know," Dallas said, grimness in her tone. "Kinah and her brother, Khalid, came up with the idea for Operation Book Worm. Khalid is considered a used-car salesman of sorts." She grinned a little.

"You've met him?" Emma was now completely taken by the Afghan brother and sister and their plans.

"Once," Dallas said dryly. "And I can see why Khalid has been able to talk corporations in the United States into donating millions of dollars for this idea. Kinah is no small-time operator, either. Their father is a Persian rug salesman, so talking people out of money is in their DNA."

"But their idea sounds more than saleable," Emma said, excited.

"It has been." Dallas leaned back in her chair. "Between them, they've got ten million dollars to throw at this operation."

"Wow…"

"Yeah, double wow," Dallas agreed. "You'll come into this by virtue of the fact that Khalid is going to use, with the U.S. Army's permission, a CH-47 transport from

Camp Bravo. He's qualified in four types of helicopters, by the way. And that's no small feat, either."

Eyes widening, Emma considered that skill. "He must be..."

"He's a genius," Dallas said. "Brilliant, mad and passionate, not to mention a damned fine combat helicopter pilot."

Emma took a deep breath. "He sounds like a Renaissance man. Many skills and talents."

"Oh, Khalid is all of that," Dallas said.

"Why does he need me?"

"He wants to land in each targeted village not only to deliver books, supplies and food, but to show you as an example of what a woman can do. Khalid wants the girls of the village to see a woman who flies that helicopter. He feels that show-and-tell is a quick way to get the girls to dream big and often."

"That's a great strategy," Emma said, understanding the Afghan's brilliant concept. "So, I'm his copilot?"

"You're both aircraft commanders—ACs. You're the same rank. You have three years less time in the Apache than he does, but he wants you in the driver's seat off and on."

"In other words, he has a live-and-let-live policy about swapping out AC status?"

"Yep. You'll find Khalid one of the most fascinating men you've ever met. He'll keep you on your toes. He wanted a woman Apache pilot who spoke Pashto because he wants that woman to be able to speak to the little girls. He wants you to become a saleswoman to encourage their education. And don't be surprised if he has you do impromptu speeches on why little girls should want an education. Khalid wants to fire their imaginations. He wants to shock them from the realm of dreams to that of possibilities."

"I'll be happy to take on this mission, ma'am," Emma said.

"For the next six months, from spring through fall, you'll work with him. He plans on having fifty schools set up along the border villages by the time snow flies."

"But," Emma said, holding up her hand, "haven't you left out one thing? You know all the border villages are wide open to attack from the Taliban? Those villagers live in fear of them. And how does Khalid protect all these villages? Once the Taliban hears of schools for girls, you know they'll attack and kill the teachers."

Dallas nodded grimly. "He's very well aware of the situation, and the U.S. Army is coordinating with him to protect these villages. They'll be moving more Special Forces A-teams *into* the villages. And air force drones will be utilized as flyovers on a nightly basis by our CIA guys stationed here when the Taliban is active. This could be a queen-maker for you, Captain Cantrell."

Emma considered the assignment carefully. If she could successfully work with Captain Shaheen and his sister, her personnel jacket would contain glowing commendations from them. Enough to bury the censure over her decision last year. And then her family, who had a nearly unbroken ribbon of service to America, would no longer have this blight on its reputation. As she sat there contemplating all of this, Emma then wondered: could she get along with this Afghan? He was filthy rich. Princeton-educated. Would he look down on her? Not appreciate what she brought to the table with her own intelligence and creativity? Suddenly, Emma felt unsure.

Dallas signed the orders and handed them across the desk to her. "Here you go, Captain Cantrell. Do us proud." She hesitated for a moment and added, "Be warned: He's a marked man. The Taliban has a huge reward out for his death. This is going to be no picnic for you. Captain Shaheen is landing in—" and she looked at her watch "—fifteen minutes. Be on the tarmac to meet him. Dismissed."

The sun was bright and Emma put on her dark aviator glasses. The breeze was inconstant across the concrete revetment area. The odor of flight fuel was strong. She watched as several ordinance teams drove out in specialized trucks, pulling their loads of weaponry on trailers. An excitement hummed through the area. Emma inhaled it and absorbed the vibrating tension. She loved that feeling, which was probably why she was an Apache combat helicopter pilot.

Some anxiety lingered about the new assignment. If Shaheen was a marked man, on the enemy's top-ten-wanted list, it was more than likely the Taliban would make good on their threat to murder him.

Then there was her own distrust of rich men who thought they could act reprehensibly without recourse. Like Brody Parker. Brody had been a rich American in Lima, Peru, and she'd met him when flying in for the original Black Jaguar Squadron. A year after falling helplessly in love with him, Emma found out he was married, with children. Stung to her soul by the lies that men could tell, she'd made a point of avoiding the opposite sex since coming to Camp Bravo. It was a clean start. She didn't need another rich, lying bastard to deal with.

Shaheen landed the Apache on a three-point landing

about a hundred feet away from where Emma stood. It was a perfect landing—gentle and not bouncy. Her eyes narrowed as she saw the ground crewman place the ladder against the bird and climb up after the rotors stopped turning. He hefted the canopy upward on the front cockpit after it was unlocked by the pilot. Emma was confused; she saw no pilot in the back seat. No one flew the Apache with just one pilot unless it was an emergency.

When Khalid Shaheen climbed out of the cockpit, he handed the crewman his helmet, and Emma smiled to herself. As the Afghan emerged, she was taken by his lean, taut form. He had to be six feet tall, which was about the top height for an Apache pilot. Most were between five foot seven inches and five foot ten inches tall. The cockpit was cramped, and anyone over six feet couldn't comfortably get into it. She tried to ignore his animallike grace as he climbed out of the cockpit and stood on the dark green and tan metal skirt. The crewman stepped off the ladder and waited nearby.

Emma took in Shaheen's olive skin, military-short black hair and straight, dark brows above narrowed blue eyes. When he smiled and joked with the crewman on the tarmac, her heart suddenly thumped hard in her chest. Shaheen was eye candy, no doubt. And dangerous… His face was narrow, his nose aquiline, cheekbones high and he had a strong chin. When he smiled at a crewman's joke, his teeth were white and even. Emma felt herself melting inwardly. Of all the reactions to have! Shaheen was like a fierce lion moving with a feral grace that took her breath away. There were no lions in Afghanistan, Emma reminded herself.

And yet, she couldn't take her gaze off the charismatic officer. He removed his Kevlar vest and placed it on the skirt of the Apache. There was a .45 pistol strapped to his waist. Emma decided that if she didn't know he was Afghan, she would never have guessed it. From this distance, he looked like a typical U.S. Army combat pilot.

The crewmen and Khalid joked back and forth, and the three of them stood laughing. Warmth pooled in her chest and Emma unconsciously touched her jacket where her heart lay. There was such gracefulness to this tall, lanky warrior. Emma suddenly felt as if she were standing on quicksand. Her reaction wasn't logical. The pilot walking languidly, like a lordly lion toward her, was married. He had to be. He had to have a wife and children. Afghans married very early. So why was she feeling shaky and unsure of herself? Emma had never had such a powerful emotional reaction to a man. Not ever, and it scared her.

As Emma stepped forward, her mouth went dry. She forced herself to walk confidently out on the revetment and meet the foreign pilot. And when his gaze locked onto hers, she groaned. Shaheen drew closer, and Emma could appreciate the curious color of his eyes. They reminded her of the greenish-blue depths of the ocean around a Caribbean island. Not only that, his eyes were large, well-spaced, with thick lashes that enhanced the black pupils. She felt as if she could lose herself within them. Emma jerked her gaze away. What was going on? Her heart pounded as though she was on an adrenaline rush. But she wasn't in danger. No, this was excitement at some unconscious level within her that she had never experienced. And that made Emma wary.

Shaheen unzipped his olive-green flight suit as he approached. Black hairs peeked out from beneath his dark-green T-shirt. He reached inside his flight suit.

And what he drew out made Emma's jaw drop. Shaheen slowed and stopped about three feet in front of her. In his hand was a huge red rose, its petals flattened from being crushed inside his flight suit, but a rose, nevertheless.

Pressing his hand against his heart, Shaheen bowed slightly and murmured the ancient greeting that all people in the Muslim world shared. *"As-salaam alaikum."* Peace to you from my heart to your heart. "Captain Emma Cantrell?" he asked, smiling as he lifted his head.

Paralyzed, Emma stared up at him. Shaheen held the drooping rose toward her. He'd obviously picked it just before the flight and carried it inside his suit to her. Emma could smell the spicy fragrance of the bedraggled flower. "I—yes," she managed in a croak. Without thinking, she took his gift and responded, *"As-salaam alaikum."* She clutched the rose in her right hand, noting that the thorns had been cut off so it would not prick her fingers.

Scrambling inwardly, Emma tried not to be impressed by this thoughtfulness. When she raised her head, she noticed Khalid's masculine smile and twinkling eyes. "I'm Captain Emma Cantrell," she said in a crisp tone. "Welcome to Camp Bravo." God, she sounded like a teenager on her first date, her voice high and squeaky. Worse, he had the same kind of swaggering, super confidence that Brody had had. They could be twins. Her heart sank. *Not this again.*

"Thank you, Emma. Please," he murmured in a low, husky tone, "call me Khalid once we get out of the military environment."

She stood looking helplessly at the rose in her hand. "Why…I never expected this, Captain Shaheen."

Officers simply didn't give other officers flowers. Clearly, he was flirting with her.

Khalid's hands relaxed on his hips, a typical aviator stance. "I went out to my rose garden this morning. I live in Kabul. It is the first rose of the season. I took my knife and cut it off knowing that I wanted you to have something beautiful from me to you."

Emma swallowed hard. Aviators never wore jewelry of any kind. Not even a wedding ring. But this guy had to be married. He was just too charming. The confusion must have shown on her face.

"Rumi, the great Sufi mystic poet, said much about the beauty of a rose." He then quoted her a passage that he'd memorized.

Emma was sure now he was flirting with her. Completely stunned by Khalid's warmth, his utter masculinity and those gleaming blue eyes, Emma choked. "But…you're married!" Well, that wasn't exactly polite, was it? No, but the words flew out of her mouth. Emma took a step away from him. Khalid's face was overcome with surprise, his straight, black brows rising. And then he laughed. His laughter was hearty, unfettered and rolled out of his powerful chest.

"I'm afraid I'm not married," Khalid said and he held up his hands, smiling over her mistake.

Emma didn't know what to do. She knew how she felt toward him—as if he were a conquering Afghan warlord who had just swept her off her feet, stolen her young, innocent heart and claimed her. His smile was so engaging her heart appreciated it by beating erratically. Brody Parker had wooed and wowed her the same way. Oh, God, it was the *same* situation all over again!

Emma gripped the red rose until her fingers hurt. Should she give it back to him? Throw it away? This wasn't military protocol between two officers. Emma furtively looked around her. Who had seen him do this? Had they seen her accept the gift? Things like this just weren't done in the U.S. Army. Could she be more distressed?

"I can't take this, Captain Shaheen." She handed him the rose.

Holding up his hands, Khalid said, "Forgive me, Captain Cantrell. My father is Sufi and I was raised with Rumi. I see all of my life through this thirteenth-century poet and mystic's eyes. I am forever quoting him, for Rumi guides my heart and my life. I hope you do not take offense to my gift. Among the Sufis we believe that love is the only vehicle to touch the face of God and become one with the source. My gift to you was merely an acknowledgment, heart-to-heart, that we are connected. And it is a gift that honors you as a person, to show that you are sacred to me and all of life. Please, do not be pained by the gift."

Stubbornly, Emma gave him a long, steady stare. "It's not acceptable military behavior, Captain. Let's leave it at that, shall we?"

Khalid winced. He pressed his hand to his heart and held her gaze. "I will maintain correct military protocol with you, Captain. Please accept my deepest apology. I am honored that you have agreed to work with me." He tucked the rose back into his flight suit.

Emma wasn't sure about this terribly handsome Afghan standing in front of her, speaking with such candor. Her heart melted over the warmth dancing in the depths of his aquamarine eyes. Given the sincerity in his voice and face, she wondered obliquely if she'd read his intentions wrongly.

"Then we're in agreement," she said in a clipped tone.

"I volunteered for this mission to help the Afghan girls get an education." Emma tried to convince herself that he was Brody Parker all over again, only even more charming and smooth than her lover in Peru had been. Emma wasn't falling for it again. Her heart couldn't take the hurt twice. Dallas's words haunted her: *This could be a queen-maker for your career.* And more than anything, Emma wanted to get good remarks from Shaheen after she finished the six-month mission. Now, she felt as though she was literally walking the edge of sword that could cut her both ways. What had she just stepped into?

# Chapter 2

Emma tensed. A range of emotions passed across Khalid's rugged face. "Look," she murmured, "I know that in different cultures, mistakes can be made."

"No, no," Khalid said, trying to muster a smile, but failing. "You need to understand the heart of our mission. By knowing what the foundation is, you can appreciate our fierce passion for our people." He held her forest-green gaze. The noise on the tarmac surrounded them. He gestured for Emma to follow him into the Ops building where there would be a room where they could talk.

Emma followed Shaheen. More and more, this felt like doom to her. She was falling fast and she needed to focus on her work. Inside Ops, the captain found an empty room. They went in and closed the door. There was a rectangular table, reports scattered across it along with pens. Emma took a seat and he sat down opposite her after pouring them some coffee.

Taking the lead, Emma folded her hands and met his stare. "My CO told me you were a marked man. I want to know what that means since I'm putting my butt on the line here."

"I have an ancient enemy," Khalid began, "his name is Asad Malik. He was born in Pakistan, along the border in the state of Waziristan. Malik was very poor, and with the Taliban, who make a permanent home in that border state, he found his calling. My father's family are Sufis. They know that education is the door to all fulfillment of a person's dreams and goals. My father has considerable wealth, and he poured it into the border villages of our country a long time ago because the so-called central government of Afghanistan ignored them."

Brows drawing downward, Khalid said, "Malik rose to become a very powerful Taliban leader. He is heartless and ruthless. He began attacking villages to which my father was trying to bring schools and education. There were many pitched battles over the years, and Malik swore to kill every member of my family."

Emma gasped. Although she knew revenge ran deep, the admittance was still shocking. "What?"

Shrugging, Khalid said, "Malik is not a Sufi. He is a terrorist at the other end of the Muslim religion. Our beliefs swing from an eye-for-an-eye attitude to one of spiritual connection with Allah." He pressed his hand to his heart. "I am Sufi. Malik is stuck in a state of twisted hatred and revenge. It would not matter what religion he embraced, he would practice what he is, despite it. He has perverted the Koran for his own goals."

Emma nodded. "Yes, every religion has its fanatics. In my year here in Afghanistan, I've lived among the Muslims and I find them incredibly generous and caring.

They aren't the terrorists that the world thinks. They believe in peace."

"Yes, we are peaceful," Khalid agreed. "It will only be through our daily life that we show the Muslim religion is not one of terrorism."

"It's a PR game," Emma said. "And I agree with you, people are educated one person at a time. Religion doesn't kill. It's the individuals within any religion who choose to interpret it according to their own darkness and wounds."

He gave her an intense look. "I have truly made the right decision in asking you to be a part of our mission. I like your free-thinking policy."

Emma tried not to be swayed by his compliment and felt heat enter her cheeks. "I try never to judge a person. I let their actions speak louder than their words." The intensity of his gaze made Emma feel as if she were unraveling as a woman—not as an officer—to this lion of a man. She mentally corrected herself once again: there were no lions in Afghanistan. Instead, Emma regarded him as the rare and elusive snow leopard that lived in the rugged mountains of this country.

"My death dance with Malik," Khalid continued, "took on new dimensions two years ago. Malik stalks the border like the wolf that he is. He continually attacks and kills the villagers who try to better their lives in any way. It is how he stops my father's generosity to lift the poor up and help them succeed. Malik does not care about such things." Taking a deep breath, Khalid continued, his voice strained. "I fell in love with a beautiful teacher. Her name was Najela. I courted her for two years and I asked her to become my wife."

Emma heard Khalid's voice quaver and noticed how he fought unknown emotions, his hands opening and closing around the heavy ceramic mug in front of him. She wanted to reach out and touch him, to soothe away the grief she saw clearly etched in his face. But Emma said nothing. She allowed Khalid to get hold of himself so that he could continue his story.

"Najela and my sister Kinah were the best of friends. And why wouldn't they be? They were both American-educated and trained in education. Najela graduated from Harvard and my sister from Princeton. They were working with my father to help set up village schools for boys and girls. I was away working for the U.S. Army and they were frequently up in this area while I flew Apaches in the southern region of my country."

Emma steeled herself. She leaped ahead and figured out that Najela was dead. At Malik's hands? She hoped not. Her heart cringed inside her chest. "Go on," she urged him, her voice tense.

Nodding, Khalid swallowed hard, took a drink of his coffee, wiped his mouth with the back of his hand and then took a deep breath and released it. "I was on a mission with the U.S. Marines in the south when I got word that Malik had captured Najela in one of the villages." His voice became low and strained. "By the time I was given orders to fly north to the village, Malik had repeatedly raped her and then he…slit her throat. I found her in a mud house that had been abandoned by the family who lived there. All I found…was her…" And he closed his eyes for a moment, reliving that nightmare afternoon.

"I—I'm so sorry," Emma whispered, caught up in his anguish. Without thinking, she reached across the table and touched his hand. And when she realized what she'd done, Emma quickly pulled her hand back. No officer should be seen initiating such an intimate action with another officer. Turning her focus back to Khalid, she thought she saw tears in his blue eyes for just a second. And then, they were gone. Had she imagined them? Emma chastised herself for losing her standards.

"Malik hates anyone and anything who tries to improve upon the villagers' lives," Khalid continued, his voice rough. "As I said, he's sworn vengeance against my family because of my father's generosity to the villagers."

Emma considered his heavily spoken words. "And is Malik out there right now? Will he be our enemy as you and Kinah set up this mission for those same villagers?" A cold chill worked its way up her spine as she saw his expression still and become unreadable.

"Yes, he is our nemesis. You need to know that this mission is dangerous so that you remain on guard. Your CO was correct in telling you I am a marked man. You will be marked too, Captain."

Eyes rounding, Emma sat up. "Aren't you afraid, Captain Shaheen? He's already killed one person you loved. You could be next." Suddenly, Emma wanted nothing to harm this man who had a vision for the girls of his country. She could see his sincerity and the heart that he wore openly on his sleeve. Khalid was priceless in her world because few men could be so in touch with their emotions and share them as he just had with her. Brody had never opened up like this. Not ever. And it threw Emma.

Khalid said, "Rumi would say a real Sufi laughs at death. A Sufi is like an oyster—what strikes it does not harm the pearl within."

Considering the saying from the thirteenth century, Emma grimaced. "Sorry, but I'm not in agreement with

Rumi. I don't feel I could be at peace if someone raped and then murdered my fiancée."

"I understand," Khalid said. "You have lived in our country where the threat to your life exists every day." He opened his hand and gestured around the room. "Afghans have been at war with the Russians. Now, we have the Taliban. Do we want to live this way? No. Do we dream of a peaceful life? Yes. I don't expect you, Captain Cantrell, to believe as we do. Najela was Sufi. I know in my heart of hearts that throughout her terrible last hours she felt compassion for Malik. He's a man so filled with hatred and vengeance that I'm sure that her compassion only made him want to harm her even more."

Shaking her head, Emma muttered, "Well, I sure wouldn't be thinking peaceful and loving thoughts if that dude was doing that to me. I'd be looking for any way to protect myself and kill the bastard."

Giving her a slight smile, Khalid nodded. "Sufis are misunderstood even by our other Muslim brethren. In fact, those who choose jihad and become terrorists hate us as much as they do the so-called infidels."

"Which is why Malik hates you?" Emma wondered.

"He hates my family for many reasons and has sworn vengeance against each of us. In part, because we are Sufis and believe in tolerance and generosity toward others. The fact my father is worth billions of dollars makes Malik hate us because he was raised in poverty. He didn't own a pair of shoes until he was eleven years old when the Taliban leader recruited him."

Suddenly, there was a deafening explosion outside. The sound and reverberation slammed into the room. Instantly, they both dove for the deck, hands over their heads. Emma hissed a curse. Tiles from the ceiling fell around them as a second explosion shook Ops.

"It's the Taliban," she growled, getting to her feet. Automatically, she pulled the .45 pistol from her belt and ran to the door. Swinging it open, Ops looked like a beehive that had been overturned.

Shaheen was at her side, looking down at her. Emma's face was set and her gaze aimed at the windows outside. He saw one of the helicopters burning, the black smoke roiling and bubbling skyward. "Do you get attacks often?"

Grimly, Emma moved toward the center of Ops. Pilots and crews were hurrying out the doors, armed and ready to fight. She knew from being here over a year that such attacks were sporadic. "No," she snapped, moving with everyone else toward the doors. "Come on, we need to help the fire crews."

Khalid didn't know Camp Bravo as she did. He trotted across Ops and found himself outside with her. Emma's eyes were searching the end of the runway and she pointed in that direction. "That's one of the places they hit us. They sit in the brush beyond the runway and lob RPGs, rocket propelled grenades, this way."

Khalid noted a squad of Special Forces speeding away in a Humvee, armed and ready for battle. He wanted to protect Emma. It was his natural reaction. Telling himself she was a warrior like him, he kept his thoughts and his hands to himself. She was all business now. Another crew rolled up in a fire engine and began spewing foam over the burning CH-47 transport helicopter, already a total loss.

Emma turned. She was glad she had her Kevlar jacket on because gunshots were suddenly being traded at the end of the runway. "Come on, this is under control.

No sense standing out here like targets." She gestured toward Ops again.

Shaheen wasn't so sure, for a minute longer, he watched the Special Forces from the Humvee spraying the bushes where the Taliban had been hiding. "Do they get inside the camp?" he asked as he followed her into Ops.

"Not so far, but we're always watching." Settling the .45 back into the holster on her waist, she added, "We're never safe here. Let's get back to discussing the mission, shall we?" Emma stopped and poured herself another cup of black coffee from the urn at the side of the Ops desk. Khalid did the same and they returned to the meeting room.

There were several enlisted men in there. They'd already picked up the ceiling tiles that had dropped from the explosion, so Emma thanked them and, once more, she and Khalid were alone. They pulled their chairs to the table and sat down. Her heart pounded and she felt tense and on guard. As she sipped the coffee, she hoped it would soothe her jangled nerves.

"Will they attack more than once in a day?" Khalid wondered. He found himself drowning in her dark, forest-green eyes, fraught with care and concern. If he read her correctly, it was concern for his welfare. That touched and warmed his wounded heart. There was something ethereal about Emma. Was it how her mussed red hair curled slightly at her temples? Was it her huge green eyes fraught with compassion? Or those lips that reminded Khalid of a rose in full bloom? His inspiration to cut the first red rose of the year from his family's garden hadn't gone as he'd hoped. "Well, let me lay out some information to you on Operation Book Worm," he said, returning to business.

* * *

Asad Malik crept away from the end of the runway with his men. Bullets were singing around them, but he knew from long experience that the Special Forces couldn't see them and they were firing blindly into the thick brush. One day, when there was time, such brush would be cleaned away. He had ten men with him. They continued to work their way through the heavy brush, their AK-47s and grenade launchers in hand. Smiling to himself, he congratulated them in a whisper on destroying one of the helicopters. It was a good day!

Dressed in baggy brown trousers, a crisscross of wide leather straps containing bullets across his chest, Malik did not think this attack was done. No. He would wait, skulk through the brush with his men and wait on the other side. Malik knew this forward base was vital to the war effort by the infidel Americans. Until lately, he'd not had enough money to buy more grenades and bullets. Now, he had a new donor from Saudi Arabia who had given him millions to support the Taliban effort.

Grunting and breathing hard, Malik knelt, hidden. He waited for his ragtag group of nine other men to catch up with him. Most were barefoot, their clothes thin and threadbare. They were all skinny, their cheeks sunken, for coming here had been hard on them. Malik usually worked other areas, but this base was crucial to the American mission and he'd wanted to strike the head of the snake finally.

"Everyone all right?" he demanded roughly as they sat in a semicircle around him. "No wounds?"

"None, my lord," one of the bearded men spoke up.

Malik grinned. "Good. Now, let's sneak around the other side of the runway. Knowing the infidels, they'll think this attack is over."

There were soft, knowing chuckles from the men, all of whom nodded their accord to follow their charismatic and brave leader.

"Come!" Malik whispered harshly, lifting his hand and moving forward. "I want another helicopter," he snickered.

Emma could see the burning intensity in Khalid's blue eyes as they narrowed speculatively upon her. They'd just finished off their coffees and got down to the business at hand. She felt giddy and thrilled with his interest in her. Sure, he respected her as a professional, but she sensed something deeper. Sternly, she chided herself for thinking he was drawn to her.

And then her heart contracted. Was Khalid interested in her or was she imagining things? That couldn't be. Khalid was the head of the mission and held power over her. His comments would eventually go into her career jacket. Maybe he was this charming with everyone. She couldn't allow herself to get involved with this intriguing, romantic Afghan warrior. But why did he have to be so damn good-looking? She vowed to savor this rugged male pilot secretly; he'd never know it. She could hide her feelings. For now.

Khalid pulled out a map from one long pocket on his flight suit leg and spread it out before them. He stood up and, using a pen, said, "This is the route we're going to follow. We'll move from one village to another." His index finger was on the map, tracing the small villages along the border with Pakistan. It bothered him that he was drawn to Emma, despite her military demeanor. Khalid refused to put another woman in the gunsights of Asad Malik. It would be too easy to become personal with red-haired, brazen Emma Cantrell.

"For the next six months," he said, straightening and moving his shoulders as if to shrug off the tension gathered in them, "you will be with me and Kinah, and you will surely be well-educated into our Sufi world. We believe that all religions have a good message for the spirit. My father, who was born in Kabul, comes from a long line of Sufis. My mother, who is a medical doctor from Ireland, continues to this day to be a Presbyterian missionary. She came to this country after she finished her residency in Dublin, Ireland. Her father is an elder in their tradition. And her entire family has been missionaries here in Afghanistan for nearly a hundred years."

Surprised, Emma's brows rose with that information. "Then…you're half-Afghan and half-Irish?" Maybe that accounted for those dancing blue eyes that always had a bit of devilry lurking in their depths.

"I am," he said with pride. "I am a good example that east meeting west can actually get along."

"Your religions are so different."

"That's what I'm trying to tell you," Khalid said, turning the map over. "The Sufis have no quarrel with any other religion in this world. We accept people as they are and respect their beliefs."

"Too bad that all religions can't hold the same ideas," Emma said. She was thinking of the evil Asad Malik.

"That's why," Khalid explained, "the jihadists who are twisted and out of touch with true Muslim traditions, hate Sufis and will kill them on sight. The terrorists among those who profess to be Muslim are threatened by the enlightened ways of the Sufi people."

Emma sat back. "And so you have no trouble being half-Christian and half-Muslim?"

Chuckling, Khalid shook his head. He spread a second map on to the table. It showed close-ups of some of the more major villages along the Afghanistan-Pakistan border. "Absolutely none. Sufis honor and respect every religious tradition on the face of our Earth. We believe all paths lead through the heart to the Creator, no matter what name you call him or her."

Emma watched as he traced a red line around certain areas. "What are those?" she demanded.

"This is Malik's territory, where he and the Taliban are constantly attacking the villagers."

Emma got up and leaned over, their heads inches apart as she studied the map. "This guy is big. I know I've heard his name."

"Yes, he's north of your base camp."

Emma straightened. "Like you said, we'll be alert."

"Agreed," Khalid said. He picked up the papers, neatly folded them once more and tucked them away in the leg of his flight suit. "So, Captain Cantrell, are you ready to fly back to Bagram Air Force Base with me? We have much to do and there's so much to show you about our mission."

Surprised, Emma watched as Khalid stood, lean, strong, his broad shoulders thrown back with unconscious pride. "Bagram? I thought we'd be working here, out of Camp Bravo?"

"Oh, we will," Khalid assured her. "I'm inviting you to have dinner with me tonight at my family's villa in Kabul. You may stay overnight. As you know, there are male and female sections to each home. I have had our housekeeper prepare you a room in the women's part of the house. After we have a wonderful dinner, I will take you to my office and show you Operation Book Worm. I think you will appreciate what I'll show you. Then, you can grasp even more of the mission and its priorities."

Shocked by the offer, Emma sat staring up at him. "But…"

"This is a work invitation, Captain Cantrell. I'm an excellent host. It's easier for me to show you what we will be doing at our villa where it is all stored, than to try and lug it piecemeal back and forth to this camp."

Emma considered the unexpected invitation and her vivid imagination took off. What would it be like to be with this Afghan warrior? And truly, that's what Khalid was. She knew he professed compassion and love for others, but her body was not reacting to him in that way. No, she felt a hunger and drive to know Khalid on a much more personal level. How was she going to keep this fact a secret? Looking deeply into his eyes, Emma realized that this wasn't at all personal to Khalid; it was merely a formality to offer her dinner. After all, Emma knew from experience that all Afghans, rich or poor, would automatically invite her to their home for dinner. It was a custom and way of life in Afghanistan.

"Of course I'll go with you, Captain Shaheen. I look forward to it."

Khalid brightened. "Excellent. If there is anything you need to pack in your flight bag before we take off, why not go get it now. I'll meet you back at Ops."

Good, he was remaining all business. As she walked with Khalid out of Ops and into the warming sunlight over the camp, Emma couldn't explain the happiness threading through her. Khalid bowed slightly where the path forked and led to Ops. The fire had been put out on the destroyed helicopter and there was still a lot of activity on the tarmac.

"I'll see you soon, Captain?"

"Yes," Emma said, "this won't take long." Khalid was all business. All military. That warm smile, those inquiring blue eyes of his were veiled.

"Good, I'll meet you at our Apache." He strode confidently back into Ops to file their flight plan.

Shaking her head, Emma trotted down another dirt avenue between the desert-tan-and-green tents. Khalid and Brody had a lot in common, but she'd never spent too much time with a man who had one foot in the east and one foot in the west. The breeze ruffled her red hair as she continued to jog down the dirt path. Making a left, she found her tent and unzipped it. Worry hovered over her. Above all, she had to keep her silly heart out of this. It was bad enough that Khalid was in the active gun sights of Asad Malik, but the Taliban leader would target her, too. In a heartbeat.

As Emma packed essentials into her canvas flight bag, she couldn't stop thinking about Khalid. He'd loved and lost his bride. That explained why he was still single at thirty, unheard of for a Muslim man. She replayed the grief that was raw and alive in his eyes as he'd shared the tragedy of Najela's death at Malik's hands.

After grabbing her toothbrush, toothpaste, comb and brush, Emma quickly finished her packing. She zipped up her flight bag and took her helmet bag off the makeshift chest of drawers. As she headed outside, she felt the sunlight warming up the coolish temperature. She turned on the heel of her flight boot and walked quickly down between the rows of tents. Despite the unexpected Taliban attack an hour earlier, the air was alive with the puncturing sounds of helicopters landing and taking off once more. The smell of jet fuel was always around. Metallic, oily smoke still hung above the camp from the destroyed chopper. The growl of huge military trucks belching blue smoke, their coughs and grinding of gears, filled the air, too. As she jogged across the camp to the control-tower area, Emma's heart took off.

Why did she feel giddy? Like a school girl who had a crush on the all-star football quarterback? Would she be able to tread on the edge of the sword with Khalid? Separate out her womanly need to know more about him on a personal level from the professional one? Emma wasn't sure. She slowed to a walk and pulled open the door to Ops. As she moved through the busy building and out the other door to the tarmac, Emma sensed her life was about to change. Forever.

# *Chapter 3*

Emma was surprised that Khalid insisted she be the AC—air commander, on the Apache that was to be flown to Bagram. She stowed her bag in a side slot of the combat helicopter. Mounting the helo, Emma was strapped into the back cockpit in no time. She tried to ignore Khalid's charisma as he climbed into the cockpit in front of her. The sergeant helped her and then tended to Khalid's needs. A sudden shiver of warning went up her spine. The whole base was on high alert because of the attack.

Looking around, lips compressed, Emma saw the remains of charred, still-smoking helicopter that the Taliban had destroyed with a grenade launcher. To her left, several Humvees contained Special Forces who were still looking for the terrorists who committed the offense. Something was wrong….

* * *

Malik lay on his belly, the binoculars to his eyes. He studied the Apache combat helicopter, more interested than usual in the pilots. Actually, one pilot. A snarl issued softly from between his full, thick lips. Allah had blessed him! There was his sworn enemy, Khalid Shaheen, in the front seat of the Apache. Mind spinning, Malik watched intently.

So, Shaheen was back in the northern provinces? Malik had his spies and they kept him somewhat updated on his enemy's whereabouts. The last Malik had been told, Khalid was in Helmand Province flying Apaches against his brothers in the Taliban. Malik knew where Shaheen lived in Kabul. He and his upstart, rebellious sister, Kinah, could be found at their family home from time to time. Was that where he was going? A hundred questions ranged through Malik's traplike mind.

"My lord," Ameen whispered near his ear, "it's time to move away. Troops are coming."

Malik growled a response; he didn't want to leave, but he knew he must. Those ground troops would have dogs with them and dogs would find them. Tucking his binoculars away, he got to his feet.

"Where to, my lord?" Ameen asked.

"A change of plans," he told the teenage soldier. "We're going to Kabul…."

Thirty minutes after completing the flight check list, Emma had taken the Apache off the tarmac. The shaking and shuddering was familiar and soothing to her. She'd felt the Taliban nearby. She'd not seen them, but she instinctively knew they were close. Emma wondered if Khalid was testing her flight skills. After all, he'd been in Apaches for four years and she had only one year of combat beneath her belt.

At eight thousand feet under a sunny April-afternoon sky, Emma relaxed to a degree. Still, she was tense about going to Shaheen's home. This was out of normal military protocol. She had no experience with Afghans except in the villages, and Shaheen was much more powerful than those people who survived in the wild mountains along the border.

"Do you like dogs?" Khalid asked through the intercom.

Emma scowled. Now, what was this all about? Shaheen had the ability to rock her world. "Dogs?" What did dogs have to do with them? It was the last conversation she would think of having with this pilot. If nothing else, Khalid was turning out to be one surprise after another.

"Yes, dogs."

"Why are we talking about them?" Emma demanded, automatically looking around outside the cockpit.

"So you will be well-prepared when I open the door to my family's villa. My father raises some of the finest salukis in the world. Two years ago, he gifted me with Ayesha, a female with a black coat, white chest and cinnamon-colored legs and underbelly. My father gave her to me shortly after Najela was murdered. The dog helped me in ways I can't explain. She gave me back my life and brought me through the darkest tunnel with her love and devotion."

Not wanting to be swayed by his words, Emma swung her gaze across the instrument panel out of ingrained habit. The chances of attack were minimal, but she never completely let down her guard. "I'm sure I can handle your dog," she said, laughing. "Hey, it's kinda nice to have a dog around. We have a few base mongrels that we feed, but they're wild and you can't pet them. I'm always leaving scraps outside my tent for a black dog that comes by every night looking for something to eat. If I try to walk toward him, he takes off at a run and disappears. I've learned to put the food in a pie tin, close up my tent and not try to befriend him."

"Ah, you are a true lover of animals, too. That speaks highly of your heart, Captain Cantrell." Khalid's job in the front seat was to keep watch on the two video screens in front of him. There wasn't much chance of attack at this altitude, but you could never quite relax on the job. He was intensely curious about Emma, but hesitant. She was a by-the-book military officer. Giving her a rose had been a misstep. Khalid had hoped it would open a door to signify a good, working relationship, but Emma had taken it all wrong.

Worriedly, Khalid realized he'd set them on an awkward course with one another. And he desperately needed a woman pilot who could fulfill his vision to inspire the little Afghan girls. How to fix what had already gone wrong? She didn't sound very interested in his dog story, either.

Brows dipping, Khalid asked himself why he was so interested in Emma. She was a tough military combat pilot. Her record showed her abilities and fine skills. He got the feeling she really didn't like him at all and was just tolerating the situation. Maybe it was the attack this morning that had set her off. He shrugged his shoulders to ease them of tension. He simply didn't know how to deal with Captain Cantrell. Most people melted beneath his charm and sincere smile. But all it did to her was make her retreat, becoming stony and unreadable. As his U.S. military pilot friends would say, he'd blown it.

How to repair things between them? He'd spent years in the States being educated. He knew Americans. Khalid sighed. Emma made him feel like a joyous young man. That wouldn't work here. Khalid turned his attention to the screens and did an automatic scan, looking for possible SAM missiles. Taking a deep breath, he hoped what he was about to say wouldn't turn her away from him.

"I did a little research on you, Captain. Your family has a history of service," Khalid said.

Something had told her that as easy-going as Khalid appeared, he was a man who researched the details of any situation.

"Yes, the Trayherns have given military service to their country since they arrived here two hundred years earlier. My mother, Alyssa, was a Trayhern before she married Clay Cantrell, my father. It's a tradition for the Trayhern children, if they want, to go into the military of their choice and serve at least four to six years, depending upon whether they are officers or enlisted. We're very proud of our family's service and sacrifice," Emma said tensely.

"You should be. I'm very impressed, Captain. That's very Sufi-like, to serve others. My Irish mother would say it is what you owe to life. That we all owe others. We can't live life alone or separate ourselves from the poor and suffering."

Emma moved uncomfortably around in her seat. Talking to Khalid was like a minefield. She didn't really want to know anything about him. All she wanted was to do a good job on this mission and then get back to base camp, her military record clean once more. Clearing her throat, she said, “She sounds like a wonderful, giving person much like my mother, Alyssa.”

“My mother has red hair and brown eyes,” Khalid informed her. “She’s an obstetrician and she has set up clinics throughout Afghanistan with the help of her church’s ongoing donations. She has spent from age twenty-eight to the present here in Afghanistan. The good she has done is tremendous. I think you must know many Afghan women die during childbirth. Most women have an average of seven children. And one out of eight women dies in childbirth. Very few villages have health care available to them.”

“That’s so sad,” Emma said as she banked the Apache to start a descent into Bagram. They had left the mountains, and now the dry, yellow plains where Bagram air base sat spread out before them. “I can’t believe how many women lose their lives. It’s horrific. I heard from Major Klein, my C.O., that there are Sufi medical doctors who have devoted their lives to the villages along the border.”

“Ah yes,” Khalid said, brightening, “Doctors Reza and Sahar Khan. I’ve met them a number of times. My mother works with them through her mission. They are truly brave. Because they are Sufi and giving service and trying to help the border villages from the farthest south to the farthest north of our country, the Taliban constantly tries to kill them. The only way the Taliban keeps hold over our people is through fear, retaliation and murder.” His voice deepened. “Reza and Sahar have a strong calling. As Sufis they render aid and help wherever they can. Reza is a doctor of internal medicine and surgery. His sister, Sahar, is an obstetrician. I cannot tell you how many women’s lives she has saved. They drive a Land Rover that is beaten up and very old. I have offered to buy them a new one, but they said no."

"Why?"

"Because it would stand out like a sore thumb and the Taliban could find them more easily. In January of each year they start in the south of Afghanistan and then they drive along the border from village to village offering their medical services for free. By the time June comes, they have reached the northernmost part of our country, and they turn around and drive back down through the same villages. Each village gets visits twice a year, except of course, the most northern one, but they stay two weeks there to ensure everyone in that village is properly cared for."

"Who funds them?"

"I do," Khalid said. "I also coordinate with several American charities who give them medical supplies. Money's only importance is how it is spent to help others."

Emma said nothing, easing the Apache down to three thousand feet. "That's gutsy, and talk about sacrifice, those two doctors should get medals of valor." Obviously, this officer was generous with his money. Brody's bragging came to mind. Was Khalid bragging to impress her? Something told her he was, and she became even more wary.

Snorting, Khalid said, "The central government refuses to acknowledge their sacrifice to our people. They aren't very happy about Sufis, either. They barely tolerate them."

"Why are Sufis so targeted?" Emma asked. She saw Bagram air base coming up. It was huge and lay on the flat, dirt plain with Kabul about ten miles away. The city glittered in the sunlight. Kabul wasn't that safe, either. The Taliban had infiltrated the city and it was dangerous for any American, military or civilian, to be there without an armed escort.

"What mystic group hasn't been a target?" he asked rhetorically. "Ah, Bagram is below us. We'll be on the ground in a few minutes."

She heard veiled excitement in his voice. Emma paid attention to the air controller giving her landing instructions. Tension accumulated in her shoulders. She really didn't want to go to Shaheen's home. It felt like a trap to her, but Khalid was her boss. If he wrote her up for a glowing commendation after this six-month gig, she'd have a revived military career in front of her. And Emma wanted nothing more than to expunge that black eye she'd given to the Trayhern family, once and for all.

"Come," Khalid said, gesturing toward a large parking lot inside Bagram air base. "My car is over there."

The roar of jets taking off shook the air until it vibrated around them. As Emma walked at Khalid's side, her bag in her left hand, dark aviator glasses in place, she felt nervous. At the Ops desk where they'd filled out the required landing flight forms, everyone seemed to know him. He had joked and laughed with many of the enlisted personnel behind the desk. His sincerity and concern for each of them was obvious. Emma saw how every man and woman glowed beneath his charisma. Brody Parker had done that, too. It seemed people who weren't as rich as he was were always enamored with him. Emma had realized later it had been because they knew he was rich.

As she walked down the line of cars, Emma reminded herself that Khalid was dangerous to her heart. He was far too likable a person. Frowning, she saw him take keys from his pocket and click them toward a Land Rover. The vehicle was a dark-green one that had plenty of dents and scrapes all over its body. In fact, there was a lot of dirt and mud on it, too.

"Hop in," Khalid invited, opening the rear so they could throw all their flight gear into the back.

Emma slid into the passenger side and put on the seat belt. The dashboard was dusty. She wondered if Khalid's home looked like his car.

Tension thrummed through Khalid as he drove through the security gates of Bagram after showing his identity card. "Have you been in the city of Kabul before?"

Emma watched him drive with care. "Yes, I have, but only with an Afghan escort on a day trip. When I fly in here, I remain on base for safety reasons." He looked around constantly. In fact, they both had their side arms on the seat between them. She knew attacks were frequent in Kabul. The road leading up to the base was asphalted, but soon they were on another highway with plenty of potholes to dodge. Heavy traffic came and went from the busy main air base that served the country.

"Not many Americans wander off Bagram," Khalid murmured, nodding. "And with good reason. They are targets. One day I hope that our country will be free of the Taliban and you can see the beauty of it."

Emma was as alert as he was, keeping a hand on her .45 pistol. Too many cars were attacked by the Taliban. That Khalid was a marked man only increased the chances that they could be attacked.

Khalid motioned with his long hand toward the city. "My parents' villa is on the outskirts, upon a small hill ringed with thick, almost impenetrable brush. I also employ guards at the base of the hill." He grimaced. "Unfortunately, anyone who is rich is an automatic target. But you will be safe at our compound. Ten-foot-high stucco walls completely surround our home. It's all one story so that it is hidden behind the walls. There is a metal gate at the entrance and a guard is always on duty. Each window has an ornamental grate across it to prevent break-ins. The front door is wrought iron, too."

"I don't know how anyone could live this way," Emma muttered. She saw Khalid give his characteristic shrug.

"We have generations of Afghans with PTSD, post traumatic stress disorder. We all have it," he said, glancing at Emma. "It's just a question of how bad it is and how much of your life it stains."

Shaking her head, she said, "I've always valued being born in the U.S., but after being over here and seeing the poverty, the murders and constant threats that your people live under, I feel very, very fortunate in comparison."

"Yes, I was grateful for my years I spent in your country," Khalid said. He swung off on a dirt road that led up to a small knoll in the distance. The road was rough and rutted because of the spring rains. "The seven years I spent there Americanized me a great deal." He flashed her a sudden grin. "I really miss American French fries."

For a moment, Emma's heart melted. His smile was dazzling and she felt the full effects of it. "You seem very Americanized. Your English is flawless and you use our slang, Captain Shaheen."

Khalid drove around some potholes, the ruts deep,

dry and hard. The Land Rover crept forward. "I love America. I love what she stands for. I want my people to have a democracy just like yours. While I studied at Princeton, I truly understood what democracy was for the first time. I brought my passion back here and Kinah and I have worked ever since to bring our country closer to that vision we hold in our hearts."

"It's a vision worth holding," Emma agreed, hearing the fierce, underlying emotion in Khalid's voice. There was no question he loved this desert country. Emma studied the rounded hill coming up. The shrubs were thick and dark green from the base up to the top of greenish-brown stucco walls. The color of the walls blended into the earthen landscape. If she hadn't been looking for the walls, she probably would have missed them. She wondered what it was like for Khalid and his sister to grow up here under such constant threats. Her admiration for him grew.

The bearded guard at the front entrance opened the gate and saluted Khalid. The sentry stepped aside as Khalid returned the salute and drove the Land Rover into the three-car garage. The automatic door started downward as he eased out of the vehicle.

Emma followed suit. They gathered their gear and he took her to a side door.

"Prepare yourself," he said, a glimmer in his eyes as he opened the door.

Emma didn't have time. The dog, a saluki, Ayesha, rushed out the door, barking joyously around them, her thick, long tail wagging with happiness. It was impossible for Emma to remain stiff and stoic. Khalid had been right: Ayesha would lick her fingers off her hand if allowed to do so.

Wiping her wet fingers on the side of her flight

suit, Emma and Ayesha bounded over the white-tiled hall with its cool, pale-green walls. Khalid's laughter and playfulness around the saluki automatically made Emma's heart pound a little harder. Truly, Ayesha was a faithful companion to the Apache pilot who petted her fondly as she danced and pranced at his side.

The hall flowed in three different directions. Khalid pointed to the left. "Your suite is the second door on the left. My dear housekeeper, Rasa, has promised you will be comfortable while you visit us. If there's anything you need, just press the buzzer on the inside of the door, and she will come to assist you."

"And you, Captain?" Emma asked.

"I'm going to my suite, get out of my uniform, grab a shower and I'll meet you in our courtyard in an hour. There's much to show you before we have dinner at 8:00 p.m. tonight."

Dinner. Her spirit sank. Emma didn't want to spend too much time with this pilot. He was too mesmerizing. Ayesha bounced around Khalid, her tongue lolling out of her long muzzle, her dark-brown eyes alight with worship for her master. "I'll see you later," she said, more tersely than she meant it to be. Emma wished mightily for a bathtub, but they weren't to be found anywhere. At base camp, there were only showers. Her flight boots thunked with a slight echo down the highly polished white-, brown- and orange-tiled hall.

The door to her suite was ajar. Emma pushed it open and walked in. What she saw made her gasp with delight. The suite looked like a five-star hotel room! Across the king-sized bed was a gorgeous lavender-and-white star quilt. And on the wall above it hung an art fabric collage of a Rocky Mountain meadow filled with colorful wildflowers. Setting her bags on the bed, Emma looked around, dazed by the quality of the furniture, the decorations and the sense of peace that filled the room.

Her mahogany dresser was an antique. She ran her hand across the polished surface and figured it had to be from either North America or perhaps Europe. As Emma opened one of the drawers, she noticed the dovetailing on each side, another sign of quality craftsmanship. She tucked away her few clothes, keeping out her silky pink pajamas and her own washcloth. Emma had learned a long time ago to carry one with her since many countries didn't provide them.

The pale-lavender walls matched the beautiful quilt on her bed. Fresh flowers in a brass vase adorned the mahogany coffee table that stood between a small purple sofa and a wing chair. Soft music played from a radio. Doilies and a long embroidered runner lay across the top of the dresser. The furnishings gave the room a 1930s flavor. She felt as if she'd walked back in time to an era when everything was made by hand. Even the rugs on either side of the bed seemed to have been handmade from scraps of cloth that had been wound into ropes and then anchored together.

Walking through another open door, Emma sighed. With a Jacuzzi bathtub, the bathroom was as large as her bedroom! She gazed at it longingly. Mentally, she blessed Khalid's westernized parents for their thoughtfulness toward their visitors. There was also a large glass-and-tile shower. The blue tiles on the walls were hand-painted with colorful wildflowers. Emma recognized some of them, others she did not. She walked closer to study them. Some were from the U.S., for sure. Others were jungle flowers and orchids.

A washcloth and a bright-yellow fuzzy towel had been

folded on a nearby table. Lavender-colored soap sat in a white ceramic dish. She picked up a bar and inhaled the fragrance. It was jasmine, one of her favorite scents. Did Khalid know that? How could he? Emma replaced the soap and turned, suddenly feeling horribly trapped by the assignment. First things first. Emma noticed a range of hair products near the white porcelain sink. She would draw a luxurious bath, soak and then wash her hair in the shower. Still in mild shock over the plush suite, she once again reminded herself that Khalid was a man full of surprises.

What next? Emma wasn't sure. She quickly shed her boots and uniform and turned on the faucet to fill the Jacuzzi tub. As she sat on the edge of the tub and swirled her fingers through the warm water, she felt her heart shrink with fear and dread. What if Khalid made a move on her? Emma could swear he liked her, but so far, he hadn't done anything off limits. The rose told her he was flirting. Did he see her as nothing more than a woman to chase and try to catch in the next six months? Brody had done something similar; he'd chased her for four months before she'd agreed to a date.

*Careful. You can't get involved with him. You have your family to think of first. You have to redeem the Trayhern's good name. Never mind Khalid is warm, personable, humorous and kind. Or rich.* Groaning, Emma closed her eyes for a moment. This mission was much worse than she'd ever realized.

# Chapter 4

"Come," Khalid invited Emma as she walked into the spacious kitchen, "let's go to the garage. I have my storehouse in there." He tried to ignore the fact that she was now in civilian clothes, her red hair still damp from the shower and falling like fiery lava around her proud shoulders. Instead of a baggy olive-green flight suit, Emma now wore a tangerine-colored T-shirt with dark-brown trousers. On her, they looked good. Too good.

"I'll follow," Emma said firmly, gesturing for him to take the lead. Emma could smell the wonderful odor of lamb cooking with spices in the oven. With how Khalid's light-blue polo shirt showed the breadth of his chest, Emma kept distance between them. He was just too much of a temptation.

Khalid opened the door to the storehouse and stepped aside to allow Emma to enter. He turned on the lights. Emma halted and stared around the cavernous three-car garage that held only the Land Rover right now. Along the walls in neat rows were thousands of books and boxes of educational items such as crayons, pencils, pens and notebooks.

"This is our vision," Khalid said, closing the door and walking into the room. "Kinah and I bought state-of-the-art printing machines. We gathered a group of Afghan widows and trained them to print out the books for the children." He went to one aisle, pulled out a book and opened it. "We've not only employed six women who had no way to earn any money. Now they are our printers and publisher. The books are written by the best authorities in education, according to Kinah. She worked a year to produce Pashto-written texts and pictures from grades one through twelve. It was a momentous challenge."

Emma nodded but remained distant. She made sure there was plenty of space between them. She heard the pride in Khalid's voice for his innovating and hard-working sister. "This is a major undertaking."

Khalid nodded and slid the book back onto the shelf. "Yes, it is." He gazed down at Emma and had a maddening urge to tangle his fingers in her damp red hair, which curled softly around her face. Did she know how fetching she looked with that coverlet of copper freckles across her nose and cheeks? Emma wore no make up, but didn't need any. She was beautiful just as she was, Khalid's heart whispered to him. But since he was marked for death, there was no way to fall in love with any woman, not even someone as tempting as Emma Cantrell. He focused on showing Emma the large room of supplies. "Once we begin Operation Book Worm, all the supplies will come from this location.

They will be marked, packed by another group of widows and then sent by truck to Bagram for us. From there, we put them aboard our CH-47 and fly them out to the villages."

"And your sister Kinah?" Emma asked. "Where is she in all of this?"

"Right now my sister is working with leaders of the first ten villages along the border where we will set up the schools. She's taking a roster of each child, his or her age, and how many children will be in each school." Khalid said fondly, "My sister is a tempest. She never sits still. Kinah's a fierce warrior for peace and the education of our people. She's a fighter who has vision, strength, intelligence and courage."

"She'd have to have all those things to do what she's doing," Emma agreed grimly, looking around in awe at the room. "Her life is always on the line out there. I'm sure you know that."

Darkness came to Khalid's normally sparkling blue eyes.

"Too aware. I have hired two of the best security guards I can find, but I still worry about her. She refuses to wear a flak jacket, which concerns me. We have ancient enemies out there." His voice lowered. "I know Malik is hunting us, Emma. He's just waiting to spring a trap to capture either or both of us. I worry it will happen when Kinah is alone and unable to defend herself…."

"And yet, you have said Asad Malik has promised your death." Emma looked around. "Where are *your* bodyguards?"

Khalid shrugged. "Now, you sound like my sister, Captain. She is always on me to have them."

"Thanks for the tour, Khalid." Emma sounded less

military and slightly breathless. That irritated her a whole lot. Emma felt an unexpected yearning for him that was like a flowing stream that turned into a wild river within her. Khalid was too good to be true. Brody had never been a humanitarian and that's where they were different. In Emma's eyes and heart, Khalid was a true hero, fighting to lift his people out of abject poverty. He had the money, the position and resources to make it happen. There was a generosity so deep within him that it made Emma stand in awe of Khalid. How many men had she met that had all these qualities? Not many. All the more reason to remain at arm's length from this fierce Afghan warrior.

"You're welcome, Captain Cantrell. Now," he said, glancing down at his watch, "I believe Rasa will have our dinner ready for us."

Emma walked toward the door, dreading the meal. Hopefully, she asked, "Are you going to split us up? I'll eat in the women's quarter and you in the men's?" In the Muslim world, men and women ate separately.

Khalid laughed and walked quickly to open the door before she got to it. "No. You are American and I honor the fact that Americans sit as families together. We'll eat in the dining room." He saw a wariness in her eyes and added, "Does this meet with your approval?" No longer could he afford to assume anything about this woman.

Emma kept her sedate demeanor. "This is not military protocol, Captain Shaheen. To tell you the truth, I'm a little uncomfortable with it all." There, the truth was out. Emma noticed the genuine concern in his face and how much her words had hurt him. She knew how important it was for an Afghan to be a host. "But I'll deal with it."

"Yes?" Khalid said hopefully. "For I have no wish to offend you again."

"I'm not offended." Emma hoped she'd smoothed the situation over enough so they could have a quick dinner and she could make a run for her suite.

Asad Malik arrived in Kabul at 9:00 p.m. He and his men had met with a local Taliban sheik at a village outside Camp Bravo. He'd loaned them two pickup trucks so that they could speed their way to Kabul. The stars were bright and beautiful above him as they pulled up at the bottom of the hill where the Shaheen family home sat.

They got out of their pickups and quietly assembled near Malik. He put on a special pair of night goggles stolen from an American soldier during a heated battle. He liked these goggles because, suddenly, night became day. Everything was green and grainy, but he could see. This was the first time he'd ever been this close to the Shaheen estate. As he used binoculars and began a survey of the home, he realized it was going to be very hard to attack.

Ameen, his second in command, came up to him. "My lord, is there a way we can assault the home?"

Malik growled under his breath, "There's heavy brush all around the hill. At the top, there is a ten-foot wall. And on top of the wall is concertina barbed wire." Dropping the binoculars, he handed them to the young man, who wore a worn brown turban on his head. "Stay here. I'm going to look around. With these goggles, I'll be able to see much more." He picked up his rifle and melted into the night, leaving his men standing quietly by the trucks.

* * *

Emma walked down the hallway and back into the kitchen. A short, black-haired woman in a long dark blue gown stood at the oven. She wore oven mitts as she pulled out the lamb and placed it on the counter. When Emma saw the housekeeper's face she bit down on her lower lip. The whole left side was terribly twisted and scarred, as if severely burned. What had happened to her? Emma had no time to think about this because Khalid cupped his hand beneath her right elbow and guided her into a huge dining room with its crystal chandelier hanging over a long, rectangular mahogany table.

Once out of earshot, Emma whispered, "Captain Shaheen, what happened to Rasa? Her face is horribly scarred."

Khalid pulled out the chair at the end of the table for her. He dropped his voice. "Rasa lived in a border village. She was fighting to get a school started for girls. Rasa was well-educated and a fighter for women's rights."

Emma sat down and looked up to see darkness in Khalid's eyes. He took a chair on her right and sat down. "Malik, our enemy, heard of Rasa's efforts and he brought his thugs into the village. They found her and poured acid all over her face and told her to stop thinking about educating girls. She was told that women were more stupid than the donkeys that hauled the loads of firewood into the village."

Emma was horrified. "My God, I'm so sorry for Rasa."

He picked up her gold linen napkin and handed it to her. "Rasa lost the sight in her left eye, too. When my father, who was trying to bring education to the villages so long ago, found Rasa, he brought her here, to Kabul. He paid for all of her medical needs. At that time, Rasa was only eighteen years old. She was so grateful that she begged my father to allow her to be the permanent housekeeper for our family. She wanted to repay my father for all his generosity toward her. Rasa remains blind in that eye to this day, and there is nothing that could be done for her. But her face is much improved over what it was at first."

"This isn't right, Khalid. Malik is evil."

Opening his napkin, Khalid nodded. "He's a murderer. One day, I will meet him on the plain of combat."

Startled by his words, Emma realized she was seeing the warrior side of Khalid for the first time. He was a combatant now, his eyes narrowed and dark, his full, expressive mouth thinned with tension. Emma felt the chill of his rage. The light-hearted Khalid had disappeared. Now she understood a little more why this man had been chosen by the U.S. Army for Apache combat helicopter training. This aviator was a consummate hunter, like the legendary and mystical snow leopards who lived in the Kush mountains.

Taking a shaky breath, Emma asked under her breath, "Does Rasa know English?"

"No." Khalid gave her a pleading look. "When Rasa comes to serve us, please do not look into her eyes. She never meets your gaze. Her eyes are always downcast and she speaks so softly that at times, I have a hard time hearing her."

Heart aching for Rasa, Emma felt how the woman's spirit had been broken by Malik's attack upon her. "Of course," she promised. "I don't wish to make her uncomfortable, Captain."

Khalid nodded and looked toward the arched entrance

that led to the kitchen. "Rasa is painfully aware that no man would ever take her as his bride. She hides beneath a burka so that no one can see her damaged face when she shops in Kabul for us. I have tried over the years to convince her she is not ugly, that she has a beautiful heart and soul. And that any man would overlook her physical face for the unscarred beauty of her heart," he sighed, "but she will not believe me. I have brought potential suitors here for her, but she shuns them." Shrugging, Khalid said, "I've given up at this point."

"Is Rasa happy here?" Emma asked, touched by Khalid's obvious grief over Rasa's suffering. He seemed to hold back unknown emotions.

"Very happy. She has adopted us as her family." Khalid saw Rasa coming from the kitchen with a tray of steaming food. "We'll speak later," he said in a quiet tone.

"Of course," Emma said.

Malik crept silently along the road leading to the estate. Crouching, his AK-47 in his right hand, the butt resting on the earth, he eyed two turbaned guards at a ten-foot wrought-iron black gate. They weren't like most security guards. No, these two bearded men were alert and looking around. Malik knew he was well-hidden by the brush on the dirt road.

After waiting five more minutes, Malik crept into the brush. It was thick but negotiable. He was tall and wiry and able to step softly and not raise alarm. Sitting down, he observed the gate head-on. The guards never left it. He could hear them talking in the distance. They carried AK-47s with two bandoliers of ammo crisscrossing their powerful chests. Judging from how they carried themselves, these were Afghan warriors and not the drivel from Kabul who couldn't fight a fly.

Slowly turning his head, Malik decided to continue to move slowly and quietly around the hill to see if there was another entrance to the estate.

"And so," Khalid said, pointing to the papers spread out on the table after dinner, "this is the full concept of our efforts."

It was nearly 10:00 p.m. as Emma pored over all the information about Operation Book Worm. "This is impressive." She glanced at Khalid, who sat to her right. "How long did it take you two to figure this out?"

"Four years," Khalid murmured. Emma's hair was dry now and curled in crimson around her freckled face. Did she know how beautiful and utterly natural a woman she was? Khalid itched to understand her on a more personal level. He knew she was single because he had looked at her personnel jacket. She had been suggested as the right person to partner with him on this effort. And she was.

It was on the tip of Khalid's tongue to ask if she had a significant other. Just because Emma was single didn't mean she was available. And why was he even thinking in that direction? He could be killed at any moment by Asad Malik. Unconsciously, Khalid touched his chest where his heart resided. Was he finished grieving for his fiancée? Was he returning to life as a man with yearnings and needs? Was his wounded heart truly healed and now calling for him to find another woman who could fulfill his dreams? But that could never happen. Khalid would never put another woman in the sites of Malik.

Emma saw the odd look in Khalid's eyes. What was

he thinking? She nervously gathered up the papers and handed them over to him. “It’s late,” she said firmly. “I know we’re getting up early tomorrow. Kinah will be here at 0800? Right?”

“Yes, my sister is flying in tomorrow morning. She’ll have the information we require. Then, the widows will be driven over here and, based upon Kinah’s assessments, we’ll get busy filling orders for each village and boxing them up. Then, you and I will trailer them to the CH-47 assigned to us at Bagram Air Force Base.”

Emma rose. “Sounds good, Captain. I’ll see you tomorrow morning.” All evening she had felt as if Khalid wanted a warm, intimate conversation with her. Oh, nothing overt. Subtle, just as Brody had been. Emma rose from the table and smoothed her slacks.

Khalid quickly stood with her. There was confusion in Emma’s green gaze. Why? There was a wariness in her expression as if he had somehow, once more, breached officer-to-officer protocol. Should he apologize? Khalid had treated her with courtesy and kept all conversations about the mission, nothing personal, during dinner. He didn’t want to chase Emma off this operation by unmilitary behavior toward her.

Malik hissed beneath his breath. There was no entrance other than the one gate to Shaheen’s estate. Making his way back to his men who were patiently crouched and holding their weapons, he took off the goggles. Ameen approached, a hopeful look on his darkened face.

“I will not throw away our lives on trying to get into that castle,” he told his men. “I swear blood vengeance on Khalid Shaheen, but this will not be the place to settle that score.” Lifting his hand, he gestured sharply to the trucks. "Mount up. We're going back to the base camp. We will watch Shaheen's movements from there and figure out what he's up to now."

By the time Emma got up and dressed in a fresh flight uniform, Kinah and Khalid were already in the dining room having breakfast. Emma had slept hard. She realized how safe she felt in this villa compared to the base camp where mortars would sometimes be lobbed at them by the Taliban. Rubbing her eyes, she smiled a welcome as Kinah rose to greet her.

"Ah, you are the red-haired pilot Khalid spoke of," Kinah said, getting up, her hand extended to meet Emma. "I'm Kinah Shaheen. Khalid's little sister." She grinned mischievously and glanced back at her brother who sat at the table.

Emma grasped Kinah's long, graceful hand. She had nearly waist-length black hair shot through with red strands, green eyes that Emma was sure came from her Irish mother and full lips. Kinah was dressed in a traditional black Muslim gown.

"Hi, Kinah. I'm Captain Emma Cantrell. Nice to meet you."

Kinah stepped back and placed her hands on her hips. "Khalid, shame on you! You did not tell me how lovely this American woman pilot is!" She gave Emma a wink.

Emma decided Kinah was every bit the trickster that Khalid was. It must be that wicked Irish sense of humor in their DNA.

Dressed in his flight suit, Khalid made sounds of protest. "Beloved sister, Captain Cantrell is here as an envoy from the States. Why would I speak of her obvious beauty?" For once, he wished outgoing Kinah would not embarrass Emma. She might bolt and refuse to work on the mission.

As she walked to the table, Emma noticed that a third breakfast setting was there for her. They had not yet eaten and apparently were waiting for her to arrive; such were their manners. "I don't know about you, but I'd love some chai. I need to wake up," she told them, sitting down. Kinah sat at the head of the table this time, her brother on her right and Emma on the left.

"Indeed," Kinah said with a smile, "I believe Rasa is fixing three cups of chai as we speak." She reached over and gripped Emma's lower arm. "We are truly grateful for your presence, Captain Cantrell."

"Call me Emma." There was such warmth in the woman that Emma found herself climbing out of her military decorum.

"Wonderful," Kinah said. "I don't like standing on protocol, either. Please call me Kinah. When we're out in the field together, you must consider yourself a part of our family." She gestured to herself and her brother.

"Well…" Khalid choked, giving his vivacious sister a pained look. "We're in the military, Kinah. I can't just call her by her first name out there."

"Pooh!" Kinah waggled her finger into Khalid's face. "We must appear bonded and friends, brother. After all, it was my idea to bring in an American woman pilot."

Emma saw Rasa come, head down, eyes trained on the floor, bearing a tray with three steaming cups of chai. She could smell the cinnamon and nutmeg fragrance wafting upward in the steam. Kinah's words caught her attention.

"Oh?"

Kinah took her chai and warmly thanked Rasa, who murmured back in Pashto. "I believe," Kinah said, resting her elbows on the table, the chai in her hands, "that little girls out in these villages need to see two strong women from two different cultures." Her eyes sparkled and she said in a whisper, "How else are my little girls to know they can dream as big as their hearts? They see me as an educator. They see you as a woman in the military who can fly a helicopter, who is an officer and who is fully capable. You see," she said, sipping her chai delicately, "little girls in the villages are often told they can't dream of being anything. They see you and me, Emma. They will get it very quickly that they *can* dream! They *can* set a goal through learning to read and write."

Moved by Kinah's passion, Emma said, "I hadn't thought of it in that way, but you're right. Leading by example."

Nodding, Kinah said, "Exactly. I expect you to give a little talk at some point, after we have the schools set up. I would like you to share how you became a pilot. What made you yearn to fly? What dreams did you have as a little girl that fueled your desire to fly a helicopter? You see," Kinah said, smiling softly, "little girls have wings of imagination. You can instill them to imagine whatever it is they desire to become."

Emma smiled a little and sipped her chai. Clearly, Kinah was a force of nature. Compared to Khalid, she was a ball of energy, hardly able to sit still, her hands always gesturing and her eyes fierce with passion. Khalid paled in comparison to his dynamo sister. The fact that Khalid was the rudder to Kinah's ship of dreams made Emma respect him even more. She could see the doting, loving look on Khalid's face for his beloved sister. She wondered if Khalid took after his Sufi father and Kinah her Irish mother. Clearly, the fire belonged to Kinah.

Emma could understand why Khalid adored his sister. Kinah, although in traditional Afghan dress, was far more a feminist that Emma ever had been. "I wonder if you picked up on your Irish mother's DNA? You're a missionary of a different sort," Emma said. "Is it not a religious calling as much as a humanitarian effort that drives you?"

"Precisely," Kinah said, nodding her head, her dark curls moving across her back. "I may only be small but I am a giant who stands over most others because my heart is connected to my dreams." She gave Khalid a warm, loving look. "And my Sufi brother knows well that when our hearts are aligned with our passions, we can accomplish miracles."

Once Rasa completed delivering their breakfast, Kinah called her over, stood up and gave the housekeeper a warm hug and thanked her. Rasa was bright-red, obviously uneasy and quickly scuttled back to the safety of her kitchen.

Kinah sat down. "You see, women like Rasa deserve more from life than having acid thrown in their face by those bastards."

Emma nearly choked on her eggs. Kinah's language startled her.

Khalid groaned again and gave Emma look of apology for his sister's bad language.

Kinah merely laughed and ate heartily.

Emma bowed her head and ate her food. She felt caught up in a whirlwind in Kinah's presence. But it was a good one. Now, she grasped Khalid's worry for his fierce, passionate sister. And given that Asad Malik hated this family, Emma understood why. If Malik ever encountered Kinah, it would be a battle of life and death. Kinah was no wilting lily. She would fight to the death rather than allow Malik to rape her, cut her throat or throw acid in her face. No, Malik would have met his equal and Emma bet that Kinah would win the day, if not the war itself.

# Chapter 5

Emma tried to still her excitement and fear as she piloted the CH-47 toward their first village. The vibration rippling through the bird soothed her. The April morning was crisp and clear. They had left Bagram with boxes of educational supplies. In the rear, on the nylon seats along the fuselage, sat Kinah. The load master, Tech. Sgt. Brad Stapleton, all of twenty-two years old, also sat in the back. He would be responsible for unloading their supplies once they arrived at the border village. To her left was Khalid, her copilot on this mission. They had just flown past her black ops base camp, and were now heading toward Asmar and then on to their final destination, Do Bandi.

Asmar was a larger village on a dirt road and further away from the border with Pakistan. Do Bandi was closer to the border and had been protected by A-teams, army Special Forces comprised of ten men. These teams lived in the village, rotating out every thirty days when a new team came in to replace it. Khalid and Kinah felt this village was safer than most and a good one to cut their teeth on. Emma couldn't disagree. There were a lot of logistics and this was their first trial-and-error run.

"Do the village elders know we're flying in this morning?" Emma asked Khalid over the intercom.

"Yes. The A-team stationed there received permission from the chieftain two weeks ago for us to visit him." He flipped her a thumbs-up with his gloved hand. "It's a go." He grinned.

Khalid reminded her of an excited little boy. Emma wasn't sure who was more anticipatory: him or his restless, dynamic sister, Kinah. Neither had barely slept last night, they were so "charged up and ready to rock 'n' roll," as Khalid had put it this morning over breakfast. Emma had slept deeply and had had torrid dreams about Khalid. As a result, she'd awakened this morning in a sour mood. How to keep her boss at bay, do her job and not get involved were *her* logistical problems to solve.

Emma took the CH-47 down to one hundred feet as they approached the first range of snow-covered mountains. They would fly nap-of-the-earth, skimming at that low altitude up, down and around through mountain peaks and passes in order not to be fired upon by the Taliban. Any helicopter that didn't do this type of herky-jerky flying was a sure target for a Taliban rocket. Emma loved flying by the seat of her pants in the hulking, slow transport. The helo was sluggish, but it was steady beneath her hands, which gripped the cyclic and collective. Her intense focus was on skimming the earth and not getting nailed with a rock outcropping or brushing too close to a granite wall with the tips of the helo's rotors.

By the time they reached Do Bandi, which sat down at the north end of a narrow, green valley, the armpits on Emma's flight suit were wet with sweat. Her heart pounded, adrenaline coursing through her bloodstream. Every time she had to fly nap-of-the-earth, the percentage of a crash rose exponentially. It was life-and-death flying, as she and her cohorts called it. But there was no other choice, was there?

As Emma brought the transport in for a landing outside the village, the twin rotors kicked up thick, choking dust that billowed hundreds of feet into the air. A huddled group of elders hid behind the mud huts to protect themselves from flying dust and debris. The CH-47 hunkered down and Khalid quickly shut down the engines. Emma saw the A-team coming out of the shadows of the line of huts. They were the first to approach. Emma ordered the load master over the intercom to open up the helo.

"I'm bringing down the ramp," Stapleton told her. "A-team is approaching on the starboard side."

"Roger," Emma murmured. She heard the grating roar echo through the helo as the ramp began to descend. The helo vibrated and groaned.

Khalid unstrapped. He wore a Kevlar vest and a .45 pistol holstered across his chest. Grinning, he felt higher than a kite flying off a hill in Kabul. Kite-running was something he'd done as a child. He'd never won, but the exhilaration of flying a kite and then chasing it was always thrilling. That was how he felt now: anticipation and joy.

Pulling off her helmet after unstrapping, Emma quickly ran her fingers through her flattened hair. She'd tied her shoulder-length hair into a knot at the nape of her neck. From her right thigh pocket she pulled out a dark-green silk scarf known as a hijab, to wrap around her head. The hijab was a sign of respect to the Muslim Afghan people. Women did not go out into public without their heads being covered. She didn't mind fitting in, although Emma found it ironic in another way. Here she was, a modern-day combat helicopter pilot wearing a .45 strapped across her chest and a delicate, feminine scarf. It was April and cold so the scarf would keep her head warm.

"Ready?" Khalid asked, switching everything off in the cabin. His job as copilot was to power down the helo after it landed. His hands flew across the console, flipping switches and turning off the radios.

Emma turned in her seat. The groaning ramp came to a rest in the dirt with a "clunk."

"Ready," she said. She gave Kinah a thumbs-up, which meant it was all right to unstrap. The woman smiled and nodded, quickly removing the harness and getting to her feet. There were about fifty boxes in the hold of the transport. Only about half were actual school supplies. The rest were donations from America of clothing and shoes for the children. There were also medical items for the A-team sergeant who was responsible for the health of the villagers. Penicillin and other antibiotics were treasures out on the frontier and Emma knew their worth was as gold to the Afghan leaders. Antibiotics were desperately needed by all border villages, but few ever received them. Death by infection was a common way to die, unfortunately.

Kinah walked down the ramp. She was dressed in a black wool robe with a bright red hijab over her thick, dark hair. She shook the hand of the captain of the A-team and then walked quickly toward the wall of old men, the elders of the village.

Emma could see her breath and knew that at this altitude, the temperature was still at freezing. She would be glad to see May arrive and warmth grudgingly coming back to these mountain villages. She had pulled on her thick, warm green nylon jacket and left it unzipped in order to reach for her .45 in case she needed it. Although Khalid felt this was a highly secure village, no one took it on faith. The Taliban had made repeated attacks on it, only to be repulsed by the A-team stationed here. The BJS Apache combat helicopters spewed out their bullets and rockets at the enemy when called in by the A-team to chase them away.

Khalid came to her side as she stood just below the lip of the ramp. "Come, let me introduce you."

"Kinah already has the elders smiling," Emma observed, giving him a slight grin. "Your sister should run the United Nations."

Khalid laughed heartily. "My sister is a one-woman army, no question. She's like a laser-fired rocket—she knows her destination and nothing will stop her from reaching it." Khalid walked toward the huddled group near the huts. "I love my sister dearly. I worry about her, though. She disdains having guards to protect her."

Emma nodded. Today, Kinah had ordered her two Afghan guards to remain in Kabul. She did not want them near her on this first, important step of their education mission. And worse, Kinah would remain behind in the village after all the supplies were removed by the load master and the A-team members. She saw the worry banked in Khalid's eyes. Border villages were not safe and they never would be until the Afghanistan government turned its eyes and heart to them. These villages took the brunt of the Taliban attacks.

Emma stood at Khalid's side as he greeted the village

elders in Pashto. She was glad she could understand what was being exchanged. There was much hand-shaking and touching of cheeks between Kinah, Khalid and the elders. Khalid ensured that Emma was introduced and she went through the same greetings with the elders. She could see that hope burned bright in their aged eyes. Not only was this village receiving protection from the A-team and the army from the air, but medicine was now available. The next step was education for their children. Emma knew that Afghans fiercely loved their children and wanted only the best for them.

Khalid turned to Emma. "Would you like to work with the wives of the leaders to distribute the clothes and shoes?"

"Of course," Emma said. Behind the elders was a group of their wives dressed in burkas, only eye slits to see through. The burkas were only worn outside; in their homes, they came off. Emma went and introduced herself. She led the four women to the supplies being stacked outside the CH-47. There were fifteen boxes of clothes and shoes. She watched as the women reverently touched the cardboard boxes. Their voices were low and filled with excitement.

Khalid was busy for the next hour. It was important to get the helo unloaded and back into the air. They couldn't remain on the ground for fear of a Taliban attack. He'd lost sight of Emma, who had gone into the village with the women. The elders had chosen an empty mud hut for the school, which was where Kinah had gone with the boxes and many curious, excited children.

Finishing up, Khalid walked down the rutted main street with huts on either side. A donkey pulled a creaking cart, the owner walking beside the gray beast. He was heading down the slope below the village in search of firewood. Dogs barked and ran excitedly up and down the street.

Khalid remained anxious since the Taliban were always nearby; it was just a question of when they would sneak in to try and attack these good people. Leaping over several ruts, Khalid walked to the house of the chieftain, sure that Emma would be there. The children were all lined up at the door, giggling and expectant. Some of the children had shoes, others didn't. Mothers with their wriggling, restive children stood patiently, hidden beneath their burkas, waiting for their turns to get their children fitted for shoes.

Khalid squeezed through the door, and Emma realized how handsome he looked. His short black hair was mussed, giving him a boyish look. She forced herself to remain neutral toward him by repeating Brody's name in her head.

"Ready?" Khalid called to her over the noise of the children. The wives of the leaders had opened many of the shoe boxes. A child sat in a chair as the mother tried on pair after pair until they found the size to fit her child's feet.

"Yes," Emma called over the din. She turned and warmly thanked one of the wives and told her she had to go. The woman smiled and pressed her burka-covered cheek against Emma's. One thing Emma had learned was that if one could befriend Afghan people, they were loyal to the death. A fierce love welled up in her chest. These villagers had courage to survive despite the terror of the Taliban always skulking nearby, hidden and deadly.

"How about a quick lunch at your base camp?" Khalid suggested on the way back to the unloaded helo.

She shrugged. There were so many fine lines to walk

with him. Emma knew if she turned him down, he might get upset. For a C.O., an invitation was often an order. "Sure," she said.

"It's not a death sentence," Khalid teased her as they walked shoulder-to-shoulder down the main street. There was such struggle in Emma's face, and he tried to put her at ease.

"Captain, you have a dry sense of humor," Emma said.

He sighed and pressed his hand over his heart. "I've been so charged," he admitted, wishing for some relaxation between them.

Though she felt bad, Emma forced herself not to feel sorry for him. Khalid was her boss, pure and simple. She wanted high marks from him after this six-month gig. He obviously saw her reluctance.

Khalid performed the mandatory walk around the helo, part of his copilot duties. He would look for anything loose, oil leaking or flight surfaces that weren't secure. Emma went directly to the cockpit. Sitting down in the right-hand seat, she got ready to perform the takeoff check list once Khalid finished his inspection tour outside the CH-47.

For the next five minutes, they were too busy to talk. Khalid called the black ops base and let them know they were taking off. Sometimes, an Apache helo would escort them, but today, there was high demand up north near Zor Barawul. The Taliban had launched another offensive against the village and it was currently being repulsed by a lot of air power. Their next stop tomorrow was that very village. Danger was always near.

"So," Khalid said as he sat opposite Emma in the chow hall back at base camp, "what would you tell the little girls about yourself?" He was obviously casting around for a way to ease the tension between them.

Emma had lifted her fork halfway to her mouth and stopped. She had spaghetti with meatballs. Khalid had the same, adding four pieces of buttered garlic bread, as well. She frowned momentarily, ate her food and considered his request. His question seemed innocent enough.

"I'd tell them that my family is a military one," she said between bites. "Nearly all the Trayhern children serve at least one tour in the service of their choice."

"So," Khalid said, relishing the warm garlic bread, "little girls would think that this career choice is expected?"

Emma shrugged. "I guess it is. My youngest sister, Casey, wasn't interested in being in the military. She joined the Forest Service and is a ranger currently stationed at Grand Tetons National Park in Wyoming."

"Is she considered an outcast?" Khalid wondered. While he hungered for a more personal connection, Khalid resisted his impulses.

Emma shook her head. "No, of course not. My Uncle Morgan Trayhern is fine with whatever we kids want to do with our lives. He loves Casey as much as any of the rest of us. His adopted daughter, Kamaria, never went into the military. She's a professional photographer and was a stringer for a number of top-flight news organizations around the world before she settled down at a Wyoming ranch."

"The girls would probably like to know how many children are in your family."

Emma smiled and explained. "Let's see. I'm the oldest. Then came the first set of twins, Athena and Juno. Two years after that, Casey and Selene. There are five daughters in our family. My mother loves the Greek myths so she named each one of us after a goddess. In my case, my middle name is Metis. She was a goddess and mother to Athena. Casey hated her name, Castalia, and so she shortened it to what it is now." Emma grinned. "My poor dad had five girls running under his feet, but my mom thought it was great," she laughed. "We're a very close, tight-knit family."

Khalid had watched her relax slightly and dared to ask a personal question. "Are you the only daughter with red hair?"

"No. My mother, Alyssa, said she has red hair and twins in her DNA. Two of my twin sisters, Casey and Selene, have red hair, too. Athena and Juno have my dad's black hair. Why?"

Khalid shared a slight smile with her. "I like the combination of your red hair and freckles. It makes you look like a young girl despite your being a mature woman, Captain."

Grimacing, Emma growled, "Don't remind me!" She sopped up some of the marinara sauce with her garlic bread. "All my life I've had to fight that little-girl look. I'll probably have to have gray hairs before anyone gets that I'm not a teenager."

Chuckling, Khalid felt his heart expand. He saw the righteous indignation gleaming in Emma's green eyes. Her mouth was beautifully shaped. He entertained the dream of someday kissing her, just to discover how soft and luscious she was. What was it about Emma that made him realize he was a man with needs once more?

As he twisted his spaghetti around his fork, Khalid asked, "They will probably ask if you have a man who loves you." He knew he was taking a chance with such a question. Emma's eyes flared with surprise. Khalid added a coaxing smile with his request, and her fine, thin red brows eased. He was glad he could influence her mood. Did he dare interpret that look to mean she was interested in him? Khalid felt torn. Half of him wanted a personal relationship with Emma. The other half did not want to put her life at risk.

Pushing her plate away, Emma picked up her mug of coffee. "No, not presently," she slowly admitted. And then the words leaped out of her mouth before she could stop them. "What about you?"

"I'm like you," Khalid offered.

"Because of Najela?" Emma guessed. She saw pain come to his eyes for a moment.

"Yes. I am just now realizing that I am ready to face life on the personal front again." Khalid did not say, *Because of you, I am inspired not only to live again, but to allow my heart to dream of you....*

Emma didn't know what to say. Clearly, Khalid liked her. She saw it in his hooded gaze, the desire banked in their blue depths. Paying strict attention to her coffee, she hoped the moment would pass.

"Now that we've started this mission," Khalid said, "you are welcome to stay as my guest at our home in Kabul. You don't need to remain here at the base camp."

"No," Emma said with finality, "I want to stay here." *That way, you won't be so available.* She was afraid of herself. Afraid of what she might do because Khalid clearly desired her. The man was more than capable of sweet-talking her into something that couldn't—shouldn't—happen. Seeing the regret in his expression, Emma steeled herself against Khalid. The man oozed charm and sensuality.

"Well," Khalid said, setting his emptied plate to one side, "if you want, my home is always available to you. I know you loved the bath."

Groaning, Emma held up her hand. "Don't remind me! I'm a bathtub baby. I hate showers."

"Then," Khalid said, his voice low and smoky, "perhaps once a week you will consider coming to take advantage of the bath in my home?"

Emma managed a polite smile. "I don't think so, Captain Shaheen. It wouldn't look proper to the military. Thank you, though, for the offer." Emma couldn't afford to make him angry at her. Yet, she was walking the edge of the sword with this very available male pilot who was interested in her.

"Pity," he remarked. "Well, then I will fly the CH-47 back to Bagram alone. I will miss you, Captain Cantrell."

"Oh," Emma said lightly, standing and picking up her helmet bag, "I think you'll have plenty to keep you busy, Captain Shaheen."

Back at her tent, Emma threw her helmet bag on her cot. She turned to sit down in the camp chair at her desk. Upset with herself, she decided that she was too easily swayed by Khalid, for whatever reason.

Tomorrow morning, he'd fly in at dawn with another load of boxes for the village of Zor Barawul. They would continue this pace daily or every other day, depending upon the distance involved.

"Hey, Emma!"

Emma turned toward the open flaps of her tent. Nike Alexander poked her head in. "Nike, come on in! How are you?"

The BJS woman pilot slipped in, threw her helmet

bag next to Emma's on the cot and sat down in the extra chair. "Okay. Just got off a hot fire fight around Zor Barawul. We kicked ass. How are you? I haven't had time to catch up with you lately. What's happening?"

"Just delivered our first boxes of books to Do Bandi. I had lunch at the chow hall and was coming back here to drop off my helmet and then go to the BJS HQ to fill out my report." Emma watched as Nike pushed the black curls off her sweaty brow. She saw the armpits of her flight suit were wet with perspiration. Flying an Apache in a fire fight made the adrenaline rocket upward. She saw pink spots on Nike's olive-skinned cheeks. Her friend was still caught up in the adrenaline charge from the fire fight.

"Was that your boss I just passed out there?" Nike hooked a thumb toward the tent opening. "That eye candy that's long and lean? Black hair? Blue eyes?"

Groaning, Emma nodded. "Yes, that's Captain Khalid Shaheen."

Nike gave her a wicked look. "Hey, if I hadn't met the man of my dreams recently, I'd definitely give that dude a second look. He's absolutely handsome."

Sighing, Emma gave her friend a dirty look. "Don't make this any worse than it is, Nike. Think about me. I have to work with the guy for the next six months and remain immune to him."

Laughing, Nike slapped her knee. "Oh, Emma! You're single. You're not involved with anyone. Why wouldn't you think about getting hooked up with him?"

Emma explained all the details to Nike about Brody Parker. As she did, she watched her friend become more serious. At the end of her explanation, she watched the excitement die in Nike's eyes. "So you see, I need a good recommendation from Captain Shaheen for my personnel jacket. I have to dig myself out of the black eye I gave us," she said, desperate. Opening her hands, Emma added, "And I don't dare let him know I like him, Nike. I fight it constantly. But I'm afraid he's just another player in disguise."

"I see," Nike muttered, sitting up, hands on her knees. "I'm hoping in my own way to overcome our mistake, too. But at least I don't have to worry about falling in love with my boss. That's an extra added strain on you."

"I'm not falling in love with him," Emma said more sharply than she'd intended. "I like the guy, yes. But love? No."

"Hmm," Nike murmured, a grin pulling at her lips, "sure don't look like it from my end. Every time you talked about him, your voice went soft and your eyes got that faraway, dreamy look."

Emma stood up, scowling at her best friend. "Nike, you're wrong."

Nike stood, laughed and picked up her helmet bag. "Okay, then prove it."

# Chapter 6

"When does Shaheen arrive at Zor Barawul?" Asad Malik demanded. He sat crouched in front of a small fire, warming his hands. The cave where he and his men hid sat across from the Afghan village, which was perched on top of a hill.

Merzad, a trusted warrior, stood attentively by the Taliban leader. "My lord, our spy in the village told our man that next week Captain Shaheen, his sister Kinah and an American woman pilot are to fly educational books and desks into this village."

Scowling, Malik took a tin cup filled with steaming chai from the cook, Omald. He looked across the fire as the boy fed the fifteen men under his command. Omald was only thirteen, an orphan Malik had taken under his wing. He had been ten when Malik had found him in a burned-out border village. He had brainwashed the child and turned him into his personal servant. Omald's job was to make him chai, feed him, take care of his horse and serve his soldiers whatever scant food they could steal.

"Do you think that they will arrive with an Apache escort?" Merzad asked, taking a proffered cup of chai from Omald.

Shrugging, Malik enjoyed the warmth of the fire. The cave was dry and cold. Outside, April rain fell. There was a gray pall over the entire area and Zor Barawul was hidden in the mists and cold mountain air. "I hope not. We never know," he muttered, stroking his black-and-gray beard. At fifty, the harshness of his life as a leader in the Taliban, was catching up with Malik. His joints ached in the winter snows and it worsened during the spring rains. Now, he looked forward to the summer heat when his arthritis stopped bothering him as much.

Merzad crouched down next to him, his narrow face set in a deep scowl. The black beard on his face was fuzzy and unkempt. All the men smelled. They went days, even weeks, without a place to clean themselves up or comb their beards and hair. He looked over at his beloved leader, a giant of a man with broad shoulders, a deep chest and powerful, sun-darkened hands covered with scars. Merzad felt a brotherly love for his fellow Pakistani. They'd grown up in the same village, survived terrible odds and gone on to carry the jihad into Afghanistan. Like Malik, Merzad felt strongly that the Taliban needed to be back in control of the country before the U.N. came in with troops to "free" the people from them.

Continuing to stroke the beard that fell nearly to his chest, Malik murmured to his best friend, "I hope to fulfill my promise to Shaheen and his sister. I killed

Shaheen's fiancée two years ago. I've waited patiently, praying daily to Allah to give me another chance to kill him and his infidel sister. We were blessed when we hit the base camp to spot Shaheen there. Our spies have kept good track of him since then."

"They are both infidels," Merzad muttered. "They might be born to a Muslim father, but he's a Sufi." The word *Sufi* came out like a growling curse from the lean forty-five-year-old soldier.

Snorting, Malik sipped the delicious cinnamon-sprinkled chai. "Sufis are our enemies," he acknowledged. "I have no use for mystics of any kind." He smiled, remembering his rapes of Najela. She had fought him, and, to this day, he bore four fingernail marks on his right cheek where she'd clawed at him. No matter, he'd had his way with her. His loins warmed to the memory of taking the feisty black-haired beauty. She'd fought every time and Malik had enjoyed the encounters. Finally, he'd grown bored with her bravery and had slit her throat as she slept. They'd thrown her body into a village where he knew his archenemy, Khalid Shaheen, would find her. Again, his lips twitched with those fond memories. He anticipated capturing Kinah. She was fiery and gave no quarter. Malik, in his own way, admired the Sufi woman, but his hatred was even more intense toward her than it had been toward Najela.

"According to our source," Merzad said, pleased, "you will have them all coming to Zor Barawul."

"Yes," he muttered, "but the leader of that village is pro-American. His village, over the last year, has been protected by A-teams, given medical and dental care from the Americans." Shaking his head, he said, "We must be careful here, Merzad. We can't just openly walk into their village and threaten them as we used to. We tried that just this week and got nowhere. I've lost half of my men to the Apaches. We must rethink and try a different strategy."

Agreeing, Merzad sipped his chai, deep in thought. "It used to be easy to come across the border and threaten the leaders of these villages. Now, this past year, they have received all kinds of aid from the U.N., the U.S. Army and charity organizations from around the world. They no longer fear us." His mouth dipped downward as did his thin black brows.

"They will fear us again," Malik muttered, finishing off his chai and handing the cup back to his servant. He slowly rose on painful knees and rearranged the two bandoliers of ammunition across his chest. Looking around the large, dry cave, he saw that his men had bedded down and were sleeping, their rifles next to them. They'd just suffered a terrible defeat at the hands of the American Apache helicopters. The best thing to do, Malik knew, was to let them heal and lick their wounds, give them hot food and chai to rebuild their confidence. He silently cursed the combat helicopters. They were the bane of his existence. His mind spun with possible plans.

Zor Barawul was considered an American stronghold now. Malik could recall when he had owned that village. The old, crippled leaders cowered before him as he rode through like a conquering hero, his men following him. *No longer.* Allah would show him a way to infiltrate the village. His whole focus was on capturing or killing Khalid and Kinah Shaheen. Then his revenge would be complete.

After ordering another cup of chai, he watched the young lad quickly pour it from the tea kettle across the grate of the fire. Malik took it and scowled. The

Shaheens were infidels. They weren't even full-blooded Afghans. The blood of the Irish ran through their veins. Malik hadn't liked it when the Shaheens began to come regularly to the villages along the border. First, it was the elder Shaheen who had thrown his money at the villagers. Malik cursed the Sufi. All of them were stupid dreamers who thought love could solve the world's problems. How wrong they were! All of the money the elder Shaheen had given the villages had created schools. Malik had been livid with rage when he'd found out that girls were being taught, and he'd come in and destroyed every one of those schools.

Of all things! Malik was enraged to find out that five years later, the stupid girls were going to be educated once more by the Shaheen son and daughter. What an utter waste of time! A donkey was far more valuable than an accursed woman! Women had little value except as brood mares to bear a man's children and further the male family line. *Stupid women! Women must know their place. I will show them, once and for all. Once I capture Kinah Shaheen I will use her and kill her. Once she's dead, I will dump her body in Zor Barawul and let the women there see what will happen to them if they so much as pick up a book.*

Emma moaned. She turned over in her cot, the layers of blankets keeping her warm. Khalid was with her in her dream. He was touching her cheek lingeringly. She could feel the roughness of his fingers as they curved and followed her cheekbone. The look in his blue eyes, hooded with intent, reminded Emma of a summer thunderstorm. Skin tingling wildly in the wake of his slow caress, Emma sighed and leaned forward. She was naked and so was he. They knelt in front of one another on a sunny, grassy slope. She didn't know where they were, only that it was warm, beautiful and the fragrance of roses surrounded them.

"You are my beloved rose with freckles," Khalid murmured, watching her cheeks turn pink as he whispered the words. "The sun may rise and set, but the rays of love emanate from your heart to mine."

As her breasts brushed his dark, hairy chest, they tightened and a deep throb began in her lower body. Oh, how Emma wanted his hand to trail downward, hold and caress her taut breasts. A softened sigh slipped from between her lips. Khalid smiled into her eyes.

"You are the rose who grows in my heart, beloved."

Her mind was starting to come unhinged as his fingers trailed across her eyebrow, down her temple and back to her cheek. "Rumi…was that Rumi?" she managed in a whisper.

His smile increased. "Rumi talks of the rose. Do his words not touch your heart, also?"

Nodding, Emma moved her hands up across his shoulders. She felt the warmth of the sun upon them. Khalid was so strong and steady, as if he knew who he was and where he was going in his life. Emma wished she felt that way. Confidence radiated from him like the sun itself. As she absorbed a sense of protection and love from him, Emma's lids shuttered closed. His fingers outlined her lips and she wanted to kiss him.

"No yet, beloved. Allow my hands to remember every inch of your beautiful being. My heart needs to map you, remember you and breathe you into itself…."

Heat throbbed through her womanly core. Fingers digging into the hard flesh of his shoulders, Emma whimpered his name, begging him to kiss her. She was not disappointed. As Khalid's strong mouth brushed her lips, she trembled. She felt him smiling against her. She smiled in return. With her eyes closed, Emma simply wanted to feel the texture of his mouth, the heat of his ragged breath whispering across her cheek, the male fragrance that was only him.

She opened her lips and pressed into his smiling mouth. They slid and melted together as if in a slow-motion dance of fusion. Emma realized in some far corner of her barely functioning mind that Khalid was courting her slowly, enjoying her with a thoroughness she'd never experienced before. There was no hurry. No rush. Just…timelessness and being rocked and cradled with his mouth sliding upon hers. There was such strength and yet incredible tenderness as he asked her to open her mouth more so that he could take her fully into himself.

Had she ever been kissed like this? No. Every sip of his lips upon hers sent wild tingles down to her breasts and fueled the need to take him completely within her. Khalid's slow exploration of her lips now moved to her cheeks. His mouth scorched a path of neediness with each caress upon her skin. He traced the outline of her brows with his lips. Soft, rose-petal touches grazed her closed eyelids. Strands of hair caught beneath his seeking mouth as he lingered on each of her delicate ears. Emma surrendered to the slow, delicious seduction by Khalid.

"You are honey, my sweet, sweet woman," he whispered into her right ear. Moving his fingers upward from her jaw, Khalid framed her face and pulled back just enough to drown in her dark-green eyes that were sultry with need—of him. "The sweetness of your heart bathes my wounded heart. Honey heals. The sugar of life nurtures new bees into being born and birthing. You are no different…." He trailed a series of kisses from her brow down to her parted lips. There, he halted and barely grazed them with his own. "And like the bees, the honey of your heart allows me to be reborn anew…."

*"Emma! Wake up!"*

Emma jerked into a sitting position, completely disoriented.

"Over here!" Nike called, her head sticking through the opening in the tent. "Wake up!"

"Oh," Emma gasped. "What time is it?" Khalid's words and fiery, evocative touches were real. Her body throbbed and ached. Embarrassed that Nike had had to awaken her, she looked at her watch.

"Oh, God," Emma groaned, "I'm late!!"

"No kidding," Nike said. "What's the matter? You having a sexy dream about Khalid?"

Emma leaped out of bed and fumbled for her flight boots beneath the cot. Shocked at Nike's intuitiveness, Emma muttered, "Oh, forget it, Nike! I was up late last night writing reports, that's all."

Nike grinned. "Oh, sure. Well, hey, Khalid's on the tarmac waiting for you."

"Okay, okay." Pulling out her boots, Emma twisted around. "Can you tell him I'll be there in ten minutes?"

Laughing, Nike said, "Yeah, no problem. Was it a good dream?"

Emma glared at her. Nike chortled and disappeared. How could her girlfriend know about that wonderful dream? Stymied, Emma tore her mind from that to getting dressed, getting to the toilet and grabbing her flight bag. She was late! She'd never slept through the alarm on the bedstand! Ever. Grabbing the clock, Emma realized with a sinking feeling that the alarm was on, but she hadn't heard it.

With a moan of trepidation, Emma hurried to make up for lost time.

Emma was breathless as she arrived at Ops. As usual, it was a beehive of nonstop activity, planes and helos landing and taking off in an invisible dance known only to air-control-tower personnel. She saw Khalid leaning against the fender of the Apache, reading a book. He was relaxed, his head bent down, his helmet bag sitting next to him on the skirt of the helo. The April day was cloudy and chilly. It had rained all night. Puddles lay everywhere on the asphalt landing strip. Ragged, scudding clouds hid the mountains that surrounded the base camp.

Sucking in a breath, Emma walked quickly toward Khalid, her flight boots splashing through several puddles. She saw him lift his head. Instantly, her heart rate doubled. Why did he have to be so handsome? Just looking at the man, who was all warrior and yet so incredibly sensitive, made her feel even more breathless than the run from the tent to Ops had. Emma girded herself for his censure.

"Good morning," Khalid greeted, giving her a warm and appreciative look. "Nike said you overslept."

"I did." Emma pushed several strands of hair off her face. "I'm sorry. I set my alarm but I slept right through it. That's never happened before."

Khalid saw how upset Emma was, her cheeks stained with heat. It only made her freckles more obvious and gave her a decidedly girlish look, at variance with the competent combat pilot she was. "Relax," he urged quietly. "We are in no rush. The weather is bad and we are going to have to wait for the clouds to rise more before we can fly nap-of-the-earth." CH-47s did not have all-terrain radar to see where they were going, and flying a hundred feet off the ground required a good set of eyes and no fog or low-hanging clouds obscuring the terrain.

"Oh," Emma said, relieved, "that's good news."

"Here," he said, handing her the book, "this is a gift for you. I realize it's not military protocol, but I would like to share my world with you a little bit. Take it. We'll go to the chow hall and get some chai and wait until the clouds lift." He picked up his helmet bag.

Emma looked down at the book. She nearly dropped it. It was a paperback called *Rumi: In the Arms of the Beloved*. Stunned, she looked up at Khalid.

"How did you know?" she croaked, confused as she held the book. How could he know about her torrid dream of this morning? Was it all over the internet? Nike had known too. Now, Khalid, of all things! Emma stood there feeling stupid for a moment. She stared at the cover. It showed several men in tall, red, Turkish caps wearing white clothing and whirling around in long skirts. Because of her one-year saturation into Pashto, Emma realized these were Sufi whirling dervishes. They would whirl around and around to music and it allowed them to go into a mystical trance to connect with the Beloved, a direct connection with God.

"Know what?" Khalid asked, confused, as he walked at her side. Emma's brow wrinkled. There was shock in her green eyes. She kept turning the book over and over, as if it were too hot to handle. Khalid wondered if he'd overstepped her personal bounds again. Was giving her a book such a crime in the military's mindset? After all, they were both captains, of equal rank. He saw no reason to think a book was too personal a gift. But, judging from the rush of redness to Emma's cheeks, the way she tucked her lower lip between her teeth, maybe it was.

Gripping the book, Emma muttered, "Oh, nothing. I'm still waking up." She hoped the excuse would sail with Khalid. It did. The worry dissolved from his handsome features. And then, abruptly, she said, "Thank you. This was a very nice gift." They were love poems! Inwardly, Emma felt as if Khalid could see straight through her, to her heart, and was fully aware of the throbbing ache that still lingered in her lower body. His eyes at times made her think he truly had paranormal abilities. Had his intuition whispered to bring her a book of love poems because, somehow, he knew how she felt? Emma always felt out of step in Khalid's presence. He thrilled her, mesmerized her, made her want him in every way possible. And he was off-limits to her for a damned good reason. Emma wasn't ready to toss her wounded heart into any relationship yet.

"Ah, yes. Well, a good, bracing cup of delicious chai will cure your sleepiness," Khalid chuckled. They made their way through muddy ruts, leaping over puddles and walking around the larger ones.

Emma glanced at her watch. It was barely 0800. The chow hall would be packed, the noise high and it was the last place she wanted to be. Right now, she felt terribly vulnerable. Was it the dream? Or something more? Emma swore she still felt every touch of Khalid, her skin still retaining memory of it. "Sounds good," she managed, her voice sounding strangled even to her.

To her relief, Khalid found an empty table in a far corner. She sat down with the book on the table and watched him thread through the men and women to get to where the Afghan widow sold the chai. Khalid had such grace. He walked with pride and almost always had a smile lurking at the corners of his sensual mouth. Fumbling with the book, Emma finally opened it. She began to read some of the poems. Instantly, heat nettled her cheeks and she slapped the book shut and pushed it away, as if would incriminate her. The memory of that very real dream was still too close, too evocative. Reading Rumi's poems was like fanning the fires of her desire once more.

Emma shook her head. Somehow, and God only knew how, she had to erase Khalid from her body and her yearning heart. But how? Emma couldn't blame Khalid for how her body was behaving. Did he know that casual smile of his just made her ache to grab him and haul him into her bed? Emma was sure he'd be shocked by her very brazen instincts. Khalid was gentleman, a throwback to another century where a man smoothly courted a woman with flowers, gifts, looks and compliments without ever touching her.

Sighing, she rubbed her face with her hands. What made her situation worse was that Emma wanted to be in Khalid's world. It was more than just sex. The mystery of the man himself compelled her. Not that he hid any aspect of himself, but her curiosity went much deeper. If Emma was honest with herself, she wanted to hear every thought Khalid had. What were his growing-up years like? How was he able to adjust to American life? What adventures had he had in the U.S. Army while learning how to fly the Apache? And how could a Sufi be a warrior? There was so much Emma wanted to know. And it was all personal. She spotted Khalid coming back, moving as quietly as fog around groups of people coming and going from the chow hall. In his hands, Khalid held two cups of chai.

Emma felt as if she were sitting on a volcano about to erupt. As Khalid handed her the chai and sat down opposite her, Emma did all she could to ignore her attraction.

"The chai will help you wake up," he observed wryly, lifting his cup in toast.

His teasing eased her anxiety. "Salud," she muttered, clinking the rim of his cup.

Khalid sat with his elbows on the table. "Have you looked at Rumi's book yet?"

"No," Emma lied. She didn't want to get on the topic of love with him. That would be like holding a grenade with the pin released from it. "These are whirling dervishes on the cover, aren't they?" Emma hoped this safe conversation would steer him away from the main topic of the book.

"Ah yes, the young men who spend years learning how to turn in a circle, remain grounded and yet, open their hearts to Allah." Khalid smiled. "They are the role models for the rest of us. I have seen some twirl for an hour or more without stopping."

Emma drank her chai, relieved the conversation was on religion and not her. "That's an amazing feat in and of itself. I couldn't twirl in a circle for probably more than thirty seconds before losing my balance and falling down."

Chuckling, Khalid said, "At one time, I begged my father to send me to a Sufi learning center. From childhood on I had seen the whirling dervishes at the festivals. They were magical! I remember standing in front of my father, his hands on my shoulders, and my eyes were huge as they whirled past us like tornados."

Emma sipped more of her chai. "I can just see you as a little kid: all eyes. That would be an incredible thing to experience." Emma recalled the magic carpet and genies of the *Arabian Nights*, and felt those myths were still alive—between them, for whatever reason. The magic seemed to leap to life every time they talked to one another. And now, she'd dropped their conversation to the personal level. Groaning inwardly, she felt trapped.

Khalid drowned in Emma's warm forest-green gaze. "Yes, I fell in love with the mystical segment of our Sufi way of life. My father gently turned me away from becoming a dervish."

"Do you regret that?"

"No. In reality, my father saw I was not ready for such schooling. I was a very adventurous boy given to taking risks and boldly exploring where few ever went." His smile increased. "He knew my love of flying. I thought as a child I could fly in the invisible ethers that the whirling dervishes flew on. My father was far more practical. He harnessed my love of flying with military service with the U.S. Army. I hadn't thought of that path, but it felt like the right one for me." He pointed his index finger upward. "When I'm flying, I feel like the dervishes, held in the invisible mystical hands of the universe. There's nothing quite like it."

"I agree," Emma said. "The sky takes away all my fears, worries and anxieties about the future."

"Hmm, perhaps we're both eagles of the Kush, eh?" he teased.

Emma laughed, and the words flew out of her mouth, "Oh no, you're a snow leopard! No doubt about that." And then, she gulped, set her mug down and realized her gaffe. Amusement glimmered in Khalid's expression.

"Indeed. You see me as a beautiful and rare snow leopard?"

Emma froze. No matter what she'd say, she would incriminate herself. *Damn!* Her heart sank into her boots. What had she just done? Was she so exhausted that she was unable to erect her defenses, keep the conversation strictly focused on their mission?

Khalid leaned forward, his voice dropping to an intimate whisper. "I often wondered how you really saw me, Captain Emma Cantrell. Snow leopards are perhaps the most beautiful and rarest of cats in the world. There are only a handful who live in the Kush. I was fortunate enough to see one, once. His coat was of soft gray-white with spots of brown that matched the mountain slope. He blended in so well that at first I did not spot him. But my friend, who was a biologist, did. I watched that cat move from one side of the rocky, unstable slope to the other. He had such feline grace, such quiet power and authority, all I could do was stare with admiration at him." Khalid sat up and gave her a dazzling smile. "So, you see me as a snow leopard. What a wonderful compliment. Thank you!" There was no question; his heart was opening to Emma.

# *Chapter 7*

When they landed at Zor Barawul, the April showers had eased up. It was almost noon when Emma powered down the CH-47 and shut off the engines. The village was a hub of activity. Two days earlier, it had been under attack by the Taliban. Now two A-teams were present. One was stationed on an outpost that overlooked the valley where Zor Barawul sat. The other team lived in the village itself.

It seemed nothing could dampen Khalid's spirits. He unhooked the jack from his helmet, pulled it off his head and seemed utterly unaffected by the violence that surrounded them. Emma marveled at that, but she figured, as her hands flew over the controls, that his Sufi perspective gave him that sense of protection.

The rains of April made the village a sea of mud. Warm in her thick nylon jacket and glad to be wearing it, Emma heard the ramp grinding down. On this particular flight, they had brought a dentist and a dental hygienist from Bagram. Emma wasn't happy about keeping the CH-47 on the ground all day, considering the recent attacks. Too often, if a bird stayed on the ground, the Taliban would sneak up and lob mortars at it. However, they'd be staying to help out and, near sunset, they'd fly the army dental team back to Bagram.

Turning in her seat, Emma stood up and saw her load master, Sgt. Steve Bailey unhooking his harness. The twenty-two-year old blond was tall and gangly. When Khalid walked back to help him organize the boxes to be off-loaded, she thought they looked like brothers bodywise. As always, Emma remained alert and on guard. She swept her gaze around the area where the helo was sitting. It was parked on the tip of the hill. There was a fifty-foot diameter landing area. The rocky slopes dropped off steeply to a valley a thousand feet below them.

Khalid eased between the cargo boxes. They were battened down with sturdy netting and nylon straps that kept the boxes from flying all over while they were in the air. He saw Abbas, a tall older village leader with a deeply lined, narrow face waiting for him near the ramp. He wore a dark-gold wool turban, a gray robe and wool cloak over his proud shoulders. His black and gray beard was neatly trimmed, his eyebrows straight and thick across his dark-brown eyes.

Emma smiled to herself as Abbas shook Khalid's hand, pumping it up and down. The leader then leaned forward and kissed the pilot on each cheek. This was a common Afghan custom and a sign of friendship. She heard Khalid murmur, *"As-salaam alaikum."*

Abbas returned the warm greeting with *"Wa alaikum*

*as-salaam wa rahmatu Allah,"* in return. That meant "And to you be peace together with God's mercy."

Emma liked the sincere greeting. Khalid had already prepped her for the important people who ran this village. At Abbas's side was his wife, Jameela. She was dressed in a black burka, only her cinnamon-brown eyes looking out through the cross-hatched material. Jameela had been college-educated in Pakistan and spoke fluent English. At her side was Ateefa, their daughter.

Emma felt her heart contract with pain at the sight of the five-year-old girl with a prosthesis on her right leg. Her black hair was clean, brushed and hung around her small shoulders. There were shoes on her feet. Emma knew most children in these border villages went barefoot all year long, even in the harsh, icy winters and cold, rainy springtime. Today, as she pulled the green scarf from the thigh pocket on her flight suit, Emma smiled to herself. A gaggle of wide-eyed, curious children of all ages peeked around the adults huddled near the last mud hut at the end of the village. They too had shoes. Not only that, they were dressed warmly in clothes that had been donated by Americans. Emma knew a lot had been done for this village and the people were grateful.

Placing the scarf around her head, Emma walked down the ramp. The A-team helped bring the boxes out of the cargo hold of the helo. Several wooden pallets had been set up by Bailey where the boxes would be placed. That way, the boxes remained dry and protected from the mud. There was an air of excitement, as if a festival were in progress. The U.S. Army dental team, consisting of two men, forged ahead of Emma. They would give their greetings to Abbas and then get on with their work.

A dental hut had long ago been set up and they came in monthly to help the villagers.

Emma waited to present herself to Abbas. When she was next, she murmured the same greeting, her hand pressed to her heart and giving Abbas a slight bow, a sign of respect. He'd never met her before and official salutations were a must.

Abbas thrust his hand out to her. *"Salaam,"* Emma said, as he shook her hand, warmth dancing in his dark eyes. He then leaned down and brushed a kiss on each of her cheeks. His beard tickled her. She returned the greeting and then stepped back. Her ability to speak Pashto to him made his eyes light up with surprise.

"Ah, you speak our language, Captain. That is an unexpected gift."

Emma smiled. "I'm working with Captain Shaheen and his sister Kinah for the next six months. He asked for someone who could speak Pashto. It makes it easier on everyone."

Abbas looked over at his wife. "Indeed, it does. Please, this is my beloved wife, Jameela. She will take you to our home where you will share a cup of hot chai with her. As I understand it, the desks for the children's school have arrived today. Perhaps you two can decide where they need to be set up? I will have my men take them out of the boxes and assemble them."

Emma nodded. "As you like, my lord. I'm here to serve." She saw the old man's expression soften and seemed grateful for their presence. Khalid had told her that Abbas was highly educated and had a degree in biology. He'd received university training in Pakistan and returned to the village of his birth. He had been responsible for breeding better animals, improving sheep's fleece and his progressive leadership had influenced a number of other border villages. The man was courageous in Emma's eyes. He had fought against the Taliban, but had caved to their demands when his people's lives were threatened. Now, with over a year's worth of U.S. Army protection and help, this village has flourished.

Jameela stepped forward and shook Emma's hand. "Welcome, Captain Cantrell. I'm so thrilled you are here with us. I am Jameela."

Smiling, Emma shook her hand. They traded kisses on the cheeks. Jameela brought her daughter forward. "And this is Ateefa, our youngest. Her leg was destroyed by a mine when she was three years old. Last year, thanks to Captain Gavin Jackson, a prosthesis was made for Ateefa. And look at her today! She has thrown her crutches away and can run and race with all her friends."

Emma crouched down and took Ateefa's small hand. The little girl was beautiful, with large black eyes and a sweet smile. "How do you do, Ateefa? I'm glad you have a leg to run around on now. How are you getting along with it?"

"Fine, soldier lady," Ateefa said shyly, putting her fingers in her mouth.

Emma chuckled. "You have a beautiful daughter."

Abbas touched his wife's shoulder. "Beautiful children from my beautiful wife. Go, Jameela. Take our guest and allow her to warm up in our house."

"Of course, my dearest husband," Jameela said. She held out her hand to Emma. "Come. This is an exciting day for all of us. The children have been longing to see their new desks. After some chai, I'll take you over to the house we have chosen to become our school for our children."

The excitement was palpable as Emma walked at Jameela's side. Ateefa and several other young children raced ahead. The main street had deep ruts created by the donkeys who pulled the carts. It seemed everyone was out to greet them. Emma felt her heart lift. This is what life was really about: helping those who had less than she did. She followed Jameela to a beautiful two-story stone building with a red wooden door. It was the only home that had two stories. All the rest were made of adobe mud bricks, or, for those who could afford it, built from stone.

Looking over her shoulder, Emma noticed Khalid with a heavy box balanced on one shoulder, leading the A-team down the street with their own boxes of desks. A number of children across the street stood at the opened door of what would become their school. They were like excited little puppies wriggling around, giggling, excitement shining in their faces. Emma smiled. It was a great day for Zor Barawul. Still, she felt tense. She sensed that the Taliban was nearby monitoring them and this sent a chill up Emma's spine as she entered the warm home.

Asad Malik watched the activity at Zor Barawul through a set of Russian binoculars. The beat-up set had served him well over the years. He'd killed a Russian officer with his pistol and divested him of anything of value, including his binoculars. It reminded Malik of their victory over the Russians who had tried to tame the wild Afghan people. They hadn't succeeded, and if he had anything to do with it, the Americans and the

U.N. would leave with their tails tucked between their legs, too.

"What do we do?" Merzad asked as he stood near the opening of the cave looking across the valley to Zor Barawul.

"Nothing," Malik murmured. "Not yet..."

Frowning, Merzad offered, "You know, we have two new boys, orphans, with us. Why not send them into the village as our spies? Let them pretend to be hungry and lost. Someone will surely help them. With all the food, money and medical gifts old Abbas has gotten in the last year, they will take in our 'lost' boys. They could become our eyes and ears, Lord Malik."

The plan wasn't a bad one. Malik dropped the binoculars back on his chest. Turning, he nodded. "That's a good plan. Our only problem is we haven't had either boy long enough to brainwash them properly. What if they run away and side with Abbas? What then?"

Merzad shrugged. "When you rescued them three months ago, they were starving. They've been treated with nothing but discipline, been given food, a blanket and I believe they can be our spies without concern."

Rubbing his beard, Malik glanced over his shoulder. Both boys were sitting near the fire, recently fed and cleaning some of the weapons for his soldiers. Their jobs were to clean weapons, help the cook, water the horses and do the bidding of his soldiers. Soon, they would be taught how to fire the weapons. For now, cleaning a rifle was crucial because it taught them about the weapons and it gave them prestige within the group. Being trusted to handle such weapons earned them respect from his soldiers. The boys desired to be a part of his family.

"Benham is thirteen. He's got the slowness of a donkey pulling a cart, though."

"Agreed," Merzad said in a low voice so no one could overhear them. "He's slow but very loyal to us."

Malik's gaze moved to the ten-year-old boy crouched nearby with a partly dismantled AK-47 on a thin, tattered blanket before him. "Fahran is the smart one." The scrawny child wore a dark-blue woolen robe, his feet bare and sticking out from beneath the dirtied material. He had black hair, startling green eyes and he reminded Malik of a wily fox.

"You have doubts about Fahran?" Merzad probed. "When you say nothing but you look for a long time, I know there are problems you are contemplating."

Malik gave his compatriot an appreciative glance. Merzad was forty-five years old and his best friend. Having been born in the same village gave them a bonding like no other. Merzad had saved his life a number of times and vice versa. Malik trusted few, but Merzad had earned his trust. "I'm unsure about him, that's all. He's very young."

"But alert and smart," Merzad offered. "He's learned how to take apart an AK-47 and put it back together as no one we've ever seen. Even now, he instructs Benham on the next step. That older boy has been at it as long as he, but Benham stumbles and is forgetful."

"Mmm," Malik said, hand on his beard, studying the two youths near the fire. "The real question is: do I trust Fahran on such a spy mission?"

Saying nothing, Merzad stood quietly. He knew better than to argue Malik in or out of anything.

"Benham comes from a farm-laborer background," Malik said, talking to himself. "He has no education whatsoever. Our men are teaching him to read by learning the Koran. Fahran has been schooled and comes from a well-educated family in his village. He reads, writes and speaks several dialects already."

"Do you think he knows English?"

"How could he?" Malik said, looking over at his friend. "He comes from an Afghan border village in the north. According to him, his parents took their schooling in Pakistan. No, I doubt very seriously if he knows English."

"If you are considering him for this mission, I can ask him," Merzad suggested. "If he does, that would be a strong reason to have him go. He could eavesdrop on the Americans. They'd never suspect someone like him would know English, much less understand it."

Nodding, Malik said, "Have one of our men ask him. Then, let me know."

"Of course," Merzad said, leaving his side.

Malik turned and placed the binoculars to his eyes once more. How badly he wanted to sneak over under the cover of night and lob a rocket or mortar round into that helo. Chances were that it would lift off before dark. They rarely left any helicopter on the ground overnight.

His mind turned back to the ten-year-old Afghan orphan, Fahran. Malik didn't fully trust anyone that smart. His loyal soldiers could read the Koran but few knew how to write. He wanted to keep them dumb. It suited his purpose. Merzad, of course, knew how to read, could write and spoke a number of different dialects, but Malik trusted him.

The boy with the bright-green eyes, his black hair straight and shaggy around his head, was quick and agile. His small, greasy fingers flew over the weapon with knowing ease. Malik had entered a village one night where his men had killed a number of Sufi families. One of his soldiers found Fahran hidden beneath a bed, shivering like a dog. They'd dragged him out, kidnapped him and brought him along with them because they needed young boys for their unit. Benham had been found in shock, wandering around outside the village, crying for his parents, who had been killed.

At first, Malik recalled, Fahran had tried to run away several times, and each time, he was caught. Finally, the soldiers kept a rope tied around his thin ankle. If Fahran tried to escape, the rope would tug in the soldier's sleeping hand and awaken him. Fahran had tried it once and was whipped soundly, his back bleeding from ten lashes. After that, Fahran seemed to accept his fate. But had he really surrendered? Malik didn't know and wished mightily that he had the answer to that question.

With a sigh, he returned to watching the activity across the valley. Merzad would find out if the boy knew English. For Malik, that would seal the deal one way or another.

"Look! Look!" Ateefa cried, sitting down at the first assembled desk. She beamed with excitement at her parents who stood in the large, cold room smiling down at her with pride. All around her men were tearing open boxes and everyone was assembling the wooden desks. Children were barely able to stand still as they waited to be assigned a desk by Jameela.

Emma stood near the wife of the leader, smiling. There was an air of celebration, the room filled with men, the laughter of children and as many families who could squeeze in to watch the miraculous event. She thought about American children who took a school desk for granted. Much of the world did not possess the riches of America, and watching Khalid and the A-team work to assemble the desks made Emma's heart warm with pride.

Jameela joined the wives of the other children and asked them to open several boxes that held crayons, notebook paper, pens, pencils, rulers and erasers. The small group of younger women eagerly descended upon the huge box, glad to be part of the activity. Immediately, all their children gathered around the boxes, touching the cardboard and anxious to see what was inside.

Emma couldn't help the men with the desks, although she wanted to. That was considered a man's job, not a woman's. Several more A-team members set up the newly assembled desks. Others hauled away the cardboard and placed it in neat rows in front of a huge green chalkboard that had been hung in place earlier in the morning.

She saw the joy in Khalid's ruddy features as he crouched and gathered the pieces to assemble another desk. Emma didn't want to feel so good about watching him. His long fingers moved with an assuredness and precision that made her crave his touch. She couldn't erase the haunting dream of him courting her, kissing her. Every time his gaze met hers, she quickly averted her eyes so that he couldn't, somehow, read what was in her thoughts and heart. What to do? This wasn't getting any easier, Emma realized with a sinking feeling.

Of course, it didn't help that she was drawn to the man who read love poems by Rumi, either. In her foreign language class she had read his poems, and she understood why Khalid was a devout reader of his work. The ancient mystic touched her heart and soul as well. Who wouldn't be touched by this man's greater awareness of the human condition, his acceptance of the fact that no one was perfect, and yet that we all deserve another chance? Emma liked Rumi a lot, but she wasn't about to confide that to Khalid since it would make their relationship that much more personal. Right now, she had enough to juggle emotionally about the Afghan pilot.

Emma watched as several children mimicked the A-team members by helping them haul the cardboard out of the classroom. It wouldn't be wasted. The cardboard would be taken to a barn for future use by the villagers. The mountains in this area had a lot of brush and very few trees. Wood was hard to come by. The cardboard would be a welcome fire starter in the mornings around here, Emma realized.

Khalid set up another desk. As they were put into working order, Jameela announced the name of the next child to be assigned that seat. Emma watched the pride and excitement in the eyes of the children, and the hope mirrored in the faces of the proud parents. Her heart opened to Khalid, who dusted off his hands and walked toward them. Kinah had the supply box. She handed out all the items to the parents, who in turn, gave them to their children. Truly, Khalid and his sister were changing the world one child, one village at a time.

The warmth in his sparkling blue eyes stole Emma's breath for a moment. It was a fierce, burning look Khalid gave only to her and it made her feel so special. Blessed by her lover's gaze, as Rumi would say. Khalid moved over the cardboard debris to reach Abbas's side. How shaky she felt after that hooded look that had lasted only a fraction of a second between them. Emma tried to ignore it.

If only she could find something to dislike about Khalid and focus on that. He was terribly human, but as for a real flaw? She couldn't detect one—yet. It could be the one thing to protect herself from wanting a personal relationship with him. The more she worked with Khalid, the more Brody Parker dissolved into her past.

# *Chapter 8*

"Come," Khalid entreated Emma as she stood near the edge of the village. The sun had just set and the grayish dusk was upon them. "Let's give the sergeant relief from staying with our CH-47. He needs to eat before we leave."

Emma hadn't seen Khalid the rest of the day. The men had been busy over at the schoolroom, and she'd been with the women and school supplies at another nearby home. Her heart beat a little harder to underscore the dark and light playing across his face. Those dark-blue eyes were narrowed and filled with desire—for her. Gulping, Emma nodded. They fell into step while avoiding the donkey-cart ruts down the center of the muddy street.

"So, how was your day?" Khalid inquired. Up ahead their transport helicopter sat like a dark hulk. As soon as the load master who guarded the helo returned from eating in the village, they would lift off and fly back to the base camp. No one kept a helo on the ground overnight out here.

"Busy," Emma admitted, smiling a little. "The women got all the school supplies divided among the children. They'll have everything they need for tomorrow's first class."

"Good. We got the desks all assembled, finished off some last-minute things in the room itself and now it stands ready for use." Khalid rubbed his hands and gave her a satisfied smile. "We've done good work today, Emma." And then he grimaced. Khalid hadn't meant to call her by her first name. That was personal, not professional. Giving her a quick glance, he saw her eyes widen considerably over the gaffe.

"I apologize for that slip," he murmured.

Emma couldn't be angry at him. The way her name whispered from his lips sent a tantalizing sensation across her skin. "I guess when we're alone, we could use first names," she said.

Holding up his hands, Khalid said, "I want what makes you comfortable. I know you prefer professional military conduct between us." Khalid didn't want that, but he had no choice. And it formed a buffer zone between them so that his aching need to kiss her, to court her, was stopped cold.

As she reacted to Khalid's earnest look, an old block in her heart melted. How long could she go on pretending she wasn't drawn to this heroic man? No matter what Emma tried to do, she could no longer erect Brody Parker's face and memory as a wall between her and this handsome pilot. "It's okay," Emma reassured him.

Relief and terror surged through Khalid. This was

new footing, and it was like going down slopes with rocks that slid from beneath him. Instantly, he felt thrown into turmoil because the expression in Emma's eyes rocked his foundation. He saw desire in her eyes. For him.

As they approached the helo, the load master came out to meet them. Emma ordered him to the chieftain's house for dinner. His face lit up and he eagerly trotted back into the village. They climbed into the fuselage via the lowered ramp. Emma automatically swept her gaze around the bird to ensure all the cargo had been removed. The fuselage sounded hollowly as they walked toward the cockpit.

Emma took the right seat and sat down. Khalid hesitated a moment, pulled something out of his large right leg pocket and then sat down. Curious, Emma saw he had a small book in his hands. Looking out the window, she searched the area for movement as a matter of habit. The A-team had a member out on guard walking the perimeter around the helo. She knew the Taliban was active at this time of day. Like nocturnal animals, they stirred at dusk and hunted throughout the night.

For the first time, Emma spoke his first name. "Khalid, did you see those two boys? Those two poor little orphans who came in earlier today asking for help?"

Nodding, he placed the book on his thigh, his hand across it. "Yes, Benham and Fahran. Abbas took them in. With so many family members being killed by each side, children are left to fend for themselves."

"It's horrible," Emma muttered. "It just tears my heart out of my chest. Those two children had no shoes and they were wearing such thin clothes. I don't know how they survived the nights in these mountains."

"That was curious to me, too," Khalid murmured. "It's freezing at night. What they wore wouldn't keep them from dying of hypothermia."

"They probably slept in tight little balls against one another," Emma said. "They're so cute. Benham is shy. He wouldn't look anyone in the eyes."

"That's not uncommon. These children have PTSD and they're traumatized to the point that they don't know who to trust any more. They're orphans of war."

"Fahran told Abbas that they came here because they heard that Americans were giving food and clothing away."

"Word carries fast," Khalid said. He watched the soft gray dusk accentuate Emma's freckles. Once inside the helo, she'd removed the hijab and ruffled her fingers through her hair, catching the strands and taming them into a ponytail. Soft, curled tendrils along her temples emphasized the anguish in her green eyes. "Well," he said, "let me read to you from Rumi." He held up the book. "My father gifted me with this set of poems when I was five years old. You can see how dog-eared and worn the book is." He gave it a fond look as he lifted it toward her to inspect.

Emma could see that the title on the small red leather book was nearly worn off. She couldn't make it out. "Oh, so you're going to read to me?" Thrilled by the offer, Emma wondered why, but didn't want to spoil the magic of the moment. She was exhausted trying to ignore his masculinity, his worldliness and kindness toward others. Maybe, just this once, it would be all right, she told herself. All right to let down her walls and just be with him in this stolen moment.

"Of course," Khalid said. He opened the book and gently laid it across his thigh. The light of dusk filtered through the Plexiglas to highlight the words written in Pashto. "He is our greatest Persian poet and mystic. His words touch the soul of a person, regardless of their faith and beliefs. He was so connected to the Creator that he transcended his own Sufi boundaries to see that all of us are loved."

Sitting back in the seat, Emma watched Khalid's darkened form in the copilot's seat. She absorbed the grace of Khalid's long fingers. He reminded her more of an artist than a combat helo pilot. "I haven't had anyone do this for me except when I was a little girl. My parents would come in and read to me. I loved that time. I remember being in bed with my stuffed bear, Mr. Brownie. Mom would play the part of the woman in the story and Dad would be the man." Emma smiled in remembrance. "That was so much fun…."

"Reading is a way to open a person's heart," Khalid agreed. "It shows care, respect and love."

Emma felt her heart thud on that comment. Khalid's warm look stirred her body. He touched her on a level no man had ever reached. Emma was afraid to tell Khalid that, for fear that she would lose control. And that just couldn't happen.

"Well," Khalid murmured, "I have chosen some of my favorite quotes from Rumi that I'd like to read to you."

Just the way Khalid softly spoke the lines in his husky voice made her feel as if warm honey were being poured over her. Touched beyond words, Emma struggled to find her voice. "That was a beautiful poem." She considered Rumi's words for more than a minute. Khalid sat quietly, hands resting over the book balanced on his thigh. He seemed at peace, undisturbed by the war-torn world that surrounded them. "It sounds as though Rumi knew through experience about love."

Nodding, Khalid said, "Yes, Rumi knew the great highs and lows of loving another just as we do. He had a great love and then it was torn from him." Khalid touched the edge of the book with reverence. "Rumi led a hard, demanding life. That is why I believe so many people around the world, regardless of their personal belief system, can relate to his poems."

Sighing, Emma looked through the Plexiglas at the graying world, "I've never known that secret sky he spoke about in his poem…." Then she caught herself, blushed and gave Khalid an apologetic look.

"There are many types of love," Khalid agreed. "Rumi, because he was a mystic and desired to know the Creator, walked through trials by fire in order to fulfill his desire. To do that, one has to experience these things as other people do. But—" Khalid smiled a little "—he knew love and many of his poems are a reflection of that. It isn't always love between a man or woman, it can be the love you have for your parents, your friends or your relatives."

"He sounds like he was a very astute observer of life," Emma said. "I really wish now that I had studied Rumi more back at language school. I like how he sees our messed-up world."

"Let me read you another poem," Khalid said, and carefully turned the page on the very old, well-used book.

Emma felt as if that poem was about her, about the walls she was trying to build within herself to stop herself from liking Khalid. Shifting uncomfortably, she refused to meet Khalid's inquiring gaze after he finished the reading. His expression softened.

"I know that something exists between us," Khalid began gently, getting Emma to look into his eyes. "I feel you pulling back, Emma. I think I understand why, or perhaps I don't at all."

*Ouch.* Emma sat up, hands clasped tensely in her lap. "Are you always this direct?"

"I speak from my heart," Khalid said. "I know no other way. Do you?"

The man was so open and vulnerable right now that Emma couldn't just fire off some sniping comment and escape from the helo. The sincerity in his darkened eyes called to her. "I…well…" she hesitated. And then, she knew she had to be equally honest with him. "Look, Khalid, you're my boss. I don't think a personal relationship is appropriate. Do you?"

"I wasn't expecting to be attracted to you, Emma." He never broke eye contact with her. "For so long, I felt nothing at all after Najela's death. In fact—" and he straightened and looked out at the darkening world beyond them "—I did not realize my heart was healing from that tragedy until I met you."

Emma sat immobile, confused. "Oh…" was all she could manage.

Khalid wrestled mightily with his past. After Najela's death, he'd sworn never to fall for another woman and put her into danger. Now his resolve was disappearing. All he wanted was a closer connection with Emma. The more he tried to stop himself, the more he felt driven to do the unthinkable.

Khalid could see the bewilderment on Emma's face. Without thinking, he stood and leaned over her. His hand slid across her jaw to cup her cheek. Bending his head, he gently placed his mouth across Emma's parted lips. Her breath was warm and sweet, her mouth soft and tasting of cinnamon chai. He felt Emma stiffen and then, surrender to his kiss. There was such hesitancy and, yet, a sense of yearning as her mouth slid provocatively against his. The moment felt torn out of time and place. All Khalid could do was taste Emma, absorb the perfume of her skin, her hair and the silk of her mouth into his wildly pounding heart.

Emma suddenly jerked out of the woven heat of the moment. She looked up into Khalid's hooded, dark eyes that burned with need—of her. "We can't!" she cried.

Khalid stepped back, hearing such fear in her voice. His mouth throbbed with the kiss, the taste of her on his lips. The book was still gripped in his hand. "I'm at fault," he murmured apologetically. "After Najela's murder, I swore I would never get involved with another woman. I never wanted her harmed as Najela had been." He gave Emma a helpless look. "I'm so sorry, Emma, I don't know what happened."

Emma felt panic. She could still feel the masculine stamp of Khalid's mouth on her own. Oh, how she wanted him! All of him! The unexpected kiss broke open the lies she'd been telling herself. His mouth resting lightly on her own, his male scent consuming her, all conspired against Emma. The raw pain in his hoarse tone was evident. Najela's death had changed him forever. Opening her hands in desperation she said, "We've both got good reasons not to do this. I'm relying on you to give me a positive rating after this mission."

Khalid shook his head, his emotions still gripping him in a powerful hold. "But I will give you an excellent report for your personnel jacket. Why are you so worried about that? You are a good pilot, you care and you're an excellent officer. How could I not give you a glowing report?" Khalid knew from many earlier heartbreaks that some women could not tolerate his Muslim-Christian background. Maybe that's what this was all about. He borrowed from both great religions, but primarily was guided by his Sufi heart and soul. His heart never led him wrong, but Khalid had encountered a few women in his life who were not as tolerant as he was, and those relationships had broken up as a result. Was Emma wrestling with this issue, too? It didn't matter. He had to be responsible. Never would he place Emma in Najela's place. He just couldn't!

Khalid sat down. Emma looked as if she wanted to run away. Searching her face, he asked, "Is it because of my religions that I embrace, Emma? Does that offend you?"

Brows raising, Emma gasped, "Why—no! Of course not!"

"What then?"

Emma sighed. She had to tell Khalid why it was important to get a good grade on this mission. As quietly as she could, because she didn't want her voice drifting out beyond the helo to other ears, she confided in Khalid how she'd allowed Nike Alexander to give up her seat in the Apache to save a Special Force's sergeant's life last year. As she finished the story about the punishment she'd gotten, the demotion and the black eye it had given her famous military family, Khalid's expression changed from confusion to surprise and then, finally, understanding.

"Ah," he said, "I see why you are so distraught. It creates great pain for you to hurt your family's untarnished reputation. I get that." Khalid sat for several moments digesting Emma's conundrum. He could still taste her on his lips. He never wanted that sweet cinnamon taste to go away. The barrier between them was greater than he'd anticipated. And now he understood Emma's fear of intimacy with him.

"Can I convince you that I will give you a good mark for this mission?" he asked in a hopeful voice.

Emma grimaced. "So many things could go wrong, Khalid. It's not a matter of trust. It's about life. What if we got together and then broke up three months from now? You'd be hurt. Angry. And you could get even with me by giving me a very bad mark on the report." Emma shook her head. "No, I can't risk that. I'm sorry."

Tapping his fingers softly on the book, Khalid said, "I wish I could regret kissing you. But I cannot." His stomach roiled, his heart pounded as if he were being pushed in several directions—between the horrific past, wanting to love Emma and knowing he never could.

Emma shrugged, dodging his inquiring gaze. She stared down at her clenched hands in her lap. She could feel Khalid struggling with these issues. Emma felt she owed him the truth. Looking up, she held his gaze. "No, I can't regret it, either, Khalid. But there are other things involved."

"Such as?"

"Such as I'm on a second tour over here. In nine months, it's finished and I'm being rotated stateside. I have three more years on my officer's contract with the U.S. Army. I have no idea where I'll be sent."

"I understand. Many hurdles."

"Yes," she whispered, feeling emotionally exhausted. "And they are all out of my control."

"But," Khalid persisted with a gentle smile, "life always throws hurdles at us. I swore on Najela's grave not to fall in love with another woman and have her harmed by Asad Malik."

Now more than ever, it was time to tell Khalid everything. He needed to know about her own heartbreak. She couldn't hold back. Emma finally broke down and told him about Brody Parker. When she was finished with the deeper explanation, she said unsteadily, "Just as you have your own reservations about getting involved again, I feel the best thing to do is to walk away. We can't jeopardize this mission…or our wounded hearts."

The words were like ice. Khalid realized he was just coming out of two years of grieving over the loss of Najela. He was acting irrationally and expecting too much from Emma. It was her right to set the agenda. "I understand," he said. "I will honor your needs, Emma. I will remember our kiss forever." Moving his shoulders, as if to remove an unseen load, Khalid added, "I do not want to be a dark shadow that stains your life and stops that wonderful smile from giving others sunlight."

Feeling miserable, Emma muttered, "I appreciate it, Khalid. I'm just sorry it couldn't be what we wanted."

Khalid rose because he saw the sergeant returning from the village. "I am, too. Here comes our load master. We need to fly back to base camp now."

"Hey," Nike Alexander called, sticking her head inside Emma's tent, "how are you?"

Emma was just easing her flight boots off her feet when her best friend slipped through the tent flaps. "Hey, Nike. Good to see you."

"Girlfriend," Nike murmured, putting her hands on her hips and studying her, "you look like hell warmed over. Bad flight back from Zor Barawul?"

Sighing, Emma gestured to the chair next to her cot. “Have a seat,” she said. After she kicked her boots beneath the cot, she got up and tied the tent flaps together. She’d just arrived back to Bravo an hour earlier. It was cold, nearly freezing outdoors. As soon as Emma had got in her tent, she’d turned on the space heater to warm it up.

Nike put her helmet bag next to the chair and sat down.

Emma poured herself some water. “Want some?”

“Yes, thanks. We forget we’re in a desert, and none of us drinks enough to stay properly hydrated,” Nike said.

Emma poured a second glass and handed it to the Greek pilot. “You look like you saw some action. There was a lot of chatter on the channel as I was flying back.”

“Yeah,” Nike said, drinking the water in gulps. “The crap hit the fan over near the border about three miles west of Do Bandi.” Nike gave her an evil grin. “We creamed about fifty Taliban who thought they could sneak across the valley in the dark.”

“Wow,” Emma murmured, “that’s good.”

“Fifty that won’t be harassing those poor Afghan villagers in that area,” Nike said. She placed the emptied glass on a table next to where she sat.

“Yes, and Do Bandi is one of the villages we’re working in to bring education to the children,” Emma said, worried. She sat down on the cot next to her friend.

“So, what’s with you? Catching the flu? Rough flight back? Get shot at?”

Mouth quirking, Emma growled, “I wish it was one of those things.”

"Uh-oh," Nike said, grinning. "Man trouble."

"It's Khalid."

"Yeah, remarkable dude, isn't he? A stud. If I didn't love my guy like I do, I'd sure consider chasing him myself," she chuckled.

Emma searched her friend's face. "From the moment I saw him, I felt my heart twang like a harp. I fought it, Nike. I put up good reasons not to even think about being with this guy."

"But?"

"We were in the cockpit at dusk tonight. He came and sat down in the copilot's seat and started reading Rumi's love poems to me."

"How sweet!" Nike got excited. "Emma, that's wonderful! How many American guys would think of doing that?"

"Oh, you would react that way, Nike. Dammit! I need a little pity here, okay?"

Nike chuckled darkly. "What's standing in your way, Emma? You're not attached. And if you like him, what's the problem?"

Emma told her. She saw Nike lose some of her ebullience over the event.

"Oh yeah, I forgot about that. He is your boss, after all. And Brody Parker led you on and then crushed your heart. He was a sonofabitch."

"I really hurt Khalid's feelings tonight. He asked me if I trusted him to do the right thing. And I said I couldn't trust him."

Nike shook her head. "I feel for both of you. Right now, you're caught between a rock and hard place. Your first duty is to your family and expunging the bad name we managed to give it."

"Yeah," Emma sighed, "I know it. To be fair to him,

he's fighting his attraction to me because he lost Najela to Asad Malik. He doesn't want to put another woman in that bastard's gun sights."

"Mmm," Nike said, "He's caught between a rock and hard place, too."

"Yes," Emma said, feeling glum.

"Well," Nike said, patting her friend's sagging shoulder, "you do the best you can, Emma. The way I look at it, if it's meant to work out, it will. No matter the reasons, if it's meant to be, it will happen. You have this mission to toe the line on and get glowing commendations."

Giving Nike a warm look, Emma gripped her hand, squeezed and released it. "I just want to try and get my career back on track and get my family's good name polished up again."

"Right on," Nike agreed.

Emma pressed her hand to her heart, her voice low with unshed tears. "The problem is I like the guy. More than a little. This sucks.

"Doesn't sound like a problem to me." Nike gave her an encouraging wink, which didn't help matters.

# *Chapter 9*

"Brother," Kinah called to Khalid from the door of the school, "come visit with me."

Khalid halted in the center of the muddy street in Do Bandi. The late-April rains were starting once more. He wore his dark-green nylon jacket and a black baseball cap to shield himself. As he glanced over his shoulder, he saw that Emma remained at the CH-47, helping a group of medical people get their supplies. He hadn't seen Kinah in two weeks and he waved to her.

When Emma looked his way, Khalid motioned with his hand, signaling where he would be if she needed him. Today, he was the pilot and she was the copilot. It was her duty to deal with the details while he could be somewhat free from those responsibilities. Emma raised her hand in return and nodded.

Happiness thrummed through Khalid as he turned. A cluster of children surrounded him at the door where his younger sister stood. He pulled out handfuls of candy from the thigh pockets of his flight suit. Little hands opened. They didn't grab or fight. Instead, Khalid could see Kinah's firm but loving training.

"Well, well," Khalid said to them, "I believe you all need this." He handed out all the candy to the children. They were polite, smiling and they thanked him. Then, they scattered to the four winds, sweet treasures in hand.

Kinah laughed and stood aside so her brother could enter the now-empty classroom. "You are like Santa Claus to them, brother. And you spoil them. Every time you fly in here, they know it's you. I can hardly keep their attention when they hear your helicopter coming toward the village."

Khalid grinned, shut the door and embraced his tall sister. She was dressed in a cinnamon-colored wool robe and a bright-red hijab covered her black curls. "I can see your handiwork, sister," he whispered, giving her an evil grin as he stepped back. "They are acting with manners. Well done." Khalid scanned the area. "This looks great," he said. There were three large green chalkboards hung on three walls. Twenty-five desks were arranged in tidy rows. Kinah was one for insisting that children learn to be organized. Each desk had a notebook, a pen and a pencil on top of it.

Kinah slipped her arm around her brother's arm and walked him to her desk at the front of the room. "Do you have an apple for the teacher, too?"

"No," Khalid admitted, still smiling. "No apple."

Pouting, Kinah released his arm and sat down in her chair. She gestured for him to sit down in the sturdy wooden chair next to her desk. "I know, you save all your gifts for Emma."

Khalid sat down and took off his baseball cap. He shrugged and said, "Well, perhaps I did remember to bring you something." He dug into the pocket of his jacket. Kinah had a great love of Kit Kats, the chocolate wafer bars. She'd been able to get them only rarely after leaving America when her education was complete. He saw Kinah's winged brows rise, and she looked with curiosity at him.

"I met Steve Hudson, an army major at Bagram. He's assigned to fly with the Apache squadrons in the south. He just happens to be a good friend of mine. So I asked a favor of him…." Khalid drew out four Kit Kats and handed them to his sister.

Kinah gasped. "Khalid! You did it!" She grabbed them. "Oh, you are such a jewel, beloved brother!" Rapidly, Kinah tore off the wrapping and took her first bite of the Kit Kat.

Khalid laughed. "You look like an addict getting her fix, Kinah."

Giggling between bites, Kinah said, "Oh, I am! But better to be addicted to chocolate than opium."

On that note, Khalid lost his smile and became more serious. "Indeed," he murmured. It did his heart good to see his vibrant, feisty sister once more. Since Operation Book Worm had begun on April second, nearly four weeks ago, he'd rarely seen his sister. Kinah's job was to bring in teachers, create an atmosphere of learning and organize everything having to do with the children's education. Her tasks were at an end today at Do Bandi. Khalid and Emma would be flying her to Zor Barawul, where she would manage the educational program for two weeks, before they headed home today.

Kinah sighed, finishing off the first Kit Kat. "That

was pure heaven. Thank you, brother." She reached over and pinched his cheek.

Khalid caught his sister's long, fluid hand and placed a kiss on the back of it. "You were looking tired. I knew Kit Kats would refuel you." He released her hand. Kinah colored fiercely and pretended to give him a stern look.

"Brother, I fly on the wings of my heart's passion. You know that. And when you love what you do, all the energy in the world is available to you."

"You have always been guided by your heart."

She returned his look. "Is there any other way?"

"No," he agreed. Gesturing around the room he asked, "So, how are you? Have things been quiet here?"

Kinah sighed. "The last week has been peaceful. The Taliban, I think, realize that with an A-team stationed here, they cannot ransack and harm the villagers. It has been a very happy, relaxed place for once."

"Mmm," Khalid said. "The Taliban goes where there is no threat to them."

"That's getting hard for them to do with the border villages," Kinah said. "You should see the difference in the people here, Khalid. They are protected for the first time in many decades. They laugh. They smile. It truly warms my heart." She pressed her hand to her breast, tears in her eyes.

"The children look clean and their hair is cut and combed," Khalid agreed. "They are joyous. I can see it deep in their eyes."

Reaching out, she gripped Khalid's arm. "What we are doing, brother, is helping. I hope you know the extent of it."

"I do. But I always worry for you. Being out here alone…"

Kinah snorted. "I'm fine, Khalid! Do not look so

anxious. Save your worry for that red-haired woman who stirs the fires of your heart." Kinah saw her brother suddenly lose all his vitality, his eyes dark. "What?" she demanded, leaning forward. "Khalid, what's wrong?"

"Oh," he murmured, "There is tension between Emma and me." Giving her an uncomfortable look, Khalid added, "We're drawn to one another, but neither can do anything about it for different reasons."

"What? The most handsome, richest man in all of Afghanistan? I know hundreds of young Afghan women who dream of you being their husband!"

Twisting in the seat, Khalid grimaced. "It's not that simple, Kinah. You know the military."

"Ohhh, my poor older brother! What could she possibly not like about you?"

Khalid held his sister's indignant look. "Emma likes me—"

"Well, there you go!" Kinah said, triumphant. "I was right! No woman worth her salt will not be swayed by your looks and kind heart."

"Kinah, let me finish…."

Pouting again, Kinah sat back in her chair. "Go on."

"Emma has a six-month mission assignment. Technically, I'm her boss as the military sees it. At the end of those six months, I must write a recommendation based upon her performance over that time."

"Emma is a hard worker!" Kinah said. "She's kind, responsible and cares. I'm sure you'll give her the praise she deserves in that report."

"Yes, I will." Khalid gave his sister a look, pleading with her to stop interrupting him. He told Kinah the rest of the story. When he finished, he added, "And so, she cannot get involved. If she did and we broke up, she's afraid I would give her a bad grade and recommendation. That would hurt her military career. And frankly, I hadn't thought of that angle at all. But she's right."

Snorting again, Kinah leaped out of the chair and began to pace the room. "This is silly stuff, Khalid. I see how Emma looks at you. I certainly see the look on your face. Clearly, you are both falling in love with one another!" She threw up her hands and looked at the ceiling. "Surely, Allah, you can get these two stubborn donkeys together? Rip off their individual blinders so they can see?"

Khalid chuckled over his sister's dramatic antics. "Kinah, come, sit down…."

"How can I, brother? Surely," she protested, turning and standing in front of him, hands on her hips, "this is really about trust."

"Yes, it is," Khalid said, looking up at her demanding features.

"Emma doesn't trust you."

"That's right. She says I'm like the man who broke her heart. He too was rich and powerful. Only, he was married with two children, and he lied to her."

"Of all things!" Kinah stamped her foot and then said, "I will talk to her. I will tell her how sweet, how kind and how sensitive you are. That you would never break someone else's trust."

"No," Khalid said, "you can't talk to her, Kinah. It wouldn't be right. I'm hesitant to get into a relationship, too." He frowned and his voice lowered with anguish. "I can't because I want no woman murdered and tortured as Najela was. As long as Asad Malik lives, I will put no other woman beneath his sword. You know that. I've purposely avoided getting back into a relationship for two years now because of that price."

Rolling her eyes, Kinah muttered, “Men! You’re all alike. I swear by Allah, you are!” She cupped his jaw and looked into his anguished blue eyes. “This must stop, Khalid. You can’t put your life on hold because Malik is a threat. We may never see him die, and what will you do then? Live life as a monk? Deny yourself the happiness you deserve?” Removing her hand she straightened. “Khalid, do not be afraid to live once again. Don’t be scared of reaching out to Emma if she stirs your heart. Asad Malik wins if you deny yourself any sort of personal life.” She marched to the door and pulled it open.

Alarmed, Khalid leaped to his feet. “Kinah! Where are you going?”

“To see your beloved,” she sang out, sailing out the door and disappearing.

Khalid groaned, knowing he couldn’t make a spectacle of himself by rocketing out of the room and running down the street after Kinah. What had he done? It would only make things worse if he intercepted Kinah in front of Emma. And his sister wasn’t one to be stopped from her trajectory. Khalid knew she cared for him and she liked Emma. It was Kinah’s way of caring: getting involved as a possible future sister-in-law. Frustrated, he stood looking at the light filtering into the classroom. Emma wouldn’t be happy about this. And his sister had a goal in mind, Kinah was mission-oriented. Groaning again, Khalid decided the best thing he could do was visit the chieftain of the village, give his regards and find out if he needed anything from the U.N. forces.

“Emma!” Kinah called, waving at her. Emma stood near the ramp after giving the medical team directions into the village.

"Hey, Kinah!" Emma's smile blossomed genuinely for the firebrand woman. "How are you?"

"I'm fine, my sister." Kinah gave her an American hug and then the Afghan greeting of kissing her cheeks. Gripping Emma's upper arms, she said, "Are you feeling well?"

Emma laughed. "Yes. Why? Do I have dark circles under my eyes?"

Kinah took her hand and pulled her away from the A-team members who were walking the perimeter of the helicopter. "Come with me," she whispered dramatically. "We must talk."

Emma warmed to the small Afghan woman. The bright-red hijab reminded her of a red light flashing on a police cruiser. Smiling to herself, Emma allowed Kinah to pull her aside. The rainy skies threatened. A shaft of sunlight shot through like a beam down into the green valley far below. The wind was chilly and Emma was glad to have on her thick nylon jacket.

"Now," Kinah said, releasing her hand and remaining near Emma, "it appears to me that your heart has dark circles beneath its eyes!"

Studying Kinah's narrowing gaze, Emma said, "What?" Sometimes Kinah spoke in symbols and she couldn't follow the intelligent woman at all. Plus, Kinah, who loved all things American, mixed and matched Afghan sayings with American slang and sometimes, it all got jumbled for Emma.

"Do you like my brother?"

Before Emma could speak, Kinah held up her index finger the way a teacher would to a child.

"Before you say anything, my sister, I want to know how you feel. Not what you think." Smiling brightly, Kinah pressed her hand to her heart. "And no, Khalid did not send me out here to harass you. I've decided to find out the truth for myself."

Unable to stop her smile, Emma quickly grasped what was happening. Sometimes, Kinah's excitement and sureness sent her like a juggernaut into a situation or in this case, into a person—her. "Did Khalid tell you why I can't like him?"

"Oh, pooh!" and Kinah waved her hand impatiently and wrinkled her fine, thin nose. "Whys do not count, sister. Only your heart counts!"

Emma rested her hands on her hips and appreciated Kinah's misguided efforts. "I'm sure he told you why I can't cross that line."

Widening her large eyes, Kinah whispered fiercely, "Yes, he told me. Emma, why do you deny your heart its yearning? My brother likes you. Allah knows, he moons like a dog that has lost its mate. He told me why you think you cannot like him, but I say this is foolishness. How often do you think love happens between two people? Not often. And you deserve happiness, Emma. I know my brother will make you ecstatically happy."

Emma held up her hands. "Whoa, Kinah. Slow down, okay?"

Laughing, Kinah shook her head. "Slow down? Does the heart ever slow down? Of course not. Emma, I know you care very much for my brother. When you think I do not see the look you give him, or that he gives you, I remember it." Kinah tapped her temple. "You are suited to one another. Perfectly. I see no reason not to allow Khalid to court you as is our custom."

Emma saw the burning hope in Kinah's eyes. She was incredibly beautiful, with a square face, a stubborn chin, gorgeous high cheekbones and a broad brow. Emma had wondered many times why Kinah had never married.

Surely, she'd had suitors. Emma made a mental note to ask Khalid sometime about that. "I love you dearly, Kinah, but there can't be any courting. I'm sorry, but my life belongs to the U.S. Army. I'm not as free to follow my heart as you think." She touched Kinah's proud shoulder. "I think the world of Khalid. You're right: he's an incredible man and truly deserves happiness after losing Najela. But I'm not in a position to do anything about it, Kinah."

Touching Emma's reddened cheek, Kinah whispered, "You are wrong, but I understand better what Khalid had told me about the two of you. I see that there are other priorities that must be sorted out first."

Emma smiled gently. She loved Kinah's fierce independence, her willfulness, her heart brimming over with a desire to lift others and give them a better way of life. "That's a nice way of putting it," she told her.

"And what if these priorities sort out?" Kinah asked, slyness in her tone.

Emma chuckled. "Oh, you're such a crafty fox, Kinah! Just be patient. I don't know what the next minute will bring. Or the next hour. In our world of the military, all I can count on is change."

"But you like my brother?"

"I do," Emma hesitantly said.

"Does he not melt your heart?"

Sighing, Emma nodded. "He can melt butter with those looks he gives me sometimes."

Clapping her hand, Kinah said, "Wonderful! I have prayed to Allah daily that my dearest brother would be healed of his wound and loss. I prayed that a new woman might enter his life, awaken his numbed and shocked heart." She gripped Emma's arm, giving it a small shake. "My brother is one of the finest men you will ever meet.

He appears kind and gentle, but he carries the heart of an Afghan snow leopard. He is a warrior, but he knows when and how to display that side to himself. He can be your best friend, Emma, if you allow him that. Perhaps that is all you can share with one another right now, but allow him that at least."

"You're such a used-car salesman, Kinah."

Kinah laughed. "Thank you, dear sister. That is a compliment! Afghans are great traders, as you know."

When the Silk Road existed, Emma knew, Afghanistan was little more than four hundred different tribes. And they traded lapis lazuli, the bright-blue stone, for much money and goods. Trading was, indeed, in their DNA. "Yes, *you* certainly are." She looked at her watch. "Kinah, I have some things I have to attend to."

"Of course," Kinah said. "I'll meet you here once I find my handsome brother."

Emma watched the elegant Kinah turn and walk with pride in her steps. Unable to be angry over her overture, Emma hurried up the ramp to find the lists that she had to check. She wondered if Khalid knew that his sister had come to plead his case with her. Somehow, Emma felt Khalid would be embarrassed by it, but who could stop Kinah?

# *Chapter 10*

Back at base camp, Emma walked with Khalid over to Ops. There they had to fill out the mandatory after-action flight reports. The April skies had cleared and now a cool breeze blew across the area. Helicopters of all types were coming in before night fell. Only the Apaches with their 24/7 ops ability ruled the night air.

Khalid opened the door for her and they made their way to a small room off to the left of the busy Ops desk. After shutting the door, Emma set her helmet bag on an empty table, grabbed the report forms and sat down. Khalid did the same.

"So," Khalid said as he looked up from his form, "my sister grilled you. I'm sorry, Emma, I didn't want her to say anything."

Touched by his sincere apology and the worried look in his blue eyes, Emma stopped herself from reaching across the table to touch his hand. How easy it was to let herself simply be lulled into Khalid's world of the heart.

"Don't worry about it." Emma pushed some strands of hair off her brow. "Kinah is a force of nature that no one can stop. She was very nice about selling you to me."

Khalid sat back and looked up at the ceiling for a moment. "I knew she'd do that…."

"Hey," Emma murmured, sympathetic. "She loves you, Khalid. She's a great sister. I have sisters, too, and I'd want them to circle the wagons to support me."

"Do they?" he asked, resuming work on his report.

"Yes. We're tighter than fleas on a dog."

Laughing at the slang expression, Khalid shook his head. "Well, I ask your forgiveness for my beloved but impetuous younger sister."

"I weathered it," Emma said dryly.

After filing their reports, Khalid prepared to check out an Apache helo. He would fly it back to Bagram Air Force Base. Emma rose and collected her gear and walked to the door. Outside the thin wooden door she could hear the noise of Operations: the laughter, the people talking, along with the sound of airplane and helo engines.

"I'll see you tomorrow at 0800?" Khalid asked as he opened the door. How badly he wanted to romance Emma, but he knew it was folly. If anything, Khalid realized his growing desire for Emma would truly have to be tabled forever. The pain in his heart was constant over that realization.

"Yes," she called over her shoulder. Emma lifted her hand in farewell. "Have a safe flight home, Khalid."

He watched Emma disappear in the crowded Ops and his heart contracted with sadness. Turning, he walked up to the Ops desk to fill out a flight plan before he left for Bagram.

* * *

Emma was jolted out of her early-morning sleep by a sergeant who came to her tent.

"Captain Cantrell?" the woman sergeant called.

Disoriented for a moment, Emma said, "What? What's wrong?"

"Ma'am, Zor Barawul is under attack. We need every available pilot!"

Adrenaline shot through her and she leaped off the cot. "Has Captain Shaheen—"

"Yes, ma'am. He's on his way to pick you up right now. You have about ten minutes before he arrives here at the base."

Emma turned on a small lamp that gave her enough light to get dressed and hot foot it over to Ops. "What's the report on the village? Do we have Apaches in there?" Grabbing her flight boots, she jammed them on her feet.

"Yes, ma'am. Two Apaches were sent there about thirty minutes ago when the attack by the Taliban began."

Emma quickly caught her red hair into a rubber band at the nape of her neck. She stood up, grabbed her helmet bag and rushed out the tent flap. The sergeant trotted alongside Emma. Overhead, the night sky twinkled with bright, white stars. A thin slice of moon hung in the sky. The air was cold but not freezing.

"What else?" Emma demanded, jogging down the road between lines of tents.

"Ma'am, they think it's Asad Malik attacking. It's his signature and the A-team is calling for reinforcements."

"Dammit," Emma muttered. Her brow wrinkled. One of the things they had done after they left the village of Do Bandi was to take Kinah north to Zor Barawul. She was to spend the next two weeks helping to get the teachers set up to teach. Was Kinah okay? Emma's heart contracted with fear for the woman.

The sergeant said, "Ma'am, I need to get back to BJS HQ."

"Fine, I'll be in radio contact with HQ on this, too." Emma lengthened her stride, fully awake now. By the time she arrived at Ops and signed in, she saw Khalid's Apache landing outside the doors. Once outside, Emma stood impatiently on the tarmac and waited until the blades had stopped turning. The flight crew quickly placed chocks beneath the three wheels.

As she quickly climbed up on the helo, she saw Khalid's dark and tense face. The other cockpit behind his had the canopy open. She hesitated for a moment. "Khalid, have you heard anything on the attack?"

"No, climb in."

Nodding, Emma swung into the seat and quickly got settled. A crew woman helped her strap in and then closed and locked the canopy before hopping down off the helo and pulling the ladder away. Time was of the essence. As soon as Emma got the helmet on her head and plugged into the communications system, she asked, "What's the last you heard, Khalid?"

"Let's do the preflight check. I'll tell you more after we get airborne," he ordered tersely.

The tension in his voice heightened Emma's worry for Kinah. Oh, God, what if she was hurt? Emma's hands flew with a knowing ease as she went down the check list for preflight with Khalid. Her heart pounded like a drum and speed was important.

The Apache shook and shuddered around them as Khalid, the air commander, got the helo up to speed.

Emma received permission from the control tower to take off. She noticed that the Apache was loaded with weapons. They were flying into combat, no doubt.

As the helo took off beneath Khalid's hands, Emma switched to the green light across her instrument panel and two screens in front of her. The green color was less harsh on her vision. Blackness surrounded them, the base camp quickly disappearing. They would fly at nine thousand feet toward Zor Barawul. Emma felt safe within the shuddering vibration of the Apache. She could sense Khalid's worry. What must it be like for him? He'd already lost the woman he loved. Now, he could lose his sister. Emma knew how close they were, how much they loved one another. "How are you doing?" she asked.

"The best I can," he growled.

Emma heard the terror in his low, husky tone. She could hear his fast and shallow breathing. "Does Kinah know what to do in a situation like this?"

"My sister is a survivor, if nothing else."

"And she's gone through attacks like this before?"

"Yes."

His voice was raw and strained. How would she feel if one of her sisters was in a fire fight with the Taliban? If the Taliban broke through, they'd kill Kinah on the spot. Lips tightening, Emma said in a soothing voice, "I know she'll be okay, Khalid. I feel it in my heart."

"Let us hope you're right," he rasped.

There was little else she could do. Emma felt a special kind of helplessness. She knew all the people at this village. Good, kind and generous Afghans who wanted nothing more than a life better than the hard-scrabble one they had to eke out in these desert mountains. And what of the A-team stationed there? Had they taken casualties? Emma couldn't stand not knowing so she dialed in the A-team frequency. Instantly, her ears were filled with the sound of gunfire, explosions and the yelling of orders between the captain and his men. No doubt, a fierce, ongoing battle. Gulping, Emma began to pray because at this point, that's all she could do.

Khalid circled the village of Zor Barawul, high up on a hill far above a narrow unseen valley below. His heart centered on Kinah, but he couldn't afford to go there. Right now, he was coordinating with the two Apaches already on station and working to kill the Taliban who had gotten very close to the village itself. In his gut, Khalid knew it was Asad Malik. Just the other day on a Taliban website, he'd read that Malik promised to kill him and Kinah. Was this the beginning of his campaign against them? Khalid had read Malik's spewed hatred against the education of girls. He'd railed against Kinah because she was a woman leading a fierce battle for peace and education.

Khalid had not told Emma about this website or Malik's promise. Grimly, he swung the Apache around as the air commander, Major Klein, ordered them to hover and fire rockets into a hillside about two hundred feet below the village. Unable to do anything but focus on the attack, Khalid worked constantly with Emma, who would handle the ordinance and fire the weapons.

Emma watched the explosions walk across the rock, dirt and thick scrub brush on the steep slopes. She heard Major Klein ordering another set of Apaches out of this fire fight, saying that they were low on ammunition. They would have to fly back to the base camp, take on another load of ordinance and then fly back here. Emma was amazed at the ferocity of the battle. The winking red and yellow lights of A-team members firing down the hill looked like Christmas sparkling in the night.

Emma worried for all the villagers, like Ateefa, the little girl with the prosthetic leg. How was her mother, Jameela? Was she holding her children and trying to keep all of them safe? In the mud homes, bullets could easily fly through the walls and kill someone trying to hide. Abbas had one of the few stone houses, but it had windows and bullets took no prisoners.

Her headphones jumped with more frantic calls from the A-team. A group of Taliban had breached the slope! She felt Khalid moving the Apache in that direction. With a sinking feeling, Emma saw the other two Apaches who had been on station flying off because they were out of ammunition. Now, it was up to them. Could they repel this attack? Hundreds of infrared bodies showed up on the slope via the one screen. The Taliban were like relentless ants crawling up the hill and cresting it.

"Medevac's on the way," Emma reported, hearing another channel. "A-team has four men wounded."

"Roger," Khalid growled. "Switch to Gatling gun. Hose that area where the enemy is getting over the top of that hill."

"You got it," Emma said. She felt the Apache bank, heard the engines thunder as her fingers flew over the console to engage the huge gun beneath the belly of their helo. At least twenty Taliban were now running full tilt toward where the A-team had made their stand. If they got past the A-team, they were into the village itself. And Emma knew they'd go house-to-house, firing inside and killing everyone without mercy. The villagers had some weapons but could never repulse an attack like this. They were helpless against these thugs.

Khalid took a big risk by flying in low. They were

well within range of the enemy firing a grenade up at them, or worse, a rocket. It was a chance they had to take. The helo shuddered violently as Emma triggered the Gatling gun. Khalid felt the floor of the helo vibrate heavily as the gun continued to fire. His feet grew numb from the shudder. He watched his other cameras because he knew Emma was engaged with the gun.

Suddenly, a bright light popped off the slope about two hundred feet below. "Rocket launch!" he yelled. Instantly, he shoved the throttles to the firewall, hit the rudders and made an effort to evade the fired rocket.

Emma cursed and quickly turned her attention to it. She hit the flares in the nose. They could possibly detour the rocket. Red flares lit up the sky. Her fingers flew to the trigger to fire their own rockets. She punched the button. Instantly, the Apache bucked from the rocket's fire. Bright yellow light momentarily blinded her. Her harness cut deeply into her shoulders as Khalid worked frantically to get the Apache out of the way of the oncoming Taliban rocket. Her eyes widened and her heart banged violently in her throat. Would the rocket hit them?

A million thoughts jammed into Emma's head as she watched, almost fascinated, as the ground-fired weapon hurtled up toward them. A rocket had heat-seeking abilities and she was sure it had locked on the Apache's overhead engines. Mouth dry, Emma suddenly felt her entire world slow down to single frames from a movie. She heard Khalid's heavy breathing. Felt the Apache screaming in protest as he continued violent, evasive maneuvers to try and outwit the oncoming rocket.

Then, at the last second, the Apache rocket locked onto the enemy fire and struck it with full force. The entire night lit up like a Fourth of July celebration.

Emma gasped and threw up her gloved hand to protect her eyes from the red, yellow and orange fireball that was no more than three hundred feet to their starboard. The resulting explosion sent a massive shock wave through the night air. It struck the Apache broadside. The helo shuddered and shook. Khalid wrestled with the controls in order to ride out the shock wave.

"Direct hit!" Emma yelled, her adrenaline pumping through her, making her anxious and yet angry. She had no time to sit and gloat over the fact they were still in the air.

"Back to work," Khalid snarled. "Gatling gun. We're going back in. The Taliban is still on top of the hill. We've got to stop them!"

For the next ten minutes, Emma's world revolved around halting the Taliban attack. Her headphones crackled with other communications. There were three medevac helos on the way. Khalid asked BJS 60 to send more reinforcements, saying that they were running low on ordinance. Emma was careful with the Gatling gun. Prolonged firing would only waste the precious ammunition. Instead, with Khalid's expert touch at the controls, she was able to use the infrared camera that showed body heat and fire it in short bursts. It saved their ammo and targeted the running groups who were trying to penetrate the village itself.

Sweat poured down Emma. Her gloves were wet, and she felt the trickle from beneath her armpits. Her gaze was glued to the television console, slipping back and forth between it and the infrared screen. Emma saw the Taliban being driven to a standstill. In the back of her mind, she worried that another rocket would be fired at them. They hovered less than four hundred feet above the fray and directly over the A-team like a big, bad guard dog. Bullets pinged off the Apache's resilient skin. The Taliban were now firing up at them, hoping to hit the rotor assembly above the cockpits and bring them down.

Time became suspended. All Emma saw was gunfire back and forth. The shuddering of the Apache vibrated through every cell in her tense body. Khalid's breathing was ragged and so was hers. This was a life-and-death effort. If they couldn't stop the Taliban from coming over the slope, the A-team would be overrun. Already, the A-team leader had called for reinforcements. They needed more ammunition. A CH-47 had been launched from the base camp with a resupply of ordinance for them, but none of it would get here in time. Emma knew it was only their being on station above the team that might tip the balance in their favor. If they hadn't hovered and stood like a gate guardian, the Taliban would have surged like a tsunami into the village, murdering men, women and children.

"Fire a Hellfire missile into that area where they've breached it," Khalid ordered her.

Emma rasped, "Roger that…" She quickly dialed in the Hellfire II. It was a brilliant idea. Why hadn't she thought of it?

"After firing it, I'm going to fly us around to attack that slope with what we have left in ordinance. If we can't stop them, everyone's toast."

"Roger," Emma said sharply, her mind focused on the missile. She flipped the switch. The Apache jerked as the missile slid off the rail. Light flared beneath the stubby wing. And then, she watched it hunt down the mass of men coming over that slope like a dark, malevolent ooze toward the village.

The entire night sky lit up again. Blinded, Emma

couldn't know how many that rocket had killed, but it had to be substantial. Rock, dirt and dust flew skyward. She felt Khalid wrenching the Apache in a sharp bank to the left. The shoulder harness bit hard into her and Emma tried to brace herself. Khalid was a skilled pilot and he knew how to push the limits of the Apache to get the maximum performance.

The helicopter thumped down, down, down the slope where there was no longer any enemy left alive. Emma tensed and held on. She worked to get the gun back online. In seconds, Khalid whipped the combat helicopter around to the slope where the Taliban had breached the hill. On the screens in front of her, Emma observed a lot of unmoving bodies. Down below them, however, was another mass trying to climb upward.

"Fire at will," Khalid muttered.

"Roger," Emma said, her voice taut. She triggered the gun again and again. The knot of Taliban scattered like a flock of birds that had had a rock thrown in their midst. "They're on the run!" she yelled triumphantly.

"Keep at it," Khalid ordered in a tight voice.

Between her skill at hitting targets and Khalid's ability to make the Apache dance like a ballerina in the sky, Emma was able to beat back the rest of the attack. In minutes, the charge was over. They swung around and around the hill looking at their infrared screens for any moving bodies trying to form another attack. Sweat ran into her eyes. Emma blinked several times. She pushed the perspiration away with her trembling, gloved fingers. She felt the Apache surge upward into the darkness.

"I think we got them," she told Khalid. Her voice was shaky; the adrenaline made it that way.

"Roger that," Khalid agreed, his voice thick with unspoken emotion.

"We're down to dregs on ordinance," she warned him.

"In five minutes, two more Apaches will arrive on scene."

Five minutes could be a hell of an eternity, but Emma remained silent. They kept flying around the thickly brushed slope below the village. Who was dead in Zor Barawul? Who was injured? She could hear the chatter between the A-team leader and the medevacs that would arrive on scene in ten minutes. Before they could land to take on the injured men, the place had to be secured and safe. That was their job: fly around and continue to be a threat to the Taliban, should they think of trying a second assault.

"Helluva night," Emma whispered into the microphone on the inter-cabin frequency.

"Yes. You're a good shot."

She heard a little relief in Khalid's voice. He was on an adrenaline high like her. Emma smiled a little. "You're one hell of a pilot, too."

"Thank you. Now we're a mutual admiration society."

Chuckling, Emma felt some of her own relief tunneling through her. "I'm worried about Kinah. I wish we could know how she is."

"I know…"

"Maybe we can get one of the A-team to go check in the village as soon as medevac arrives and takes their wounded back to the hospital at Bagram?"

"That's what I was thinking," Khalid said. He swung the Apache out in wider arcs as they approached the base of the hill where the village sat. "I wish we could land. But I know we can't."

Emma grimaced. "Take it from one who once did and suffered as a result, you don't want to do that."

Khalid smiled, but grimly. He kept his hands on the collective and cyclic, continuing to widen their hunt for whatever was left of Malik's group. He hoped Malik was dead. "No, I don't want to go there. When things get organized and calmed down, we can ask the captain to send a team member in to locate Kinah."

Emma saw the other two Apaches arriving on station. It felt good to see the combat helicopters loaded down with ordinance. "Whew, the cavalry has just arrived. Good to see them."

"Hey, Red Dog One," Nike Alexander called to them, "I hear you've been stomping the hell outta the Taliban. Good work. Doesn't look like there's anything for us to do. Bummer! Over."

Chuckling, Emma keyed her mike. "Roger Red Dog Three, we didn't leave much for you to clean up. Over."

"And here I wanted to dance on those bastards' heads," Nike chortled. "Over."

Khalid laughed and so did Emma. "We're going to hang around for a while longer, Red Dog Three. Over."

"Roger that. More Apaches are good. It will give those bastards second and third thoughts about regrouping to hit this village again. Any idea of casualties yet? Over."

"No, Red Dog Three. No sense of how many are dead or wounded. Over."

Emma sat back and tried to relax as Khalid urged the Apache to five thousand feet. She watched as the other two combat helos scoured the area, hunting like hungry wolves for any survivors. Grateful to this incredible machine, Emma knew they had saved Zor Barawul. At least this time. She wondered how Khalid was handling the fact his sister might be dead or injured. How badly she wanted to land, but they didn't dare break that regulation.

Emma switched to inter-cabin and asked Khalid, "You doing all right?"

"As best as I can. I'm worried for Kinah…."

"What if we get permission to fly back to camp and then we pick up a CH-47 and fly back out here? It will be dawn by that time and we'll be able to do it. That way, we can land and you can find Kinah. It might take an hour, but at least you'd be on the ground." A CH-47 had no nighttime gear on board and was only flown in VFR conditions where the pilot could do a line-of-sight visually.

"Good idea, thank you."

"I'll call BJS and get permission to head back to base," Emma said.

# *Chapter 11*

"Kinah!" Khalid called as he ran into the village shortly after Emma had landed the CH-47. Dawn crawled up the horizon, allowing them to fly back to the battered village. The A-team leader, Captain Jason Cunningham, had radioed in just as they landed the Apache at their base camp. They'd found Khalid's sister. Kinah had been wounded in the fierce fighting but had waived her right to be brought back on the medevac. There were men on Cunningham's team that needed medical treatment before her own wounds, she'd told them.

As he rushed into the schoolhouse, Khalid saw that hundreds of bullets had punctured the mud walls.

Kinah sat holding the two orphan boys in the schoolroom. "Khalid!" she cried, relief in her tone.

"Sister!" he rasped, his voice cracking with emotion. Kinah's hair was in disarray. Small oil lanterns burned and shed light into the gray space. Beneath each arm huddled one of the young orphans, Benham and Fahran. Both were pale, their eyes huge with fear. She sat on the floor, her back to one wall near the desk. She was not wearing a hijab. Tracks of tears streaked down her dirtied, tense face, making Khalid even more anxious.

"They said you were wounded," he whispered, kneeling down and tentatively touching her shoulder. He tried to keep the fear out of his voice as he searched for blood.

"Just a scrape," Kinah protested, sniffing. She held up her hand and showed him a graze of a bullet across her wrist area that had been hidden by her robe. As Khalid gently cupped her shoulders, she struggled to battle back her tears. Her lower lip trembled. "Khalid, it was awful! So many people were killed! I hate the Taliban! They did this to us!" More tears fell and made tracks through the fine dust across her face.

"I know, I know," Khalid soothed. He crouched before them. Gently touching each boy's head, he asked them in Pashto if they were all right. Each jerkily nodded they were okay. Khalid could see they were in shock by the glassy look in their eyes.

"I was in here," Kinah whispered, "with them. They wanted to help me clean up the room. Such good boys." She wiped her eyes and sniffed. "It was just shortly after dusk." Looking around at the holes and the cool air flowing through the schoolroom, Kinah sobbed once and then gulped back the rest of her tears.

"I dragged the boys beneath my desk and huddled with them in my arms. We were all crying, Khalid. We were so afraid. I've been in fire fights before, but this one was the worst I've ever weathered. I was fearful of the Taliban overrunning the A-team. Poor Captain

Cunningham! He and his men fought fiercely. All I wanted to do was keep the boys safe and survive this awful hell on earth!"

Touching her curly, dusty hair, Khalid gave her a sad smile. He pulled a green linen handkerchief from his pocket and gently dabbed her dusty cheeks. "It was bad," he agreed. "But you survived, Allah be praised. And so did these boys." He gave them a smile in hopes of letting them know they were now safe. "Are they wounded?"

"N-no," Kinah sniffed. She took the handkerchief and wiped her eyes. "A medic already came by and checked them over. He wanted me to leave for this silly scratch on my wrist and I told him no. The boys are fine. Just scared."

Who wasn't? Khalid nodded and helped each boy to stand. They shook like leaves in the wind. He then gripped his sister's hands and pulled her to her feet. Khalid briefly held her, placed a kiss on Kinah's damp cheek and looked deeply into her frightened eyes. His sister had been in two other villages where fire fights had broken out a year ago. This one, however, had scared her even more and shadows lurked in her brown eyes. "I want you to come home for a while, Kinah. Let the U.S. Army get this place more secured. Then come back here."

"No," she muttered, giving him a defiant look. Breaking free of his embrace, Kinah brought the two boys to her side and held them. Each clung to her robe.

Sighing, Khalid nodded. "I thought you'd say that."

"We can't leave. That would be a sign of defeat, Khalid. You know that." Kinah scanned the room riddled with bullet holes. "No, I refuse to run! I would say this is the work of Malik." Her brows dipped and anger tinged her husky tone. "That desert rat is behind this, Khalid. My gut tells me so. Last year up north at the other village where I worked so hard to get the people to build a schoolroom, he came in and shot hundreds of holes through it."

"Yes," Khalid said quietly, "I believe he's behind this attack." And he said no more. Both of them were aware of Malik's promise to kill them. It had almost happened last night. Khalid wanted desperately to remove Kinah from the village. As he looked into the stubborn set of her chin, he knew it was useless to insist.

"Where's Emma?" Kinah asked, wanting to move on.

"At the helo. We brought in a medical team and other emergency supplies." He glanced toward the door that had been splintered by gunfire. "I need to get back to help her. Will you be all right here?"

"I'm fine, brother. Go. I'm taking these boys to my home. They need to get washed up, find clean clothes and be fed some food. That's where I'll be."

Khalid leaned over and pressed a kiss to her damp cheek. "We will come to see you later," he promised, his voice thick with emotion. Turning on his heel, Khalid left the nearly destroyed classroom. A number of the desks were in shattered ruins, too. His heart ached for his sister. This time around, Kinah had been brutally impacted by the attack. The other two times last year were nothing in comparison to this one. Khalid could see that she grappled with the trauma of it all. Who didn't in this demoralized village?

Emma glanced up to see Khalid striding down the muddy street toward where she stood with the list of supplies in hand. How was Kinah? Anxious, she passed the list to her load master. A number of men from the village assisted what was left of the A-team to offload the emergency supplies. Five soldiers were on their way to Bagram for treatment of their wounds. The medical team, consisting of a doctor, a nurse and a medic, was already in the village helping those who had been hurt, but not badly enough to be medevaced to Bagram for treatment.

Meeting Khalid, she asked, "Kinah? How is she?"

Khalid told her. The morning was dawning clear after the storm clouds of yesterday. Emma's fine, thin brows moved downward as he finished.

"She's been traumatized," Emma growled, unhappy.

"Yes, this time it really got to her," Khalid agreed, his voice distraught.

"She won't leave?"

"No. Wild horses wouldn't drag her out of here now."

Seeing Khalid's worried, forlorn eyes, Emma wanted to reach out and embrace him. "I'm sorry, Khalid. War is ugly business. Everyone is hurt by it," she said, hurting for him.

"You should have seen those two orphan boys. They were shaking like little trees in the aftermath."

"The worst is how the children are affected," Emma agreed. "But they're with Kinah. She'll be a rock for them and she'll get them through this."

Khalid looked around. Bodies of the Taliban had been put to one side of the flat landing area. A number of Afghan national soldiers had come with them on their flight, and now they were going through each man's clothing to find identification. It wasn't a job he would want.

"Malik's behind this," he rasped to Emma as they walked back to the helo. Most of the crates were out of the bird and the last of the A-team men hefted supplies on their shoulders and took them into the busy village.

"It sounds like his signature calling card: destroying the schoolroom. The bastard," Emma whispered, angry.

Walking up the ramp, the load master, a twenty-year-old blond technical sergeant handed her another list. Emma stopped and signed it. She was AC, air commander, and therefore responsible to see the shipment was out of the helo and delivered to the proper village authorities. Khalid walked past her and sat in the left-hand seat. He moved his knees aside so she could slide between the seats and sit down in the right-hand seat. Even though she was the AC, Khalid was the head of this mission.

"What now?" Emma asked. Khalid's profile was silhouetted against the sunlight suddenly flooding into the cockpit.

"I need to talk with Abbas. By the way, their family is okay. Shaken up, but no injuries. Many of their windows are shattered, but they can be replaced."

"Good," Emma sighed. "I'm relieved." Living in a stone house rather than a mud one had its advantages in a fire fight.

Khalid glanced around. No one was near their helicopter. Driven by the anguish of his sister facing death so bravely, he couldn't help himself. Last night as he and Emma had fought the Taliban, he'd known that they, too, could die. And they nearly had when that rocket was fired at them.

Khalid's eyes narrowed upon her, burning with desire. Taken off guard by his sudden predatory look, she didn't see it coming. One moment he was in the chair and the next, he was standing. He cupped her face with his long hands and leaned down, sweeping a powerful kiss against her mouth. Emma stiffened momentarily. The heat of his mouth rocked her lips open. She felt his warm breath, smelled his spicy scent and tasted chai.

Her world dissolved beneath the swift, hungry kiss, his mouth sliding hotly against hers. Oh! Emma didn't know what to do. For so long, she had yearned for Khalid's mouth on hers once more. She wanted to feel his sensuous, exploring lips against hers, inciting her, teasing her and letting her know just how much he loved her.

Mind spinning as she hungrily returned his passionate kiss, his fingers moving through her hair and holding her prisoner against his searching mouth, Emma heard the word *love* reverberating through the halls of her wildly beating heart. Right now, Khalid's mouth was playing her as if she were a beloved instrument in his hands. His lips drifted from her mouth to her cheek, to her closed eyes and finally, back to her parted, wet lips. There was such tenderness in Khalid's slow exploration of her as a woman. And Emma wanted this. She wanted him.

Khalid's soul absorbed Emma. Never had he wanted a woman more than her. That shook his internal world. His grief was gone. In its place an assuredness that this magnificent and courageous red-haired American woman was priceless to him. Her mouth was soft and pliant, giving and taking. He'd been afraid she'd reject him, but, to his relief, once his mouth slid across hers in invitation, she'd responded just as eagerly and passionately as he. Perhaps it was the combat last night, their near-death experience? Khalid wasn't sure. What he did know without reservation was that he was falling in love with Emma.

As he sipped at her wet lips, Khalid smiled and whispered against them, "You are the sunlight to my darkness, beloved."

Just the way he whispered *beloved,* made Emma moan with pleasure. As she drew away, his face inches from her, the tender light burning in his blue eyes, she didn't know what to do or say. "Oh, Khalid," she managed in a strangled tone.

"I know," he said apologetically, releasing her. "We're in a very confusing situation." He stared down at her full mouth glistening in the wake of his worshipful kisses. Fighting himself, Khalid sat down. He reached out and gripped her hand. "We could have died in combat last night."

Emma closed her eyes, as she heard the urgency in his voice. She worried about someone seeing them kiss or holding hands. It was forbidden by military law. Opening her eyes, she cast a quick glance around. They were alone, and relief sped through her. She drowned in his pleading gaze. "In our business," she said in an unsteady tone, "we can die at any time, Khalid. You know that." He had been right, though. Last night's combat had been raw and violent. She was still edgy from it. So was he. Plus, Khalid had thought his sister might have died in the attack. Emma realized the pressures upon him and knew that he needed a safe harbor. She was that harbor.

Nodding, Khalid forced himself to release Emma's hand. It was a hand he wanted to kiss, one finger at a time. His dreams were erotic, with his loving Emma an inch at a time. "Yes, you're right. I'm still on an adrenaline high from it."

Emma tucked her hands in her lap. "We're both jumpy. We have a right to be." She lowered her voice and searched his stormy gaze. "You could have lost Kinah last night. I understand, Khalid. We all need someone at times like this."

The silence settled in the cockpit. Khalid's heart pounded with love for Emma. He knew he could not speak of it. Not yet, at least. And he had to get past the six-month mission before he broached it with her. "People need people," he agreed, his voice suddenly weary. "I'm just glad you're here. Thank you." He reached out and grazed her hand. "I didn't exactly give you warning, did I?"

Emma drowned in the heat of his voice and eyes. Khalid's ability to seduce her was more than impressive. She'd never met a man who could touch her heart and soul at the same time. But Khalid did. "No, you didn't," she admitted, her voice barely above a whisper. What should she do? As much as she tried to push away her desire for Khalid, their attraction kept growing. Emma felt out of control, but reasoned that it had to do with the combat.

"It was good."

His eyes crinkled at the corners. Sometimes, Khalid reminded her of an Irish elf, a trickster who was completely unexpected in his actions. Like this kiss. How long had she waited for it? Emma wanted to tell Khalid of her dreams of making love with him, but she didn't dare. "Yes, it was very good," she said. "But I'm confused, Khalid. I'm not sure what to do."

"Then," Khalid said, hope in his voice, "perhaps we

can learn to be good friends who support one another in times like this?"

"I don't know where professionalism and personal needs begin and end with you. I'm at odds with myself." She touched the area of her heart. "I wish we'd met somewhere else. The military is a rough place to find romance, much less keep it and grow it."

Joy raced through Khalid as he heard Emma's softly spoken admittance. She couldn't look at him, her gaze down on her tightly clasped hands. He wanted to unleash his excitement and hope, but he reined it all in. He had to respect Emma's need to get past this mission. "You have trusted me with yourself, Emma. I will hold you in my heart and hands as if you were a dear friend."

Tilting her head, Emma studied Khalid's serious features. "I've been in other situations where my boss and I did become friends. It never influenced us when we were flying or what we had to do in our respective jobs."

"And you are okay with that between us? To allow our friendship to flourish like a red rose bud?" Khalid asked hopefully.

She melted beneath his burning blue eyes that spoke so fervently of untold and unexplored possibilities. Perhaps, someday, Emma cautioned herself. "I can't think of having a better friend than you, Khalid."

# Chapter 12

"You're looking pretty down," Nike observed of Emma as they sat in the chow hall at dinner time. The place was noisy, crowded and plenty of A-teams were mingling with the combat and transport pilots.

Emma pushed the mashed potatoes around on her aluminum tray. "Yeah, some stuff happened in the last twenty-four hours, and I'm conflicted about it."

Nike had her appetite. She dove into the steaming mashed potatoes and gravy. "Khalid?" she guessed.

Looking up, Emma frowned. "Yeah. How'd you know?"

Nike wiped her mouth with a paper napkin. "Oh, come on! He's in love with you. Don't you see it?"

"Mmm…."

Nike cut into her sirloin hamburger. "The guy clearly loves you. Now, I wouldn't ordinarily judge things like that, but it's written all over his face every time I see him with you. Has he let you in on his secret?" She grinned wolfishly.

Unhappy, Emma set her cutlery aside and sighed. "Yes and no. He kissed me this morning." Emma saw Nike's black, thin brows raise with surprise and then she saw fear in her friend's eyes—for her. Holding up her hand, Emma quickly added, "No one saw us."

"That's good. Because you think getting busted over us landing on that hilltop was something? If Dallas hears about you kissing another officer in a combat zone, your ass is grass, my friend. You'll never be more than a captain, even if you're allowed to stay in for your twenty years."

"I know, I know."

"So, you want his attention? He seems like such a heroic figure, Emma. He's doing so much for his people here in his country. He and his sister are out on the front lines every day making a difference." Nike popped some food into her mouth, chewed for a few moments and swallowed. "What's not to like?"

"I didn't want his attention, Nike, but he's a man with a mission."

"You like him?"

"Yes." Emma's brows curved downward and she stared at the food on her tray, her stomach in knots. "There's nothing to dislike about Khalid. That's the problem."

Nike studied her critically. An entire A-team took up the picnic tables to their left. She lowered her tone and leaned forward so only Emma could hear her. "What is the problem? That he's Afghan and you're an American citizen? That your family, if they heard about you falling in love with a foreigner, would go bonkers? Or…? You supply the third reason."

Emma glanced toward the A-team. A sergeant came and sat to her right, his tray filled high with food. She knew these men ate MREs out on their thirty-day missions and that hot food was a rarity in their lives. "My family is very open-minded about whom I might fall in love with. My mom and dad aren't prejudiced."

"Yeah," Nike said, "but he's a Muslim, Emma. Did you consider that angle? I mean, the Trayherns are a military dynasty. I'm sure you probably don't have that religion in your family."

Emma shrugged. "Not yet. My family accepts all religions, Nike. They have a live-and-let-live attitude. I like my parents' take on it: a religion is something you live daily. It's not about going to church once every seven days and then not living your beliefs the other six days. In Khalid's case, I respect and admire him for his dedication and beliefs. He clearly lives them every day whether it's dangerous to do so or not. That's commitment."

Nike considered her words. "I just wonder if your parents would be so open-minded if you married the guy, though."

Shocked, Emma sat up. "Married?!" She'd said it a little louder than she'd thought. The entire A-team to their right collectively lifted their heads and stared at Emma. They soon turned, bent their heads and continued to shovel in the food as if they'd never get any more.

Heat flushed from Emma's neck upward and stung her cheeks. She rolled her eyes, having no one to blame but herself for speaking too loudly. Nike grinned, clearly enjoying her reaction. Emma leaned forward and whispered, "I haven't thought of marriage, Nike."

"Well, I didn't either when I met Gavin, but that's what happened," Nike chuckled, resuming eating her meal.

"Did your family have issues with him being an American army captain because you're from Greece? Did your parents get upset with the fact you are going to marry someone who wasn't Greek?"

Nike wiped her mouth, took a sip of her coffee and said, "No, they didn't. My dad was in the military for twenty years and is now a commercial pilot for a major Greek airline. He flies around the world. My mother is cosmopolitan, too. The only thing that gives them stress is that when I marry Gavin at the end of our tours, we'll continue to be in the army. And so, we're not going to be home in Greece. They'd like that, of course, but understand we have to go where the army assigns us."

"Yes, but eventually, you will retire," Emma said. "Would you live in Greece or the U.S.?"

"We don't know that yet. My parents want us to live in Athens near them. But Gavin's farm parents want him to come and settle down near them in Nebraska. We're not promising either set of parents anything at this point."

"And Gavin isn't Muslim," Emma muttered.

"True, but you know what? I have a lot of friends who worship different gods. As long as they don't push their religion on me and I don't push my beliefs on them, we're fine. Everyone has to be more open-minded."

"It's only the fanatics of any religion who cause trouble," Emma agreed.

"So, if Khalid's religion isn't really an issue with your parents or you, why are you so hesitant?"

Emma picked up her fork and ate a few kernels of corn from her tray. "I just need time, Nike. I didn't expect to like this man. I didn't realize how heroic he really was deep down. Khalid has worked for the good of the common people here in his country ever since he returned from the U.S. And it's not like he doesn't have money. His father is a billionaire times ten. He uses the money to lift people out of the terrible poverty we see here."

"Yeah, he'll need billions to do that," Nike muttered. "With all the bribes that are expected, I'm sure he goes through plenty of dough."

Emma groaned. "Yes, bribery has been a way of life for Afghan people for thousands of years. It's awful. I don't see what or who is going to break this cycle, Nike. The chieftain of the region is always looking for money from Khalid."

"Oh, you mean Jawid Khan. He's a crafty devil," Nike agreed with a slight smile. "But he's like all chieftains. They have over four hundred and fifty different tribes that make up the country of Afghanistan. They've had this system enforced for thousands of years."

Emma continued to nibble at the corn. "Khan is only forty-five years old and, really, he's the one who is part of the Northern Alliance that has been fighting the Taliban for the last decade after the Russians gave up and left."

"I heard he's a pretty colorful guy. I've never met him."

"I haven't, either," Emma said, "but Khalid knows him well. He can't do business in Khan's villages without his blessing."

"And of course," Nike said, smiling, "the blessing is in the form of money greasing the chieftain's palm."

"Right on," Emma said.

"But, I hear from Mike, Dallas's husband who works up the strategy with the general, that Khan is a pretty decent fellow. He's continued to use his five hundred horsemen to seek and root out Taliban all along the border."

Emma nodded. "Khan is a good guy of a sort. I just wish this bribery would go away."

"But how else is Khan going to feed his men, take care of his horses and get ammo to fight the Taliban?"

"I know, I know," Emma muttered. "It's a system. I don't have to like it."

"It's so old that I don't care what the commanders say about winning the hearts and minds of Afghans. I don't think it's ever going away," Nike admitted.

"I understand from Mike that Khan is coming to Zor Barawul. After this last attack on Khan's main village, he's shifting his forces to protecting them in a proactive manner."

"He's going up against his old nemesis, Malik," Nike said.

"Yep, those two hate one another. I'm hoping that with five hundred horse soldiers in the valley, Malik will think twice about doing what he just did to that village."

"Malik's not dumb. He's a cagey fox," Nike agreed. "He'll probably shift his force north or south of Zor Barawul."

"Yeah," Nike said unhappily, "to Do Bandi, another of Khan's villages he's sworn to protect."

"At least we know the players," Nike said, lifting the cup to her lips and sipping. After she set the white mug down on the table, she added, "And Khan is a pretty good guy. Maybe Zor Barawul will get the peace it needs in order to really establish that school for the girls and boys."

Emma lifted her fingers and crossed them. "I hope so."

"You going out there tomorrow?"

"Yes, with Khalid. Kinah's in the village and we're bringing in a dental team for the children."

"You'll probably meet the colorful Khan, then. He's supposed to be arriving there by tomorrow morning, from what I understand."

Emma at his side, Khalid stood by the ramp of the CH-47 as Chieftain Jawid Khan, astride his prancing white Arabian stallion, rode up. In his hands, he had a box of dates from Saudi Arabia, one of Khan's favorite delicacies. The forty-five-year-old chieftain was tall and erect in the saddle. He wore a dark-green robe embossed with gold threads. The geometric designs across his powerful chest and sleeves emphasized his authority. On his head was a turban that matched his intelligent forest-colored eyes. Khan's beard was trimmed and neat but showed silver among the black hair. Khalid smiled to himself. Khan was from a thousand-year-old family line that had ruled this part of Afghanistan. The man was married and had ten children. The last twenty years of his life, he'd lived on horseback and fought, first, the Russians with the Mujahadeen, and for the last ten years, the Taliban, whom he hated with equal ferocity.

The stallion snorted and danced to a stop. It was decked out in a dark-green leather bridle and martingale, with gold tassels sparkling in the morning sun. The entire village of Zor Barawul had come out to welcome their leader and his five hundred horsemen now surrounding the entire mud and stone village.

Khan's narrow face broke into a smile. He'd lost one of his front teeth many years ago to a bullet that had grazed his mouth as he'd charged up a valley to destroy a Taliban machine-gun position. The bullet had chipped the tooth, but that hadn't stopped him from continuing the charge up the hill. When the fight was over and won, Jawid Khan celebrated with his men. He'd had his second-in-command, Naraiman, pull what was left of the tooth without any anesthesia. Out here there were no painkillers. Khan's men had roared and cheered as Naraiman used a pair of rusty old pliers to get the job done. Khan knew men would only follow a leader who didn't show weakness to pain or suffering.

Dismounting with a flourish after two of his soldiers ran up to hold the stallion's reins, Khan grinned widely. He opened his arms toward the lean pilot in the dark-green flight suit. "Khalid, my brother!"

Khalid bowed his head to the mighty warlord and handed him the box of dates. "My Lord Khan. Welcome."

Khan looked at the dates and grinned. He handed them to another awaiting soldier. "Brother, you look well." He moved forward, kissed each of Khalid's cheeks and then shook his hand. Then, he turned and studied Emma whose red hair flashed like fire in the morning sunlight. She wore a hijab to match the color of her hair. "So, who is this beautiful red flower?"

Emma held out her hand to the warlord. She murmured the usual words of welcome and expected him to shake her hand. Instead, after giving her the formal greeting, Khan swept forward and kissed each of her cheeks, denoting that he considered her a trusted friend, not just an ally.

Breathless, Emma felt the soft brush of his beard against her cheeks. The man was very good-looking, despite the gap in the front of his upper teeth. His skin was darkly tanned, the squint lines at the corner of his green eyes deep and fanned out. Khalid had warned her that Khan was a flirt with all women, whenever he could get around Muslim law. In his position of power and authority, he regularly broke Muslim customs.

"So, Captain Cantrell, you are more beautiful than the stories that are carried to me." Khan stepped back and grinned up at the tall Afghan pilot. "Khalid, you are a blessed man."

"I think so," Khalid said with a slight bow of his head. "Come, we have gifts for you, my lord." He led Khan to the rear of the helo. "We have five hundred pounds of grain for your horses. We've brought in a pallet of five-gallon plastic jugs of water." Khalid knew that in this desert, food and water were scarce for man and animal. It was a worthy gift for the warlord, who appeared properly impressed.

"Very good, Khalid!"

"And," Khalid said, walking up inside the helo and bringing out a gunny sack that he held gingerly, "a special gift for you."

"Eh?" Khan's thick black brows rose as he took the gunny sack. Bottles clinked inside. "Is this what I think it is, brother?"

"It is," Khalid said, smiling. Khan had gone to school in France. He had a degree in Business Administration. While there, Khan had acquired a taste for good burgundy. Oh, Khalid knew that Muslim law forbade the drinking of alcoholic beverages, but that had never stopped Khan. "There are six bottles of burgundy in there, my lord. I think you will enjoy tasting them. A little reminder of France."

Khan grinned. He had sent his family to live in France. He left them every spring and returned to them as winter set into his country. No one fought on horseback during the season of ice and snow. In France, his family was out of harm's way. In the winter, Khan ran several multimillion-dollar businesses in France that kept his family accustomed to their rich life. "Thank you, brother. You make my heart smile." Khan handed over the gunny sack to another soldier. He gave him orders to take it to the stone house which was always maintained for his visits to Zor Barawul.

Turning, Khan rubbed his hands together. "So, let us sit, have hot chai, breakfast and discuss things." He turned and gestured toward Emma. "Come, sister. You will join us as we talk strategy against my brother, Malik."

Emma was shocked by the invitation. Khalid had warned her that the westernized Khan paid no attention to the Muslim law that said men and women should not eat together. She saw Khalid barely tip his head forward. "I'd be delighted," she told the warlord in Pashto.

"Excellent! Come!" He slid an arm through one of each of theirs and led them through the village. The villagers lined the rutted, dusty street. They cheered their proud warlord, for without him, they would have been destroyed by the Taliban long ago. If not for Khan's threatening presence, his five hundred loyal men on horseback, this village would have been utterly destroyed long ago. They had reason to cheer for their brave and caring warlord.

"And so, Malik attacked with at least two hundred men last night?" Khan asked, popping a date into his mouth. His men hovered nearby. The room had been prepared with expensive Persian carpets and many pillows and the scents of chai, curry and honey filled the air.

Khalid sat in the position of honor to the right of the warlord. Emma sat on the left. "Yes, my lord. And they almost overran us. Our three Apache helicopters made the difference."

"I wish I'd been here!" Khan said. He smiled over at Emma. "I understand you fly this Apache?"

"I do, my lord."

"Isn't that amazing, Khalid? A woman flying a combat helicopter."

Khalid understood Khan's amazement. In his country women were kept back from such achievement, something he wanted to change one village at a time by educating the women. Once they were educated, they could take places of more power, and their voices would be respected by the elders. "As you know, women in the Americas and Europe are not held under a man's thumb."

Grinning, Khan took a cup of chai from an old, bald man who was his chef. "Yes. One day, brother, I hope to see our women in those powerful machines."

Emma gulped and hid her surprise. Was Khan that forward-thinking? She stole a look over at Khalid, who seemed pleased. She knew these two men had at least a fifteen-year relationship with one another.

"I believe we will see our women rise to whatever they dream of becoming," Khalid murmured tactfully. "I hope in another decade, our country can be at peace, not at war."

Frowning, Khan sipped his chai. "So, tell me of Malik. Give me the details."

Khalid told him everything. When he was done, he added, "If you are going to stay in this area, it will be helpful. My sister, Kinah, refuses to leave this village until all is in order. We have teachers coming in to teach and they must feel safe here. Otherwise, they will leave."

"Of course, of course." Khan handed the emptied china cup to his cook. "But you know I have many villages to protect. I cannot remain here forever."

Khalid nodded. "How long can you stay?"

Pulling thoughtfully at his beard, Khan said, "Perhaps a month, brother. But I will need your help. I intend to root out Malik from the caves on the other side of this valley. I will not sit idle. And to do that, I need ammunition, food for my men, water and grain for my horses. We will hunt by day and return back here to Zor Barawul at dark."

"Whatever you need," Khalid promised, "you will have." Ammunition for their AK-47s and older rifles was vital. "And we have an A-team who will ride with you. They can call in bombs from B-52s and other aircraft should you flush out Malik and his men."

Khan rubbed his hands together in glee. "Excellent! We had another A-team ride with us for a month up north and they did a good job of calling in the bombs on the Taliban."

"Captain Cantrell and I will fly back to the base camp," Khalid said. "We'll let General Chapman know what your needs are. It may take three or four days to get in all your supplies…."

"That is fine. My men could use a few days of rest," Khan said before smiling over at Emma. "We will rest. I will pay my respects to Abbas and the other elders. I will find out Malik's tactics from them. And then, when you return with our supplies, we can make our plans."

Getting up, Khalid said, "We'll leave now, my lord. Thank you for your generosity and food."

Emma quickly rose, bowed and murmured parting words to the smiling warlord. Outside the rock house, Emma walked at Khalid's side. The everyday rhythm of the village was once again in place. The children were playing, dogs were barking, women in burkas were hurrying down the street. Several carts drawn by small gray donkeys moved along the main thoroughfare. "Wow, Khan is something else!" Emma exclaimed.

"Yes, he's quite a colorful character," Khalid said, smiling. Down at the end of the street sat their emptied CH-47. The load master waited near the ramp. "Khan liked you."

Emma snorted. "I respect him for what he's done to try and keep his people in his villages safe."

"I meant," Khalid amended, grinning, "he was very drawn to you. I think he was enamored with your red hair."

Groaning, Emma muttered, "Great."

Khalid chuckled. "Don't worry. He knows that I favor you."

Feeling heat tunneling into her cheeks, Emma gave him a dark look. "We're friends, remember? Not an item."

Holding up his long, expressive hands, Khalid laughed as they stepped out of the village and onto the landing zone where their CH-47 sat. "Yes, yes, of course." Emma's worried look dissolved. Khalid was falling in love with this red-haired woman, with her dancing green eyes. For her sake, though, he had to slow down. She was obviously tense about the possibility of their relationship going beyond a friendship. He'd given much thought to Najela's murder and now was awakening from his loss. Kinah's words had shaken him. She had been right: he couldn't continue to live in a vacuum and ignore his need for a deep, satisfying relationship. Still, Khalid was nagged by Malik's presence and worried for Emma.

As Khalid entered the helicopter, Emma on his heels,

he cautioned himself to remain patient. He had. Yet, he wanted to kiss her again. This time, he would trail a series of kisses from her silky, flame-colored hair all the way down every inch of her body to her toes. Khalid did his best to tuck all his longing away and sat down in the left seat as the copilot. Today, Emma was the AC of this mission. As he slipped into his harness and Emma sat down in the right-hand seat, Khalid wondered privately if she was falling in love with him. Was there hope for them despite this war?

## *Chapter 13*

The early-June weather was welcome to Emma. She pulled off her helmet as Khalid squeezed between the seats and walked toward the opening ramp of the CH-47. The sunlight was bright and she was glad to have her aviator glasses on. Getting up, she set her helmet in the copilot's seat and smiled to herself.

Ever since Jawid Khan had made his presence known in the southern part of his territory, the warlord seemed to have chased Malik and his men out of the area. Despite Khan's presence, Emma didn't trust Malik. He had twenty years of hard-earned camouflage techniques and could dig in, hide and still be nearby without anyone knowing about it. On the other hand, Khan knew how to dig rats out of a tunnel and he and his men had systematically scoured every cave along the other side of the valley, ridding themselves of pockets of Taliban. Khan took no prisoners and Emma saw the fierce horsemen in a completely new light. They were ancient warriors come to life. There was no mercy between enemies. Ever.

Today, MREs—Meals Ready to Eat—oats for the horses and more burgundy for Khan had been flown into Zor Barawul. Pulling the rubber band off her ponytail, Emma allowed her shoulder-length hair to flow free for a moment. She then combed her fingers through the strands and whipped her hair up into another ponytail. She grabbed her green silk scarf and wrapped it around her head. Once it was secured, she set off to visit with Kinah and see how things were going with the school.

There was an air of celebration in the village. A number of children who had been let out of school early were with Kinah, waiting anxiously at the edge of the landing area. The dust had cleared. Khalid worked with the A-team Special Forces soldiers and the load master to remove the supplies from the bird. About fifty of Khan's horsemen sat just out of range of where their helo had landed, their faces alight with expectation. They didn't necessarily like the MREs, but it was food. Many times, the horsemen had only meager supplies to last days at a time when out hunting the Taliban. Some days, they had nothing to eat.

Kinah waved and grinned. She refused to wear the burka that the other women of the village donned when outside their house but she wore the hijab. Her bright red scarf emphasized her black hair and flashing eyes.

"Emma!"

Emma grinned. "Hey, Kinah! How's it going?" The knot of children remained around her friend. She spotted the two orphans, Fahran and Benham, among the group. Ever since the horrific attacks by Malik a month earlier, the two had seemed inseparable. Kinah had saved their lives and they doted upon her.

Emma handed out candy to the children. Little hands shyly reached out, along with murmurs of thank you. She loved that these children were always polite and didn't grab a handful of candy and then run off. They knew how to share.

"I'm fine, sister." Kinah embraced Emma and they shared cheek kisses with one another. "Look at you! How long has it been? Two weeks? And Khalid looks very happy, too." She gave Emma a sly look. "So, love flourishes, eh?"

Emma stepped back and smiled. "We are just *friends,*" she emphasized.

"Mmm, friends. Indeed." Kinah smiled and looked across the sun-splashed narrow valley at the caves that were a part of the rocky landscape. "Friendship is always a good beginning basis for a relationship."

"It can only be friendship," Emma said. She fell in step with Kinah, the children providing a phalanx around them as they walked into the village.

"As you say, my sister," Kinah murmured, a sly smile still lingering across her mouth.

Emma wasn't taking the bait. She knew Kinah wanted her to fall in love with Khalid and marry him. Emma waved as a number of women in burkas came outside their mud homes to greet them. The village had a palpably, happy atmosphere. It was amazing how the people rebounded once the Taliban threat had been removed. Apaches had flown in almost daily during the first two weeks when Khan had begun to root out Malik and his men from the valley caves. The Americans had worked in concert with the warlord to eradicate the threat.

Kinah stopped at the school, opened the door and stepped inside. Emma followed and so did the curious children. Closing the door, Emma saw that all the bullet holes had been patched over with new mud. The temperature was pleasant, in the seventies and the windows in the schoolroom provided good light.

Emma scanned the room and looked approvingly at Kinah. "This is a wonderful space. It's as good as new. How are the kids doing?"

"They are learning to read and write not only in Pashto, but in English. I have told them that English is the accepted universal language for our globe. They must learn it in order to grow."

Emma nodded, glancing toward the books, the chalk, the crayons and at the children's art that adorned the walls. "Good. That's a wise move. Little kids are sponges and it's the right time to teach them foreign languages."

Kinah counted heads and then gave the children an unexpected recess, much to their delight. They would get fifteen minutes to go out and play. The classroom fell into silence as the last child left and closed the door. Kinah sat down at her desk and gestured to Emma to take a seat on the wooden chair next to it.

"My brother looks very happy, my sister. Have you two been growing closer as friends?"

Emma cleared her throat and sat down. "Yes and no. The military doesn't foster much else between officers other than follow the Code of Conduct. Fraternization is not allowed."

"Yes, that is what Khalid said."

The door opened. It was Benham, the thirteen-year-old orphan.

"Mem sahib, come quickly!" he called urgently.

"There is a baby goat stuck in a thick bush down on the side of the hill. We need your help in order to free it."

Kinah frowned. "But, Benham, where is the boy who tends those goats? It is his job to free it."

"No, no, mem sahib. This baby is far down the hill. Fahran and I can hear it bleating. It is in trouble! Can you help us? Please?" He gave her a pleading look.

With a sigh, Kinah got up. "Very well. I'm such a sucker for babies who get tangled up in all that brush."

"I'll go with you," Emma said, rising. She pointed to her flight uniform. "I can probably thread those thickets a lot more easily than you can in your robe."

Grateful for the company, Kinah nodded. They followed Benham out the door. He led them down behind the classroom. Emma saw nothing but a lot of thick green bushes. Some were two or three feet high and others, six to ten feet high. She saw holes in the ground where brush had been blown away by Apache rockets earlier. The wind was breezy as they stood on the lip of the hill. It was a steep, rocky descent. Benham scrambled like a mountain goat in his new leather shoes down the reddish slope.

"Come, come!" he hollered enthusiastically, waving them to follow him.

Emma heard a faint bleat. It was way down the hill. She wore a .45 strapped over her Kevlar vest across her chest, and she swept the area critically for enemy. Yes, Malik and his men had just been cleared, but Emma sensed the enemy was never very far away. Malik was a coyote. Looking over at Kinah, she saw the woman scowling.

"Over here!" Benham called pleadingly, as he slipped

and slid farther down the rocky slope. "You don't want the baby goat to die, do you? I'll need help!" He slipped in between two thick bushes and disappeared. The goat bleated again.

"Let me do this," Emma said, holding out her hand as she took a step down onto the narrow, sliding earth and rock. "You stay up here, Kinah. You'll just get in trouble with that robe you're wearing."

"Are you sure, sister? This isn't the first time I've helped untangle a baby goat or sheep from that awful brush."

Grinning, Emma slid farther down the slope, arms out for balance. "My turn."

"Be careful…"

"Don't worry," Emma muttered, sliding and correcting constantly, "I will be."

Kinah noticed the other orphan, Fahran, suddenly appear out of the brush. He was farther down from where Benham had disappeared. His face was white and he seemed frightened. Kinah waved to him and called, "Emma is coming to help you. Just stay with the baby. She'll be there in a moment."

Fahran looked back toward the brush. He clung to a branch in order not to fall farther down on the steep talus slope. He opened his mouth and then shut it. Then, he looked at Emma who slid down the slope toward him. Dust rose in her wake. Rocks tumbled all around where she placed her flight boots. More than once, Emma fell on her butt, got up, dusted herself off and kept moving toward where Benham had disappeared earlier.

"It's all right," Kinah called reassuringly to Fahran. The ten-year-old orphan had a soft spot for all babies, animal or human, she had discovered. Maybe because he had lost his own family, he was sensitive to the plight of others. Fahran clung to her gaze as if she were going to cast him off some day, but Kinah always reassured him that she would be there for him. "Emma is coming! Just stay where you are, Fahran!"

Emma disappeared into the brush. The shrubs were long-armed, poking at her, and the leaves swatted her face. Breathing hard, she watched where she put her feet. She could barely see anything, the brush was so thick. The goat bleated frantically now, but she couldn't see him, only hear him.

"Benham?" she called.

"I'm here, I'm here," the boy's voice drifted toward her.

"Keep talking so I can find you!" Emma called, holding up her arm to protect her face from thick foliage.

"You're coming the right way," Benham shouted. "Hurry, hurry! The baby goat is bleeding! You must rescue him!"

Groaning, Emma threw caution to the wind and crashed forward through the brush. She heard the baby goat. It was shrill and bleating, as if completely frightened out of its wits. "Damn goats," she muttered.

Just as Emma turned around to avoid a huge group of limbs and allow her body to create an opening, a man's hand grabbed at her shoulder.

Emma was jerked hard into the brush. Grunting and terrified, she looked up to see an Afghan soldier grinning at her. His fist was cocked, and it smashed down into her face. The moment his fist connected with her cheek, Emma felt an explosion of pain. And then, darkness.

"Khalid! Khalid!" Kinah screamed as she ran down the street toward the helicopter.

Khalid jerked around. His sister was white-faced, her eyes wide with fear, her hands above her head to get his attention.

As he handed the load master the supply list, Khalid stepped off the ramp. What was wrong?

Kinah raced to him, out of breath. "Khalid, something terrible has just happened!" She rapidly told him the story.

Frowning, Khalid knew that slope was precarious and steep. "Are you sure?"

"Yes, yes," Kinah sobbed worriedly, "I kept calling for Emma. She never replied!"

"What about the boys?" he demanded, feeling sudden fear.

"They're gone, Khalid!" Kinah pressed her hands to her mouth, tears streaming from her eyes. "Oh, brother, I think Emma has either been killed or taken prisoner by the Taliban! Otherwise, she would have returned my calls and the boys would have reappeared."

A cold terror bolted through Khalid. There was no way to get a horse down that slope. He ordered Khan's soldiers to get off their animals and follow him. As he raced down the center of the village, his throat ached with fear—fear for Emma. Khalid jerked his pistol out of the holster.

Kinah watched from the top of the hill as Khalid and fifty of Khan's men searched every inch of that slope over the next half hour. She had directed them to where she last saw Emma, and they had literally torn the shrubbery apart looking for her.

After a frantic search across the slope, Khalid scrambled back up the hill. He was breathing hard, his face a mask of fear. "I'm going to call this in to our base," he told Kinah. "Emma is gone."

"Oh, no…" Kinah moaned. She grabbed Khalid's arm. "I'm so sorry, so sorry. I should have known it was a trick. This is Malik's work. He's used the two orphans to lure Emma into their trap. Oh, Khalid, why didn't I see it? Why didn't I recognize this was a trap? What will they do to Emma?" Her eyes were wide with terror.

Khalid gulped hard and pulled loose from his sister's grip. "I've got to go. I'll get back to you as soon as I can. Use the radio I left with you if Khan's men find anything or if you hear anything from a Taliban envoy."

Kinah gulped and rasped, "Yes, yes, I will, my brother. This is terrible! Emma's in danger!"

She was in more than that and Khalid knew it as he raced down the dusty road toward the helicopter. His mind spun with what had to be done first, second and third. His heart was pounding in agony. *Oh, Allah! Emma is a prisoner of the Taliban!* He knew it in his gut and heart. Najela's dead body swam in front of his eyes. Running up the ramp, Khalid snapped orders to the load master to get the supplies out of the helo pronto. Fifteen men from the village raced forward to follow him.

With a steady voice, Khalid talked to BJS 60 ops, telling them everything. A CH-47 did not have infrared or television cameras. He couldn't just lift off and fly around to try and find Emma and her abductors. He'd have to wait until an Apache was free of other duties to fly over here to begin a search pattern or he'd be shot out of the sky.

As he sat there in the cockpit of the helo, Khalid felt as if his whole world had turned black. Fear gripped him. Instinctively, Khalid felt this was Malik's work. The man was a sly enemy. And despite Jawid's best efforts to purge the valley of the Taliban, Malik had somehow managed to avoid detection.

He knew Khan and his soldiers were down in the valley. He picked up the radio and called the warlord. There was no signal. That wasn't unusual; among the sheer cliffs a radio signal could easily get lost. Khalid wiped his dry mouth with the back of his hand. His heart ached with fear for Emma. Malik would kill her. Worse, he would probably behead her. That was what the Taliban did to infidels. And especially if a woman soldier or pilot was captured, they were broadcasted as examples.

Khalid felt his heart explode with new grief and awareness. For so long, he had tried to tell himself he was not falling in love with Emma. That they were from very different worlds and countries. Yet, he *had* fallen in love with her! He closed his eyes, his hand pressed to his chest. There was such agony that he could barely breathe. He wanted Emma in his life. For the rest of his life. How could she be gone, ripped suddenly and unexpectedly from his life, from his heart?

Opening his eyes, Khalid felt a new emotion. It wasn't love. It was hatred. Despite only being half Afghan, the blood of the warrior was genetically as much a part of him as his Irish mother's side was. His eyes narrowed as he looked out over the green floor of the V-shaped rocky valley. Emma did not deserve this. None of it! She loved the Afghan people and these villagers loved her in return. She had made so many friends. True, loyal friends for life among them. She had done nothing wrong, and yet, Malik had captured her.

Getting up, Khalid cautioned himself to wait. He couldn't just take off and go find Emma. The infrared on an Apache could spot body heat miles away. It was their only chance to find her. Without hesitation, Khalid skidded down the ramp. The men had made short work of getting the rest of the boxes out of the hold of the cargo helo. His boots created a metallic echo as he left the ramp and stood in front of the men who had finished searching the slope.

One man, who had part of his arm missing, came forward and handed Khalid a green scarf. "This belonged to mem sahib," he told him. "We found it among the brambles near the base of the slope. There are footprints of five men. And we found where they hid their horses." He pointed toward the other side of the valley. "We can track them, Captain Shaheen. We have good daylight, half a day. Can we go after them?"

Khalid felt torn. The Afghan warrior in him wanted to leap upon a horse and lead these crafty men who knew how to track in even the worst of circumstances. Yet, as an officer in the U.S. Army, he had to wait for that Apache gunship to arrive. None was available for at least three hours. By then, Malik would escape. Holding up his hand, he told the man, "Hold on. I'll be right back. Mount up and get me a horse."

Khalid made a radio call to BJS 60 and told them what was going on. To his relief, Major Klein gave him permission to ride with Khan's men to start tracking Malik in hopes of finding Emma. She ordered him to take a satellite radio with him so they were in contact at all times. Klein understood there were no Apaches presently available and their only chance to find Emma was to do it the old-fashioned way: with men on horseback tracking their enemy.

Khalid pulled open his helmet bag. Inside was a curved dagger in a leather sheath. He removed it and set it on the seat. Glancing over, he imagined Emma sitting on the other seat. His heart contracted with such anguish that tears drove into his eyes. Khalid blinked them back, forced down all his emotions. He jammed all the extra cartridges for his .45 pistol into the leg pockets of his uniform. He found it comforting to strap on the dagger to the right side of his waist. This dagger had been in his father's family for eight hundred years. It had belonged to a caliph and had been a present to one of Khalid's relatives who was a powerful warlord in the region. Touching it, his fingers brushed the jewel-encrusted leather sheath. Khalid silently swore he would use it to cut Malik's throat.

# Chapter 14

Fahran bit down hard on his lower lip. He crouched within a grayish cave that had poor light. For an hour, they'd ridden hard with their prisoner—the woman he and Benham had lured down the slope of Zor Barawul. Frightened, he watched as Lord Malik shoved the woman, Captain Emma Cantrell, off her feet. He hid his face, his back up against the cold, jutting rocks. Fahran felt no pain for himself, but anguish for the semiconscious woman.

He saw Benham standing near the knot of Taliban soldiers who encircled the woman. Her hands were tied in front of her and she was helpless against the jeering, cursing men. How could he have done this to Emma? How? Tears leaked into Fahran's eyes and he looked away as Malik lifted the toe of his boot and savagely kicked the woman in the ribs.

He heard Emma cry out. Suddenly, she went limp

within the circle; dirt was smeared across her face and through her hair. Gulping and sobbing, Fahran stood up on tiptoe to see if she was dead. He bobbed his head from one side to another to see if she moved. Oh, why had he been talked into this by Lord Malik? Emma had always been nice to him and Benham. She'd brought both of them special gifts that no one else received. She'd even brought him the pair of fine leather shoes and the socks he now wore with pride.

Guiltily, Fahran gazed down at his shoes. They had been expensive, that he knew. To denote their worth, there was fine leather craftsmanship and colorful stripes on either side. Fahran had never had a pair of shoes in his life until Emma brought them for him. And how had he repaid her? Wiping his eyes, he crept closer. Was Emma dead? Had Lord Malik killed her with his boot? Gulping, Fahran wedged in between two soldiers.

Emma Cantrell lay unconscious within the circle of men, her face dirty and pale. Fahran thought surely she must be dead. His gaze shot to Malik who swaggered into the circle. The warlord's eyes were black with hatred. He kicked Emma again, this time in the shoulder. She moved like a rag doll, no sound issuing from her slack lips. Benham was grinning like the idiot he was. He liked hurting Emma.

What could he do? Fahran blinked back the tears, for he knew if any of these rugged, hard soldiers saw him cry, they would give him the boot, too.

"Leave her," Malik boomed. He looked around. "Come, let us eat in the other cave. They will never find us here." He grinned triumphantly.

The soldiers shouted a roar of approval. This cave was a very secret place and to get to it, one had to follow a series of tunnels. Their horses were tied up in a smaller, nearby cave. They would eat a hot meal, the smoke being carried down into another cave that no one could climb into.

Malik spied Fahran. "You!" he growled, pointing his finger at him. "Take care of this bitch when she wakes up."

One of the soldiers next to Fahran gave him a pistol from his belt.

Fahran gulped and nodded. "Y-yes, my lord," he whispered.

Suddenly, everyone was gone. Fahran could smell the wonderful scent of curry on the cool breeze moving silently through the series of caves. He stared down at Emma, who was motionless. Frightened that she was dead, Fahran dropped the pistol onto the dirt floor and knelt at her side after everyone had left.

Gently, he put his dirty hand on her shoulder. "Mem sahib Emma? Are you all right? Please wake up? Please," he choked in a whisper as he leaned near her ear, "don't be dead…."

The cave was cold. They always were. Fahran took his jacket, which Emma had brought him, and he carefully laid it across her shoulders and back to try and protect her from the draft. Hesitantly, he touched her cheek. She was so pale. Her freckles stood out in dark-brown spots across her ashen flesh. Terrible memories of his family dying a year ago slammed into him. He had leaned over his mother who was bleeding from the mouth, ears and nose after the bomb had exploded. She too had had her olive skin turn ashen just like Emma's. *Oh, Allah! Emma cannot be dead!* Why, oh why had he listened to Benham when he was given the order by Malik to lure either Emma or Kinah down the slope? Benham had swaggered, proud that he, of all people, had been chosen to initiate the trickery.

Malik had told Benham to take Fahran, too. Benham, of course, was in charge, Malik had assured the thirteen-year-old, patting him on the shoulder. Fahran hadn't wanted anything to do with the plan. Yet, he knew Benham would kill him if he didn't go along with it. On the way across the valley, Fahran had tried to find a way to detour Benham from the plan, to no avail. Benham had captured a baby goat and tied it in a thicket. He would jab it every once in a while with a sharp stick to get it to bleat. They'd hunkered down with the baby and watched Emma coming their way.

Two of Malik's best soldiers had then sneaked up and waited for Emma. When she'd gotten tangled in the thick brush, they'd attacked her. In seconds, she had been knocked unconscious. It had been easy to drag her to the horses tied below. One soldier mounted and the other hung her across his horse's withers. Benham leaped upon his horse and Fahran rode behind him, clinging for dear life as they thundered down a narrow trail that would lead them across the valley to their hidden cave complex.

Emma groaned. Pain made her open her eyes. At first, everything was blurry. Pain was radiating from her left shoulder. Her left hand felt numb and she couldn't feel her fingers. Her head throbbed. And so did her cheek and jaw. Blinking, she realized Fahran was kneeling next to her, his little face anxious.

"Mem sahib! You live!" He touched her jacketed shoulder.

It took long moments for Emma to realize what had happened—and where she was. Fahran jabbered on in Pashto, telling her everything. Her ears were still ringing, probably from the blow she'd taken earlier to the head. Fahran started to cry.

"I—I'm so sorry, mem sahib Emma. You did not deserve this. I—I couldn't do anything. I tried to get Benham to stop the plan. Oh! I thought you were dead after Lord Malik kicked you in the back."

Emma lay with her cheek against the fine, cool dust of the cave floor for nearly five minutes, trying to absorb what had happened. Fahran's tears rolled down his taut face making tracks through the dust on his cheeks. She tried to reach out with her left hand, but pain made her grunt. Her arm fell helplessly to the floor.

"Fahran," she croaked, "help me stand up. Can you do that?" Emma saw the pistol laying in the dirt about fifty feet away. She knew from Fahran that he was supposed to guard her. A mere ten-year-old. Hatred for Malik gave Emma the strength she needed. As she sat up, holding her left arm tight against her body, she closed her eyes until the dizziness passed.

Fahran anxiously circled her. "What are you going to do, mem sahib?" He told her what Malik had done to her. That he'd kicked her twice.

Emma opened her eyes. She knew her left shoulder blade had been dislocated by Malik's kick. "Help me stand. I need to reset my shoulder blade."

Fahran gripped her right hand. Between them, Emma got to her feet. She staggered. Fahran threw his small arms upward and around her hips to steady her. It was enough. Emma heard voices wafting through the cave complex. She guessed the Taliban soldiers were not very close. The voices were muted. *Good.*

"Help me get to the wall," she ordered, her voice low with pain. Every time she took a faltering step, the agony made her groan. Gritting her teeth, she relied on Fahran's strength to get her to the wall of the cave.

Leaning against it, breathing hard, she felt Fahran's hands continue to steady her. "I'm—okay," Emma told the boy. "Stand back."

Fahran backed away. He gave Emma a quizzical look. What was she going to do?

Emma sucked in a breath. *Oh, God, this is going to hurt….* She hurled her back against the cave wall as hard as she could. There was a *snap* and her shoulder blade seated back into its correct position. Emma blacked out from the overwhelming pain and fell, unconscious, to the floor.

Fahran cried out and raced forward. Emma was dead! What had she done to herself? She lay on her stomach, her arms flung away from her body. Dropping to his knees, he sobbed out her name and shook her shoulder, trying to awaken her.

Emma groaned. She felt Fahran's small hands gripping her flight suit near her right shoulder. The moment she groaned, he leaped way, frightened. The pain in her shoulder ebbed now as she pushed herself up into a sitting position. Fahran's eyes were huge. Tears glimmered in his dark eyes. "I'm okay," she rasped.

With a moan, Fahran walked toward her, unsure. "A-are you dead? Or are you alive?"

Emma forced a smile that was more like a grimace. "I'm alive, Fahran. I dislocated my left shoulder." She vaguely gestured toward the cave wall. "I threw myself into the wall to reset it. Do you understand?"

"N-no."

Emma felt stronger, more clear-headed. Her left shoulder ached, but nothing like before. She tested her left arm and lifted it a little. There was pain, but it was now manageable. Worriedly, Emma couldn't feel three of her fingers on her left hand. Had there been nerve damage when Malik kicked her unconscious? Had his boot severed those nerves? Fear struck her as she slowly opened and closed her left hand. If she couldn't get back sensation in those fingers, she would never be allowed to fly again.

"You must come with me," Fahran urged, coming over to where she sat. He whispered the words fiercely and kept looking toward the exit where the Taliban soldiers had left.

"Where? Where am I, Fahran? Can you help me get out of here?" She saw him screw up his small, thin face. He looked down a dark tunnel that lay opposite. Some grayish light came through it.

"You are on the other side of the valley opposite Zor Barawul," he told her. Anxiety raised his voice and he sounded reedy. "You must follow me, mem sahib Emma. I know another way out of here! But it is dangerous. And only small people can slide through the opening."

Emma nodded. "Am I small enough?" Her heart beat with hope. She heard the drifting voices of the soldiers. Would they come back and check on her? Emma knew Malik would kill her.

"Yes, yes, you are." Fahran held his small hands about an inch apart in front of her face. "It is late afternoon. We can wriggle like escaping rabbits away from Lord Malik." Anxiously, the boy looked at the opening. "They are eating and drinking now. There's a great celebration because you were captured."

Grimacing, Emma got to her feet. She gripped Fahran's slender shoulder. "Show me the way to get out of here. Can you take me out of these caves and get me clear of Malik and his men?"

"Yes, yes, I can." Fahran walked over to the pistol and then brought it back to Emma. "You keep this. I cannot kill anything."

Her heart broke over the boy's sudden, sagging face, tears in his eyes. Emma took the pistol and made sure there was a bullet in the chamber and the safety was off. "I understand," she told him gently. Patting his dusty hair, she added, "Let's go to Zor Barawul, Fahran. Take me home."

The sun slanted steeply on the western horizon when Malik heard the cry of a guard. It was the soldier standing at the mouth of the second cave. Malik had been crouched in front of the fire, eating a juicy, warm rabbit leg. The scent of curry and hot tea filled the small, warm cavern. Malik stood up, the leg of the roasted rabbit in his left hand.

"Lord Malik!" the soldier panted, running into the cave. "Riders! Lord Khan and his men! They're coming our way!"

"Mount up!" Malik roared. He took several more tearing bites from the rabbit and then threw it away. Turning, he said to Benham, "Get the American bitch. Bring her here to me."

"Yes, Lord Malik!" Benham pirouetted and raced for the smaller cave via a tunnel.

Everyone else quickly stored their meager utensils in rags and hurried down another tunnel to where all the horses were tethered. Malik scowled. It would be impossible for Khan to find this place. This cave complex had never been discovered. Touching the dagger at his waist and then his pistol next to it, Malik picked up his AK-47 and ran down the tunnel toward the saddled horses.

Benham gasped as he skidded to a halt in the other cave. Breathing hard, he looked around. Where was the American pilot? And Fahran? Suddenly scared, Benham wondered if she had overpowered Fahran and run. But where? Anxiously, Benham searched the entire cave. Nothing. There were no voices, no noises. No—anything. Suddenly afraid, Benham spun around and raced as fast as he could. Lord Malik needed to know his prisoner had escaped.

Malik had just grabbed the reins of his white stallion when Benham burst into the cave. His black-and-gray brows drew down. "Where's the American?" he roared at the approaching teenager.

"Gone!" Benham cried, sinking to his knees. All around him, riders and horses swirled. The tension was electric, dust raised by the horses suddenly whinnying and prancing around.

"What are you talking about?" Malik thundered as he mounted. He rode over to the cowering youth.

Benham choked out what he'd seen. "I-is there another way out of there, my lord?"

Scowling, Malik snarled, "Yes. It's a small, narrow passage." He glowered at the big, lumbering Benham. "You're too large to go in there to see if you can find them." He jerked his head around and barked orders above the din. A very small, wiry soldier came running forward.

"Siamak, go into the tunnel where the American was being kept prisoner. She's escaped into it. Find her. Kill her. Then, join us near Do Bandi. I'll see your horse is left here for you."

Nodding, Siamak bowed and took out his curved dagger from his belt. "As you wish, my lord." He turned and ran out of the cave.

Turning, Malik raised his hand and roared, "Follow me!" He jerked his stallion's reins and then trotted down another twisting, winding tunnel. Someone had lit a torch, the yellow and red flames flickering ahead of Malik.

Malik grinned savagely. He knew that this half-mile long tunnel, barely ten feet high, would lead them to a brush-covered opening that Khan knew nothing about. Within half an hour, they would be gone. Malik seriously doubted if Khan would even find this cave. It was all but impossible.

Gasping for breath, her shoulder burning, Emma crawled and wriggled through the blackness. Only Fahran's small shoes near her face kept her hopes up.

"A little more!" Fahran gasped.

Hope sprung up in her. It felt as though she'd wormed her way through the narrow, twisting tunnel forever. Every time she reached with her left hand to pull herself forward, the burning sensation deepened in her shoulder blade. She tried to use her right arm, but it was difficult. Her head throbbed and Emma wished mightily for some aspirin.

As they inched around a curve, Emma gasped. Light! She saw sunlight coming in through massive bushes that grew in front of the entrance. She saw Fahran's head bobbing up and down as he quickly scooted forward on his belly. Within three minutes, they were out of the tunnel and standing outside the thickets.

Holding her left arm against herself, Emma looked around. It was near sunset. The sky was a deepening blue as the rays of the sun shot across the tops of the peaks above them. Fahran dusted himself off the best he could. Emma glanced down at her flight suit: she was dirty from top to bottom. She turned toward the small, narrow inlet. “Fahran, is there a trail down to the valley?”

“Yes,” he said, suddenly smiling, relief in his face, “this way!”

Khalid rode with Jawid Khan, who had shown up with more men as they rode down through the valley. Khan’s white stallion was a pure Arabian, small and powerful. Khalid’s black gelding scrambled to keep up as they took a narrow, steep and rocky path up the side of a hill. Above them were caves. His terror over Emma being taken had tripled in the last two hours as they rode at high speed.

At the top of the hill, Khalid pulled his stallion to a skidding stop. His eyes were narrowed and he jabbed his finger to the left. Khalid squinted. He could see dust clouds rising far above them.

“What?” Khalid demanded, coming abreast of the panting white stallion.

Khan grinned. “Dust clouds indicate a large group of Taliban, brother. That is Malik! Let’s go!” He spurred his stallion up the steep hill, pulling out his rifle from the sheath as he did so.

Khalid didn’t question the man. Khan knew signs of Taliban better than anyone. His gelding was shiny with sweat, foam on his neck as he plunged up the hill on the heels of the white Arabian.

Khan gave a war cry of triumph as he breasted the hill. Khalid quickly saw why. There, no more than a mile away, in a slight meadow area, were twenty fleeing Taliban. And leading them on a white stallion was Malik himself.

"Do you see Emma?" he shouted to Khan, who was busy cocking his rifle.

Looking through his binoculars, Khan shook his head. "She's not among them. Once we get them, we'll find her location!" Khan whirled around, gesturing violently to his two hundred horsemen. For once, the odds were on his side. Normally, the Taliban outhorsed them and had more ammunition than they did. But not this time.

"Lord Khan!" Khalid shouted and pointed to the sky as two Apache helicopters hove into view. He pulled out his radio to direct the pilots to fire on the Taliban, "Malik is mine!"

Grinning wolfishly, Khan nodded. "As you will, brother. Let the Apache helicopters finish him off!"

Khalid knew he shouldn't feel happy about killing twenty people, but he did. Since Emma wasn't with them, he had the luxury of using the Apaches. As he called in the air strike, he wondered where she was. Had Malik hidden her in a cave? More than likely. Was she even alive?

## *Chapter 15*

Emma was startled by two Apache helos flying overhead. They were firing off major expenditures of rockets. She heard the thuds, the explosions high up on the ridge above where they stood on the valley floor. Fahran clung to her, his head buried against her. Emma held him with her right arm, her left arm nearly useless. For about ten minutes, the combat helicopters circled like buzzards over an unseen prey. She couldn't see who or what they were targeting, but guessed it was Malik and his horsemen. Grimly, Emma watched. She hoped the son of a bitch died.

"Come on," she urged Fahran. Looking up, she noted that the sun had set, but the well-used trail was easy to see. "We've got another mile before we reach the village," she told the boy.

Where was Khalid? Emma knew he'd be looking for her. They scrambled up the steep and rocky shrub-strewn slope. Breathing hard, slipping and sometimes falling, Emma thought she might be more mountain goat than human. Fahran, who was much lighter and smaller, climbed ahead. Sometimes, he would turn and hold out his small hand toward her. Emma's left shoulder ached badly and her left arm felt better if she didn't use it. She had to get to a doctor as soon as possible once she got back to the village.

As they huffed up the last, steep slope, Fahran cried out and pointed to the left. "Riders!"

Emma gasped and hunkered down on the gravel slope, the sharp stones biting into her knees. About a mile away on another trail that led directly to the village, she saw a band of over two hundred riders at a hard gallop. In the lead was Jawid Khan. Her eyes narrowed. Yes! Khalid rode next to him! Her heart tumbled and for the first time, Emma allowed the suppressed emotions to surge up through her. Khalid! He'd gone out on horseback hunting for her. And he was safe. Gulping, Emma fought away the tears.

"Come on, we'll meet them at the village," she told the smiling Fahran, her voice hoarse with tears.

The last thing Khalid expected to see when he galloped into the village of Zor Barawul was Emma standing in the center of the village with bedraggled-looking Fahran in hand. He skidded his gelding to a halt and leaped out of the saddle, his booted feet hitting the ground at a run.

"Emma!" he called, his voice cracking with emotion. How pale she looked. Emma held her left arm against her body, her right hand protectively drawn across Fahran's thin shoulders.

"Khalid!" Emma didn't care who in the village saw

them. She rushed forward after releasing Fahran. Emma extended her right hand toward him. Khalid's eyes filled with anguish and joy. As he approached, he gripped her hand and then closed the distance.

"You're alive," he whispered, leaning down and kissing her mouth tenderly.

Emma's world anchored only to Khalid's warm, cherishing mouth against hers. She moaned softly and leaned against his strong male body. He took all her weight and carefully held her, as if she were a priceless glass vase that might shatter at any moment. The warm moistness of his breath reminded Emma of life, instead of death. She could have died. She knew that. Emma loved Khalid with a fierceness that swept through her as he took her mouth commandingly a second time.

Breaking contact with her, Khalid looked critically into Emma's softened and teary green eyes. They were marred with pain. And relief. And love—for him. Was that really possible? Stunned, Khalid hadn't expected to see that. Did Emma love him? Her eyes were shining with joy—for him alone. Her lips trembled and then she fought back the tears.

"Malik dislocated my left shoulder in the cave," she whispered. She looked down at Fahran. "He helped me escape, Khalid. He's the real hero here. Fahran risked his life to show me another way out of that cave complex."

Khalid tousled Fahran's dusty hair. "Thank you, my brother."

Fahran looked shyly up at the pilot and managed an embarrassed shrug.

"There's a medevac flying in right now," he told Emma, his fingers wrapping around her right arm. Sweat and smudges of dirt covered her face. Even her red hair was dust-coated. "Can you walk? Or do you want me to carry you?"

Giving him a half laugh, because it hurt to move with the inflamed and injured shoulder, Emma said, "God, no. Just keep a steady hand on me, Khalid." Worried because three of her fingers were still numb, Emma wanted to see a doctor as soon as possible. The people of the village came out and offered help. Khalid thanked them and told them that Emma would be flown back to the base for medical treatment.

Near the edge of town, Kinah rushed over. She had concern on her face and her eyes were dark with worry. Emma assured her she would be okay after they carefully hugged one another.

"Malik's dead," Khalid told his sister with grim satisfaction. "The two Apaches came in and destroyed his entire army. There's not much left of any of them." He had wanted to race down that slope and meet Malik on the field of battle. Instead, Khalid had called in the combat mission over his portable radio. The two Apache helicopters had loosed an arsenal of ammunition that had killed every Taliban rider. Including Malik.

Emma closed her eyes for a moment. Then, she looked down at Fahran, who refused to leave her side. "Benham was with Malik?" she asked the child.

"Yes, he was, mem sahib."

Nodding, Emma told Khalid what had happened. She saw the medevac flying over the mountain crest and heading directly for the landing zone just outside the village. Khalid gently placed his arm around Emma for just a moment, his embrace butterfly-light.

"We'll get you to Bagram. I know all the doctors there. We'll get you to an orthopedic and neurology specialist, Emma. He'll make you well." He bored a look into her fatigued eyes. All he wanted to do was kiss her senseless and hold her tightly against him and protect her from a world gone mad. But he could do none of those things right now. Khalid swallowed his frustration. He had to be patient. Emma was worried about her numbed fingers. All he could do was be at her side.

Kinah came forward and grasped Fahran's hand as the medevac landed, the blades whirling and kicking up dust clouds. "I'll take care of him," she called to them. "Be well, Emma. Brother, let me know how she is?"

Khalid nodded. Kinah had a military radio that was always on her person. Plus, the A-team that was stationed at the village could always be contacted to let her know the latest news. "I will, my sister."

Once the medevac had shut down, Khalid led Emma to the open door. Welcoming hands ushered her into the helo. As Khalid climbed in and made sure Emma was being taken care of, a bit of relief sank into him. Khalid had terrible memories of finding Najela dead. He didn't think he could go through the same thing again.

"I can't believe it," Emma told Khalid as she walked into his home near Kabul. "Thirty days leave." Her left arm was in a sling and she had been given pain medication for her dislocated shoulder.

Khalid opened the door. "I can. Come, we'll get you into your suite and you can take a long, hot bath." The sky was dark, with sparkling stars, the wind hot off the desert. Inside, air conditioning welcomed them. He shut the door. Rasa, his housekeeper had been called earlier, and she stood attentively at the end of the hall near the living room.

In Pashto, Khalid asked Rasa to escort Emma to her

suite. He leaned over and pressed a kiss to her hair. "If you want to go directly to bed, do so. I will be up for a while." He motioned toward the kitchen. He'd eaten little in the last twenty-four hours.

Emma nodded as she noticed the darkness beneath Khalid's eyes. "Okay," she whispered. "I'm not hungry, just dirty and tired. The bath sounds perfect. Good night." After hours in the medical facility at Bagram, being poked, prodded and X-rayed, Emma felt so fatigued that her feet moved like chunks of concrete across the tiled floor. She'd had serious bruising on her cheek and ribs, but nothing was broken, thank goodness. Bath and bed sounded wonderful. She smiled at the housekeeper, and the woman nodded and smiled shyly in return.

"Only good dreams," Khalid said, giving Emma a raw look of love.

"Good dreams," she murmured. Emma looked over her shoulder to see Khalid striding silently into the kitchen. What she wanted was to be with him. To bathe, get her hair washed and slip into Khalid's bed and be held in the loving protection of his arms. It was another dream....

Swallowing, Emma understood that it couldn't be. At least, not right now. The doctor at Bagram said she'd suffered nerve damage to the three fingers of her left hand. Worse, he had no idea if she would get feeling back in them or not. And, the final blow to Emma was that she could not fly until—or if—she got full use of her fingers back. Emma felt as though the world had crashed in on her. She reminded herself she'd get out of the dirty flight suit, clean up and, she hoped, sleep deeply. Tomorrow morning, she would be in a better frame of mind.

* * *

Emma sat up screaming. The shout that erupted from within her startled her awake. Breathing raggedly, she shakily touched her perspiring face. Even with her eyes open, the light from the moon coming in the window, she could still see the hatred for her in Malik's eyes. That had been seconds before he'd kicked her in the ribs and knocked her unconscious.

"God," she muttered, throwing off the sheet and planting her bare feet on the cool tile floor. The slight movement of air conspired to help her focus on the present, not the past. Emma moved her left arm tentatively. She was on pain medication and now it moved easily and without any problem. Getting up, she found the lavender silk robe at the bottom of her queen-sized bed. As she pulled it on, Emma wanted to escape the room—and Malik's leering face. Maybe a hot cup of tea would help.

Heart pounding, Emma made her way through the darkened halls to the living room. This was her favorite place in Khalid's home. There were leather couches strewn with colorful pillows and a beautiful Persian rug lay between the two massive couches. She halted and gasped. "Khalid!"

"Emma." Khalid swallowed his shock at seeing her and quickly stood up. He'd been leaning against some pillows propped up against one of the massive sofas. Dressed in a dark-blue cotton robe, he stared at her in confusion as she anchored at the door.

He saw the dark circles beneath Emma's eyes even as the moonlight sprawled through the massive picture window. Her flesh gleamed. It was then that it hit him: she'd had a nightmare. More than likely a reaction to her trauma. "Please," Khalid whispered, "come in. I can leave if you like?" He had no desire to make her feel trapped. The wildness in her dark-green eyes haunted him. Khalid saw the fear etched in them. Praying it was not fear of him, he lifted his hand and opened it to her.

"I—uh…no, stay." Helplessly, Emma said in a shaky voice, "I had a nightmare about Malik just before he kicked me. I woke up screaming. Did I wake you up, too?"

Khalid watched her with such gentleness in his eyes. "No. I've been up for a while." He motioned to the book near the pillows. "I was reading and hoping to get tired enough to go to sleep."

Emma saw how very old the book was. The leather was frayed and worn. Somehow, just talking with Khalid was helping calm her down. "I wish I could read a book and feel safe…feel…okay," Emma gulped. Clinging to Khalid's dark gaze, all she wanted to do was run to him. As if reading her mind, he walked toward her, his arms opening, silently asking her to come to him. Emma didn't shy away from her raw feelings for Khalid.

Moving into his arms and feeling his strength and tenderness, her face pressed to his neck and jaw, Emma released a long, trembling sigh.

"You're safe with me, beloved," Khalid rasped near her ear. Tendrils of her unbound hair tickled his chin and lips. Inhaling her feminine scent, he felt Emma sag completely against him, her arms sliding around his waist. He closed his eyes and savored her trust of him. Without thinking, he pressed small kisses upon her mussed, clean hair. "It's going to be all right," he breathed against her ear. "We have one another, Emma. The world might unhinge, but we love one another. And with love, we can get through anything. Together."

Tears beaded along Emma's lashes. "I feel so weak, Khalid. So scared. My whole life is upended. What if I don't get feeling back into my fingers? My God, I can't fly. The army won't allow it. Where will I go? What will I do? All I've known is the army and flying."

Khalid absorbed her sob. Emma's fingers dug into his robe and chest. "Let it out, Emma. I'm here…I'll hold you against the storms."

Emma had never felt so safe or so loved as in that moment. There was something so exotic and ancient about Khalid. He was a warrior at heart. A man who could wear his heart on his sleeve without apology. And he knew when to be tender and sensitive. She had never found all these qualities in one man before. She had in Khalid. As hot tears spilled out of her eyes and streaked down her cheeks, Emma trusted Khalid with her life. She cried out her fear of having no future as a pilot, of having her world suddenly turned upside down and not knowing where she was going to land. Only the safety, the stability of Khalid's strong arms holding her tightly against him was real.

Eventually, Emma's sobs ceased. She hiccuped a few times. Khalid gently moved her toward the sofa and they sat down together. She eased back into his arms and he simply held her. With her head resting against his shoulder, her silky hair against his jaw, Khalid closed his eyes. He could feel Emma's heart pounding against his chest. Felt the touch of her hand against his damp robe. He tenderly slid his fingers through her mussed hair. This was the first time Khalid had explored her and it made his heart swell fiercely with love for Emma. He felt her nestle her cheek more deeply against the crook of his shoulder. The fast beat of her heart was slowing now.

"Crying is a good thing," he told her. "I remember

when I was a little boy and my pet canary died, I cried for days afterward. He was my friend and at seven years old I didn't understand that things could die. My parents encouraged my tears and they held me. I was lucky to have their understanding. I learned about death and that I could be held with love in the aftermath."

Just hearing Khalid tell his story soothed Emma's fractious state. She sat up and wiped her cheeks free of the spent tears. "I feel like I'm dying, Khalid." Emma held up her left hand and looked at it. "I have this horrible gut feeling that I'm not going to get rid of the numbness in my fingers. That the army will ask me to give up my commission." Emma searched his eyes. "What will I do then?" The question was hard to ask, but she felt as if Khalid saw into her soul and never judged her.

Reaching up, he pushed a few errant tendrils of hair away from her face. "Beautiful Emma, you are young. You have your whole life ahead of you. Sometimes, we have one door shut in our face. But as soon as that happens, another will open. That is the way it is."

Emma nodded, barely able to keep from staring down at her hand. "My family is a military one, Khalid. Most of us serve our country. Casey didn't, but that's okay, too. She's my younger sister." Dragging in a deep breath, Emma expended it and frowned. "The army won't wait long to see if I can fly again. If I can't, they'll release me. What good to them is a pilot who can't fly?"

Touching her left hand, Khalid stroked each of her long, artistic fingers. "Listen to me, Emma. I have had many dreams for you—and me." He snagged her glance and smiled unsurely. "I have dreamed of asking you to marry me. To be my partner. I have dreamed of us flying books and school materials all along the border of my country—together." He held her left hand. "The military might not let you fly, but there is nothing to say you can't fly a commercial helicopter. You know, I own a fleet of them. I have three. I have used them for years to help Kinah fulfill our destiny with our Afghan brothers and sisters. You know me as flying for the military, but my life is much broader and deeper than that."

Amazed, Emma stared at him. Her heart pounded. Khalid wanted to marry her! She vaguely heard the rest of his words, her gaze locked with his. There was such tenderness in his eyes for her. Real love. Not some passing infatuation, but love. Emma knew the difference. She twined her fingers between Khalid's. "From the moment I met you, Khalid, I fought my attraction to you. At first, I thought you were just like Brody Parker. But over time, I knew that wasn't so. Every time we kissed, I wanted so much more from you. I wanted to know everything about you. How you grew up. What held your interest. What experiences you went through to make you the man who is sitting here with me now."

Lifting his hand, Khalid cupped her cheek. "And I fought loving you, Emma. After Malik murdered Najela, I felt as if my whole life was over. I couldn't conceive of ever loving another woman." He grazed her cheek. "Until I met you. Then, everything changed for me, Emma." Touching the area of his heart, Khalid whispered unsteadily, "I felt as if my life were given back. A second chance. And once I realized I loved you with a fierceness to match the breadth of my life, I wondered if you loved me. You know in the military we can't show our affection with one another. It's not allowed."

Emma nodded. "I know…and I wanted so badly to tell you, Khalid, but I was scared. We're from different countries. Different worlds. I was worried how our parents would get along. I was worried about a lot of things, so it stopped me from telling you how I really felt." Emma closed her eyes as his fingers trailed down her cheek to trace the length of her slender neck. Khalid had to know the truth. "Where would we live? What kind of life would be expected of me by you? I had so many questions and no answers."

Khalid dropped his hand and held on to her searching gaze fraught with worry. "My mother is Irish. My father is Afghan. I was raised in a home where nothing but love and respect ruled. My father, whom I know you will love, is a man of great heart. He respects everyone. Their beliefs. Their individualism. My mother is tolerant of all peoples. She sees only their hearts and their dreams."

"Your parents are like mine in that way," Emma said.

Khalid managed an unsteady smile. "When one is raised in such an environment, Emma, how can one have problems with any other? I believe you have the right to ask those questions, but you must base the answer on your experiences with me. I can't believe that your family is prejudiced against anyone from a foreign country. You show a tolerance and respect similar to mine, so I know your family is heart-centered too. It's not the color of a person's skin or their particular beliefs that really matters."

"It's the only way I want to see the world, too. My parents taught us the real measure of a person was their humanity to others," Emma whispered.

Khalid tapped his heart with his hand. "Yes. The only question I ever have of anyone is whether they are coming from their heart. You come from your heart, beloved, just as I do. Is it not possible that two people who come from the heart can love and marry? That their families would also be celebrating such a union? When you marry for love and come into that sacred union with only love, then the best of all worlds has been born."

Emma saw how her doubts had no merit whatsoever. Khalid's voice was low with feeling. The more she knew the man, the more deeply she fell in love with him. Khalid was complex, with so many layers, and yet, he had a global perspective she didn't see as often in others. And that drew her powerfully to him. "You're right," Emma admitted quietly, brushing her fingers across his hand.

"Love moves mountains," Khalid told her. "No one can be untouched by love. I have dedicated my life, Emma, to doing things from my heart for others. Yes, I am rich monetarily, but I prefer the richness that comes from the heart. It's not something money can buy. That is why it's so important to help my people here in Afghanistan. Kinah is the same. She sees our money as simply a way to a means. One that will lift our people, one child at a time, to be educated. Because getting an education will lift our nation out of the past and bring it into the present."

Emma saw the fervency in Khalid's narrow eyes. And she heard it in his voice. "You're a family of dreamers who put your vision into reality."

Smiling faintly, Khalid took her hand and pressed a soft kiss to the back of it. "I like that. Yes, that's true, beloved. Right now," he whispered, sitting up and framing her face, "all I want is you at my side, Emma. I want you as my partner for life. I cherish your ideas, how you see the world and how you see me. I want to fulfill your dreams, too. What is a life lived alone? It is empty and hungry. I want my life entwined with yours, Emma. Will you marry me?"

How could she say no? Khalid's words fell gently across her heart in such a way that Emma could not see her life without his larger-than-life presence in it. "Yes, I will marry you, Khalid. I'm not sure where our lives will lead, but it's going to be an adventure."

Leaning forward, he brushed her lips, parting them. "Beloved, no matter what we do, we will allow our hearts to lead the way…."

## *Chapter 16*

Khalid picked Emma up and cradled her in his arms. She kissed his cheek and inhaled his dizzying male scent as she wrapped her arms around his broad shoulders. There was joy in his eyes, a fierce love for her that stole her breath. This man, who bridged two major religions, was living proof that east could meet west from the heart. Khalid was unique and Emma sighed as she rested her brow against his cheek. Her mother, Alyssa, had always said that whomever she married had to be more than just a man. She had been right: Khalid was archetypal in the best of ways. Having been born and lived in such a loving home where the Christian and the Muslim religions were joined, he'd absorbed the best from both. And now, she was going to live with this man who held the hope of the world in his heart.

Emma smiled faintly as Khalid nudged the door to

his master bathroom open with his toe. "Ah…water. I like where this is going, Khalid…"

He gently placed her on the thick blue Persian rug in front of a huge glass-enclosed double shower. "Care to join me?"

Grinning, Emma watched as he stepped into the blue-and-white tiled shower and turned on the water. The multiple shower heads released warm water that fell like soft raindrops. "Just try and stop me."

Khalid smiled in response, then felt the temperature of the water. "Just right. Are you ready, beloved?"

Without hesitation, Emma slid the lavender robe off. She wore only a silky tank top and shorts that fell midway on her thighs. "I am. You?" She gave him a challenging smile.

Khalid had no shyness about removing his blue robe. He was completely naked beneath. If Emma was disappointed in him, her large, beautiful green eyes did not reflect that. As her gaze moved from his throat, down across his darkly haired chest to his flat stomach to his narrow hips, he saw her cheeks turn pink and those copper freckles darkened. Reaching out, he settled his hands lightly on her shoulders.

"Do I pass your inspection?"

His teasing made her laugh. A sudden, happy giddiness surged through Emma as she looked up into his glinting, narrowed gaze. "Oh, yes, you do." She saw how pleased Khalid was, and maybe, a bit relieved. After all, he was a flesh-and-blood man and Emma knew he was probably worried she might not be pleased with his body. She felt him move the thin silk from her shoulders. Her skin flushed and then prickled pleasantly as he coaxed the material off her torso and exposed her breasts. In a moment, Khalid had removed the soft material and set it on a nearby shelf. His gaze moved hungrily across her body. She felt his desire even though he hadn't made a move to touch her. Her breasts tightened and the nipples hardened beneath his intense look.

Pushing the silky pajama pants off, Emma let them pool around her feet. She smiled and moved into the warm streams of water that issued from opposite walls within the huge shower. Gripping his hand, she said, "Come on in. The water's fine."

In moments, Khalid had closed the shower door, and the steam began to gather, moving in fine, thin ripples around them. Emma moved boldly into Khalid's arms. She wanted him and wasn't going to be coy about it. To her delight, his very male mouth curved over her brazen move. As soon as she slid her wet body up against his, his arms circled her. Leaning up, she claimed his smiling mouth. Emma unleashed all the hunger from the last months against Khalid. His mouth was strong, giving and taking against her own. As his tongue moved across her lower lip, she felt his hand slide teasingly down her spine. His fingers splayed and outlined each of her vertebrae, the water intensifying his burning touch. Khalid drew her powerfully against him and Emma gasped. She felt him smile and returned it. The water was like another set of her lover's hands as it curved and curled around her face, wetting her hair, the strands thickening and lying in fine sheets across her shoulders.

Khalid's mouth tore from hers and he trailed hot, hungry kisses from her jaw down the graceful line of her neck to her shoulders. With her left shoulder, he was tender and careful. Her skin sizzled with pleasure and danced with each slight brush of his exploring mouth.

As Khalid eased her back, his hand splayed out against her spine to hold her steady, their hips melted into one another. His kisses sought and found each of her taut breasts. Emma sighed and gripped his tense arms that held her captive.

He tenderly mouthed each of her nipples, making her moan. The water sluicing across her face, down her shoulders and trickling in and around her breasts only increased her pleasure. Each kiss along the curve of each breast heightened Emma's need of him. Khalid's masculine power was nearly overwhelming. She felt him trembling and Emma intuitively understood he was holding back his fierce love for her. Because of her injured shoulder, she knew he was being gentle so that he wouldn't create more injury for her.

As Khalid brought her back against him, the water spilled over them, the heat and steam curling around them like the fingers of a thousand other tantalizing hands. He slid his hands down, down, down until he cupped her hips. And then Khalid lifted her against him. Her arms slid around his shoulders as he gently settled her against him. Inch by inch, he slowly lowered her down upon himself.

A raw, guttural sound of pleasure rose in Emma's throat. She threw her head back, her body melted hotly against Khalid's as she brought him within her throbbing core. The moment was powerful, the water running around them, fusing them even more wonderfully to one another. Emma leaned her head downward, found his mouth and kissed him hard. She didn't want him treating her like some fragile glass that might break. After all, it was only her shoulder. Emma felt him smiling beneath her mouth. In moments, Khalid was moving her, holding her and kissing her hungrily in return.

The steam swirled around them. The silken water fused and inspired them. Emma gripped Khalid's broad, powerful shoulders, suddenly tensing as the heat of her body burst open and flowed in a tidal rhythm. A groan of complete pleasure tore from her wet lips. She felt Khalid tense, a growl from deep within him rolling upward. The sound was like thunder, shared and absorbed between them.

Closing her eyes, taut as a bow against Khalid, Emma surrendered all her love into this man who held her in his arms. For long, golden moments, only he existed—a part of her, a part of her pounding heart rhythm in tune with his. She thought she'd known love before, but she really hadn't. The love that Khalid had shared with her, the respect, the joy was rare. And beautiful. And fulfilling.

As water coursed down her head, the strands of her red hair clinging to her wet face, she leaned over, framed Khalid's face and kissed him. Nothing had ever been as wonderful as this moment for Emma. She understood now what Khalid had said earlier about living from the heart. It was effortless and joyful. As their mouths cherished one another, took and gave, Emma knew this man was greater than most. Her spirit had seen his. She truly saw Khalid's heart and his love for her. And searching his soft blue eyes, Emma knew he looked into her soul with nothing but love. Together, they could do a lot in their own unique ways to help the world. What else was there but love? In her dizzied mind, her thoughts disjointed, Emma was ready to accept whatever life would hand her. After all, she had a man who loved her with a fierceness that took her breath away. All else would fall into some kind of order after that.

* * *

"I'm really sorry," Nike told Emma as they stood outside the HQ of the BJS 60 squadron. "I know Rachel would be here to support you today, but she's off on a mission."

"Don't be," Emma told her best friend. She smiled a little. On her left hand was an emerald ring that Khalid had given her a month ago. Rachel, her cousin, had wanted to be with her when she found out the army's decision, but a sudden fire fight along the border had broken out and all available women pilots were called to the Apache gunships to go help turn the tide.

Nike grimaced. The July sun was hot overhead, the nonstop sounds of helicopters landing and taking off nearby permeating the vibrating air. "You got feeling back in one finger, but not the other two. I don't know why the army refuses to let you fly. This is so stupid."

"Let it go," Emma counseled gently. "The army says a pilot has to have feeling in all ten fingers. Not eight. I'll be okay."

"I won't be," Nike griped. Upset, she jammed her hands on her hips. "The army should give you more than four weeks to heal up! Who's to say you won't get feeling back in those fingers two or three months down the road?"

"What are they going to do with a pilot who can't fly?" Emma asked. "Major Klein was very sorry she had to give me their decision. She said if it had been up to her, I'd still be with BJS 60."

"I know. Everyone in HQ knew when the decision by the army higher-ups had come down. Major Klein was in a really ugly mood for a couple of hours after that. That's how we all knew they'd decided against you staying. You seem to be at peace about this," Nike said. "Khalid's influence?"

"In part, yes." Emma put on her aviator sunglasses and settled the black BJS baseball cap on her head. "My family is fine with what has happened. Khalid and I have a plan. I'll now be a part of his family nonprofit charitable organization. I'll be allowed to fly commercial helicopters that he and his family own. And really, it's a good thing because I can fly into the safe villages with resupplies and the army won't have to do it." She grinned and began to walk with Nike toward the tent area. Emma would pick up the last of her clothes and other personal items from the tent she'd lived in for over a year, and then be escorted off base. For a new life. A new adventure. And with a man she loved and who loved her with a fierceness that made Emma feel as if she were floating on a cloud of nonstop joy.

"When it's all said and done," Nike told her, brightening a little, "you'll be allowed back on base because Khalid is assigned here."

"Yes, I will." Emma gave her an evil grin. "Down, but not out, Nike. I'm going to move my stuff into his home in Kabul. A week from now Khalid gets thirty days of leave from the army and we're going to fly home to San Francisco to be married. My entire family, uncles included, are coming. Even Rachel, my cousin, is being given leave to attend, thanks to Major Klein. She knows how much it means to my family to be there for our wedding."

"That's great. I wish I could be there, too."

"So do I. I was surprised Major Klein let Rachel go. This is our heavy season for Apache demands and we're now a pilot short because I had to resign my commission."

"I think Major Klein is a good C.O. I know she didn't want you to resign, but she can't buck army regs as much as she might have wanted to. You and Rachel will be back a month from now," Nike said, gloating. "And we'll just pick up where we left off, girlfriend." She threw her arm around Emma's shoulders and gave her a quick squeeze.

"We will," Emma promised her, voice thickening with tears. Nike was an incredible friend, someone she never wanted to lose touch with. Today, her life would change forever. It was a bittersweet moment for Emma. She'd been the casualty of this war in one way. In another way, this war had brought her the man she would love forever. And, she would have her cousin Rachel here with her. If she had learned anything, Emma had learned a long time ago that the only thing she could count on was change.

Emma opened up her tent. Nike followed and in quick order they had her personal belongings in the duffel bag. Her shoulder had healed up completely in the past month and it was easy enough to carry it over her right shoulder. Nike walked with her in the hot sunlight. The smell of aviation fuel, dust and the noise of trucks coming and going was a constant.

Emma was glad to be going home. Her family was in high gear to give them a July wedding at Golden Gate State Park near San Francisco's Golden Gate bridge. And San Francisco was one of Khalid's favorite cities in the world. Yes, Emma thought, it would be a whirlwind month filled with overflowing happiness for her entire family. But especially for her and for Khalid who loved her tenderly every night before they slept in one another's arms. She was excited to have the Cantrells and the Trayherns embrace Khalid and his family who would also be there for the wedding. They were a global family in so many ways already. Now, east was marrying west. She liked being a forerunner. And she loved Khalid, a man who had one foot in western civilization and the other firmly rooted in his beloved Afghanistan. She would love this fierce global warrior forever.

* * * * *